REAPING DAY

BOOK THREE OF THE HARVESTERS SERIES

LUKE MITCHELL

Cover design by Yocla Designs

Cover illustration by Hokunin

Editing by Lisa Poisso

Proofreading by Dj Hendrickson

DEDICATION

"I never intended on writing a dedication, because I didn't write this book for someone else. I wrote it for me. I wrote it because I've found a great passion for writing, and I love it so much that I thought I just might try to make a career of it. So there you have it. This book is dedicated to me—selfish prick that I am!" – Luke R. Mitchell, *Red Gambit*

Well, a selfish prick, I may still be. But as I've watched thousands of readers step into my little made up world (and heard from some who've actually found something of value there), I can't help but feel that something has intangibly shifted. Sure, I'm still writing because I want to, but it's becoming clear to me that I'm no longer writing for myself alone.

So this one's officially for you guys—the readers who are making this deluded dream of mine a living, breathing reality.

Thank you for reading. You guys rock.

PROLOGUE

After nearly a thousand years spent traveling the universe, Nan'Cagor had yet to grow comfortable with the feeling of being in deep space, though he could never quite place the exact thing that so unsettled him. There was the silence, of course—the deep, nearly complete absence of any sound but the faint hum of the ship's systems and the stirring of their cargo, audible to his ears even from several compartments away. But it was far more than that. It was the feeling of the profound nothingness that stretched out in all directions around them, as far as his mental senses could reach.

It was the Void, and it was unnatural.

As far as Cagor was concerned, feet—or tentacles or whatever else that century's host body happened to be sporting—belonged on the ground or in the water. Wings in the air weren't so bad either. But no matter what, he was sure that life should be firmly rooted to the gravitational pull of a proper planet, not floating in the vast emptiness of space.

Still, he'd take space travel any day over the doom they'd left behind. The only question was whether they'd brought enough food to avoid simply falling into the slower doom of the cursed blood sickness. Apparently he wasn't the only one thinking about feeding.

"Cagor," Al'Krastor called. "Food."

The crimson glow of Krastor's eyes was paler than usual. Cagor nodded to his superior and went to assess their stock.

The sounds of their cargo grew more audible with each step down the dim oval hallway, at least until he drew up to the hatch and the room beyond went abruptly silent. He availed the hatch with his mind, and it jumped to his will, peeling off to the side to reveal the large compartment currently acting as their pantry.

He stepped into the room but paused at a whimper from the small girl to the right. The girl and her mother both cowered when he looked their way, silent tears streaming down the older woman's face while the younger one tried to bury her frightened sobs in her mother's lap.

"How many times must I tell you?" Cagor said. "You are not in any danger here. You need not cry and cower every time we come."

The mother only stared back at him with bloodshot eyes and flowing tears.

Cagor sighed, a mannerism he'd picked up from the humans. He looked around, taking in their sad stock. They weren't the finest Earth had had to offer, but the twelve humans would have to do. Pathetically short life spans, disease, inbreeding—these were all problems Cagor and his companions would no doubt have to address at some point, but it was better than nothing.

And right now, he was hungry.

He pointed to one of the men brooding in the corner—one of the older, weaker specimens in the group. "You. Come with me."

The man's face pulled into a snarl, and he spat on the floor by way of reply.

Cagor rolled his eyes (another human affectation) and reached out with his mind. The old man promptly went bolt upright, hopped to his feet, and marched over to Cagor as if he'd been possessed by the spirit of blind obedience.

Of course, it was only Cagor himself that had possessed the man.

Cagor turned and left the room, his new puppet following eagerly at his heels. The hatch crawled shut behind them, and Cagor headed back to the front of the ship with their dinner in tow.

Al'Krastor eyed the tribute distastefully when they entered, but he didn't hesitate. As soon as the old man was within reach, Krastor grabbed the human's arm and bit delicately into his forearm with a bored look. The Al slurped up a few deep gulps of the blood flowing from the bite before gesturing their third, Nan'Solga, over for his turn.

Cagor suppressed the protest on the edge of his tongue and waited his turn. Solga was only a Nan himself, equal to Cagor by every right, yet Krastor continued to favor the bastard over him in every way.

No matter. For now, it was enough to be alive.

Solga finished his portion and waved Cagor over. Cagor took the old man's arm and drank his fill. Then, with a careful shift of thought, he released a flood of healing factors into his saliva and set to work licking the man's wound shut. His skill at healing wasn't particularly admirable among his kind, but nonetheless, the wound was mostly closed when he stepped back a minute later. It'd be fully healed within one of Earth's day cycles. Not that they'd be needing to feed again from this one so soon. Each of the three raknoth didn't need more than a few gulps every couple of days, and they could easily rotate their feeding stock to keep the humans fresh and healthy.

Cagor was just debating whether he should take a stand and tell Nan'Solga to deal with stowing the man back in the pantry when the ship suddenly called out to them in alarm—a buzzing telepathic pulse that was impossible to miss.

Cagor exchanged a tense glance with his companions and reached with his mind for the ship's instruments.

"No," Al'Krastor said quietly beside him. "It cannot be."

Cagor sensed it a second later: an incoming ship, not unlike their own.

Terror clutched at his senses. Across from him, Solga's eyes flared bright crimson with panic.

"It's…"

Solga didn't need to complete the thought. They all knew.

Somehow, by the worst odds of the universe, the Masters had found them.

Krastor looked at them, the stark paleness of his eyes betraying his despondence. "Let me do the talk—"

A section of the hull exploded inward with a wrenching crash. Sudden and furious winds tugged at them as the ship's air rushed to make its feeble donation to the Void. Cagor and his companions dug into walls and consoles with sharp claws. The old man they'd fed on found no such purchase and was rocketed rapidly into the void with the escaping air.

The hull was reacting now, folding over to seal the breach. It wasn't quick enough.

The Master who'd no doubt opened the breach to begin with pulled himself through the hole and landed on his feet with a heavy thunk as the hull sealed above him.

Cagor had never seen this particular rakul in person, but he recognized the hulking, bipedal mass of muscles and sharp edges from the memories his kin had shared with him.

"Kul'Gada," Al' Krastor said, dropping to his knees and bowing his head in deference. "Master. We bow before you and praise your—"

Kul'Gada's thick tail flicked into the wall with a bang, denting the wall and silencing Krastor. The Kul regarded them in silence, eyes burning with crimson fire more intense than any Cagor had ever seen.

Seconds ticked by. Cagor and his companions waited, eyes to the floor, too terrified to move.

"Traitors." Kul'Gada's voice poured into Cagor's mind like a choir of rasping whispers with the weight of an ocean behind them.

It made Cagor cringe. Cringing turned to trembling as Kul'Gada splayed the fingers of one hand and his digits smoothly elongated into foot-long appendages that were more blade than claw.

Al'Krastor half rose from his cowering bow. "Master! We—"

Kul'Gada stepped forward and hacked Al'Krastor's head into multiple pieces with one sweep of his bladed hand.

Nan'Solga, to his credit, elected to go down fighting once their imminent doom was confirmed. The raknoth roared and lunged for the rakul. Kul'Gada caught Solga's head in his open palm and slammed the raknoth to the deck hard enough to shatter his skull.

Kul'Gada straightened and stepped on Solga's broken skull for good measure. It crushed under his weight with a sickly crunch.

Cagor watched, slack-jawed and utterly beyond action as he tried to find the will to move, to fight—to do anything but cower silently, frozen in place.

Then Kul'Gada's mind fell on his with all the inexorable mass and pull of a black hole, and Cagor was truly and completely powerless to so much as blink as the Kul drank in his every memory and thought of Earth—cursed Earth, with its cursed blood and impetuous humans and its doom, past, present, and future.

"You were wise to flee," Kul'Gada's raspy multi-voice finally whispered in his mind what felt like years later. *"Your brethren will beg me for such mercifully quick deaths before I am through with them."*

For a thousand years, Nan'Cagor had toiled and trained and vied for position among his peers. He'd listened to his elders' lectures about the intergalactic supremacy of their strength as a species, about how he and his ilk should be grateful to count themselves among the raknoth and how they should always bear the name with pride. For the most part, he'd listened. He'd believed. But now, a thousand years later, there was no pride to be found—no dignity in the shriek that escaped his throat as Kul'Gada grabbed his skull and squeezed.

CHAPTER ONE

Of all the items on the long list of things Rachel Cross had never expected to see in her life, it had never even occurred to her to add a raknoth drinking—or, technically, *preparing* to drink—tea, and especially not one doing it with all the poise and delicacy of a Victorian monarch at that. Yet here she was, and there sat the blood-sucking aristocrat in all his pompous glory.

In the interest of not looking at him one second longer, Rachel instead glanced around the spacious room for the thousandth time, seeing but not really observing the collection of fine ceramics and luxuriously dark, shiny wood furniture that graced the space with its oh-so-eloquent presence. She suppressed an exasperated huff (only for the hundredth time) and settled for squeezing her staff and clenching her toes until her feet cramped.

The collection probably would have gone for an arm and both legs back when people had cared about such things, back before they'd had to shift their focus to more pressing concerns like whether they'd be able to grow enough food for the winter and whether they'd be able to escape the notice of marauders while they did it.

But fancy, gaudy, stupid, unnecessary trinkets weren't the reason she was about to blow a gasket.

The impetus of that impending calamity was the imperious little brat who sat in front of them, taking his sweet, deliberate time in fixing his tea—the making of which was apparently of life-and-death necessity before he could be bothered to properly hear them out. Or maybe he was just fucking with them. Who drank tea these days anyway?

The raknoth, apparently. Or at least this one.

She never would have expected to use either of the phrases, "little brat" or "fixing his tea," in reference to a raknoth, and yet here she was, about to burst a blood vessel, and there he was, stirring that steaming cup ever so gingerly with his ridiculous little spoon.

Last time she'd ever agree to play nice.

She glanced over at Lea and decided that if the beautiful Resistance fighter could keep her composure through this nonsense, she could at least give Nan'Ashida one more minute before she put him through one of his rustic adobe walls.

Whether he knew it or not, the little prick spoke up just in time.

"Tell me, Krogoth," Ashida said to the raknoth sitting across the table from him. God, even his voice was annoying. "Have you ever been on a safari?"

"Never," Krogoth said.

"A shame." Ashida raised the tea cup to his lips with three fingers and took a delicate sip, then he let out a contented sigh.

And now she'd seen everything.

"I've always found them to be invigorating," Ashida continued. "The perfect glimpse into the true way of the world—predator and prey, hunter and hunted. Survival"—he pointedly shifted his gaze to her and Lea before looking back at Krogoth—"of the fittest."

Rachel rolled her eyes so hard the muscles at the tops of her eyeballs threatened to cramp. "Cool story, dude." Lea tensed at the sound of her words, but Rachel pressed on. "It's a shame some scaly green assholes had to go and blow the world to shit. Probably wasn't so invigorating out there during the dark days. Probably still isn't."

A crimson glow awakened in Ashida's eyes, and a look of distaste warped his features as he regarded her.

Given his clear raknoth superiority complex, she was kind of surprised she could read Ashida's expression at all. Many of the raknoth, like Zar'Krogoth with his rust-red hide, elected to retain their reptilian appearances—what Jarek referred to as "going full raknoth"—around the clock. Having dealt with more than enough raknoth in just the past couple of weeks to keep her sated for life, she was getting a bit better at reading the expressions of their scaly snouts and smooth, angled eyebrows, but there was still a lot of guesswork involved.

With Ashida opting to maintain the appearance of the human host whose driver's seat he'd laid permanent claim to, though, his disgust was clear. He had the dark skin of a native Kenyan, which only made the creepy crimson glow of his eyes stand out that much more. He could have hidden the ominous luminance, she knew. That was how the raknoth had managed to take their planet and pull the strings that had ended up wiping out nearly ninety percent of the world's population fifteen years ago. They hadn't needed to break a sweat or raise a finger—save for the one that had pressed the nuke button.

She kept that thought firmly in mind as she held Nan'Ashida's gaze, hoping he'd choke on his stupid tea.

"How can you think to work with these pathetic creatures, brother?" Ashida asked Krogoth. "The lion would not think for a moment to lower itself to the company of the hare. It is unnatural. And unnecessary. This lot"—he flicked a hand toward Rachel and Lea, somehow conveying disgust with the motion—"will be centuries in their graves before we'd ever have any reason to expect the harvesters would come here. And if that should ever come to pass"—he gave a haughty laugh —"I don't see how our *food* could hope to stand beside us on the battlefield."

He went to take another sip of tea and froze, which seemed a little ironic, because that was exactly what his cup of tea had done: frozen solid. At Rachel's will, of course.

She harmlessly dispersed the heat she'd drawn from the tea and met Ashida's confused look with a wide grin. "Not bad for a pathetic little hare, huh, asshole?"

Krogoth looked between the frosty cup and Rachel and said nothing. But was that amusement on his features?

"How dare you?" Ashida said once he'd gotten over his indignant rage enough to speak.

Rachel focused on the cup and channeled the smidgen of energy it took to send the tea cup and its solid contents sailing across the room. It smashed against the wall with one big satisfying crash and fell to the floor with a series of smaller ones.

Ashida was on his feet in an instant. Rachel tapped into the batteries she kept clipped on her belt as a soldier might keep spare magazines. It took considerably more telekinetic horsepower to drive the raknoth back into his seat than it had to hurl a little teacup, but it was worth it.

And they'd been worried she wouldn't be a good diplomat.

The dark wooden chair under Ashida gave an indignant groan as he slammed into it. Ashida gave his own threatening growl. Then, after a moment of struggling, he bellowed, "Release me!"

Rachel looked at Lea, trying to keep the considerable exertion off of her face. "You think a lion's ever said something like that to a hare?"

Ashida might have been a pompous bastard, but he was also a raknoth, and they weren't so easily matched for physical strength, even by an arcanist like herself. She doubted she could have kept him contained for more than a minute if he really cut loose.

Luckily, Krogoth helped her maintain the integrity of her little show, whether deliberately or not. "The point is well made," he said, raising a hand for her to stop. "Enough."

She gladly released her telekinetic hold on Ashida. Channeling fatigue swept in. She leaned casually against the wall to keep her knees from shaking and kept her eyes on Ashida. Raknoth weren't exactly legendary for their self-restraint and levelheadedness.

In testament to the fact, Ashida bounded to his feet and batted his chair aside, toppling the rich wood violently enough that it cracked when it hit the ground.

Krogoth had risen to his feet as well, keeping easy pace with Ashida.

Rachel probably would have considered a bath in battery acid before she'd trust Krogoth with her life, but she wasn't going to complain about him throwing in a hand to protect it either.

Fortunately, his aid wasn't necessary. Ashida only stood there, shoulders heaving in the aftermath of his sudden outburst.

Finally, after a long silence, he looked at the cracked chair on the floor. "Look what you have made me do," he said quietly.

Rachel managed to keep her voice level. "We have more important things to worry about than nice furniture and tea time, Ashida. The rakul are coming, whether you wanna believe it or not."

"Bah," Ashida said.

"You and your men could be what turns the tide when the fighting starts," Lea said, probably trying to appeal to his obviously considerable ego. "The army you command is formidable. If you'd be willing to glyph your men against telepathic influence—"

Ashida gave a harsh bark of laughter. "If I did that, my men would no longer be *my* men, little girl." He looked at Krogoth, his face showing the first signs of hesitation Rachel had seen. "You truly believe this madness, brother?"

Krogoth gave a slow nod. "I saw the messengers flee for the Masters myself. Harvest will fall."

"Bah." Ashida considered Rachel. "If that is truly the case, why not simply offer up the humans when they arrive, as we were always intended to do?"

Rachel held her tongue so Krogoth could explain it without all of the expletives and insults she'd be compelled to include.

"You know why," Krogoth said. "The day we decided to cut off contact with the Masters was the day we signed our inevitable death warrants. It was always a question of when. Even if they would forgive us, they certainly wouldn't think to spare the humans just because we've grown to require their lifeblood. There is no moving on to the next planet. If the humans perish, so too will we."

"Perhaps the Masters could—"

"The Masters will gladly cut us to ribbons and display our true corpses for all to see. We have already undermined their authority.

They will have already returned to Rakzaied to replace our numbers."

"But—"

"As far as the Kul are concerned," Krogoth said, "we are already dead. They simply come to complete the formality."

Rachel thought she could see the moment the weight of Krogoth's words shimmied past Ashida's denial and settled firmly down on his chest.

"I will have to consider," Ashida began, but Krogoth was already turning for the door, beckoning Rachel and Lea to join him.

"Do as you wish, Nan," Krogoth said. He spoke quietly, not pausing or turning back. Ashida would hear nonetheless. "But do not make the mistake of believing that you will be any less doomed than us for your hesitance to raise arms against the Masters."

If Ashida had a comeback, he didn't manage to spit it out before they left.

Outside, they tromped silently through the complex. It was decadent to the max, all rustic, cream-colored walls and impractical red-tiled roofs. The courtyard sported a running fountain, and on the balcony above it, two girls were *sunbathing,* of all things. Like Rachel, they looked to be in their mid-twenties. Unlike Rachel, their skin glowed bronze, and their curves were voluptuous beneath the skimpy bikinis that left so little to the imagination.

Bikinis. Sunbathing.

Now she really had seen everything.

She exchanged a look with Lea. Unlike Rachel's fair skin, Lea's was a lovely chestnut brown, but it certainly hadn't gotten that way from tanning, and Rachel was reasonably sure neither one of them had ever thought to wear a bikini in the past fifteen years, if ever. The thought of walking around so exposed made her skin crawl.

Maybe no one had explained to the girls on the balcony what manner of monsters roamed the lands these days.

There were the raknoth, of course. But then there were the marauders too, those wayward souls who'd fled their humanity when the bombs had fallen fifteen years ago and had yet to return to it.

People wanted to hate the raknoth, but it was hard to ignore just how many humans had taken a leaf out of their book when the shit had hit and treated their fellow humans as resources to be taken advantage of.

Hell, maybe it had always been that way. Maybe people had just gotten a little bolder once there were no real organized governments to make them pay for it.

God, she was starting to think like Jarek.

She wondered if they should try to get the girls out of there, but they looked happy enough. She didn't see any obvious bite marks on them, and they even waved down to her and Lea as they passed the fountain.

Hell, maybe they had better lives than she did.

Or maybe Nan'Ashida had telepathically raped their minds into dumb servitude and ordered them onto the balcony just to complete the decor he'd so obviously imagined in fine detail.

The thought made her want to hit something.

She still couldn't quite believe she or anyone else in the Resistance had agreed to the tenuous (and tenuous was probably even too sturdy a word) alliance with the raknoth—the very same assholes who'd destroyed their planet. The same wretched bastards who'd been responsible for the deaths of her family.

She'd be lying if she said it hadn't been keeping her up at night, but so had the visions Haldin had shown her of the rakul. It wasn't quite fair to say it was any fault of Haldin and his friends, but it sure would have been nice if the Enochians had brought anything other than disastrously bad news with them on their galactic trip to Earth.

For now, shirking imminent death had taken the reins, no matter how deplorable the thought of working with the raknoth was.

That said, she'd be damned if she wasn't going to stick Alton Parker in a corner and get some answers the first chance she got. As far as she knew, Alton was the only surviving raknoth who knew the details of what had happened to her mom and her family, and he'd been a little too conveniently indisposed and removed on their world-wide alliance recruitment tour these past weeks. Soon, though, she'd get him alone. One way or another.

They reached the front gate and waited under the guards' stares as it slowly crept open for them.

"What an asshole," she said when they were on the other side and the gate was groaning shut behind them.

"Your behavior toward our host in there was most undiplomatic, Rachel Cross," Krogoth said.

"Our host was a prick," she pointed out.

She diplomatically withheld the point that Krogoth, by general virtue of association, among other things, was a prick in her eyes as well.

Krogoth shot her an even stare, and then he emitted a chuffing growl of laughter. "You speak truth. Were we not on a diplomatic mission, I would have extracted the respect he failed to show me."

"Hey, we could go back. No arguments here."

By "extracted respect," she was pretty sure Krogoth meant, "removed Ashida's insolent head." She wasn't a scholar of raknoth sociology, but he probably would have been in his rights to kill the Nan for his lack of respectful address, especially now that he'd ascended from the title of Al to Zar—coincidentally after he'd removed Zar'Golga's head a couple of weeks earlier. She could think of a lot worse ways to spend the rest of her morning than watching Krogoth repeat the act on Ashida.

"Rachel…" The look Lea shot her was decidedly disapproving.

Krogoth gave another guttural chuckle. "The lady warrior is fierce," he said to Lea. "Perhaps there is yet hope for us in the coming war." He glanced at Rachel. "Even if it is her kind we have to thank for our current predicament."

Rachel only just managed to hold back the gasp at the words that hit like a sudden gout of icy water down her back. Krogoth and Lea paused, and she realized with an internal curse that she'd frozen in shock.

Krogoth couldn't know… Could he?

Alton might have been the only one left who'd been around for the business that had left Rachel without a family, but she had no idea how many of his kin had known that the virus that'd left them mortally dependent on human blood had been born of an arcanist's enchantment, and that said arcanist had in fact been Rachel's mom.

Something told her it was better if no one who didn't already know—least of all one of the three most powerful raknoth left on the planet—ever found out.

"See?" she said, weakly trying to force a wink at Lea. "You say undiplomatic, he says fierce. Krogoth gets it."

"*He* said undiplomatic," Lea said, not missing a stride though Rachel was pretty sure the younger Resistance fighter had guessed roughly what was going through her head.

Aside from Jarek and the Enochians, Lea and Alaric Weston were the only ones who knew about her mom's role in all of this, and neither one had seemed hasty to spill the beans and add yet another source of tension to an alliance that was already more a teetering tower of dry kindling next to a bonfire than a secure fortress.

"Whatever." Rachel waved a hand, hoping Krogoth would chalk up any oddness to the fact that she was a human and an arcanist rather than anything more sinister. Hell, the raknoth probably didn't care enough to even notice odd behaviors to begin with. "Let's just go home."

Krogoth was already turning to continue on, clearly having lost interest in their petty human chit chat. Rachel exchanged a relieved look with Lea, and they followed after the Zar without a word.

Yeah. She was definitely going to be having that talk with Alton the first chance she got.

Thinking of the Enochians on the way to Krogoth's ship, she checked her comm and realized she'd missed a call from Haldin.

She dropped back just outside the ship to return the call. Lea joined her as the comm holo sprang to life with an idling icon and a chirping tone.

There was a small crackle of static, then the holo enlarged and shifted into a pixelated, stuttering image of Haldin Raish's pretty boy eyes and thinly bearded jawline. The odd purplish hue of the wall behind him confirmed he was aboard the borrowed raknoth ship that had brought the Enochians to Earth.

"Hey... achel," came Elise's choppy voice from somewhere off screen.

They must've still been somewhere in the mountains. Not that Rachel's connection was all that much better right now.

Haldin turned with his comm and, frame by choppy frame, Elise came into view on the couch next to him, beautiful and raven-haired, as did Johnny and his flaming red hair, sprawled out and resting his legs over both of them.

"Hey. You guys look cozy over there."

Elise frowned at Johnny. "Certain parties may... -main unclear on the... -er points... couch etiquette." The connection seemed to stabilize, and Elise continued. "I'd like to say it's a culture shock thing, but we did bring these couches from Enochia."

Johnny raised a helpless hand. "Sometimes a guy's gotta sprawl! It can't be helped." His gaze shifted from Rachel to Lea, and he waggled his eyebrows. "Hey, Lea."

"Hi, Johnny." Lea's tone was level, but she didn't quite manage to keep the smile from tugging at her features.

Rachel resisted the urge to roll her eyes. Not that Johnny couldn't hold his own in a fight, but half the time it seemed like he'd flown here for no other reason than to bring them bad jokes and cheesy pickup lines from across the galaxy.

When the video connection sputtered out and died, leaving them with only audio, Rachel decided it might actually be a mercy.

"How did it go?" Haldin asked, his voice a bit clearer now that they weren't wasting precious bandwidth.

Straight back to business. That seemed like Haldin's style, all right.

"Iffy," Rachel said. "We definitely left Ashida with a lot to think about. I'd say it's fifty-fifty whether the little prick comes around, though."

"How about you guys?" Lea asked.

When Haldin spoke, Rachel pictured him with a sour frown.

"Worse," he said. "We didn't even get a maybe. Those idiots wouldn't even—"

He paused, distracted by something on their end.

"They didn't believe us," Elise finished for him.

"Seems to be a lot of that going around," Rachel said. "If only we could just up and leave the stubborn bastards behind."

"Damn those pesky hundreds of millions of helpless innocents," Johnny agreed in a tone that made her picture him hunching over and waving his fist like a bitter old man.

Yeah. That was the kicker, wasn't it?

"Have you guys heard any word from Jarek?" Rachel asked.

"No," Haldin said. "I was just about to try him."

"Stay on. I'll add him."

Rachel swiped through the holo menus and threw Jarek Slater onto the call from her contact list. They waited for nearly half a minute, their comms chirping in unison.

She was about to give up and drop Jarek from the call when the chirping halted in a soft click.

"I'm sorry to say that now is an exceptionally bad time, ma'am," Jarek's AI companion, Alfred, said in his smooth English tone. "Jarek wishes me to inform you that he'll call you once the, uh… negotiations are complete."

She stymied the river of questions that poured through her head. "Exceptionally bad time" sounded an awful lot like "active warzone" to her ears where Jarek and Al were concerned, but he was too far away for her to do anything in a timely manner.

"Keep him safe, Al."

"Of course, ma'am."

Al cut Jarek's line from the call with a soft click.

"That didn't sound great," Haldin said.

Rachel shook her head, too busy trying to ignore the gnawing feeling in her gut to remember the Enochians couldn't see her.

What the hell had they been thinking, sending a cowboy and a freakin' Jarek to Japan?

CHAPTER TWO

Jarek Slater poked his armored head around the corner of the stone wall. "Was it something I said?" he called.

A burst of gunfire from the front of the large, ornate house was the only answer he received.

He jerked behind cover and pressed his back to the stone wall, smooth and cool through Fela's tactile sensors.

"I'd hazard a guess that your comment about the nuclear fortitude of the Japanese people didn't help matters, sir," Al said, talking through Fela's speakers rather than directly into Jarek's ears so that their companions could hear as well. "And I told Rachel you'd call upon commencing negotiations."

"Well thank you, Mr. Robot."

"Al has a point," Alaric said beside Jarek. "It wouldn't kill you to hold the wise cracks for fifteen minutes."

"You can't prove that." With a careful thought, Jarek slid his helmet's faceplate open so the wiry old Resistance commander could see the pointed stare Jarek fixed on his straw-woven hat. "And besides, you're not exactly alleviating racial tensions walking in here looking like a goddamn cowboy samurai."

He didn't miss the way Alaric's eyes drifted to the long, lovely claw

18

trails Zar'Golga had left across his face a couple weeks ago. He was almost getting used to it by now, though that wasn't to say he was a fan.

"And further besides," Jarek continued, pushing the thought aside and leaning past Alaric to address the raknoth behind him, "I thought we were supposed to be in the company of friends here, Stumpy."

Al'Drogan—also known as the Red King by many and as Stumpy by Jarek—showed Jarek a frown under sandy blond hair and lightly glowing crimson eyes. "Because all raknoth must be such great friends, yes?"

Jarek willed his faceplate closed. It snapped shut with a decisive click. "Mayhaps mistakes were made," he said as the helmet's internal tactical display came alive.

The faceplate Pryce and Al had cobbled back together from the one Golga had wrecked with a far-too-close-for-comfort club swing wasn't perfect, but it was far better than nothing.

Armored as it was, he hesitated to poke his head back out. The house guards had only fired a few warning shots, presumably because they weren't looking to shoot the ever-living crap out of their master's estate, but he wasn't so sure the silence would last once they caught sight of him again.

"So do we have a volunteer to go first?" Jarek looked pointedly at Drogan. "I vote the bulletproof raknoth, personally."

Drogan only crossed his arms.

"Dammit, Stumpy. My armor doesn't regrow like your hide. You could walk straight up there and give those guys a good whack on the head—no problem."

"Do not talk to me about whacking anything," Drogan muttered.

Jarek smiled and reached up to pat the hilt of his beloved Big Whacker, the same sword he'd used to relieve Drogan of his hands a few weeks prior, before this entire alliance between human and raknoth had even been a twinkle in their wide, desperate eyes. Drogan's hands had since grown back, and creepily fast at that, but he hadn't stopped calling Drogan by the nickname Stumpy, if for no other reason than that it seemed to get under the raknoth's skin. Or hide. Whatever.

"Fine," Jarek said. "I'll go do all the work. Again. Might I trouble you for some cover, Commander?"

Alaric drew his mismatched revolvers and nodded. Jarek drew one of his own pistols. It wouldn't do to go killing potential allies, but a little suppressing fire might let him close on the gunmen without putting Fela through more abuse than need be. The poor exosuit had already been through too much lately. They all had.

He flicked a salute to Alaric and took off underneath the ornately carved arch that spanned the wall's entryway.

Under his own power, Jarek was pretty fast. Aided by Fela's strength and stability, "pretty fast" was upgraded to "impossibly fast" —at least for a human. At a full out sprint on nice flat ground, he could hit nearly sixty miles an hour.

The rock garden sand pit wasn't exactly nice running terrain, and the Big Whacker strapped to his back, not to mention the people shooting at him, didn't really promote textbook running form, but he was still well into the manicured yard before the first shots dinged off his armor.

He fired back in their general direction. Behind, Alaric's revolvers added their own voices to the chaos in the courtyard. There was a pained cry from the front porch as Jarek rounded a giant boulder at the corner of the house. A second cry followed, and the thunderous roar in the courtyard dimmed to a few traded shots every couple of seconds.

"I thought the plan was not to shoot our potential allies," Al said in Jarek's earpiece.

"Yeah. And then there's the hat too. Guy's clearly out of control."

In truth, he would bet money—if anyone had cared about money anymore—Alaric had only winged a couple of the gunmen to give the rest of them pause.

"Do you have a plan, sir?"

Jarek holstered his pistol, looked up to the first of the giant house's multiple slanted layers of roofing twenty feet above, and smiled. "Have you ever known me to be a man without a plan, Al?"

Before Al had time to point out the alarming frequency of times he'd led them into dangerous situations without a scrap of a plan, Jarek gathered himself and jumped. With Fela's legs, he easily cleared the edge of the rooftop and landed in a light crouch.

From the vantage point, he could see Alaric's revolvers poking around the wall to fire a couple of blind shots.

Jarek took off over the slanted, rust-colored rooftop. Several tiles cracked underfoot as he went. Al dropped four pins on his tactical display, designating the locations of the gunmen. Nearing the first two pins, Jarek went into a slide and allowed the roof's slant to carry him over the edge.

As he shot out to open air, he grabbed the rooftop edge and swung back under to land between the two men on the stone porch. Or at least he tried to.

Tiles shattered and slipped under his grip, and instead of reversing direction and swinging onto the porch, he ended up landing in the well-groomed bushes in front of it.

"Shit!"

"Well executed, sir."

He looked up from the tangle of greens and his retort died at the sight of the two repeater rifles trained at his face.

"Ah. Hey, fellas."

For a brief moment, the two Japanese men only stared at him in surprise. Then they snapped to it, tensing to fire.

Jarek leapt up and swatted the barrels aside hard enough to tear the rifles from their owners' grasps. He landed on the porch and sent one of the guards into the wall—no, through the wall, it turned out—with an open palm strike to the chest. Feeling an inkling of remorse at the damage, he caught the second guard's wrist to keep him from drawing his sword, bopped him "lightly" atop the head, and dumped him off the porch and into the bushes. That would keep him dazed for a minute or—

"Behind you, sir."

Jarek spun in time to deflect an incoming blade with a raised forearm. Said blade clapped thunder, and he realized it was a freaking shotgun bayonet he'd just narrowly avoided.

"Holy shit, dude." He yanked the weapon free, swept the guard's legs out with a kick, and planted a foot on the man's chest before inspecting it more closely. "This is hardcore."

Ahead, the last standing gunman snapped something at him in Japanese.

"He says, 'Put down the weapon, steel demon,'" Al said. "Or something like that."

"Great." Jarek held the gun non-threateningly to his side. "Well tell him we came here to talk and that we wouldn't have—"

Footsteps from inside. Rapid, padding thumps of—

Shit!

"Incoming!" Al cried.

Jarek was already dropping the gun and throwing himself backward. Too late.

The wall to his left exploded outward with a tearing sound, and what felt like a small freight train plowed into his side. Only the freight train appeared to have arms, mint green ones that wrapped around his midsection as they flew off the porch and into the courtyard below.

Jarek grabbed at strong mint green fingers and waited until the moment they hit the ground to rip and roll.

In a contest of pure strength, Jarek would have had his work cut out for him, even with Fela's strength. Breaking free in the wild tumble of their landing, on the other hand, was easy enough.

He reoriented himself as they bounced to a halt and drove a heel straight into Minty's face as the raknoth scrambled to regain his feet.

The blow sent Minty tumbling backward and bought Jarek a moment to roll to his feet.

"I was wondering if the adults were gonna come out to play. We need to talk to your boss. Uh, unless you are the boss… Sorry, I'm not great with faces. Zar'Kole?"

Minty pulled himself to his feet and brushed some dirt from the shoulder of his dark kimono. "Zar'Kole is not here, human. And I have no interest in talking."

"Ah." He caught a glimpse over the raknoth's shoulder of Alaric and Drogan entering the courtyard. "Is it all right if I call you Minty, then?"

Raknoth tended to fight as if they were invincible, which made sense seeing as they nearly were against most foes. This one was no different.

He lunged straight for Jarek's throat.

Jarek caught the raknoth's wrists and pivoted to drive an elbow into his temple. Minty ducked the blow, hooked an arm through Jarek's armpit, and stepped forward into what felt like the setup of a raknoth-powered body slam.

Jarek lifted his legs, and Minty reflexively supported his weight long enough for Jarek to replant his feet on the raknoth's thigh and torso and kick off as hard as he could. The grating shrieks of claws on armor made him flinch, but the kick landed him back on his own two feet with Minty staggering backward to catch his balance.

The raknoth gave a battle roar and was tensing to spring at him again when Drogan stepped in on his flank and drove him to the ground with a devastating punch to the head.

Jarek threw his fists to the air. "Stumpy with the KO!" He walked over, grabbed Drogan's hand, and raised it in victory. Or tried to.

Drogan shook his hand free in clear irritation. "Do not touch me, Jarek Slater. And he is not even… KO-ed, as you say."

In testament to Drogan's statement, Minty was staring between the two of them, clearly perplexed by the fact that Drogan wasn't tearing Jarek's head off.

"Okay," Jarek said. "So no KO. But wouldn't you say he looks thoroughly… stumped?"

It was hard to tell what with the lack of pupils and the uniform red glow, but he was pretty sure Drogan rolled his eyes.

"What is wrong with you?" Minty asked, rubbing at the spot where Drogan had decked him.

Jarek shrugged. "Hey, even we get bored sometimes. Well, maybe I shouldn't talk for Stumpy here, but I—"

"Jarek…"

The tone of Alaric's voice made him turn immediately. Four more raknoth stood under the stone arch of the entryway, watching them with crimson eyes. Minty gave a satisfied, hissing chuckle behind them.

Alaric drifted casually away from the newcomers and toward Jarek and Drogan. "I think our six o'clock is here," he muttered when he was close enough. Not that the raknoth wouldn't hear it from across the courtyard anyway.

Jarek traded an uncertain look with Drogan then gave the four raknoth a wave.

"Hey there, fellas. I don't suppose you'd have a minute to talk?"

<hr>

If Jarek had felt bad knocking a goon-sized hole in the wall of Zar'Kole's home earlier, he felt even worse when the raknoth invited them peacefully inside. Kole, it seemed, didn't share Minty's aversion to talking before hitting. Lucky them.

Inside, the abode was eloquent in its simplicity. Wood floors, paper-thin walls, and a nearly complete lack of clutter. Guards eyed them wearily and fingered weapons as they passed. Jarek didn't need to tell Al to keep his robot eyes peeled in every direction as they settled in to talk with Kole's four raknoth posted around them.

"Oh dear," Al said, speaking quietly in his earpiece. "Do please refrain from… well, being yourself, sir. I don't like our odds, and Minty back there still looks like he wants to eat you."

Jarek didn't turn to verify Al's assessment, he knew his companion was right. Drogan was pretty good in a rumble, and Alaric was quick on the draw, but the latter didn't do them much good against raknoth, and they were heartily outnumbered.

"Lips sealed," he murmured.

"What was that?" Kole asked.

God, it was creepy how much they heard.

Jarek willed his faceplate open as a sign of good faith. "Just talking to the voices in my head."

"Clever, sir," Al said quietly.

He suppressed the urge to tell Al to shove it as Kole considered him for a stretch.

"You may leave us," Kole finally said, directing his gaze to each of his raknoth in turn. "Let our guests rest easy knowing they will not be attacked again as long as they do not give us cause." His gaze lingered on Minty as he said the last part.

The raknoth left without a word, and Jarek did rest easy—or unclenched, at least.

Once they were alone, Kole sank to his knees on the thinly-matted floor and sat butt-to-heels, gesturing for Jarek and the others to join him. Drogan sank easily to the floor to mirror Kole's position. Jarek traded a look with Alaric, and they both sat cross-legged by some unspoken agreement.

A flicker of amusement played across Kole's features. The host he occupied had been Japanese and maybe in his late fifties. Jarek was under no delusions that the raknoth wouldn't rip the life out of him given cause, but for now, he looked kindly enough.

"You've come to warn us about the harvesters," Kole said once they were all settled. "And to ask for my help in defeating them, if I'm not mistaken."

How did he—

"You heard the messengers call?" Drogan asked. He looked taken aback himself.

Kole tilted his head back and forth. "Perhaps. Certainly, I felt a troubling disturbance as I dreamed two weeks ago. Meditated, rather," he added at Drogan's clear confusion. "Dreamed is a poor choice of words."

Drogan nodded, still looking uncertain. "And this disturbance?"

"At first I thought little of it. The thought continued to nag at me, though, which is why I finally went to speak with our ship today. Our messengers confirmed that it had not been my imagination. They felt it too. Your Zar was capturing messenger scouts, wasn't he? And now they've escaped?"

Drogan shot Jarek and Alaric a pointed stare. "The nest was compromised."

Jarek held up a thumb and forefinger. "We had a tiny bit of a misunderstanding. Lives were threatened. Stumps were made. I think the important takeaway is that we all screwed this pooch together."

Kole cocked his head as if picturing such an act.

"The true point is that we believe the Masters come for us presently," Drogan said. "And, annoying as some of their numbers may be, I do not see how we can survive without the humans, which leaves us at an impasse."

Jarek refrained from mentioning how, speaking of annoying things, he personally thought it was kind of annoying how the raknoth had come to their planet out of the blue and then decided to blow it to smithereens after the humans had thwarted their original plan to feed them to the harvesters, who were now kind of ironically coming to eat all of them together. In the interest of not starting a fight with the only raknoth who hadn't outright refused to listen to them, the poetic justice alone would have to do.

Four gold diplomacy stars for Jarek.

"It was only ever a matter of time," Kole said. His tone was tranquil, and his gaze distant. "Unfortunate that the lives of our peoples have become so irrevocably intertwined, but so it is. And so we will do what we must."

"So… does that mean you're in?" Jarek asked. "Just like that?"

Kole smiled, and it wasn't creepy or predatory or ominous. Just a sad smile. "We have all been 'in' since the moment my kin first decided to wreak nuclear havoc on this world and mask our continued existence from the Masters. Truly, my kind have been 'in' since the moment the rakul sent us to Earth, and since the moment your own kind decided to try to stop us. This has been centuries in the making, and if it must come to a head now, I will not fight it."

So… did that mean he was in? Jarek still wasn't quite sure.

"You will fight beside us, then, when the time comes?" Drogan asked.

"If the time comes. Yes. But first I would speak to the Masters. The messengers in our ship should suffice to reach them. I will commune with the rakul and see if we might not find peace this side of bloodshed."

Drogan tensed. "Do you think it wise to contact them before they arrive? If we are wrong—"

"Do you believe you are?" Kole asked. "Do any of you?"

Silence.

"Neither do I," Kole said. He rose to his feet in a smooth motion. "And even if you were, harvest has always been an inevitability. At worse, we quicken its fall. Either way, I tire of living in fear. Now is the time."

Jarek clapped his hands together after a length of hesitant silence. "All right, then. Lucky for us, we brought our hiking boots. Let's do it."

Kole gave a small shake of his head. "It is almost certainly better if I speak with the rakul alone. You should continue to rally what forces you can."

Coming from most people—or raknoth—that probably would've put Jarek's back-stab alarm at blazing conflagration status. There was something about Kole, though. Jarek didn't trust the raknoth, not by a long shot. Jarek didn't trust anyone that wasn't Al or Pryce. Rachel might be getting dangerously close to worming her way onto that list as well, but sure as shit not Zar'Kole. Still, Jarek didn't get the feeling that Kole was actively trying to screw them over.

But you never really knew until you knew.

"It would help if we had your endorsement," Drogan said. "Krogoth's ascent by challenge to Zar has not been well accepted by all."

Kole raised a hand for pause. "Krogoth slew Golga?"

"Technically, I'd say our people did most of the work," Jarek said, "but Krogoth definitely finished it."

"Golga would not fight the Masters," Drogan said. "He had to be removed if we had any hope of surviving."

Kole's hand slowly lowered. "I believe that. Golga was powerful.

Had he not been sent here with us, he might have soon joined the ranks of the Kul. Very well. I will send an envoy with you to represent my commitment to standing with those who would fight for survival. Lietha."

Their old pal Minty stepped into the room with barely a moment's pause. "Master, please do not—"

Kole silenced his underling with a raised hand. "It should not be for long. You heard everything?"

Minty—or Lietha, apparently—hung his head. "Yes, my Zar."

"Then you will be my voice in this expedition for now. Go with Al'Drogan and see to it that we are ready should the worse happen. If peace cannot be found, I will join you soon."

Lietha nodded, pulsing crimson eyes held toward the floor.

Drogan rose to his feet and bowed. Jarek and Alaric followed suit, after a fashion.

"I thank you, Zar'Kole," Drogan said. "And should it come to pass, I will be honored to fight by your side."

Kole inclined his head, bidding them farewell.

Jarek paused at the door. "Do you really believe there's a chance? For peace, I mean."

Kole was silent for several seconds, then he gave his head a small shake to confirm what his wistful expression already said.

Jarek swallowed, gave Kole a silent nod, and turned to follow the others.

At least they'd have the Zar on their side when the shit hit, right?

Maybe. But would it even matter?

On paper, the day might have been a victory, but somehow, as they headed back to the ship, Jarek couldn't seem to find anything other than cold dread in his chest.

CHAPTER THREE

Rachel's head continued on its shaking swivel as if by its own free will.

"I just don't get it."

She looked around at the others, searching for some confirmation that she had not in fact slipped into some bizarre reality where this all made perfect sense. "How the hell is Jarek the only one who got a yes?"

They were back in Newark, in the spacious workshop of Jay Pryce, tinkerer extraordinaire, celebrating the end of the raknoth-recruiting world tour.

"Whoa!" Jarek cried from above. He and Pryce appeared at the top of the spiral staircase in the corner, descending with a pair of wooden crates. "Why's that a surprise? You of all people know my charms are irresistible!"

Rachel snorted and rolled her eyes, then immediately regretted it when the Enochians shot her knowing grins.

Jesus. One kiss and suddenly she had to micromanage every little movement to avoid "sending signals." She could almost hear their thoughts. Oh, was that a lingering gaze? Oh, was Rachel deflecting because she secretly wanted it?

It was the end of times, and their fearless group of world-class fighters had all decided to go back to grade school.

Jarek wasn't helping with his constant not-so-subtle references to the kiss they'd shared in the tight hallways of Resistance HQ a couple weeks ago, just before the shit had well and truly hit.

She'd made it clear enough that he should just drop it and focus on more important things, like not dying. Part of her even wanted him to listen. The other part...

Wasn't important right now, she reminded herself. Because if there was anyone here she needed to get alone in a quiet room tonight, it was most certainly Alton Parker, who was finally here within her reach after weeks of evasive bullshit.

She shot a furtive glance at the raknoth and—

Oh god. Was everyone still waiting for her to say something?

"Whatcha got there?" she asked as Jarek and Pryce reached the bottom of the steps with their crates.

Nice one. Smooth as a raknoth hide.

What they had there turned out to be booze. A veritable horde of it —beers and whiskeys, all home-brewed by Pryce, of course. It was easy enough to see from the eclectic mix of items in the shop around them that Pryce lived for learning, poking, prodding, and otherwise finagling his way through the inner workings of the natural world. Given his and Jarek's shared love for alcohol, it made sense that home brewing and distilling had made their way high on the list of Pryce's favorite hobbies.

Rachel traded a hesitant look with Lea. She'd always had a bit of an aversion to anything capable of muddling her senses, especially when she had important business to tend to. The recently added condition that the fury of a bunch of intergalactic conquerors might come falling down on their heads at any minute paradoxically made her both crave a drink and fear it. But if there was any place in the world that was safe to kick up her boots, it was probably here. And if said important business, namely a firm talk with a blood-sucking alien, was going to happen, god knew she could probably use a touch of the liquid courage.

So she moved in to join the others in eagerly inspecting the stash Pryce and Jarek had deposited on the worktable. All of the others except Haldin, Elise, and Johnny, that is.

The three young Enochians were eyeing the crates uncertainly.

"You guys had alcohol on Enochia, right?" Rachel asked.

The words sounded stupid as soon as they'd left her mouth. Of course they had. It wasn't like basic chemistry ceased to exist outside the boundaries of Earth.

"Alco-huh?" Johnny said. "We just had something we called crack. Fun stuff. Kids loved it."

"He's messing with you," Hal said. "Of course we had alcohol… You guys take it rectally too, right?"

"Oh, boys…" Elise smiled at Rachel. "There's plenty of the stuff on Enochia, but we sheltered youths haven't ever really had any of it."

"Speak for yourself, lady," Johnny said. "You don't know where I've been."

"You're right," Elise said. "I always heard those Legion parties were out of this world."

"I think you mean out of *that* world," Johnny said.

Elise stuck her tongue out at him.

Jarek distributed mismatched glasses and cups across the table, shaking his head all the while.

Rachel's eyes drifted, as they seemed to every time she saw him now, to the dark red lines running diagonally across Jarek's face—not quite scars yet, but not far off. He caught her staring, and she averted her gaze, heat rushing to her face. Jarek had gone out of his way to make it known that the wounds didn't bother him and were, in fact, pretty damn badass.

She was pretty sure it was proof that he actually felt the exact opposite, and while she found the wounds more mesmerizing than hideous, she'd done her best to avoid staring. Whatever he might say, Jarek Slater was every bit as human as the rest of them, with all the self-conscious insecurities that entailed. Or so she told herself.

"Never had alcohol…" Jarek was saying, still gently shaking his head. "Yeesh!"

"I agree," Al called from Fela's collapsed form over by the shelves. "Strutting around with those unreasonably healthy livers. The gall of them."

"Yeah, yeah, Mr. Robot. Like liver disease is really what's gonna get any of us."

Jarek looked like he wanted to take the words back as soon as he said them. But they were out now, and the room went uncomfortably quiet as the weight settled over them. Because he was right.

Rachel had seen by proxy the raw power of a single rakul, and they were looking at as many as a dozen of them on their hands. Whether any of them wanted to admit it or not, it was a real possibility none of them would—

Jarek slapped a hand to the table hard enough to jolt them out of their respective funks. "Right then! Let's drink some drugs, kids!" He clapped a hand to Pryce's shoulder. "A round for the house on me!"

"I suppose I'll just throw it on your tab then," Pryce muttered, but he was smiling as he opened a bottle of whiskey and began to pour.

"Oh, you old rapscallion, you," Jarek said, taking glasses of amber liquid from Pryce and passing them out to the others. "What about you, Alton? Want one?"

Rachel's heart quickened at Alton's name.

After this drink. They'd toast, they'd drink, and she'd politely ask him for a word. No problem.

Alton gave a shrug that was more yes than no, and Jarek handed him a filled glass.

"Good on you, man." Jarek shook his head. "Alaric pulled the ol' commander duty card on us, and when I asked Stumpy and that Lietha dude if they wanted to partake in this team-building exercise, they were all, 'We do not imbibe the foul liquid, human.'"

"Interesting words from people who drink human blood to survive," Haldin said, followed in short order by an apologetic glance at Alton.

"Most of my kind are not particularly interested in or well equipped for what humans think of as friendship," Alton said, not seeming to particularly mind the jab. "We rarely socialize outside of our own clans. And as for the 'foul liquid,' I happen to enjoy the taste of it at times, but it has little effect on my physiology. We are perfectly capable of synthesizing our own pharmaceutical aids internally should the desire rise."

"Damn," Jarek said. "There's a skill I wouldn't mind having."

"Maker bless your boring human body, sir," Al said, this time from Jarek's comm.

Once everyone had received a glass, they all raised their drinks in cheers, a custom that turned out to be familiar to the Enochians as well.

"To saving the world, I guess," Jarek said.

"No pressure," Johnny said.

Rachel clinked her glass to Jarek's, and others all piled in.

"Cheers."

Everyone drank. Franco, Lea, and Jarek set to clapping Pryce on the back and clamoring about how fantastic the whiskey was. Phineas and Alton sipped their drinks stoically. The rest of the Enochians' reactions mostly involved strong grimaces and sputtering coughs.

Rachel, for her part, held it together as dragon fire burned its way down her throat—or at least thought she did until she caught Jarek grinning at her like she'd just done something especially cute. She narrowed her eyes at him and he turned back to his conversation with Pryce, grinning all the wider.

Once the burning receded, Rachel didn't so much mind the warm tingles the drink left shooting through her throat and slowly percolating up to her face and head, nor did she mind the subtle overtone of confidence that floated in as she fixed her eyes on Alton.

It was time. And he seemed to know it.

"You'd like to talk?" his voice asked quietly at the edge of her mind.

Rachel nearly jumped.

As far as she knew, he hadn't looked at her once in the past several minutes, but apparently her attention had not been lost on him.

"Yeah," she sent back, glancing surreptitiously at the others. *"Mind stepping upstairs for a bit?"*

Without a word or a shared thought, Alton turned and strode over to the tight-winding spiral staircase in the corner. Aside from a pair of curious frowns from Pryce and Jarek, no one seemed to think it particularly odd behavior.

Rachel waited until Alton disappeared above, then she finished her drink and followed, doing her best to ignore the stares on her back and the roiling apprehension in her gut.

"YOU'VE BEEN AVOIDING ME," Rachel finally said after what had been at least a full minute of tense silence.

She stood in Pryce's cozy living quarters, facing Alton in the armchair he'd chosen.

Alton tilted his head, not quite disagreeing. "We've been busy."

"You've ducked out of every room I've walked into since Golga's attack."

Was that an amused smirk that crossed his face?

"You tried to murder brick and asphalt using my body as a battering ram last time we properly conversed in person," Alton said.

She held his unblinking gaze.

What did he want, an apology? The conversation he was referring to just so happened to be the same one where he'd told her that it was his own people—and not just the raknoth people at large, but his own clan—who'd been responsible for both Mom's death and the attack that had robbed her of Dad and Grams. Emotional volatility should've probably been a given.

If he hadn't wanted a pissed off arcanist on his hands, maybe Alton should have tried to stop his bastard ilk from killing her family.

"I need answers," she finally said. "And not just a vague summary. Details. What was my mom really up to? What went wrong?" She forced herself to unclench. "Who killed her, and where were you during all of this?"

Alton was watching her closely now. "Having second thoughts?"

"What? About working with the guys who literally blew the planet back into the dark ages? How could I have doubts about that?"

Alton's eye roll was so subtle she wasn't rightly sure it had even happened.

He sank back into his chair and crossed one leg with an affected sigh, taking his sweet time about it. "I've already told you most of what I know."

"Bullshit."

Alton held up a hand for peace and quiet. "I'll tell you the rest if you sit and promise to behave."

The sudden urge filled her to flip the armchair with him on it. "Seriously?"

Alton waved toward the couch opposite him.

Did the bastard really have to be so smug about everything?

Still, she was the one who needed answers, so she reigned in the violent thoughts, dropped onto the couch, and settled for speaking a piece of her mind. "I don't like you."

That was genuinely amusing to Alton, judging by the twitch of his lips, but there was bitterness in his expression as well. "Then you are among good company on this planet, human and raknoth alike."

Rachel was almost taken aback for a second. Now that she thought about it, she couldn't recall having seen Alton interact with any of his own kind beyond brief passing in the past couple weeks, but... It didn't matter. What mattered now was getting the answers she was owed.

She was about to press again when Alton started of his own volition.

"I was there the day it happened."

Aching pain informed her just how tightly she was grasping her own fingers as she waited silently for him to elaborate. If Alton had been there—Jesus, if he'd been involved...

How could she bring herself to accept that?

Alton was watching her, quiet and calm, assessing. "Everything I told you was true. I never saw your mother. But I also stood obediently by as Zar'Faenor compelled four violently-inclined men to go to your house and tie up loose ends. I did as I was told and played jail keeper to your mother's co-conspirators while Faenor went to join the hunt. I did not kill your mother, but I cannot say my actions were completely removed from the deed."

"And who did?" Rachel asked quietly, leaning forward. "Who killed her?"

Alton thought about that for a few moments before speaking. "She did," he finally said.

"What?"

He shifted in his chair. "She gave them a good chase, from what they told me afterward. If it had just been her, she might have even made it on the run for a while. But it wasn't, of course. She had her family to look after." He met her eyes. "She drew them away from your house on purpose."

His words settled in Rachel's stomach like hunks of cold iron. "But what did you mean by… She didn't…?"

"They caught up to her in the woods west of your home. The plan was never to kill her—not until she'd reversed our condition, at least. She knew that. She also knew that she had no hope of resisting when scores of us stood by, ready to break her mind and make her do it. It wasn't until Faenor arrived that she truly made her decision, though, I think."

Rachel waited, too ill to speak. She felt like she had the first time they'd emerged after the bombings, that terrible empty moment when she'd realized with utter certainty that everything she'd ever thought of as home was irrevocably gone forever. An image crept into her head, unnerving in its clarity—her poor, beautiful mom, defeated and afraid, standing in the open forest off the old Wissahickon trails, held captive in the steely grip of two raknoth, with several more all around. Something about it was wrong—too real, too detailed for mere imagination.

"Zar'Faenor was never one to mince words or play games. When Lilly found out you were in danger…" Alton cocked his head. "You are of course aware of the ways one might project their senses further than normally possible?"

It was a rhetorical question, and Rachel didn't bother answering it. She was too busy dreading where this was going.

"Psychedelics were clearly not on hand," Alton said. "Sleep and deep meditation would have been far too easily counteracted by the raknoth holding her."

"She died." Rachel's voice came out a whisper, heavy tears pressing at her eyes.

"She stopped her own heart in the blind hope she'd somehow be able to help you from miles away. And, I take it, she succeeded. They tried to resuscitate her, of course…"

But Rachel had stopped listening.

She'd had so many questions to ask Alton, so many important details to clarify. But now the room spun, every thought and memory and moment of crying rage that she'd ever expended over her past shifting as if gravity itself had reoriented. It was like something had broken—a dam she hadn't noticed holding back all the incongruent memories she hadn't known she'd had. Fragments of that horrible day oozed forward, indifferent to her plight as she tried to hold them back.

The blood. The helpless, dull shock that had roared in her ears and rendered movement impossible, like being pinned under an enormous waterfall against cold, hard stone. The terror she'd felt as those men, those mindless demons, had turned their sights on her.

And the small voice that had whispered that it was going to be okay just before everything had gone dark—the voice that couldn't have been hers.

Mom.

She wanted to say the word out loud. Wanted to let the tears spill over and scream it until her voice left her. But she only sat there, silent and still, under Alton's gaze.

"She took control," she whispered. "That's why I never remembered. It was—" She shakily swallowed a sob and clenched her teeth. She wouldn't cry. Not here. Not in front of this, this—

A loud series of whooping cries from below broke through her thoughts, reminding her of the party happening just downstairs. It was bizarre to imagine them down there, having fun, completely unaware that her world was shattering right over their heads.

"She gave her life for yours," Alton said. "And to save the rest of the world from my kind, I imagine she was hoping. With her died our hope of curing her arcane blight."

"I... She..."

She couldn't get the words out. Wasn't even sure what they'd be if she could. A deep, aching loss pulsed in her chest, growing stronger with every second and every detail that snapped into place in her new perspective.

Rachel had always assumed it had been instincts that had taken control all those years ago—that she'd snapped and somehow managed to lash out with her powers so violently that she'd taken down two of her attackers, scared the others away, and summarily lost consciousness. People did crazy things in crazy times, right?

That she couldn't remember any of it didn't seem so odd, as certifiably fucked up as the entire scenario had been. Sometimes minds broke. Sometimes they shut things out. But this was something else.

She had no way of knowing for sure, of course. There would be no evidence to prove anything Alton was saying, aside from the fact that her mom had died in the woods, surrounded by monsters.

But something deep inside of her was suddenly certain that she hadn't survived that day on her own, that her mom had reached out from the place between life and death and taken hold of Rachel's body, wielded her like a weapon to defend her in a way she hadn't known she was capable of.

Her mom had died to directly protect her.

Too much. It was too much.

Because, after everything she'd told herself over the years, all the time she'd spent wondering what might have been if she'd only been stronger and all the time and patient care John and Michael had put into convincing her that none of it had been her fault and that there was nothing she could have done differently to save her family, she could finally see it clearly.

It wasn't her fault. It was theirs.

The ache in her chest was unbearable now. In that moment, she would have done anything to see her mom one more time. To tell her that she loved her. To tell her anything.

But she couldn't. Would never be able to again.

Alton and his friends had seen to that.

"Rachel," Alton said quietly, seeming to sense some shift in the air, "I'm not proud of—"

"Get out." The bite in her voice surprised her more than it seemed to affect Alton.

He nodded and stood with slow movements, then ghosted toward the stairs. On the top step, he paused, as if intending to say something.

"Don't," she snapped. She couldn't hear him talk right now, couldn't stand looking at him one more second without putting him through the window. "Just… just get away from me."

Alton nodded, and descended the stairs without another word.

For a long while, Rachel sat unmoving, head reeling with the new information that had dropped so suddenly, so unexpectedly on her grasp of the past. In hindsight, she wasn't sure how she'd expected anything else out of this conversation. It wasn't like there'd been any possibility of good news.

But this…

This was insurmountable. Unforgivable. Her mom—her poor, loving mom…

"Goldilocks!" came a cry from below—unmistakably Jarek. "You gotta come check this shit out!"

Fear rose in her chest at the thought of going down there, at seeing the others laughing and carrying on while her little world continued to quietly fall apart, unbeknownst to any of them. To any of them but Alton, that was. Alton who'd sit there quietly himself, pretending to feel remorse, to be something other than the cold monster who'd stood by and—

"Goldilocks?"

She narrowly caught the mindless yell that leapt for the top of her throat like an escaping prisoner. Slowly, carefully, she let out a heavy sigh instead.

There was no escaping it. Not now. She could go down there and put on a mask, or she could stay up here and risk Jarek's impending checkup and well-meaning but ultimately unwanted questions.

So she grabbed her glass and headed for the stairs.

CHAPTER FOUR

It turned out that "this shit" Jarek had been so insistent on Rachel checking out hadn't even actually gotten underway yet. As she descended the stairs from Pryce's quarters, Rachel spied Haldin huddled over an empty beer bottle at one of the work tables, studying the glass cylinder with rigid attention. Across the table, Elise watched him with rosy cheeks and a loving grin.

"There you are!" Jarek cried up at Rachel, then he scuttled over to join Haldin and Elise.

Johnny and Lea were there as well, though they seemed somewhat distracted with Johnny's attempt to teach her some manner of secret handshake.

Everyone looked like they were at least a few drinks in.

The adults—Jarek excluded, of course—had retired over to the benches of the other work table, not so curious as to hover around waiting for the big event (though Pryce looked like he was seriously thinking about it—his neck craned drastically and his gaze attentive).

What little amusement Pryce's expression and the room's energy tickled into her chest died the instant she realized Alton had stepped out. Or maybe it was more accurate to say the moment she thought of

Alton at all, seeing as his presence probably would have only made her angrier.

Just give them a few minutes, she told herself. A few minutes pretending all was well, then she could duck out, go get some sleep—or some peace and quiet, at least.

"No way," Jarek was muttering as Rachel drew close to the table and Haldin slid a hand over the brown glass bottle. "There's no way."

"For the record," Rachel said, "drinking and channeling don't mix well, if that's what you're thinking."

Haldin looked up with a guilty grin. Jarek made a shushing sound toward her and encouraged Haldin on.

Haldin shrugged and closed his eyes. The glass bottle in his hand began contorting and shrinking down like a plant decaying in fast forward.

"Holy shit," Jarek muttered.

The bottle started stretching into a long, narrow stem, its motion smooth, liquid. The glass pooled at one end, forming a large lump that segregated itself into discrete chunks. A flower, she realized. He was making a glass flower.

In what little time they'd had to discuss the matter, Rachel and Haldin had come to the conclusion that their abilities operated around the same principles, yet she'd never seen anything quite like this, reshaping matter by will. Was that why they'd called it Shaping on Enochia? Watching the process unfold, ideas about how such a thing could be possible began to float through her mind.

The glass ceased its wriggling and resumed its existence as normal, albeit flower-shaped, glass. It wasn't exactly a masterpiece sculpture, but considering the focus she suspected it would take to pull something like that off, it was pretty damn good.

"Damn, dude." Jarek jerked his head in Elise's direction. "If she doesn't sleep with you tonight, I might."

Hal was busy frowning at his creation. "It, uh, got away from me a little there." He held the flower out to Elise, his eyes a touch cloudy, and gave Rachel a guilty grin. "You were right. Shaping and whiskey…"

"It's perfect," Elise said, taking the slightly rough flower, and she looked like she really meant it. "Thank you, love." She leaned over the table to kiss him.

For some reason Rachel didn't care to fathom right now, the loving display only itched at the growing irritation in her chest.

"How come you never make *me* flowers?" Jarek asked Rachel with an exaggerated frowny face.

She couldn't help but laugh, troubles momentarily forgotten. Maybe it was the way he said it, or maybe it was just the way he was leaning on the table with both elbows, chin propped between his palms.

"Follow me across the galaxy first, and we'll see," she said.

Jarek's eyes didn't leave hers for a second. "Maybe I will."

"Make sure you bring movies," Johnny said, leaning in around Haldin. "Lots of movies. What?" he added when he turned back to the look Lea was shooting him. "It's a long-ass trip."

Rachel hesitantly accepted another small pour of whiskey and retreated step-by-inconspicuous-step to Pryce's workbench as the youths resumed their game of drink and the older crowd continued discussing whatever they were discussing—probably something along the lines of *A Thousand Questions, Enochian Edition,* if the riveted look on Pryce's face was any indication.

She pulled herself up to sit on a section of workbench, taking care not to disturb any of Pryce's precious tools. She leaned against the wall and watched as Jarek adopted a paternal air and led Johnny and Hal through the act of shooting their next round of amber fire in one go. It was a crime according to Pryce, but Johnny and Hal traded a glance, shrugged, and followed Jarek's lead.

Rachel almost smiled as the three celebrated their victory over the dastardly liquor. Jarek had been uncharacteristically somber when he'd returned from Japan, despite having landed what sounded to her like a big win. Her own shit aside, it was nice to see him acting like himself again.

But then he had to go and call after Alton, wondering where the raknoth had wandered off to, and the sick anger crept back up to play.

What did Jarek care where Alton was, where any raknoth was? She'd already been weary enough of the way he liked to act all buddy-buddy with Drogan and Alton, but now…

Jesus, she should get out of here, go do something else.

Michael. She should be spending time with Michael rather than sitting here, drinking booze she no longer had any thirst for and watching her allies have entirely too much fun for their current circumstances.

Her brother's nightmares had become all too common ever since he'd been front and center for the giant telepathic blast of escaping messengers a few weeks ago, which was especially unfortunate since he seemed to do little but sleep the days away lately. Michael had always been fond of his sleep, but this was well beyond that. He'd even had a few more violent episodes—seizing and screaming and flailing, remembering little afterwards.

It was terrifying to watch. Worse, she didn't have a damn clue what to do about it.

The nightmares may have just been nightmares, but she had a feeling the bad attacks had some external trigger, probably messenger-related. In what scraps of conversation she'd managed with them, Alton and Drogan had both wagered the messengers were too… incorporeal for Rachel to be able to shut out of Michael's head completely.

That hadn't stopped her from trying. She'd added half a dozen glyphs to enhance her brother's telepathic shielding, both with external devices like the cloaking pendant she wore on a chain at her neck and with tattoo-style glyphs like Jarek and many Resistance fighters had. Nothing seemed to make a difference. Maybe because messengers were still creeping past her defenses, as the raknoth had suggested they might.

Or maybe because Michael's exposure to such a raw, powerful psychic power had simply left him traumatized. Psychologically scarred. Objectively, it might have even been a better explanation. She just didn't want to believe it.

An external source like the messengers triggering Michael's

episodes was a problem that feasibly had some solution. If his psyche had simply been overloaded until something had broken, on the other hand, that was much murkier territory.

Alton had originally suggested Michael's symptoms should fade with time, but, all things considered, she wasn't so sure Alton had a firm grasp on the concept of psychological damage. Hell, maybe none of the raknoth did, for that matter. To live as long and take as many lives as a raknoth did without going batshit insane, she was pretty sure some amount of psychopathy was required.

Whatever the case, she had a feeling she'd feel better about spending her time with Michael right now.

Before she could work up the will to make her excuses and slink off, though, Elise broke away from the young crowd and glided over her way, her normal eloquent grace only slightly marred by the drink.

Great. Just what she needed right now.

Still, Rachel couldn't quite bring herself to completely turn down Elise's friendly gesture and jet out as the younger Enochian hopped up to the bench top beside her.

Rachel nodded toward Elise's empty glass. "How are you feeling?"

"Warm." Elise wrinkled her nose and smiled, her cheeks flushed. "And kind of fuzzy. It's nice."

Over at the table, the boys were downing another shot of whiskey, each holding a beer as well now—aside from Jarek, who was holding another whiskey. Apparently he needed one for shooting and one for sipping.

"They're really going for it," Elise said.

"Yeah... Guess Jarek has that effect on people sometimes."

She felt Elise's glance and tensed, immediately regretting the direction she'd just opened up, but the Enochian didn't say anything.

Maybe she liked Elise after all. Except...

Except now that she was sitting here next to her, all Rachel could think about was that Elise and the other Enochians had lived aboard a small ship for almost an entire year with one of the raknoth who'd willingly participated in the murder of her family. They were roommates with the bastard. Friends, even.

"Why did you even come here?"

Elise was looking at her as if she'd been slapped before Rachel fully processed that the words had indeed left her mouth.

What was going on with her? Why was she this… this… lost? This angry?

She'd known what was coming, had a pretty good idea what had happened. She'd made peace with it. The details about her family's final hours were just that. Details. They didn't change anything, really.

So why did she want to scream when she thought about their little floundering human-raknoth alliance?

Elise was still watching her, looking like she was wondering if she should just buzz off and leave Rachel to her thoughts.

"Sorry," Rachel said. "I'm just…"

Wondering how the hell you people convinced yourselves befriending a raknoth was a good idea?

Maybe a touch strong. Something told her she'd be making a mistake to start questioning the raknoth, and Alton in particular, too strongly in front of the Enochians.

"I guess I'm just wondering why you were all willing to give up your lives on Enochia just to maybe help some people you don't know from another planet. I mean, I get it. You find out there are more humans in the universe and that they might be in trouble, and you want to help. I probably would too. But you guys have a whole planet to go back to. You've seen what's coming for us." She turned to Elise. "You don't have to…"

What? Die here?

"It's not your fight, is all I'm saying."

Elise studied her silently for a stretch. "And it is yours?" she finally asked. "We have some space on the ship, you know. We could take you and Jarek with us. Michael and Lea too. Pryce and Alaric. But I'm guessing you'd all have the same answer as us."

Rachel said nothing.

"And maybe we do have a planet to go back to," Elise said slowly, "but maybe not for long. If the rakul roll through Earth, I doubt it'll escape their notice that their raknoth seeded another planet with humans. Enochia would probably be their next stop. We can't let that happen." She shook her head. "We can't leave any more than you can."

Elise's gaze drifted to Haldin, her vibrant blue eyes looking worried.

Worried about what, though? Their lives? The safety of their planet? Or was it something more?

Whatever it was, Elise seemed to shrug it off as she turned back to Rachel with a somber look. "It's not fair or right or anything else along those lines, but it doesn't matter. This fight belongs to all of us now."

Jesus. How old was this girl, again? Johnny, Haldin, and Elise couldn't have been older than nineteen or twenty, but to listen to them sometimes—or to Haldin and Elise, at least—their souls might have been triple that.

Mature beyond their years or not, though…

"So that's it? One of the raknoth terrorizing Enochia tells you guys there are bigger fish to fry and you all hop on an alien ship out of some sense of civic duty?"

Elise studied her. "One begins to wonder if their efforts and good will are unwanted."

Rachel tried to bring herself to indicate that that wasn't what she was trying to say, but her throat and mouth seemed especially uncooperative where anything apologetic or reasonable was concerned right now.

Maybe Elise sensed and accepted that Rachel was dealing with something bigger than trust issues over their motives. Or maybe she was just some manner of matronly saint. Either way, she was calm and open as she continued.

"I guess it's fair to say we're not all shiny heroes who wake up every day thinking of nothing but saving the world. Or worlds. Left to our own devices, I don't think any of us but Hal would've ended up here." She cocked her head as if acknowledging some outside point. "Or have survived the raknoth's original plans on Enochia. But Hal's…"

"On a mission?"

Rachel wasn't entirely sure why she picked those particular words beyond the fact that, with the exception of tonight's festivities, Haldin always seemed to be walking around with the weight of a world or two on his shoulders—the quintessential picture of a man on a mission.

Elise bobbed her head in agreement, the beginnings of a sad smile stretching her mouth. "He is certainly that. If there's one shiny hero among us, it's him."

While every thought of Alton still seemed guaranteed to spike her blood pressure, hearing Elise talk about the enormous enigma that was Enochia was at least partially beginning to calm Rachel's nerves. When she spoke, the hard edge was fading from her tone. "And what does that make you guys?"

"We're his family," Elise said, without hesitation. Her gaze took on a distant quality. "He's lost people. I mean, we all have, but…"

Rachel watched Haldin turn over the glass flower in his hands with a dark frown. "He doesn't seem like the type to forgive himself so easily."

Takes one to know one, right?

"No," Elise said. "He's never really stopped blaming himself for the one. For any of them, really. He's learned to deal, but it's always there."

Takes one to know one indeed.

"It's good he's had you through all of it, then. I'm sure it helps."

Elise's expression suggested it wasn't quite so cut and dried, but she said nothing.

Across the room, Haldin and Jarek had begun debating defensive hand-to-hand tactics now, complete with wobbly demonstrations.

"Great," Rachel said. "Graduating from drunken channeling to drunken sparring."

Elise's smile only looked gently pushed rather than forced. "Aren't we lucky?"

"Ringside seats," Rachel agreed. "Not bad. The Soldier of Charity versus the Enochian Enigma."

"The Demon of Divinity."

Rachel glanced at Elise, sensing it wasn't just a random nickname.

"It's what they called him back on Enochia," she said. "The people who wanted him hanged after the first execution went sideways."

"Oh." Rachel hesitated, unsure whether she should ask more. Then, "Sideways?"

Elise smiled for real at whatever she read on Rachel's expression. "It's definitely been an adventure, I'll say that much. I keep telling Hal we should start writing some of it down. I think it'd be good for him. For us."

"I think I'd read the shit out of that."

"So why Soldier of Charity?" Elise asked, after a marginally more pleasant silence.

"I still don't know the whole story. I just know he joined up with some mercenary outfit back in the day and they didn't turn out to be the world-saving do-gooders he'd thought they were. He decided to stop them, and I guess shit got messy. After that, I guess he developed a reputation for helping the people who needed it instead of the ones who had something to give him for it."

"So he's a smart-ass with a strong moral compass?"

"You forgot man-child, but yeah, something like that."

"Well, at least he's got it where it counts." Elise gave her a mischievous grin. "Plus he's not too hard on the eyes."

"Just on the ears and the brain," Rachel said.

Elise wasn't wrong, of course. Even with the fresh battle scars, Jarek was a handsome guy, and Rachel would've been lying if she said she hadn't spent some time lingering on the memory of their kiss and imagining more well beyond a stolen hallway peck. But there was no place for blossoming relationships in their worlds right now, and even if there had been, she wasn't about to crack open and spill these thoughts to Elise just because they shared the same anatomy.

Lucky for Rachel, she was saved from having to when her comm buzzed with an incoming call.

Commander Stacy Daniels, read the display.

Shit. Make that *unlucky* for her.

She set her glass down and hit Accept. The commander appeared on the holo, looking troubled.

"Michael?" Rachel asked.

Daniels gave a slight nod. "He's okay, but I wanted to let you know he just had another episode."

"Shit." Rachel took a deep breath, trying to loosen the sudden anxious pit in her stomach.

"We have people with him," Daniels said. "You should get some rest."

"No, I'll be over. I should be with him. Thanks, Stacy."

Daniels gave her a sad smile. "See you soon then."

"I'm sorry, Rachel," Elise said quietly once the call had ended. "Is there anything we can do?"

Rachel hopped to her feet and handed Elise the remainder of her whiskey. "Finish this. Celebrate. Have fun." She tried to force a smile. "Don't worry about us. Michael always was a bit of a party pooper."

CHAPTER FIVE

Night was falling in Newark, lacing the air with a faint chill as they made their way around the block to the small park where Jarek's ship was parked. Rachel suppressed a shiver and glanced over at Jarek, who'd insisted on accompanying her, and on donning Fela to do it. Never leave home without the big guns, he'd said. She ran a thumb over the glyphed surface of her staff and couldn't say she disagreed with him. Still...

"Are you sure this doesn't count as drunk driving?"

"You gonna put me under arrest, officer?" There was more than just amusement in the alluring grin he shot her. "Look, just because the tykes back there can't handle their booz—"

A metallic thunk announced Jarek's discovery of the garbage container he hadn't noticed in his path. The container tipped over with a crash, spewing old trash onto the run-down sidewalk.

She snorted. "You were saying? About the tykes and the booze?"

He narrowed his eyes, and his faceplate slid shut and locked with a small click.

She couldn't help but smile. "Pout then."

Out here, in the cool night air with Jarek and away from the crowd —aside from Lea, who'd also tagged along—she felt temporarily lighter, more centered. Then the ship came into view, and her smile faded as Michael and the rest of tonight's shitstorm shifted firmly back to the forefront of her thoughts. A glance back told her Lea was feeling the same worry where Michael was concerned.

Lea and Michael were close, that much had been obvious since Rachel had first seen them together. Lea might have even had a thing for Michael, but Rachel wasn't sure how the Spongehead felt about it. She hadn't had much of a chance to see the two interact before Michael had been caught in the messenger burst.

Whatever there was between them, Lea hadn't thought twice about slipping away from the party to come with her and Jarek.

The flight to HQ wasn't long at all, and Jarek thankfully raised no objections to letting Al handle the piloting.

They set down in the graveyard of old, rusted shipping containers that had recently been the front for the secret entrance to the underground Resistance HQ. Now that the late Zar'Golga's forces had literally blown the roof off HQ and the need for secrecy had passed right along with Zar'Golga's life, the Resistance was expanding the base out into the shipping yard.

It was a major upgrade, as far as Rachel was concerned. HQ 1.0 had been a claustrophobic's nightmare.

Unfortunately, Michael's quarters were still down in the old section, so she took a deep breath and tried to ready herself for the walls to close in.

The Resistance crew in charge of renovations had already cleared the old common room of its considerable debris and added both a raised, mostly translucent dome and a staircase entrance from the lot above. Even in the night hour, the base was fairly alive with the expansion efforts, with work lights scattered around the yard and the sounds of power tools and busy voices drifting in from all around.

Plenty of those sounds ceased and turned to cold stares as the three of them reached the dome and descended into the old common room. Much as they'd fought and bled for these people, Rachel knew she and Jarek weren't the most popular kids on the block right now. How could they be when they'd brought home a group of oddly human aliens and driven the Resistance into allying with the very creatures they'd been formed to resist?

It wasn't like they'd had many choices. When the baddest badasses in the galaxy were coming to eat your entire planet, you couldn't really pick and choose which allies you wanted to take for the fight, right?

Maybe.

The fact that the Resistance and Krogoth's forces had formed what tenuous alliance they had was proof enough that everyone understood it was probably their only real option for survival, but it didn't mean anyone had to be happy about it.

Rachel sure as hell wasn't, especially not after her talk with Alton tonight, but that hadn't seemed to stop her, Jarek, and the Enochians from becoming the blame targets for half the Resistance.

Whatever. She couldn't blame them too much. Most of the men and women in the Resistance had lost friends or family to the raknoth and their forces. And that wasn't even to mention the tiny fact that the raknoth had caused the Catastrophe fifteen years ago. Destroying the planet and preying on them ever since... It was a lot to try to forget overnight.

If Rachel hadn't seen the monsters coming for them, she wouldn't have considered an alliance with the raknoth for even a minute. As things stood, she wasn't sure they wouldn't be better off trying to find another way even now.

And sure, maybe it hadn't completely been a one way street. But so what if the Catastrophe had been the raknoth's response to the viral would-be-genocide her mom had unleashed? It wasn't like the raknoth had been planning on letting Earth live on happily ever after before that. If things had gone to plan, it would only have been a matter of time until they'd called the rakul to come harvest the planet anyway.

So boo-freaking-hoo.

As far as Rachel could tell, they all would have been better off if her mom's virus had done its job and wiped the raknoth from the face of the Earth.

Jarek's voice broke the darkening stream of her thoughts as they wound their way through the common room and down a narrow hallway. "You okay over there?"

"Fine," she muttered, in no mood to talk any of this out right now.

She didn't have to worry too much. The people of the Resistance would never think of the raknoth as anything but the lesser of their current enemies—certainly not as full, welcome allies. For now, maybe they could all just fall in line and focus on surviving. Maybe.

She kept her eyes front and center as they made their way through the base, engaging neither the accusing stares nor the friendly hellos they got from the few Resistance members who seemed to maybe not resent them for breathing.

When they made it to Michael's room, he was sitting on his twin-sized bed, elbows resting on his knees and face buried in his hands. It struck her how much thinner he looked these days than he had even a month or two earlier. The thought only fed the angry flames building deep down.

Rachel was only a little surprised to see Lea's mother, Commander Stacy Daniels, still with him, sitting quietly in the corner of the small room.

Rachel went straight to Michael, sat down beside him on the bed, and draped an arm across his broad shoulders. Lea went to hug her mother, and the two talked quietly. Jarek hovered back outside the doorway to give Rachel and Michael the pretense of privacy.

"Hey, Spongehead," Rachel said softly, reaching up to rub the short but puffy sprigs of Michael's hair.

His dark skin looked ashen, and when he looked at her, the whites of his eyes were bloodshot.

"Rachel," he said slowly, as if it had taken him more than an instant to recognize her. He glanced at Commander Daniels. "I told them they didn't need to bother you every time this happens."

"And I told them they'd better. You're never a bother, Spongehead."

He frowned and sniffed the air. "You've been drinking."

"Just celebrating a safe return. It doesn't matter. This is more important."

Michael's mouth formed a humorless smile. She rested her head against his shoulder and looped her arms around one of his, wishing she had something better to say.

"What's happening to me, Rache?" he asked after a length of silence, his voice almost a whisper.

It broke her heart to see him like this, so tired and frail. And so completely beyond her ability to help.

She squeezed his arm and leaned back to fix him with a serious look. "I don't know. But I'm going to figure out how to fix it, even if it means going out there and stomping the floor with every one of these rakul bastards until there's no one left to beam bad vibes your way. I promise."

"I hear that," Jarek said, stepping into the room. "Even brought my stomping boots to help."

This time, Michael's smile was a bit more sincere. Especially when Lea came over to give him a hug. When they pulled apart, though, Michael wasted no time in sinking wearily back to the bed.

"Do you want me to tell them what you saw?" Commander Daniels asked.

Michael gave a bitter smile. "I think I can still manage that much, at least." He looked around at them uncertainly. "I don't know much. The… visions, or whatever they are, are really intense when they're happening, but I never seem to remember more than a few random scraps once they pass."

Lea rested a hand on his shoulder.

"Hey, we've all been there, Mikey," Jarek said.

Rachel shot him her best shush look and squeezed Michael's forearm in support.

"I remember a room," he said after a while. "I think it might have been a raknoth ship, kind of like the one the Enochians came in."

"Was there anything else?" Rachel asked softly.

Michael nodded. "Raknoth. There were raknoth. Three of them, I think. And there was this voice, this terrible voice."

"What did it say?" Lea asked.

"Traitors." Michael shuddered. "I think they're getting close. The rakul, I mean. I don't know how to explain it, but I have this feeling."

Rachel traded a concerned glance with Lea and wrapped her arm back around Michael. "We'll be ready. We're going to figure this out."

If only she'd felt half as confident as her words sounded.

Michael looked less than convinced, but he didn't argue. "What Alton told you about my exposure leaving me, uh, marked… Did he say anything about what that would mean when the rakul came?"

Rachel was pretty sure she managed to avoid visibly bristling at the mention of Alton. Inside, it was a different story, but she did her best to relax and remind herself that Michael came before the other stuff.

"He said you might hear more than you wanna hear. He didn't seem very certain about it, though. Why do you ask?"

"I, uh…" He shook his head. "I don't know. I just have this feeling like I'm connected to the rakul somehow, like I'm seeing these snippets straight from them."

"I think," said a strong voice from the hallway, "that Michael Carver is correct."

They all whipped around to see a middle-aged man with sandy blond hair step into the room. Only it was no man at all, Rachel realized with a jolt of alarm. It was Al'Drogan, playing at being human, just like Alton Parker always did outside of battle. The physical deception was probably the only reason the Resistance soldiers on his flanks were only fidgeting restlessly with their weapons instead of training them on the back of the raknoth's head.

Alaric was just behind Drogan, along with a Japanese man that a quick mental sweep confirmed was, like Drogan, also not actually a man. It must have been the raknoth Zar'Kole had sent back with Jarek —Lietha, that was it.

"Hey, buddy," Jarek said to Drogan. "What brings your stumps 'round here?"

It was a damned good question. "Allies" or not, the raknoth presence on base just begged for the slipping of itchy trigger fingers. And the way Rachel was feeling right now, she couldn't guarantee it wouldn't be her finger—or mind, at least—that did the slipping.

"Zar'Krogoth asked to stay informed of Michael's... episodes," Daniels said behind them.

"He neglected to mention he'd be sending his second in command by when we did so," Alaric said, pushing past Drogan and scooting in to check on Michael.

"And a call wouldn't do?" Rachel asked.

"Not that we're not thrilled to see you two and all," Jarek added, "but..." He nodded out to the hall where four shotgun-toting Resistance soldiers were watching the raknoth with all the laxity of cats in a dog kennel.

The raknoth paid the soldiers no mind.

"We wished to hear Michael Carver's accounting in person," Drogan said.

He took a step toward them to allow Lietha entry into the too-cramped room. That made Rachel tense enough on its own. Then she caught the slightest flicker of red in Drogan's eyes, and it registered in a flash exactly why he'd come here.

"No." She stood and planted herself between Michael and Drogan. "You're not rooting around in my brother's head. Fuck that."

Jarek glanced between her and Drogan, then understanding dawned. "Ah. Stumpy, you tricky old bastard."

It was like the air in the room had thickened with strained silence made corporeal. Outside, the soldiers had somehow managed to tense harder.

"We must inspect what Michael Carver has learned about the rakul," Drogan said.

The raknoth stepped closer, and this time Jarek barred his way with a raised hand before Rachel could grab her staff and tell the raknoth precisely what he was free to inspect.

"Easy, Stumpy," Jarek said, shooting a glance back at Rachel. "You don't wanna go sticking that mind of yours anywhere near Mikey without asking nicely first."

"And the answer is no, by the way," Rachel said.

She plucked her staff from the side of the bed. None of them could afford for this to break into a fight, but she wasn't about to step aside and let Drogan have free reign of her brother, even if Michael's head was too well protected for it to matter.

"If you have questions, fine," she said. "But keep your mind to yourself."

Drogan took on the expression of a parent explaining why they in fact couldn't spend all day playing and eating treats. "His unconscious mind might well hold information he is unable to access himself."

"His unconscious mind is in no condition to have anyone poking around in it," Rachel said. "And he's glyphed against telepathy six ways to Sunday anyways."

"Not so tight as to repel the messengers, it would seem," Drogan said.

The son of a bitch.

"Wrong tree, dude," Jarek said. "Wrong tree."

Behind Drogan's shoulder, Lietha frowned. "What tree? Does the human always talk like this?"

"Incessantly," Drogan said.

Jarek put a hand to his chest. "I doth resent that. And for the record, calling people things like 'the human' isn't winning you any friendship points, Minty. Would it kill you to learn our sad little names?"

Lietha's eyes were smoldering embers as he pointed. "That one is Michael Carver."

Jarek pointed back. "Hey! Better. If you're really feeling funky you could even just call him Michael. Or Mikey. He loves Mikey. Tell them, Mik—"

"Merciful void, enough," Drogan said. "Very well. We will settle for hearing Mikey's accounting for now."

Jarek grinned appreciatively.

Rachel could have cursed him and his never-ending little games just then, but at least Drogan seemed to have dropped his mission to prod Michael's mind for now. She even managed to start breathing again as Michael began catching Drogan and Lietha up to speed on what he'd seen.

When Michael mentioned the three raknoth aboard the ship, Drogan's already stiff posture tightened further.

"What else?" Drogan asked.

Michael shook his head. "Not much aside from the voice. I think it was calling the raknoth traitors, and it kind of seems like it was coming from my point of view, but... I don't know. It's all pretty hazy."

The fire was waking in Drogan's eyes. "Describe this voice."

"It was kind of like a bunch of whispers all mashed together into one. It was creepy."

"And there was nothing more? No sense of timing or location? No mention of any others?"

"Things kind of flashed out at the end." Michael glanced at Commander Daniels. "That must've been when my episode got violent here. I think whoever was talking might have killed those raknoth."

"I do not doubt it," Drogan said. He traded a short look with Lietha. "And I believe we may have no need of delving into Mikey's mind after all."

Apparently some part of Michael's description had rung a bell for the raknoth—and not a happy one, from the sound of it.

"What did we miss?" Rachel asked.

Drogan looked hesitantly around the room. "Three of our own clan fled the planet with our only functioning ship only days ago."

"Funny," Alaric said, "that seems like just the kind of thing you might think to report to your allies during a time of war."

"It was an internal affair," Drogan said. "Let us not pretend either one of our peoples want this alliance. The illusion of dissension in our ranks would not help matters."

"If Krogoth can't keep his own people in check," Commander Daniels said, "the dissension isn't an illusion."

"Do not speak to me of order and discipline, human."

Gun hands tensed. Nostrils flared.

Rachel focused her will, preparing to channel energy from her batteries if need be.

"Okay!" Jarek cried, spreading his hands between the two parties as wide as he could in the cramped room. "I'm hearing a lot of us and them language, guys. Let's all remember that this here is a *we*." He held up a finger. "*We* are all gonna die bloody *together* if *we* don't get our shit together. Yeah?"

"I might prefer the release of death to another minute of your rambling," Drogan said.

"Oh shit. Was that…" Jarek looked around the room. "Was that a zing, Stumpy?" He extended a fist to the raknoth. "Look at you, slummin' it with the humans. Put it there, buddy."

"Gah." Drogan turned for the door. "Come, Lietha. Let us escape this buffoonery and report our findings." He glanced back at the commanders. "We should begin final preparations. If the deserters were attacked tonight—"

"That puts the rakul only a couple days out," Alaric said. "Which sorta leads us back to the 'need to know' nature of that information."

That exact question had been bubbling on the tip of Rachel's tongue before the pissing contest had started. She didn't have a clue how fast or far those raknoth could have fled in a couple of days, but it stood to reason that the rakul would be able to cover the same distance as fast, if not faster.

Drogan dipped his head. "It is possible. We must be ready. And soon."

Her stomach sank. They weren't ready. Not even close.

Most of their "allies" were still scattered about the world, unconvinced of the coming threat. They barely even had a plan outside of building some heavy duty traps and throwing every bullet, blade, and claw they could at the bastards when they showed up.

And what would happen to Michael as the rakul closed in? Would his attacks grow more frequent? More violent?

"Drogan," Rachel said. "Is there any other way we can keep the rakul out of Michael's head?"

Drogan considered that. "I do not see how we might fix the chinks the messengers have found in his barriers when neither you nor I can see them. The messengers will preferentially flow toward those familiar to their kind, and given our recent hiding and Mikey's extreme exposure, he is likely the foremost on that list."

"Do they know I'm seeing these things?" Michael asked.

"I cannot say for certain, but it is possible they do not." Drogan's nostrils worked at the air as he thought. "Maybe even likely, considering you have no innate telepathic ability. I do not expect the rakul will make much use of the messengers once they reach the planet, but your insights might still grant us some advantage."

"And what if it goes the other way?" Rachel said. "What if the rakul do know and they use him like a nav pin? What if they deliberately trick him to lead us into a trap? We need to stop this connection. How do we do that?"

"If it becomes problematic," Lietha said, "we kill him."

His words carried all the weight of someone explaining they might need to spray down a bothersome hornets' nest. For a few seconds, Rachel was almost too surprised at the raw callousness of it to even be outraged.

"What?" Lietha said to whatever look Drogan gave him. "Mikey cannot receive these visions if—"

Drogan silenced his partner with a sharp shake of his head.

Somehow, it didn't exactly convince Rachel to drop the energy she'd already reached for, nor did it particularly put her at ease or calm the fire in her chest when Drogan turned back to her, his eyes pulsing crimson fire.

"We slay the rakul," he said, his expression composed and his tone matter-of-fact. "All of them."

CHAPTER SIX

Jarek paused at the bottom of the ship's ramp, frowned up at the bright morning sun, and shot a wistful glance back at Fela's compact form. "Did I mention I've got a bad feeling about this?"

"Oh really, sir," Al said in his earpiece. "What's the worst that could happen?"

"Zombies, Al." Jarek shook his head and set off for HQ. "It's always zombies."

"Ah, of course, sir. How could I possibly overlook such a distinct threat?"

Jarek refrained from answering as he passed a few Resistance boys with a neutral nod, then decided against saying anything at all. He didn't need Al scrubbing through his vocal patterns and discerning just how anxious he was at leaving Fela behind for the first time in weeks. Of course, Al would just pick up on his irregular silence instead now.

Perks of having a robot for a friend.

Anxiety aside, though, if he was actually going to make a point of "showing trust" as Al kept putting it—or doing the meat-suit strut, as Jarek preferred—he might as well avoid looking like the guy who walked around cackling with the voice in his head.

"""

They wouldn't want anyone to go thinking he was crazy, would they?

"I *can* be there inside of two minutes, sir," Al said, unbidden.

Apparently Jarek's nerves were shining through. Or maybe Mr. Robot was a bit nervous himself as Jarek moved deeper into the HQ traffic, which was escalating with the morning sun—more and more troops, new recruits, and helping hands getting to the day's work expanding the base above ground and fortifying the perimeter.

"Why do I feel like a kid whose overbearing mom just dropped him off for his first day at high school?"

"Why am I always the mom in your analogies?"

"Because you're a total mom-bot," Jarek said, earning himself a confused frown from a woman who was busy with a tablet full of what looked like base floor plans. He found an easy grin, and she pursed her lips and went back to her tablet.

"That said," he mumbled, openly meeting one of the many stares that followed him across the lot, "never hurts to have a codeword. Just in case."

"Might I suggest 'zombies,' sir?"

"Har har, Mr. Robot."

The guards at the new main entrance gave him the thorough stern-eyes up and down but waved him on.

"This is an important step, sir," Al said.

"No kidding." Jarek stepped through the doorway and started down the stairs to the HQ common room. "A whole flight of 'em, really. Can't help but notice they're all leading down."

"If we're serious about whipping this team into shape," Al said, ignoring his comment, "we need to be a part of it. Remind them there's a human inside the suit. This will all go a lot smoother if they accept you as one of their own."

Jarek reached the bustling common room and looked around. "Our old pals the Iron Eagles knew too damn well there was a human inside the suit. Remember how that turned out?"

"Only too well, sir. Though I do seem to recall a cool voice of reason telling you to be careful back then. And perhaps it's simply the second coming of the apocalypse speaking, but, for what it's worth, that voice believes this time could be different. Let them be your friends, sir."

Most of the room's occupants were merely passing through, but there were a fair amount scattered around the couches and chairs, taking a moment to catch up or plan next moves. Of those, it felt like at least half had turned to give him a smattering from the wonderful spectrum of stink eyes, and of *those*, the most prominent by far came from a stout man with a bulldog face—Rodgers, if memory served.

"Yeah, I can feel the love already," Jarek mumbled.

Technically, he hadn't really done anything to the stout guard himself, but Rodgers had been the one on armory duty the night Michael had slipped Jarek in to reclaim his stolen—or *apprehended*, as Nelken had since put it—exosuit from the Resistance's temporarily greedy paws.

Suffice it to say, Rodgers didn't seem to have taken kindly to being made the guard who'd lost the Resistance's only one-of-a-kind super weapon. And if the dirty looks his pals all shot Jarek were any indication, Rodgers wasn't about to be super-fanning for Jarek's reputation anytime soon.

Never mind that they were staring at one another across the exact same space where Jarek had duked it out with the world's most vicious raknoth to defend HQ not two weeks prior. No. The rubble had been cleared, and the petty little shit had piled back in to take its place with a rapidity that almost made Jarek laugh. Almost.

He realized he was fingering the bottom of the claw trails Zar'-Golga had left across his face in that fight. The mindless prodding was quickly becoming a habit.

He dropped his hand, sighed, and turned to skirt through the busy room.

"This is why we work alone," Jarek said in a quiet sing-song tone as he went.

"Give it time, sir."

"Not so sure we have much of that to give, buddy."

Not if Michael's visions and their star-hopping calculations had any amount of reliability, at least.

Their dark-skinned prophet was asleep when Jarek gave a soft knock and poked his head in. Rachel, on the other hand, was sitting on the cot she'd dragged into Michael's room, back to wall and knees to chest, head bowed.

She looked up at Jarek's entrance, and the look in her eyes stopped the playful kiss he'd been about to blow her in its tracks.

"Everything okay?" he asked quietly.

Rachel's gaze flicked to Michael then drifted around the room as if searching in earnest for an accurate answer to the question.

"Everything's fine," she said, equally quietly, after a few seconds too long.

She looked lost, enough so that Jarek had half a crazy inkling to go give her a hug and tell her it was going to be okay. The non-robotic voice in his head told him that wasn't the best idea. Rachel wasn't one to be coddled, and things between them had been... not quite right since she'd given him the cold shoulder after the big HQ rumble.

So he settled for cocking his head and shooting her his most disarming, *Hey, you can tell me... It's me!* look.

No dice. She gave him half of a forced smile and tilted her head in a clear sign he was good and welcome to move on and butt out.

He hesitated for a long moment, then shrugged and quietly backed out and closed the door.

Something was bothering her, that was for damn sure, but he wasn't going to win any points trying to push in when she wanted space. He'd catch her later, hopefully alone for a change, and crank up the ol' Slater charm until he got to the bottom of it.

Michael's most recent episode had probably just aggravated the wound she'd been sporting ever since the nest had burst and left him... whatever he was. Or, hell, it could have just been a case of the sombers on account of the Super Monsters coming to eat them. None of them had to look too far for reasons to be less than ecstatic right now.

But a slippery little feeling in his gut told him something else was up. He hadn't missed the fact that she'd disappeared with Alton for a bit last night, or that she'd looked a light breeze away from meltdown mode upon returning.

It wasn't hard to imagine what they might've discussed, and if Alton had broken hard news to her on that front...

He'd find out soon—even if it meant pushing harder than advisable and getting his goose pleasantly cooked. But for now, he had another stubborn tree to go bark at.

Yep. He was definitely looking at a twice-cooked-goose kind of day.

Alaric answered Jarek's knock looking every bit as surly and stern as he always did, and more than a little weary. His eyes traced down and up Jarek's unarmored body, noting Fela's absence without betraying any surprise.

"Looks like you woke up on the trusting side of bed this morning."

"Hey, gotta start somewhere right?" Jarek raised a fist. "Go team, and all that fun stuff."

Alaric considered Jarek for a stretch, then stepped back and opened the door in invitation.

"Care for a cup of coffee?" Jarek asked as he strolled past Alaric and into the room.

Alaric closed the door behind him. "Isn't that my line?"

Jarek shrugged, looking around the room. "You look like you need it worse than I do. Love what you've done with the place, by the way."

Alaric's frown deepened as he followed Jarek's gaze around to the blank walls and hard, cold emptiness of the tiny living quarters. "Son, I've got a raknoth warlord playing hardball, a base full of jittery children, and about three hours of sleep to my name. I don't need a coy wise-ass on that list."

"Yeah, that's kinda what I wanted to talk to you about. The hardball thing, I mean. Not the coy wise-ass. He's here to stay, for better or worse, till death do us part."

"Funny"—Alaric sank to his cot and waved Jarek to sit in the chair at his small desk—"I don't remember agreeing to any vows."

"Well," Jarek said, flipping the chair around so he could sit facing Alaric with his elbows on the chair's back, "sounds like death might be trying to do us part sooner than later anyway, so…"

Alaric waited quietly if not patiently while Jarek tried to parse out the best way to propose what he wanted to without getting shot. In hindsight, this probably hadn't been the best day to make his Fela-free debut in Resistance HQ.

"What is it, son?" Alaric finally asked. "Just spit it out so I can deal with it or try to get some sleep."

"Promise not to shoot me?"

Alaric considered that then made a noncommittal nod toward the rack on the opposite wall that was currently home to his battered long coat and his fully loaded gun belt.

Taking that to mean Alaric was either too tired to bother with shooting him or that he'd at least have fair warning, Jarek tilted his head in concession. "Right then. Out with it. I think we should use Seth to—"

Jarek paused at Alaric's swelling intake of breath and the full body clench that was evident across the room.

"—to smooth relations between us and Krogoth," Jarek forced himself to finish. "So yeah, Krogoth let Rachel and Lea tag along on his recruitment tour, but if he's not letting us in on any particulars of his operation over there… Well, Seth is the closest thing we have to an inside man, and he's not doing anyone any favors sitting over there in the brig."

Alaric looked like he was regretting not having his pistols in easy reach. "Seth isn't a tool to be used," he said, his voice deadly quiet. "Not anymore."

Jarek suppressed a flinch at Alaric's tone.

Calling Alaric's relationship with his son, Seth Mosen, complicated was like calling a raknoth kind of strong. Understatement Central. Case in point, Alaric had kept the crazy bastard—his son—locked up since they'd captured him two weeks earlier and resolutely insisted on visiting him each and every day for another hefty helping of *go to hells* along with a side of *I wish it'd been you—it should have been you.*

Alaric sure wasn't the first father who'd ever had to deal with having let their kid down by not being there. He might've been the first, however, who'd had to deal with his son murdering his own mother, Alaric's wife, and blaming Alaric for not having had the courtesy to join her in the grave.

It had taken Alaric five years, some less-than-gentle prodding from Jarek, and a small army of Reds to even get Alaric back to this side of the country, and Jarek didn't blame him one bit for that. It didn't matter that it had been the work of Zar'Golga's extensive mental and physical reprogramming—and not Alaric's perceived failings—that had driven Mosen into the deranged killing machine he was today. Not to Alaric, at least.

To Alaric, all that mattered was that his son had gone off the deep end and that now, for the first time since it happened, he thought he had a chance at getting him back.

Call him a pessimist, but Jarek wasn't so sure that was going to work out if they continued on with keeping Mosen locked up like a good little psycho son. Of course, he couldn't exactly phrase it like that to Alaric.

"Look," he started slowly, "I know sending Mosen—"

"Seth."

Jarek tilted his head in peaceful acknowledgment. "I know sending Seth over to Camp Krogoth is probably just about the last thing you wanna do right now, but I think it's a good move. Give him something to do, space to breathe."

If looks could kill…

"Do you remember what he did last time he had space to breathe?" Alaric growled.

Jarek knew only too well what Mosen was capable of. But, "Holding him here isn't accomplishing anything, Alaric. We need better communication between our camps if we have any hope of actually fighting together, and, much as I don't wanna piss you off, I have to point out that it might give you and Seth something to talk about aside from the usual—Hey!"

Alaric had reached under his cot and yanked free a snub-nosed revolver he must've kept hidden there for emergencies.

"Whoa!" Jarek cried, flinging his hands up. "Easy, man! I—"

But then he caught it too.

An odd, shimmering something had filled the room like softly glowing mist, so faint Jarek hadn't even noticed it at first, occupied as he'd been with treading on eggshells.

He waved his hand through the air, but the phantom light didn't swirl or disperse as he'd half-expected. "What the shit is this?"

Alaric shook his head, mouth agape as he flicked his gaze warily around the room. "I have no idea."

Outside, someone shouted in a distant hallway. A few seconds later, heavy boots thundered by the door.

Jarek exchanged a concerned look with Alaric then rose and checked the pistols holstered at his thighs while Alaric belted on his own guns.

"If we could go one damned day without some fresh hell…" Alaric mumbled, pulling on his coat.

He was only one sleeve in when something thumped into the door. Hard.

Silence. Then a low growl.

Jarek drew a pistol and traded a speculative glance with Alaric.

"Sir," came Al's voice in his earpiece, "there's something seriously wrong out he—"

Bam! Bam!

The sharp cracks of an insistent fist on the door. Whoever it was followed with a maddened bark, and then the door flew in with a crash.

A single man stood there, garbed in rag-tag Resistance armor and practically foaming at the mouth with anger.

No, not just anger. Jarek had seen all shades of angry. This guy's eyes were stark raving mad with mindless fury.

"Davidson!" Alaric barked. "What the—"

Davidson charged into the room with a strangled yell.

Jarek's insides shriveled at the frantic madness in his eyes, but instincts kicked in, and he caught Davidson's wild swipe with a raised elbow.

The guy wasn't pulling his punches—or aiming them particularly well. His arm hit Jarek's elbow hard enough that Jarek grunted in pain. The low crack told Jarek Davidson's arm might have just broken, but that didn't seem to bother the crazy bastard too much. Instead of reeling in agony, Davidson stepped in and made for Jarek's face with his teeth.

Jarek darted back a step and caught his raging pursuer hard across the head with a whip of his pistol butt.

Davidson crashed into Alaric's desk and toppled unceremoniously to the concrete floor.

"Jesus, dude!" Jarek cried after him, adrenaline bouncing him on the balls of his feet. "What the shit?"

He tried to take a deep breath, tried to center himself.

But Davidson wasn't done.

The crazy bastard shook off the blow that absolutely should have left him stunned stupid on the floor and instead scrambled for Alaric.

"Davidson, stop!" Alaric barked.

Jarek started forward, sure the maddened soldier wasn't about to miraculously start listening now.

Alaric, apparently coming to the same conclusion, spat a curse and kicked Davidson in the head before Jarek could.

This time, Davidson was at least too stunned to do much more than groan and roll around on the floor.

"Al, zombies," Jarek said quietly.

"Understood, sir. On my way. May I ask—"

"Fucking zombies, Al!" Jarek snapped with entirely more fire than he'd intended.

So maybe he'd watched one too many zombie flicks. So maybe raving, teeth-gnashing madmen kind of scared the shit out of him. They could all sue him later, just as soon as they figured out what the hell was happening.

"Right you are, sir. I'll just pretend these people aren't beating each other senseless out here."

"What?"

"That's what I was trying to tell you, sir."

"Shit." Jarek turned to Alaric, who was watching him like he was half-expecting Jarek to pull a Davidson. "This is happening out there too."

"Son of a bitch," Alaric muttered.

Beside them Davidson was starting to try to pull himself shakily back to his feet, eyes completely unfocused, a low growl rumbling from his throat.

"Come on," Alaric said, striding past Jarek to the door. "We need to… Shit, I don't know. Find restraints, for starters."

Jarek gave Davidson one last glance and hurried after Alaric without complaint.

In the hallway, Jarek pulled the door shut behind them. Shouts and screams seemed to be coming from every direction of the base.

"I need to get to Rachel," Jarek said.

As if in reply, Davidson slammed into the door behind them and began pounding on it.

Jarek clutched the doorknob, ready to fight his pull, but apparently doorknobs were beyond Davidson's current state of mind. He simply kept beating at the door with a mindless cry.

"You two!" Alaric shouted down the hall to a man and woman who'd rounded into the hallway, weapons at the ready and frantic confusion in their eyes. "You know what's happening?"

"No, sir," the woman called as they jogged over, looking relieved to find someone who wasn't currently bat shit insane.

Jarek couldn't say he blamed them.

"Come with me," Alaric told them. "We're gonna rally everyone we can and get to the commons."

"Yes, sir."

"I'll meet you there," Jarek said, starting in the other direction for Michael's room.

Alaric looked for a second as if he might argue, maybe even pull the Commander card and order Jarek to stick with the group, but then he turned to his new recruits. "Let's go."

"Don't get bit," Jarek called after them.

Alaric spared him an incredulous glance, then he waved his soldiers on and they disappeared around the corner.

"Just sayin'," Jarek mumbled to himself, prowling toward the opposite end of the hallway, gun at the ready.

He still wasn't sure what the hell was going on, though he had a sinking feeling there was something telepathic in play, possibly of the funky psycho harvester broadcast variety. Whatever it was, if nearly a decade of binging movies to kill his unfortunate abundance of spare time had taught him anything, it was that when perfectly sane people all of a sudden started biting, you sure as hell didn't want to be one of the ones who got bit.

He'd just reached the end of the hallway and was pausing to listen when he damn near ate his own words.

It was hard to tease out one thing from another with all the activity and shouts coming from all over the base—hard enough that Jarek only caught the shuffling footsteps and quiet groaning growl a second before the woman stepped into view and caught sight of him. She was tall with dark hair. And complete madness in her eyes.

Jarek didn't have time to finish his shout of, "Don't do it!" before she sprang at him with a shrill scream.

He caught her by one wrist, spun, and slammed her to the wall, pinning her there with an elbow to the throat. She paid the—what had to be considerate—discomfort no mind and continued bucking against him with surprising strength.

"Dammit, lady, I don't wanna—Shit!"

He turned at a movement to his left, dropping his grip on her wrist to reach for his other pistol. Then he processed the two men standing there with lucid eyes and raised stun guns.

"There's two more of 'em," the right one growled.

Jarek abandoned the pistol grab to raise his free hand in surrender. "Wait! Don't shoot! I'm not a crazy person. Yet."

The two exchanged a glance, then the one who'd spoken took aim and fired.

Jarek threw himself away from his new berserker friend with a yelp and came away blessedly free of any stunner leads. The same couldn't be said for the dark haired woman, who lunged after him but didn't make it more than a step before she began convulsing and went to the ground in a disturbing display of growling, shrieking twitches.

"Jesus, cowboy," Jarek said. "Maybe an ounce of warning next time?"

The shooter calmly held his gaze as he loaded another stun cartridge by feel. "I thought the Soldier of Charity knew how to take care of himself."

And with that, he gestured to his partner and they set off the way Jarek had come.

"Thanks," Jarek called after them. "Dick!"

At least someone had had the good sense to break out the stun weapons.

"Worst first day of school ever, Mr. Robot," Jarek said as he turned down the next hallway and continued toward Michael's room. "And where the hell are you, by the way?"

"Almost there, sir." Al sounded tense. "Navigation is… parametrically challenging at the moment."

"As in people are trying to kill you?"

"Emphatically, sir."

"I'd tell you to try being inanimate, but"—Jarek turned into Michael's hallway and spotted Alton Parker stalking his way, eyes shimmering faint red—"I might be needing you here, buddy. Nowish."

Jarek had one second to try to process how bad it would be for a raknoth to fall into mindless rage inside Resistance HQ before Johnny's flaming red hair darted into sight behind Alton.

"Take my pendant, you stubborn ass!" Johnny cried. "We can't afford to—"

Alton shook his head and said something Jarek couldn't quite pick out.

Johnny was saying something back and reaching for his neck when two wild-looking men hurtled out of a room they were passing and straight for them.

To his credit, Johnny reacted with impressive speed and neatly pulled his attacker into some kind of hip throw that left the guy pinned and frothing on the ground.

Alton, on the other hand, had closed his eyes in a silent snarl as his attacker crashed into him like a particularly big-headed puppy challenging a full-grown bear. The raknoth's face twitched like he was fighting for control, then he reached out and, almost gently, shoved his maddened attacker to send him, airborne, back into the room he'd come from.

"How ya doin', Red?" Johnny called, still struggling to control his own berserker. "You still with us?"

Alton opened his eyes, which were decidedly redder than they had been pre-ambush, and turned to Johnny right as another pair of Resistance troops scuttled into the hallway, weapons readied.

"Oh, fuck!" one of them gasped, pointing his gun.

"Don't!"

Jarek, Johnny, and the other Resistance soldier all yelled the word at almost the same time.

None of them made a lick of difference.

Two gunshots cracked down the hall. Alton jerked, then tilted his head back and gave a roar that shriveled bits of Jarek's anatomy.

Johnny backed away from Alton, slowly raising his hands. The guy he'd had pinned sprang to his feet and lunged for Alton, who apparently seemed like the most interesting thing in the hallway at the moment.

He was sure as hell the most dangerous thing.

Alton swatted his would-be challenger aside like an unwanted beach ball. The guy hit the wall with a sickening crunch and lay still.

The shooter prepared to fire again, but his partner grabbed him and pulled him frantically around the corner, which to red-eyed, raging Alton must've looked something like a fleeing rabbit looks to a hungry wolf. He tensed to spring after them.

"Shit," Jarek muttered. Then, much louder, "Hey, Parker!"

Alton showed a moment's hesitation, but didn't turn.

Only one thing to do, then.

"Sorry about this, buddy," Jarek called, raising his gun.

Johnny sharply shook his head at Jarek, wide-eyed.

Jarek sighted on Alton's back and pulled the trigger.

Alton whipped around, all of his red-eyed fury settling firmly on Jarek, and charged with a resonant roar.

Jarek backpedaled, two options cloying for place in his mind, which couldn't seem to get beyond screaming that there was a pissed off raknoth helling down the hallway toward his pathetic meat-sack form.

Run or dodge, or run or dodge, or—Shit!

Alton closed faster than seemed physically possible. Jarek threw himself to the side. Not enough. Not fast enough. Alton reached out a clawed hand, and—

Something dark flashed past Jarek and slammed into Alton in a full-on tackle.

Fela.

"Al, you magnificent bastard!" Jarek cried.

Alton staggered backward, wrestling with the suit, which had wrapped its arms firmly around his waist. Or maybe not that firmly.

Al had only driven Alton back a few feet before the raknoth got his balance back.

"Uh-oh," Al said.

Then Alton pivoted and chucked Fela into the wall.

Jarek needed to do something—needed to buy a few seconds to let him suit up.

But before he could so much as think the word *distraction*, Alton whirled and advanced on him.

"Run, sir!" Al cried, scrambling Fela back to her feet.

There wasn't time for that.

Jarek twisted under Alton's wild grab and nearly cried out at the brush of Alton's arm on the top of his head. One misstep, one hesitation, and—

Alton twisted after him with a heavy backhand, and Jarek threw himself backward.

He hit the floor hard, unforgiving concrete slapping the air from his lungs, and kicked to scoot away. Alton stalked after him like a primitive predator, basking in the kill to come.

Jarek raised his gun, knowing it was futile.

Alton dove forward.

Halfway to Jarek, something caught the raknoth in an invisible embrace and held him there, floating in midair. Then that something slammed Alton into the wall hard enough to pulverize half the cinder blocks he struck.

He roared once, looking furious, but his struggles seemed to be weakening.

Jarek tilted his head back and caught an upside-down view of Rachel striding toward them, one hand gripping her staff and the other outstretched toward Alton.

She looked pissed—more pissed than Jarek could remember ever seeing her—and something told him it wasn't solely because Alton had been about to enjoy a fine Jarek tar tar.

At least Alton seemed to be calming down now, for whatever miraculous reason. He'd ceased his struggles completely when Jarek glanced back, and the raknoth fire was draining from his eyes.

Rachel's boots clicked closer until Jarek was staring along the lovely curve of her leg and up to the eyes that were somehow exuding more fire than Alton's. She spared him the briefest of glances. "What the hell were you thinking?"

"What does it look like?" Jarek said between pants. "I'm here to rescue you."

CHAPTER SEVEN

Jarek had never been a fan of scavenging. God knew he'd done plenty of it in the years following the Catastrophe. It had been a necessity to survive. The best thing he'd ever found, though, hadn't been food. Not by a long shot. That honor almost certainly went to the storage drive he'd happened across camping out in an abandoned apartment one night. More accurately, it went to the contents of that drive.

Movies. Thousands of them, a cinematic sampler of the century's works.

Sure, movies weren't much use to a starving man. But to a fed man whose social circle had pretty much consisted of Al, an occasional visit with Pryce, and whatever band of marauders or mercenaries happened to be trying to kill him that week?

That drive had been worth a thousand cheeseburgers.

On one of the countless nights he'd spent in the following years lounging in his ship and watching his way through the better part of two thousand movies, he'd happened across a movie called *28 Days Later*. The sight of the title had brought back memories of his dad. He couldn't even remember why at first, but eventually it came to him. He'd wanted to see it back in the day, before the bombs fell. Somehow, he'd seen an ad somewhere and had set to work bugging his dad to take him.

His dad, of course, had calmly explained that the movie wasn't age-appropriate for Jarek and that, besides, the film was just a remake of an old classic and probably an enormous pile of flashy crap anyways. The one from the turn of the century, his dad had said, that was the one Jarek would have to watch—in a few years, maybe.

Remembering that little snippet of his dad, Jarek had been struck by one of those sudden, mournful pangs of loss that were routine and yet always unexpected. He'd breathed a heavy sigh. And then he'd watched the crap out of that movie.

Whether or not it stood up to the standard of the one from the early 2000s, Jarek couldn't have said. Regardless, it was thanks to *28 Days Later* that he had some loose framework to classify what in the ever-living hell had just swept through Resistance HQ.

"That," he said, "was some straight up rage virus shit right there."

Rachel frowned up at him from Michael's bedside, clearly not following. Behind her, Lea looked a bit pale.

He didn't blame her.

"That wasn't a virus," Rachel said. "It was—"

"Messengers," Jarek finished. "Yeah, I put that part together. I'm just saying—never mind. Not important."

"Are they done out there?" Rachel asked, glancing back at Michael in clear concern—probably more for whatever was happening in his head than what might happen to his body.

Jarek poked his head out the door, eternally grateful to be back in Fela's sturdy embrace again. Across the hallway, Alton glanced both directions and gave Jarek a small nod.

Jarek listened with Fela's auditory sensors and came to the same conclusion as Alton settled back into his remorseful raknoth pose.

The impromptu rage storm seemed to have abated, and HQ was beginning to pick up the broken, or bitten, pieces.

"All clear," Jarek said.

Which probably meant now might be a good time for Alton to fill them in on what the shit had just happened.

Jarek had some vague understanding, of course. Something—presumably the rakul—had sent some violently bad vibes their way, apparently using messengers, and people had started trying to kill each other. What was less clear was... well, pretty much everything else.

Did this attack mean the rakul were close? Could they do it again? Had the event been local or worldwide? All those and a thousand more like them.

At least most of their cloaking glyphs seemed to have held up to the messenger juju. Well, except for Michael's, but that was a separate issue as far as Jarek knew.

Many of the Resistance soldiers' minds had been shielded behind glyphs much like Jarek's, but not all of them. Apparently, the glyphing device the Resistance had procured from god knew where had been lost, destroyed, or maybe even stolen during Golga's attack a few weeks prior.

Whichever it was, now that HQ had dropped its game of flying under the radar, there were plenty of new faces around—faces that hadn't been properly warded against the potential for being telepathically goaded into completely losing their shit.

As far as they'd pieced together, it had mostly been those ones who'd gone promptly and utterly ape shit crazy fifteen minutes ago. Michael, on the other hand, hadn't stayed conscious to rage out like the others, but he had been having the worst seizure Jarek had seen when Rachel peeled Jarek's nearly-flattened ass off the floor and swept him into the room.

Thankfully, with an army of trained, unaffected soldiers around, coming together and containing the ragers had happened quickly and effectively enough. That hadn't made the raving wild people any less disturbing, though. Bullets and blades and mean-hearted thugs, Jarek could handle all day long. Mindless human rage puppets that made rabid dogs look like well-mannered socialites, though?

Apparently that one had direct access to his freaky button.

Who knew?

Luckily, they hadn't had to deal with any more berserkers after

Rachel had shown up. None but Alton, that was, though the raknoth hadn't actually put up any more of a fight after Rachel's first big girl body slam.

In fact, even speaking as the one who'd nearly been eaten, Jarek thought Rachel had been a bit extreme in how brutally she'd contained Alton—how hesitant she'd been to release him when his sense returned, how savagely she'd told him to stay the hell out of Michael's room once she finally had.

On some level, and probably not a particularly deep one, if Jarek's intuition was worth much, Rachel had wanted to kill Alton in that hallway. And whether it was their alliance or good old reason and morality that had guided her hand in pulling it back together, Jarek thought it was safe to say the urge hadn't simply come from nowhere.

Something was going on between her and Alton. He was sure of it now. But whatever it was, he doubted he'd be helping anyone by interjecting himself—at least not before they'd collected themselves and processed this lovely new crap storm.

"So you wanna tell us what that was all about?" Jarek asked Alton when it became clear no one was readily going to speak.

Alton didn't look up. "From what I gathered, there's at least one Kul nearby—most likely Gada—and he wanted to let us know he's not very happy."

"You don't say."

"How nearby?" Rachel called from the room. "And how the hell strong are these things that they can remotely control that many people and you all at once?"

"Clearly quite strong," Alton said. "Now that I know to expect it, I should be able to maintain control if it happens again, but... Well, it's lucky you stepped in when you did, Rachel."

Rachel somehow managed to convey distrust, displeasure, and maybe a touch of loathing all in one monosyllabic grunt. For Jarek's part, he didn't think Alton sounded like a man—or a raknoth, rather— blowing smoke up their tailpipes, but it wasn't like he had any real insight into the telepathic mind games.

"As for distance," Alton continued after a pause, "I might wager a day's travel out, but it would only be a wild guess."

A buzz from Lea's direction drew Jarek's attention.

"The commanders want us in the council chamber," she said.

Alton glanced up at them and over at Johnny. "Perhaps we should go find Haldin and Elise."

"Actually," Lea said, "I think they'll want to hear what you have to say about…"

She trailed off with a helpless wave of her hand, apparently unsure exactly what to name the ethereal golden rage storm that had just swept the base off its sound feet.

Johnny tapped at his comm. "Sounds like Hal and Elise are almost here anyway. They just got caught up in the, uh… thing."

"The furor," Alton said.

"Yeah, right," Johnny said. "That."

"Did he just say furor?" Jarek asked, trading a bemused look with Rachel. Or trying to.

She didn't look so bemused. "That's what you're choosing to take away from all of this?"

Before he could say anything, Lea lightly cleared her throat.

"We should probably all get over there."

"We'll find Hal and Elise and meet you guys there," Johnny called in from the hallway.

Alton didn't argue or give anything more than one last expressionless look at Rachel before he turned and fell in with an unusually apprehensive-looking Johnny.

"Rache?" came Lea's voice from behind, hesitant.

Rachel plunked her staff to the ground harder than necessary and used it to hoist herself up from the foot of Michael's bed. "Fine. Let's get this over with."

Jarek teetered with the words on his tongue.

He could just let all this go and move along. That was absolutely the easy play here. But he couldn't quite shake the feeling that something had gone awry for Rachel, something that seemed more and more like it might sabotage everything they'd been fighting for. Something that seemed to already be doing that to whatever existed between the two of them.

Now wasn't exactly an ideal time, but when rage parties—or furors or whatever the hell anyone wanted to call them—and super monsters could drop down on their heads without a moment's warning, it seemed prudent to apply some *you take what you can get* philosophy to these things.

He fixed Rachel with a serious look. "Can I talk to you for a minute?"

At the edge of his vision, Lea glanced back and forth between them. "I'll, uh, see you guys over there?"

Rachel held Jarek's gaze for a stretch, then finally turned to Lea and gave a short nod.

Once Rachel had broken the staring contest, Jarek did the same. "Wouldn't miss it for a hole in my head."

"Yeah..." Lea looked vaguely uncomfortable, as if she could smell a fight brewing in the air, but, after only a small hesitation, she nodded and pushed past them, only stopping to touch Michael's peacefully sleeping shoulder. "They'll be starting soon," she said at the door.

Then Lea was gone, and Rachel and Jarek were alone—Rachel making a quiet point of keeping her attention directed to her sleeping brother, and Jarek taking an acute refresher course on just how loaded and uncomfortable silence between two people could be.

But why so uncomfortable?

"What is it?" Rachel finally said, her voice quiet but decidedly not soft. When she looked up at him, her eyes weren't either. "What do you want?"

Ah. Right. That was why.

Some uncharacteristically wise portion of his mind nipped the retaliatory words bubbling up in his chest. He let the heat out as a steadying breath instead.

"I wanna know how you're doing." He waved an encompassing hand. "With all of this. These past couple weeks... I know it can't be easy."

"Do you?"

Was that accusation in her eyes?

"It's hard to tell what with all the 'Stumpy' this and the 'buddy' that." She gave her head a sharp shake, her breathing clearly elevated now. "Alton would have killed you if I hadn't stopped him. And for all I can see, you're not even pissed about it."

Yep. Definitely accusation, mixed with a healthy dose of scolding.

"I had it under control," he said, more by reflex than anything else. "And yeah, I'm not happy at having to play rabbit to Alton's bloodhound, but—shit, I don't know! I don't understand what's happening in your heads. He says he can control it now that he knows to be on guard, I can't know if that's bullshit or not. So talk to me, Goldilocks. Tell us what's going on. Tell me what you know that I don't."

She skewered him on the end of a tight-lipped glare. "What I know is that we crawled into bed with monsters. They're not your friends, Jarek. No matter how much you want them to be."

The way she said it, the desolate gravity in her tone…

"What the hell's going on with you?" he asked before his better mind had time to massage the words into something softer. "What did…"

No. Probably better not to mention Alton specifically and launch her into the defensive stratosphere.

He softened his tone. "Did something happen?"

The stiffening of her posture and the edge that crept into her eyes told him his caution had been insufficient.

Defenses fully engaged.

"We need to go," was all she said as she pushed past him for the door.

"Rachel."

She paused in the doorway but didn't look back.

"Thank you," he said. "For saving me back there."

"You shouldn't have needed saving—shouldn't have…"

Tension built in her shoulders and flooded out in a heavy sigh. Finally, she glanced back at him over her shoulder. "Come on. They're probably starting."

She set off into the hallway without waiting for his response.

Jarek watched her go with an unpleasant swirling of frustration, failure, and flabbergast.

"Man," he mumbled, shaking his head. "This day just keeps getting weirder and weirder."

"Chin up, sir," Al said in his earpiece. "It's only the end of the world."

RESISTANCE HQ's council room was about as impressive in its grandeur as your average basement, but Rachel supposed they weren't there to admire the decor. They were, as far as she could tell, there to talk Furor 101 with Professor Alton Parker and to generally go weak in the knees at just how screwed they seemed to be right now.

"You're telling us that the rakul could use these messengers to drive an entire damn planet insane if they wanted to?" asked a hard-faced Commander Nelken, still sporting the leg brace the doctor had put him in after a hefty hunk of the common room ceiling had come down on him in Zar'Golga's attack.

Rachel watched Alton exchange an uncertain look with Drogan and Lietha, who'd come either at Krogoth's behest to learn what they knew or maybe just to hold their sad little human hands through the scare.

She waited for an answer, knowing damn well she wouldn't be able to believe any of it for the absolute truth.

It wasn't just that she couldn't trust a word out of any of their mouths. Sure, despite everything else, she couldn't ignore that Alton and the others had never seemed to intentionally lie (as far as she knew, at least). But the problem was more that she wasn't so sure any of them could be considered credible sources after Alton had fallen prey to the furor himself—a detail that hadn't yet been brought to the council's attention.

"The entire planet would be a stretch," Alton finally said. "But something on the scale of a city is possible."

"This is not standard practice for the rakul," Drogan added. He looked irritated to be wasting his time listening to the humans dither, and Lietha even more so. "Perhaps they suspect humans are more easily swayed by such tactics than the species they've preyed upon in the past."

That started a round of murmurs from the attending council members.

"Helpful, Stumpy," Jarek murmured in his seat next to Rachel.

No one else in the room could have heard him—except for a raknoth.

Lietha frowned in Jarek's direction, but Drogan's lips twitched upward in mild amusement.

To his credit, Alaric didn't seem the least bit perturbed as he replied from the commanders' table. "Well, seeing as they may decide to make it standard practice against our people, what is there to be done about it, aside from cloaking everyone we can?"

Lietha showed teeth that looked just a little too sharp to be human. "Humans cannot rampage if they are dead."

The murmurs caught fire.

At least until Rachel called, "And we could say the same thing for the raknoth, couldn't we?"

That shut everyone up nice and quick.

"Are you implying the raknoth could experience similar... symptoms in future events?" Commander Daniels asked from the head table.

Rachel half-expected Jarek to give her a little leg kick or otherwise tell her to shush up until they had a proper handle on this thing, but he was too busy looking at her like he'd only just seen her for the first time.

"*Careful, Rachel,*" a voice murmured in her mind. Haldin. "*I know you're angry, but think what this could do to the alliance.*"

"Any sentient mind could theoretically fall prey to telepathic attack," someone was saying out loud. Haldin again, she realized.

Jesus, how much control did he have?

"Hound, human, raknoth," Haldin continued, "all technically fair game, except—"

"Except that raknoth are not so easily overwhelmed as humans," Lietha said. "Telepathically or otherwise."

That started another round of conversation—this one much less murmured and much more inflammatory. Rachel couldn't say she blamed the council for getting irritated with this shit.

Haldin shot Lietha his own irritated look then glanced back to Rachel, probably wondering if she was about to blow the lid on Alton's slip-up.

She thought about it. They probably deserved it, and she wasn't sure she was doing anyone any favors keeping it quiet for now.

But something about the way Jarek was looking at her gave her pause.

"Enough," Nelken's voice boomed through the room, restoring some order before she could further stir the pot. Nelken joined Haldin in scowling at Lietha. "Need I remind you that your continued existence is contingent upon ours?"

Drogan shot a warning look at Lietha. "We do not forget so easily."

"On the bright side," Haldin said into the tense silence, "our cloaking fields do seem to dull the effects to some extent. It wasn't a surefire switch out there today, but most of the people near us eventually regained their senses once we had them covered."

Alton bobbed his head, latching onto Haldin's lifeline. "The messengers could feasibly penetrate the cloaks to some degree, depending on the quality of the work and the individuals they're protecting, but I imagine they'd offer sufficient protection in many cases. That said, those already affected by the furor may not simply recover once they've been cut off from the signal, so to speak."

"As in, they may be psychologically damaged by these attacks?" Commander Daniels asked.

"It's entirely possible," Alton said. "And those who aren't may still take some time to calm down."

That might have explained Rachel's experience with the lone berserker who'd charged into Michael's room early on in the chaos. It was hard to say for sure, as she'd pinned him to the wall and forced his mind into unconsciousness before he could hurt anyone, but she'd thought she'd glimpsed a hint of sanity just before she'd taken him down.

Jarek's ruckus with Alton had started down the hall before she'd had much chance to think about it.

"Outside of somehow mass producing and distributing glyph stamps," Nelken said, looking between her and Haldin, "is there anything we can do to protect people on a large scale in the event of another attack?"

Protect entire cities of scattered people from unbelievably powerful telepaths? No problem, right?

At least Nelken seemed to have taken it to heart when she'd told him a week earlier that she wasn't even sure how their old glyph stamp device would have worked, much less how to make one. Of course, Nelken hadn't been able to offer much in the way of explanation either, other than that theirs had passed through several different hands prior to reaching them—several hands who apparently knew little more than that the thing had been crafted by a man named Ren.

Luckily—or not—Haldin looked less dubious at Nelken's question than Rachel felt. "We could make bigger versions of our cloaking pendants to cover, say, a building at a time," he said. "Maybe even entire blocks."

Yeah. Of course they could. Except that powering such a monstrosity would require more energy than—

"It's mostly a matter of how much power we can feed them," Haldin continued. "The demands get pretty high pretty fast." He turned to Rachel. "How many arcanists do you know?"

"None that are still alive, as far as I know."

"Guess we have some work to do, then," Haldin said.

"And little time in which to do it," Alton added.

That started a slow wave of uneasy murmurs until Nelken called the room back to order and turned the discussion to the matters of non-lethal options for dealing with future furors and lethal ones for dealing with the rakul.

For the latter, Drogan finally saw fit to fill the council in on limited details of their forces' preparations. Krogoth had his men building a variety of traps in the old central park across the river, where Krogoth was hoping to force the confrontation. Only a quarter of the roughly eighty raknoth on Earth had given any promise, however tenuous, of standing beside them in battle. Of particularly concerning absence from that list were Zar'Taga, with his clan of ten raknoth, and that prick Nan'Ashida, who had no raknoth with him but controlled a considerable army of humans.

Rachel had begun to tune out when, midway through Drogan's report, Lietha glanced down at his comm and hurriedly left the council room. That alone didn't seem so weird, but when Drogan hastened to conclude his spiel and promptly marched through the double doors after his companion, Rachel couldn't help but wonder what was going on.

She leaned closer to Jarek. "Do you think—"

"We should follow them? Methinks yes."

Not exactly what she'd been about to say, but she didn't disagree, either. If something was up again this soon…

She ignored the look of irritation from Nelken as well as the looks of suspicious curiosity from the gathered council members and followed Jarek to the back. The double doors closed behind them to cut off what sounded to be a fascinating discussion of the Resistance armory's current non-lethal inventory.

Hell, maybe the two raknoth had just been supremely bored.

But the tense look Drogan and Lietha were exchanging just down the hallway didn't look like a case of the post-meeting yawns. Their eyes were both emitting soft crimson. Something had them agitated.

Drogan caught sight of them and turned without a word to shuffle Lietha along toward the exit.

"What gives, Stumpy?" Jarek asked, speaking at normal volume though Drogan and Lietha were well down the hallway. "Don't pretend like you can't hear me. You're gonna frighten the children walking around like that, man."

Fela's sensors must've picked up some reply from Drogan, because Jarek chuckled. "Tell me how you really feel, buddy."

He made a micro-flinch as he said the last word and shot her a surreptitious glance. She was too focused on the questions in her head to understand why at first.

Buddy. There it was again.

Whatever. She sure as hell didn't want to restart that conversation anytime soon. And in the meanwhile, she wasn't cool with being left out of this one.

She cleared her throat and reached out to unceremoniously swat at the two raknoth minds with her own.

Both raknoth frowned back at her.

"We can talk in the ship," Jarek said. "It'll only take a minute."

Drogan and Lietha paused and shared a glance that made her think they were communicating telepathically, probably so Jarek wouldn't overhear.

What the hell had them so wound up?

Lietha looked supremely irritated as Jarek and Rachel caught up to them and the raknoth broke off from whatever private conversation they were having.

"Very well," Drogan said to Jarek. "We will talk. But it must be quick. And discreet."

"Stumpy"—Jarek clapped a hand to Drogan's shoulder, drawing an immediate scowl from the raknoth—"that's the only way I know how to do things."

CHAPTER EIGHT

"Okay," Jarek said when the ramp of his ship had sealed behind them with the odd groan-clack one-two it had adopted since he and Pryce had resurrected the craft from its unfortunate tumble with Zar'Golga. "Just us now, Stumpy. So, again, what gives?"

Drogan and Lietha traded a look, and Lietha answered instead. "My Zar has made contact with Kul'Gada."

"That's what he stayed to do, right?" Jarek asked. The last he'd seen Zar'Kole, the raknoth had looked like he'd been fixing to go ask a lion to stop eating meat. "So what happened?"

"He stayed," Lietha said.

"Yeah," Jarek said. "That's what I—wait, what do you mean?"

"He intends to meet Kul'Gada in peace."

"Guy stomps out three fleeing raknoth and Kole wants to meet him in person to talk?"

Lietha looked at Drogan instead of answering Jarek. "We cannot allow this to pass. Kul'Gada is impetuous, temperamental. He will cut my Zar down for daring to even suggest a negotiation."

"Zar'Kole knows the nature of the monster he thinks to face," Drogan said. "Better than any of us."

"You will do nothing, then?" Lietha demanded. "You will let the greatest of our Zars die?"

Drogan dropped Lietha's crimson glare. "I did not say that."

"So what are we waiting for?" Jarek asked. "Rally the troops. Scramble the squad. Call the guy for Christ's sake."

"He will not answer," Lietha said.

"And Krogoth will not send raknoth to aid a Zar who chooses to risk his life so," Drogan added.

"Can you blame him?" Rachel asked, speaking for the first time since they'd headed out for the ship.

Jarek considered her, wondering yet again exactly what had transpired between her and Alton.

She stared right back in quiet challenge.

Rachel's lack of raknoth love aside, Jarek couldn't really argue that Kole wasn't acting like a bit of an unreasonable old bastard right now.

"What about the rest of Kole's guys?" he asked, turning back to Lietha, who was openly glaring at Rachel. "They're all just twiddling their thumbs while he goes off to tame the big scary monster?"

"The rest of our clan are far more obedient than I," Lietha said. "They worship our Zar's wisdom as if it were divine law. They will not stop him. I am surprised the youngest of our Nans even dared to go as far as to inform me of the Zar's decision."

"Well… shit!" Jarek said. "When is this going down? How much time do we have?"

"I do not know," Lietha said. "Nan'Alnar only told me that the Kul draws near."

"And Krogoth can't reach out to him?"

"Krogoth is no great admirer of Kole's," Drogan said. "I doubt he would greatly lament his loss."

Great. Clan politics. A bunch of multi-millennia-year-old beings and it all still came down to the same petty crap.

"And you would?" Rachel asked.

Drogan tilted his head in acknowledgment. "Zar'Kole is as honorable and strong as he is cunning and wise."

"Clearly," Rachel muttered.

Lietha bristled and took a step toward Rachel. "You dare ques—"

Drogan barred Lietha's way. "Current decisions aside," he said, glaring at Rachel, "Zar'Kole is an admirable leader. His loss would do us no favors."

Jarek didn't doubt that, but was it worth risking more necks trying to pull his peaceful old ass out of the fire? Objectively, he was pretty sure they should sit back and let Zar'Kole martyr himself to his scaly heart's content.

Hell, maybe Kole would even get somewhere. Maybe they'd sign the Great Rak-Rak Treaty of 2042 and the rakul would shrug, say, "Hey, not worth the effort," and stomp away to let their wayward raknoth and their lowly human blood bags sort out their own considerable shit.

But probably not.

And as much as he'd like to wash his hands of the situation and focus on preparing to fight the rakul alongside those allies who didn't appear to have a death wish—not to mention handling the new ragepocalypse on the home front—he couldn't quite shut out that damned noisy conscience of his telling him that Kole was worth saving, raknoth or no. And moral dilemmas aside, if Kole was half as strong as Zar'Golga had been, they'd be wanting him on their side.

"We need to go get him," Jarek said.

The only question was whether he could convince the commanders to see it that way. He was about to voice his concern when Al spoke quietly in his earpiece.

"Commander Weston is coming, sir."

"Shit," Jarek mumbled.

The surprised looks trained on him turned to curious ones.

"Our disappearance has not gone unnoticed, methinks," he said.

Maybe this was a good thing. Alaric had met Kole, had seen that he was strong and reasonable and probably far more likely to win the trust—or at least the cooperation—of the Resistance. If anyone in Resistance command would be willing to lay it on the line to keep the old Zar alive, it would be Alaric, right?

Jarek crossed the cabin and slapped the hatch switch. The ramp gave an indignant pair of clacks and began its mournful descent to reveal Alaric standing at its edge, looking as if he'd been about to reach up and knock on the ship's hull.

"Howdy there, cowboy," Jarek called. "Just the man we wanted to see."

Alaric shifted his suspicious stare from Jarek to the raknoth and back again, jaw steadily chomping on a mouthful of chew all the while. "Somehow I doubt that," he finally said, plodding up the ramp. "Anyone care to tell me what's going on?"

"Jarek was about to propose something stupid," Rachel said.

"I resent that," Jarek said.

And, joking tone aside, he really did—not so much because of her words as the aggressive tone behind them.

This shit was starting to get old fast.

"We've got a Kole problem," Jarek added to Alaric, trying to keep his head in the game.

Alaric listened attentively as they filled him in.

"Shit," he agreed when they'd finished. "I need to bring this to the council." He glanced at Drogan. "Zar'Krogoth should be consulted too."

"Krogoth will not raise a finger to help Zar'Kole," Drogan said, "no matter how much we will need him in the coming fight."

"Well then," Alaric said, "maybe Zar'Kole should get his ass outta Dodge while he can."

"That's what I said," Rachel muttered.

Jarek shifted his weight, not liking where this was headed. "Yeah, but—"

"We can't extend ourselves so far," Alaric said, his expression firm. "Not when this Kul'Gada could just as soon drop down on our heads at any moment."

"We need Kole alive, Alaric. He's probably the only one our people might be willing to—"

"You need to stay here until we get this sorted out properly," Alaric said. "No gallivanting off with dreams of saving the day. Is that understood?"

Try as he might to conjure up his cheerful charm, Jarek couldn't seem to find a carefree joke to turn aside the sudden feeling of the chains of command wrapping tight around his chest and arms.

"Is that an order?"

Alaric studied his face for a long stretch. "That's an order. No one leaves until the council has discussed this with Krogoth."

With that, Alaric gave them all one more stern look, turned on his heel, and strode down the ramp and back toward HQ.

Jarek watched him go, feeling the chains tighten.

This wasn't what he'd signed up for. In fact, it was exactly *why* he'd avoided signing up for anything and everything since he'd learned his lesson well and good nine years earlier. Or maybe not so well and good, considering.

It had all sounded tolerable when the mission was simple, their goals unified. But the problem with agreeing to give yourself over to an outfit like the Resistance was that you just couldn't count on anyone else to always see shit straight when it started to bend.

Of course, it wasn't like the Resistance owned him. Sure, he'd agreed to participate in their command hierarchy and everything, but it wasn't like there was some supreme court of law that would be waiting to strip his suit and toss him in the ol' irons if he took matters into his own hands. And why shouldn't he?

Because bucking the reins would probably only drive the wedge deeper into the heart of this piss-poor alliance they all had going on—not to mention further ostracize him personally from the Resistance. It might even lose him any chance at having their support in the fight that was probably going to end up finding all of them, one way or another. Which would be ridiculous, sure, but Jarek had a feeling the force of nature that was human spite wasn't about to just lay down for something as trivial as the end of the world.

"Goddammit," he whispered.

As Drogan, Lietha, and Rachel all looked at him, Jarek knew that, no matter how solid the logic arrayed against the idea, he couldn't just rationalize his way out of it. He needed to do something.

"I don't suppose you have some master plan to rescue Saint Kole?" he asked.

Lietha looked affronted by the question. "I will take whatever ship I must and fly to my Zar," he said, red eyes brightening. "And if anyone tries to stop me, I will—"

"Okay," Jarek said. "So no plan. Got it."

Lietha gaped at him, too furious or indignant to make a sound.

"I'll take you," Jarek said before the raknoth decided to try to take his head off instead.

"You can't," Rachel said.

She looked tired, disappointed, as if she'd been waiting for him to say those exact, distasteful words all along.

"We can't wait for the council to somehow magically convene with Krogoth for once." Jarek waved a hand at Drogan. "We've got his envoy right here. Plus, they're gonna say it's a bad idea anyway."

"It *is* a bad idea," she said.

"But it's our bad idea."

Rachel was less than impressed.

"You think this is funny?" she asked, quiet anger flickering in her tone.

"We can't just let him die, Rache."

"He's probably eight or nine thousand years older than both of us combined. I think he can make his own decisions."

Jarek held her gaze, uncomfortably aware of the weight of Lietha's and Drogan's stares. "And what about the people living down the mountain in Katashina? None of them decided to be ground zero for the heavyweight round. Do they deserve to die too?"

She hesitated, jaw tight. "We might not even be able to stop it, for all we know. If Kul'Gada is even a fraction as powerful as the rakul Haldin showed me, it's insane for us to try to take him out away from our seat of power."

Lietha looked like he wanted to refute the statement and declare he'd rip the Kul's throat out himself, but apparently his fear of the rakul trumped his indignant fury.

"I think we're all totally with you on that one, Goldilocks," Jarek said. "Which is why I'm thinking a snatch and grab is in order."

Her eyebrows raised. "You want to kidnap a Zar and drag him back here?"

He shrugged. "I wanna convince Kole it's best to have his peace talk where his friends are all within easy stabbing distance of his enemy. If a little elbow grease is required for said convincing, so be it."

Rachel looked at Lietha. "And you don't have anything to say about that? No, 'You dare lay hands on my master, pathetic human?' or anything?"

Lietha showed teeth that were quickly becoming sharp fangs. "Zar'Kole must live. Even if it must be at the intervention of… humans."

"We'll be there and back in the blink of an eye," Jarek added.

Rachel splayed her hands incredulously. "It's literally across the world."

"Two blinks of an eye."

She shook her head. "This is ridiculous."

"As is this pointless dallying," Lietha said, shifting impatiently. "We do not require your aid, human. If you do not wish to be here, perhaps you should step off the—"

Lietha's compact Japanese frame lifted off the deck and slammed into the bulkhead before he could finish telling Rachel exactly what she could step off of. After a brief moment of stunned inaction, he gave a growled curse and started struggling.

Drogan stepped forward with a low warning growl of his own.

Jarek planted a firm hand in his chest and took a calculated risk in turning his gaze away from the raknoth and back to Rachel.

"Goldilocks…"

For a long few seconds, Rachel did nothing aside from furrow her brows at the strain of keeping Lietha telekinetically pinned. Then her face contorted in a snarl, and Lietha dropped back down to rock the deck with a small thump.

Jarek didn't need to catch Lietha when he threw himself at Rachel. Drogan was already on top of that.

"This is a bad idea, Jarek," Rachel said, her eyes not leaving the struggling raknoth until it became clear Drogan would not be letting Lietha pass. "We should wait."

Would that he could.

But leaving a good ally and a bunch of innocents hanging in harm's way? Going against his instincts because of orders? Because it was the safe thing to do?

If Jarek was built for anything in particular, it wasn't that.

He was thinking about what he could say to make her understand when it properly occurred to him what she'd just said.

"We?"

She rolled her eyes, and there was nothing playful about it. "If I can't convince you not to run off like a dumbass, I'm sure as hell not gonna let you do it alone with two…" She looked at Drogan and Lietha once more, then shook her head and pushed past Jarek for the cockpit with a muttered, "Whatever."

Behind, Lietha finally stopped his struggling.

Jarek traded a long, somber look with Drogan, told Al to close the hatch and plot the course, and headed for the cockpit after Rachel, trying to remember any other time he'd felt so wholly unsatisfied in getting what he'd wanted.

FLYING AT TOP SPEED, it turned out that *two blinks of an eye,* or at least the first half of it, was still going to end up taking about ten hours.

This had been a terrible idea. Rachel grew more certain of it with each passing mile.

The rakul were too close—within a day's travel by every estimate they had. What if they arrived at HQ while she and Jarek were off on a wild goose chase with a couple of raknoth? What if there were more events, more furors, and something happened to Michael or the others?

Any one of a thousand things could go wrong, and somehow she'd still let her concern for Jarek pull her into this exercise in lunacy. But maybe it wasn't all for naught.

For one thing, there were the innocent Japanese civilians whose proximity to Kole made them ripe targets for Kul'Gada's fury if and when he arrived there. Much as she loathed to admit any such thing right now, Jarek was right: they couldn't just ignore that.

At the very least, though, they should have told Resistance command what they were doing before jetting off. Not that they wouldn't figure it out the instant Alaric finished briefing them and the commanders realized the four of them had disappeared from HQ along with Jarek's ship.

What they would do when they did realize... Well, that might be the least of their concerns right now.

"Time zones, man," Jarek was saying in what had to be his thousandth attempt to spark some conversation from her.

For some reason, she hadn't exactly been in a talking mood since take-off.

"It's been 2 PM for like nine hours," he continued. "Am I the only one who thinks that's weird?"

Given that the raknoth had chosen to heed her not-so-subtle disdain and remain in the back cabin for the flight, Rachel had to assume the question was directed at her.

She fixed him with her least captivated stare.

He shrugged. "Well excuse me for my undying childlike sense of wonder."

"Childlike implies you're no longer a child," she said.

Hope lit in his eyes. "Touché, my golden-haired—"

"Incoming, sir," Al said through the ship speakers.

They were both upright and alert in an instant.

"Talk to us, Al," Jarek said. "What are we dealing with?"

"It's... Oh!"

"Spit it out, Mr. Robot."

"It's the Enochians, sir. They're hailing us locally."

Jarek traded a frown with her. "Locally?"

"See for yourself," Al said.

The speakers crackled.

"Nice of you to invite us along," came Haldin's voice.

"Hey, you know how it is," Jarek said. "You step out for a quick run to Japan thinking no one's even gonna notice and then all of a sudden you've got no net coverage, and you can't turn back 'cause a wise old raknoth master—who coincidentally happens to be acting pretty freaking unwisely—has his life hanging in the balance. You know, that old chestnut."

"Uh-huh," Haldin said.

"Speaking of which, how did you guys—"

The dark purple hull of the Enochians' raknoth ship raced by overhead with a roar of rushing air. It gained at least a hundred yards' lead in the space of seconds before slowing to match their pace. The odd material of its hull seemed to eat the sun and then give it back as a fluid glow rather than a gleam or a shine.

"This ship is pretty fast," Haldin said. "We left HQ two hours ago."

Jarek cocked his head in a *not bad* expression.

"I'm assuming you didn't come out here for a race," Rachel said.

"Not exactly."

Jarek looked wary. "Alaric didn't happen to send you out here to throw us in irons, did he?"

"He did express pretty explicitly that we should bring back you, uh…"

"Chicken-chasing fools," came Johnny's voice.

"Right," Haldin said. "That. But they decided we might as well try to grab Kole too while we're at it."

Huh. Maybe—just maybe—this whole expedition might not end up being the worst decision ever.

"Huh," Jarek said. "Well rock on, then, team."

There was a pregnant silence, the kind that sat heavy in Rachel's stomach for some instinctive reason she couldn't quite place.

"There's something else," Haldin said. "New intel."

Rachel traded an uncertain look with Jarek. "What is it?"

"Michael had another episode—a mild one, but he caught flashes of some kind of attack, maybe another furor. He didn't recognize the place, but Alton thought it sounded like it could've been Japan, from what Michael told us."

"What?" Rachel heard herself say.

"What?" Lietha echoed from the cockpit doorway, eyes blazing scarlet fury. "The attack has already begun?"

"We're not sure what's happening," Hal said, "but—"

"You must fly faster!" Lietha spat, and the floor hissed and smoked where the stuff landed.

"Dude!" Jarek said. "Not cool. We're flying as fast as we can."

Lietha spun and punched a hole straight through the cockpit bulwark. "Cursed void!"

"Motherfucker!" Jarek cried. "You wanna get your pal under control back there, Stumpy?"

Lietha's skin was shifting to mint green scales as he rounded on Jarek. "You think to—"

Drogan grabbed Lietha and dragged him, biting and gnashing, into the back cabin. There was a loud crash and then Drogan's low growl of, "Control yourself."

The ruckus calmed.

"This is why we can't have nice things," Jarek muttered.

"Is Michael…" Rachel started to ask toward the console. Then it dawned on her.

New intel. Interpreted by Alton. Out here where net coverage was largely nonexistent.

"When did Michael see all this?"

"Twenty minutes ago," came Michael's voice, "give or take. And I'm fine."

The sound of Michael's voice—of Michael's voice on the *local* broadcast, more specifically—made her feel like she'd just fallen out of the moving aircraft.

"You brought him with you?!" she cried.

"I'm not luggage, Rache. Or an invalid, despite what everyone seems to think."

"I know that, Spongehead. But you're also sleeping eighteen hours a day and having routine seizures. You don't belong in the middle of a fight right now."

"With any luck, there won't be a fight," Haldin said. "Assuming it's another furor, we'll stabilize the situation in Katashina and get Zar'Kole's people out safe. Then, if we can, we should get word about all this to Al'Brandt in the Himalayas. We haven't been able to reach them by comm. Having the one guy who seems to be able to see what the rakul are up to might help us do those things and get everyone back and ready to fight before they find us."

"Or home base," Jarek said.

"Right," Haldin said. "Which is why we need to move fast."

"Well excuse me if my primitive subsonic flying machine isn't up to your standards," Jarek said.

"Looks like we're almost there anyway," Haldin said.

Well wasn't that all just tidy and swell, then? Never mind that they'd dragged Michael out here like a defenseless rakul compass.

Jesus, when was life ever going to be simple again? Or safe? Hell, she'd settle for just getting back to an average of non-life-threatening.

Something told her that wasn't going to be happening anytime soon, though.

As they closed on Katashina, Jarek caught the Enochians up to speed on Kole's bold plan for martyrdom, taking particular care not to say anything too insulting about the decisions of Lietha's Zar. Judging by the fact that the steady growling from the back cabin never got above a low rumble, he must have succeeded.

They were flying high over Tokyo and Jarek was leading a discussion on how they might best accomplish a snatch and grab with a stubborn super-powered raknoth when they first noticed the dark spot on the northwestern horizon.

Something about the spot made Rachel immediately uneasy. They were already too late. She was suddenly sure of it.

"No..." Lietha hissed from the doorway. He was gaping at the steadily approaching dark spot ahead. "It cannot be."

"Oh dear," Al said quietly. He zoomed the view on the cockpit display, and the cause of Lietha's consternation became clear.

The wafting columns of darkness were unmistakable.

Katashina was burning.

CHAPTER NINE

Jarek had seen a lot of bad shit in his life. Hell, he'd made some pretty grisly displays with his own two hands. When they crested the last ridge and stared down into the wide ravine of Katashina, though, even he wasn't ready for the magnitude of the violence that had taken the sprawling village.

On the flight in, the long-abandoned ruins of Tokyo proper had been peaceful and quiet. The sight of the smoke that had filled up more and more of the skyline as they'd reached the northwestern edge of the city and skirted over low mountains had planted the seeds of dread.

Now, crawling slowly over the carnage, those seeds blossomed into much more. Shock. Revulsion. Anger.

He wanted to cover Rachel's eyes and tell her not to look, but he couldn't seem to look away or move, and the sounds of her raspy breaths beside him told him it was already too late anyway.

Some buildings were already burnt to ashes, but several of the bigger ones were still in their death throes, spewing their contribution to the thick plumes of smoke they'd spotted from a distance. The property destruction was the least shocking feature of the scene, though.

Dozens upon dozens of bodies littered the streets between the smoking shells of the village buildings, twisted together in a sick collage that told of brutal violence and reckless abandon. The disturbingly meaty smell on the air made him think plenty more must have been caught in the burning buildings as well. Most disturbing of all, though, were the smaller bodies tangled in the bloody mess. Children…

A wave of nausea hit him, harsh acid rising in his throat.

"Jesus Christ," Rachel whispered.

Jarek reached over to grab her arm for support, but she didn't seem to notice.

Thankfully, he had Al to set the ship down. He knew better than to think Al wouldn't be disturbed by the sight below, but his companions "hands" would still be far steadier than Jarek's right now.

Al guided the ship past the horrible scene and into the low mountains where Kole had built his isolated home. They touched down to a soft landing a little ways from the perimeter of Kole's estate.

Like much of the village below, the house was in the late stages of its transition to burning embers.

The groan-clack of the ship's boarding ramp beginning to descend snapped Jarek out of dark thoughts and back to the moment. He turned in time to see Lietha slide through the crack of the still-descending ramp and take off running.

"Hey, wait!" he called, but it was only half-hearted.

Drogan held his gaze for a long moment, his expression unreadable, and turned to follow Lietha down the ramp at a more controlled pace.

Jarek said nothing. There was no danger here anyway. He was fairly certain of that. They'd seen it all from above, and shocked or not, Al would've been scanning to spot anything they'd missed. Whatever had happened here, they'd missed it.

They were too late.

He stood and numbly made for the back of the ship, stopping on the way to grab his sword and wait for Rachel. She stopped beside him, leaning heavily on her staff.

He wanted to pull her to him, to hold her so tightly that her physical presence would force every single thought from his mind, but something stopped him. Maybe it was the look in her eyes.

"You don't need to see this, if you wanna stay on the ship," he said.

She set her jaw and walked down the ramp, staff clunking heavily with each step. He braced his stomach and followed.

The Enochians were gathering outside of their own ship, most of them looking green at the gills. Michael looked the worst of all, his revulsion at the scene behind them only stacking onto the sickly look he'd been cultivating since the messenger nest had burst.

Rachel went to give her brother a somber hug, spoke a few quiet words with him, then told him to stay put while they went to have a look.

By unspoken agreement, Hal, Johnny, Elise, and Alton peeled off to join Rachel and Jarek while the rest of the Enochians hung back to watch the ships with Michael.

Jarek took deliberate care to place himself between Rachel and Alton as they trekked along the path to Kole's house.

"You guys sense anything?" he asked.

"No survivors," Alton said. "Not here, at least." He took three heavy sniffs of the air. "And Kul'Gada has been through here."

Ahead, an awful wail split the smoky afternoon sky. Lietha, he could only assume.

"Yeah," Jarek said quietly. "I kind of got that impression."

They reached Kole's house and passed under the stone archway to find Lietha staring numbly up at the smoldering wreckage of his home. Ahead, Drogan was prowling around the perimeter of the rubble, sniffing here and there for some scent.

"Where are they?" Elise asked quietly.

Across the courtyard, Drogan snapped around and pointed. "Kul'-Gada came here from the west."

Lietha stirred from his stupor. "Our ship." He straightened, his voice more urgent this time. "The ship!"

With that, Lietha sprung into a wild sprint and leapt over the west perimeter wall with no signs of stopping on the other side.

"Lietha!" Drogan called.

No answer.

"Someone really needs to have a teamwork talk with that guy," Jarek muttered.

"We should follow," Drogan said. "Zar'Kole would have been using his ship's messengers to speak with Kul'Gada before his arrival. Perhaps he is still there with his clan."

It was clear enough that Drogan didn't really believe they were about to find Kole and crew alive and well, but no one argued. They headed back to the ships, swapped Michael over to fly with Jarek and Rachel, and headed west, flying low and slow enough for their telepaths to sweep for Lietha. It turned out they didn't need telepathic senses to find the raknoth.

"There, sir," Al said only a couple miles later, zooming the display.

Lietha had somehow already managed to make it to the top of what the map identified as Mount Hotaka. And he wasn't alone.

"Cursed void," Drogan said behind them, his voice uncharacteristically soft.

A raknoth ship, similar to the Enochians' but smaller, had come to a rough landing near the crest of the mountain. Four green raknoth bodies scattered the trail between the ship and the peak, most of them in multiple pieces. And at the peak was a fifth body, the one Lietha stood over now.

Drogan dropped the ramp and leapt out of the ship before they'd landed. Once Al had set them down, Jarek and Rachel followed along with Michael between them.

Outside, Lietha had fallen to his knees and was huddled over the still form of Zar'Kole. Jarek knew it was Kole only by the kimono he wore, the same one he'd been wearing when he'd last seen the Zar. It was the only thing he could be recognized by.

The raknoth's head had been hacked clear of his shoulders and crushed into an indiscernible pile of gore. Dark raknoth blood stained the grass all around it.

As they watched, Lietha gathered Kole's body up in his arms and tilted his head back to bellow a mournful shriek at the sky. Drogan fell in behind Lietha and rested his hands on the raknoth's shoulders in support, or maybe restraint.

Even the most hate-filled Resistance soldier might have felt a stirring of sympathy at the sight.

Rachel turned away.

When Jarek finally tore his eyes away from Kole and down the trail, the sight of the other four dead raknoth was no less gruesome. One had been cleanly beheaded. Two lay with their heads caved in but still attached. In addition to severe head trauma, the last raknoth had been ripped clean in two, straight through the torso.

The sight sent a shudder through Jarek, for more reasons than one.

He was intimately aware just how hard it was to hack through raknoth hide, and they were no slouches on the battlefield. Something that could have ripped five of them apart like this… that wasn't a creature he wanted to meet in a dark alley—or at all, really.

He looked back at Kole's body and clenched his fists, anger and fear beginning to bleed through the raw shock.

Why the hell had Kole insisted on staying here when he knew that thing was coming for him? He'd said himself he had little hope of a peaceful resolution. And now they'd lost what had probably been their most powerful ally outside of Krogoth's clan.

The crazy old bastard.

Jarek didn't realize just how tightly he was wound until Rachel put a hand on his arm.

"Are you okay?"

"Fine," he said.

She looked less than convinced but didn't make a point of saying so as the Enochians slowly trickled over to join them near Kole's body.

For a while, no one spoke. The sun beat down on them, the wind buffeted at their clothes and hair, and they stared at the remnants of brutal violence, lost in their own thoughts.

Jarek made the mistake of looking back the way they'd come, and the plumes of drifting smoke hit him like a bag of bricks with the reminder of just how many people they'd been too late to even try to save.

"What the hell are we dealing with here?" he asked, not really to anyone in particular. "Was it really just one of them that did all this?"

"I was just wondering that myself," Haldin said, still staring at the four raknoth who'd been crushed or torn to pieces.

"The rakul are warriors without equal on the battlefield," Drogan said. "You should understand that by now."

"Yeah," Jarek said. "Just a bit different seeing the aftermath with your own eyes."

"You can see why so many of our kind have been unwilling to believe the rakul were coming," Alton said. "Easier to simply deny such horror."

Elise waved a hand at the dead raknoth and back toward Katashina, looking a few shades too pale. "What do we do against… against all of this?"

Franco was reaching to put both hands on his daughter's shoulders when a horrible throaty voice startled them all.

"We kill the Masters. Cowardly tyrants." Lietha stood and shoved off Drogan's touch. "We tear the rakul to pieces until their cold, shriveled bodies lay bared and we crush them into oblivion. We kill them all!" The last words were roared more than spoken, and with that, Lietha stalked off toward his fallen clan members.

Jarek couldn't say he disagreed with the general principle of the statement, but it was kind of hard to forget they were talking about a group of twelve immortals who'd never been defeated. Well, except for one of them, once, by one Zar'Gada—the same Gada who'd promptly taken his earned rank as Kul and just so happened to be the first on the scene to destroy them right now.

One victor over god knew how many thousands of years, and apparently even that son of a bitch hadn't thought it a good idea to press on. Or maybe that was just what power-hungry raknoth dreamed about—or fantasized, seeing as they didn't really sleep—over the millennia: growing up big and strong so they could stick it to a Kul and take his place.

Either way, the known history of rakul slaying wasn't exactly an encouraging one.

"So what next, then?" Rachel asked once Lietha was over mourning his kin.

No one was eager to answer that question.

All this destruction rained down by a single rakul. And eleven more out there... What could they do about that? The first pangs of true fear stirred in Jarek's chest.

What if there was nothing they could do about it? What if the rakul were just too strong—worlds out of their league?

"Ah, c'mon guys," Johnny finally said. "We're not dead yet. Let's say —hypothetically, of course—we're all feeling good and fucked right now..."

"Speak for yourself, fire-crotch," Jarek said.

He wasn't in any manner of joking mood—not by a long shot. But faking a cavalier tone for the others was better than giving in to the part of him that wanted to simply sit down and stop. Give up. Do nothing.

Johnny pointed appreciatively at Jarek. "There we go! Not your finest work, but I like the spirit." He clapped Haldin on the shoulder, earning himself a somber stare, then continued on, unperturbed. "Look, we have three options." He started ticking fingers. "We can all pile into our ship and hightail it the fuck off this planet—not very cool. We can sit here dreading these faceless horrors that eat raknoth for breakfast until they come around to eat us too—not very smart. Or, we can get our shit together and make sure that, if we die, we at least do it right. Way cooler. Now who's with me?"

He was met with heavy silence and sullen stares that said everyone would just as soon Johnny cut it out and let them all wallow in their eminent doom.

Jarek took a deep breath and resisted the urge to let it out in a sigh.

What they needed was a morale boost, and, as completely as he'd failed to prevent the devastation around them, he'd be damned if he wouldn't help now.

So Jarek patted the hilt of his sword and stepped into the center of the loose huddle with Johnny. "You've got my Whacker at your six, Red."

"Interesting choice of words," Johnny said, "but I'll take it."

Jarek shot an expectant look at Rachel and tilted his head to the spot beside him.

She gave a little shake of her head.

He gestured more emphatically, and, with a hard roll of her eyes, she took a half-step toward them.

"Yeah," she said slowly. "Guess you've got my staff back here too, alien boy."

"See?" Johnny said toward his fellow Enochians. "I told you guys the aliens had a thing for putting things in strange places. C'mon, guys. Hop off those mope-mobiles."

With deliberate motions, Elise drew her staff, extended it with a springing pop, and twisted once more to deploy the vicious spear head at one end. "You've got my spear up front."

"Ah," Johnny said. "Looks like it's gonna be a rough day for Johnny."

Franco and the other Enochians filled in behind Elise.

That left only Haldin and Alton.

"Buddy?" Johnny said.

Haldin sighed and stepped in. "This is kind of ridiculous, but of course I'm with you."

"Phew," Johnny said, "that would've been super awkward otherwise."

Alton shot a glance at Rachel and stepped into the huddle almost self-consciously.

"C'mon, Stumpy," Jarek called. "You too."

Drogan frowned at him and looked over at Lietha before stepping in one step closer.

"Okay." Johnny stuck his hand into the center of the huddle. "Bring it in, guys. Yes, I'm serious."

Slowly, they each stepped closer, adding hands to the pile. Drogan was the last, hesitantly looking between the huddle and Lietha over by the crashed ship until he finally extended a single finger into the huddle.

"Scud, guys," Johnny said once they were all in. "I'm not gonna lie, I was kinda hoping we were all about to agree to run for it. But now that we're all here…"

"Crazy bastards on three?" Elise said.

Johnny smiled. "Crazy bastards on three."

Johnny counted, and they all cried the mantra with energy none of them probably truly felt—or most of them did, at least. Drogan's and Phineas' voices seemed oddly absent from the energetic display, and Rachel's mumble was only barely audible.

As soon as they broke their huddle, what little energy they'd conjured evanesced in a blink, and the inevitable weight settled back on Jarek's heart.

Team spirit and well-meant promises to one another aside, people were still dead. Far too many of them. And the rakul were only getting started.

Jarek had failed today. And as terrible as he felt, he knew the full weight of it hadn't yet settled over him.

An entire village. Hundreds—maybe even a thousand—dead and gone. Kole and his clan. All gone.

And for what?

They needed to do something, to dust themselves off and get moving—warn Al'Brandt in the Himalayas or get back to HQ and sharpen their sticks. Because, hopeless or not, they had a rakul out there that needed killing, and plenty more to come.

But first they needed to round up Lietha. The raknoth still didn't look far off from rampage mode, his eyes ablaze and his body caught between pale brown skin and mint green hide.

When Lietha kneeled down and began laboriously tearing off one of his dead clan member's ruined heads, Jarek worried it was a lot more than anger issues they had on their hands.

Had Lietha lost it? Gone mad with grief?

He was about to ask Drogan when he and Alton went over and joined Lietha in tearing off more heads.

"Dude…" Rachel said quietly. "What the fuck?"

"They leave their dead floating in space," Haldin said. "Kind of like how you guys bury yours in the ground. They call it the void. It's… sort of sacred to them."

So that's what all that *cursed void* stuff was about?

Jarek didn't have long to think about it before a particularly horrendous ripping sound pulled him back to the moment with a cringe.

"Fair enough," Jarek said. "But what's with the heads?"

"It's where the majority of their true bodies take up residence in their human vessels," Haldin said. "From what I understand, it's pretty hard to disentangle raknoth from human if they die inside, so in that case, they take the head."

Jarek looked at Hal, wondering not for the first time what the hell he'd been through to learn all of this.

"I've seen enough raknoth die," Hal said in answer to Jarek's stare. "And a year's a long time to spend couped up in a ship with one."

Fair enough.

Lietha came for Kole's head last and collected it with tender care. When the gruesome work was done and the heads all loaded aboard Kole's ship, Alton returned to them to tell them that Drogan and Lietha were going up to release the fallen to the void and that it shouldn't take long.

They watched the raknoth ship hum to life and lift up, shaky at first but quickly stabilizing as it soared up and up.

Jarek watched until the pin-point of the distant ship was lost to sight, then he turned toward the dark columns of Katashina's dying breaths and went to wait.

GIVEN their casual ease with dispensing it to others, Rachel hadn't imagined the raknoth would overly stand on ceremony where death was concerned. Whatever raknoth funeral rites consisted of, though, it apparently wasn't a ten minute affair. Then again, she also wasn't exactly sure how deep they'd go into space and how long it would take to simply get there and back again.

All she really knew was that it had been foolish to go running off halfway across the world with a pair of raknoth on what, at best, had been a long shot at rescuing Kole. At worst, it had been exactly the kind of reaction Kul'Gada had been hoping to elicit.

Even now, the Kul could be headed straight for HQ. That would be just their luck, wouldn't it? And if the party got started while she, Jarek, and the Enochians were all sky gazing in Japan…

Not for the first time, she found her gaze lingering on Alton, wondering if the raknoth could feel his master right now, could hear him whispering commands in his ear.

Her conventional understanding of telepathy told her that was impossible unless Gada happened to be hiding nearby. No human telepath could ever hope to consciously reach more than maybe a mile, but the rakul—as well as all the raknoth ships, as she understood it—had the messengers, and those ethereal little sprites, whatever the hell they were, meant the rules she knew were out the window.

Case in point, the furor that had gripped HQ and the surrounding area for miles—to the best of their knowledge before Gada had even arrived on the planet.

Alton shook his head at something Haldin said to him, and Rachel forced herself to look away and down at the uninteresting boarding ramp she was sitting on.

Could the rakul really still be holding all the strings?

If so, the raknoth were putting on a good show, pretending to fight back. But that's what they did, wasn't it? From planet to planet, species to species, they put on good shows. They snatched a body and slid in. They made themselves unquestionably part of The Team. And then, when the time was right, they called in their masters to come revel in the hunt.

They were intergalactic turncoats for Christ's sake.

And sure, there was the matter of their recently acquired blood ties with humankind that suggested this time might be different—that the very survival of the raknoth was dependent on this time being different. But was that enough? Enough to trust their scaly allies after everything?

She kneaded her brows with her palms and shook her head, attempting to cast the thoughts away like beading drips of water.

Whether or not she could trust they were all on the same side, none of them were doing anyone any good sitting here atop the quiet mountain, as peaceful as it was.

They needed to get back.

She looked over to the right, where Jarek had trekked a little way off on the pretense of going to enjoy the grassy ledge that overlooked Katashina.

Given the unmissable columns of smoke still rising from the village, though, and the defeated slump of Jarek's shoulders, Rachel highly doubted there was anything resembling enjoyment going on in his head right now.

She should go to him.

For half a second, she wanted to do more than that. Thoughts and images flicked through her head, the two of them alone atop this mountain, locking themselves in Jarek's ship and forgetting everything else, losing themselves in pleasures that required no thoughts, no pain and strife and—

As quickly as they sprang up, she quashed those thoughts with cold deliberateness.

None of that was going to happen. Not when they had alien claws at their fronts and their backs. Not when any moment could see Gada or any of the other rakul dropping down on top of them or sending in a raging horde of innocent civilians.

Not when there was every reason to believe he could wind up dead tomorrow—hell, today even.

What she needed to do was go dust him off enough that he could get his shit together, get back to home base, and be ready to move when Gada reared his head again. So with that thought held firmly in mind, Rachel stood, brushed off whatever dirt might have clung to her butt, and stomped down the ramp and toward Jarek's perch.

Gentle quietness pressed in around her as she left the ships and the sounds of conversation from Michael and the Enochians behind her faded to little more than distant murmurs. With the light breeze on her cheeks and the soft grass underfoot, it would have been utterly peaceful out there if not for the sinister smoke columns ahead and the smells of charred wreckage that wafted in on that easy breeze.

Jarek didn't turn as she approached, not even when she was reasonably sure he'd heard her coming. She sank to the grass beside him wordlessly, sitting close, but not quite touching.

What's up? The words hung on her tongue, unneeded. There was no point asking him what he was thinking about, what was bothering him. The blackened remains of Katashina in the distance below shouted all the answer she required. So she sat quietly for a little while, trusting Jarek would speak when he was ready.

"I just wanted to save the crazy old bastard," he finally said after some time. "And now"—he waved an armored hand helplessly toward Katashina—"all this…"

She put a hand on his shoulder. "I know."

He turned slowly, his eyes refusing to leave the scene stretched out before them. When they finally did, his gaze flicked first to her hand and then to meet her eyes. "But?"

She relinquished her touch on his shoulder and folded her hands in her lap. Was it really that evident in her tone? Or was Jarek just tuned to her -isms well enough that she couldn't slide her doubts and hesitations past his scrutiny?

"Well," she said quietly, "Kole did have every chance to save himself."

When she paused from pointedly studying her folded hands to shoot a glance his way, Jarek's gaze was piercing, and she didn't hold it long.

"What happened between you and Alton?" he asked.

She did her best to keep the ripple of shock from rising from her gut up to her face. "What does that have to do with anything?"

In the edge of her peripheral vision, he shrugged. "You've just seemed a bit miffed. Okay, pissed. More than usual, I mean."

"They killed my family."

The words poured from her mouth like angry gouts of flame before she'd even thought to say them. She glanced back toward the ships, wondering if Alton had heard the words she hadn't meant to let out.

"I think it's safe to say I have good reason to be a little skeptical," she added quickly, focusing back on Jarek. "And I'd think you would be too after our friend"—she tilted her head in Alton's direction—"nearly pulped you back at HQ."

Jarek nodded slowly, looking less than convinced. "Maybe so. And I wholeheartedly agree you have more reason to be pissed than most. But I'm not really sure what that has to do with Kole."

"I'm just saying we need to be careful. And remember who has and hasn't tried to kill us in recent past."

"I'm not sure we have the luxury of keeping our allies at arm's distance for the rakul apocalypse, Rache. You don't trust them, I get it. But—"

She jerked her hands up. "But what? You're seriously going to lecture me about trusting allies after you disobeyed a direct order and ran off to save a raknoth? And what good did that do, by the way?"

The weight of her words caught up to her, and she started to look away, suddenly embarrassed. Jarek beat her to it. The shadow that descended over his face told her she'd crossed a line, but he didn't snap back at her, didn't even crack a joke. He just turned back to the embers of Katashina and hung his head.

Why had she said that? She'd made her point. Taking the extra shot had been unnecessary. Mean, even.

But how could he be standing up for them after everything? It was irrational. Naïve. Everything Jarek pretended not to be.

Wasn't it?

"Jarek, I didn't—"

"No need to apologize, Goldilocks." He didn't look up. "You're right."

"It's not your fault, Jarek." She waved a hand at the village below. "You didn't do this."

"No." He shook his head, looking like he didn't remotely believe her words or his own. "I didn't."

Silence stretched between them as Rachel tried and failed to think of anything to say that wouldn't be redundant and utterly useless. Anything she said would only make it worse. She silently cursed Kole for his harebrained peace plan.

Minutes stretched by, and she found herself looking back at Alton, unable to help but think she wouldn't have shed tears if it had been him instead of Kole. Would that really have made anything any better, though? Was it really Alton she was even angry with?

She turned back to face the village.

Sure, Alton had been complicit with the operation, and tangentially involved, but he hadn't been the one who'd hounded her mom out into the woods, sent men after her family, and pushed her until she'd been desperate enough to do what she'd done to rescue Rachel.

Alton hadn't been the one. But he was the only one left, if what he told her of his clan was all true.

A subtle rise in the barely audible hum of chatter back by the ships caught her attention. Beside her, Jarek was listening intently, aided by Fela's enhanced feedback.

"It's HQ," he said to her questioning gaze.

She turned and saw Michael come around Jarek's ship at a jog, headed their way and waving a hand in a *we gotta go* fashion.

"It's the furor," Jarek said, rising to his feet. "It's happening again."

CHAPTER TEN

Jarek watched the dark purplish material of the raknoth door hatch wriggle its way closed and suppressed a shudder. He let the tension out as a long sigh instead, looking around the rather spartan room.

He'd have preferred to make the return journey on his ship, but given that time seemed to be of vital essence right now, they'd opted to all pile into the Enochians' ship and bolt back. Jarek's ship was following at its own pace, flown by the ghostly remnant of Al they kept on board the ship's computer for situations like this—the entity he and Al called "Ship Al."

And so here he was, lurking in the first empty room he'd found.

Aside from the odd assortment of rune-etched knick-knacks and dark staves that suggested this might be Hal and Elise's quarters, the room consisted of little more than a bed and a few drawers.

That was just fine. It wasn't like he'd wandered into the quiet room seeking a view.

Why did he feel this terrible?

So they'd let Kole down. It wasn't as if Jarek had never made major league mistakes or let people down before. Hell, in his bright-eyed teens, he'd accidentally thrown in with a band of veritable psychopaths thinking he was actually going to save the world from itself. Compared to that…

It was only one old raknoth, right?

One old raknoth, his loyal clan, and an entire village of innocent people, actually.

The weight of it all pressed back in, pushing him down to sit on the bed and bury his face in his hands.

He'd been too late. And now god knew how many people were going through the shit back at HQ, and they were going to be far too late to help them too, super-fast raknoth ship or no.

They'd fucked up. He'd fucked up.

It was the truth. He couldn't fight it. And much as the thought made him want to test the durability of the nearest iridescent purplish wall, there was nothing he could do about it now.

For once, he should have listened to Alaric.

Footsteps approached from the corridor outside, light and hesitant —Rachel's, he guessed. They paused outside the hatch, and he pictured her raising her hand uncertainly to knock.

No knock came, though, before the hatch disentangled itself from the wall and peeled back to reveal a tight-faced Rachel.

It wasn't a mystery how she'd known which room to try—his mind might be warded from her senses, but Fela wasn't, and he could only imagine the exosuit stuck out like a sore thumb once Rachel had learned what to look—or feel—for.

She padded into the room, avoiding his eyes until she stood in front of him and no longer could. She looked tired, and not a little bit like she didn't want to be there just now.

Jarek watched her, trying to wrangle up some snarky comment—anything to ruffle her feathers and break this odd funk that seemed to have settled its way snuggly between them.

Nothing came.

So, instead, he resorted to sweeping his gaze around the room as if taking it in for the first time.

"A whole year in here, huh? What do you suppose they've been doing for fun all this time?"

Rachel looked from the staves in the corner to the bed and finally back to Jarek with the faintest of head shrugs.

A grin tugged at his mouth as he traced her likely conclusion but died as the traces of amusement faded from Rachel's face.

"I'm sorry," she said quietly, spreading her hands in a *there, I said it* gesture.

"I'm not sure why." He shrugged. "I mean, I'm sure we could keep it up for a good year or two if we put our backs into it."

She wasn't buying the diversion. Not today.

"It wasn't your fault. None of this was, or is, or…" She sighed and came to plop down beside him.

He met her hazel eyes, so full of pain and frustration and raw emotion that he thought they might simply burst with it at any moment. And there, buried beneath all that negative energy, that tiny, glimmering flicker of want and need that peeked out through everything else and called to its bonfire-sized counterpart somewhere between his head and his free-falling stomach, well outside the bounds of reason and control.

That fire roared inside him, turning all other thoughts to dull background buzz, imploring him to reach across the single foot of emptiness between them and pull her mouth to his, to brush away all the stupid bullshit and—

Rachel turned away from him and directed her gaze down to her empty hands, and the fire dimmed, choked out by the expulsion of oxygen from his rattled lungs.

"You asked what happened between me and Alton," she said, still looking down.

Jarek willed his befuddled brain to catch up with the sudden redirection. "Yeah?"

She plucked one of the rune-etched pendants from the nearby drawers and studied it, bobbing her head as if preparing herself to say something distasteful.

"He told me how my mom died."

"Oh."

It was probably the least useful syllable he could have uttered, but it fell out all the same.

"I, uh…" He swallowed his search for helpful words at the look she gave him and settled for rubbing at the back of his head. "It *wasn't* Alton, was it?" he finally asked, when he couldn't stand the silence any longer.

She tossed the pendant back on the dresser, her expression darkening. "Does it really matter?"

He opened his mouth and promptly closed it, deciding that *maybe* was almost certainly not the answer she wanted to hear right now.

"Do you wanna tell me?"

Rachel was staring at the not-quite-corner where wall bent and floor rose to meet one another in a smooth curve, looking like she wasn't quite sure she knew the answer to that question.

"She saved me," she finally said after what felt like minutes of silence. "Stopped her own heart so she could reach out far enough to help me. That's why I don't remember stopping them, the… men who attacked us." She shook her head. "It was never me. It was her."

She looked up then, and the tortured look in her eyes put a dull ache in Jarek's chest.

"She died to save me. Because of them."

Shit. What did he say to that?

He took her hand. "I'm sorry, Rache."

The words sounded horribly inadequate in his ears, but what else was there?

In a way, Jarek's dad had died to save him too. And sure, the raknoth had been involved, but they hadn't played any more of a direct role there than they had in any other of the billions of deaths they'd caused in the Catastrophe. Somehow, swapping notes with Rachel didn't seem like the thing to do right now.

"I thought…" She pulled her hand free, stood, and looked uncertainly toward the room's closed entry hatch. When she looked back at Jarek, she spoke quietly. "I don't know. I thought I could live with it. That working with them was the only way. But…"

"It's hard to forgive something like that." He searched for something more but came up short.

Rachel nodded her agreement, not seeming to mind.

Suddenly, her recent snappiness, particularly where Alton was concerned, was much less mystifying. Knowing the raknoth had been involved in her mom's death at all had been bad enough, Jarek was sure, but this… This was just a kick in the nuts that could easily morph to a nail in their collective coffin.

Not that many people on either side gave two shits about what Jarek and Rachel thought, but human-raknoth relations were already bad enough, and they'd just gotten a sneak peek at what a single rakul was capable of. If they went into battle with Rachel riding the fence about their raknoth pals…

"I know this isn't what you wanna hear right now, but—"

"Don't say it then." Rachel's eyes were half-defiant, half-imploring. "Don't tell me we need to all suck it up and play nice for the good of the world. They're monsters, Jarek. And you saw what happened back at HQ when their master called."

"Come on, Rache, that's not fair. That was like mind control for Christ sake."

"That's exactly what it was," she snapped. "And if it happened once, it'll happen again. Have you forgotten what your pal Drogan did to Michael? To Pryce? How can you just forget about all that?"

Jarek bit back his immediate retort and forced himself to take a breath as Rachel paced stiffly around the room.

Clearly, this had been ruminating in her mind for a while now. Hot words wouldn't end up doing either of them any favors.

He held up his hands in a gesture of peace. "I'm not forgetting. No one's forgetting. Have you missed the Resistance boys walking around with their torches and their *death to the raknoth* stares? They might as well be printing it on t-shirts over there."

Rachel paused her pacing to meet his gaze. "Maybe they should be."

"Jesus, Goldilocks."

"What? You want me to show sympathy for the devil? They're not our friends, Jarek. Not Alton, not Drogan. Not even Kole."

He tensed. Two controlled breaths.

Why did that piss him off so much? It wasn't like she was being wholly—or even partly—unreasonable. Hell, maybe she was right. Maybe his "pragmatic" attitude in making the best of a bad but necessary situation had in fact been a delusional one. But still…

"You never even met Kole."

She let out an exasperated huff. "Does it really matter? Do you really think he was any different? That any of them could be? They've spent thousands of years snuffing out more sentient species than the two of us could count on our fingers and toes. Does that sound like the kind of creature that could ever be trusted?"

"Look, I get—"

"Don't." She jabbed a finger his way. "Don't pretend like you understand just to cozy up and try to convince me otherwise. They killed my family. And, in case you forgot, they killed yours too, so don't—"

Something snapped, and Jarek was on his feet before he knew it.

Rachel watched him, tense and ready.

She couldn't have known. Couldn't have known about the drunk driver who'd beaten the raknoth to the punch in stealing his mother away. Couldn't have known because he hadn't told her or anyone else. Because his pre-Catastrophe life was gone. It belonged to someone else.

But as the memories flashed through his mind—the crumpled blue and gray heap that had barely been recognizable as a car, the look on his dad's face when he'd sat down to tell Jarek the news…

"Fine," Jarek growled. "Fine then. Let's just sit here and watch the fucking world burn together, shall we? What's the point anyway, right?"

The twisted glare contorting Rachel's face faltered, as if she'd glimpsed something of the old pain her words had stirred in his chest. Tense silence strangled the space between them, both wanting to drop the angry stares, neither wanting to make the first move.

Footsteps in the corridor drew his attention before either of them could—fast, heavy. Someone running.

That was never a good sign.

"Someone's coming," he said.

Apparently Rachel had already sensed as much. "It's Elise."

True to her word, when the hatch peeled open a few seconds later, they both looked to find the raven-haired Enochian breathing hard and looking a bit flushed.

"It's Michael," Elise said without preamble. "He's having an episode."

Jarek traded a concerned look with Rachel, their squabble forgotten for the moment, and they trailed Elise wordlessly out of the room and up the corridor to the cockpit.

At their entrance, the ring of Enochians in the center of the cockpit stepped back to reveal Michael's seizing form on the ground. From what Jarek had witnessed of his other attacks, this one looked to be on the tail end. Michael's convulsions were sporadic, subdued, his muttering infrequent.

Rachel was at his side in an instant, though she knew as well as the rest of them there wasn't much to be done other than to wait it out. After an unsettling minute of dwindling jerks, twitches, and semi-violent flopping, Michael went still. Rachel gathered up his head and stroked his hair, whispering comforting words.

"Mountains," Michael groaned. "I saw mountains. Flying by below."

Haldin exchanged a dark look with Alton and Franco before turning his gaze to Jarek.

"The Himalayan clan?" Jarek asked.

"Could be," Haldin said. "I assumed he was busy stirring up the furor back home, but if Gada's back on the prowl, Al'Brandt's temple is the next closest to Kole's."

That didn't bode well for their Himalayan allies. Unless...

"You happen to notice where the sun was, Mikey?"

"Ahead," Michael said. He winced as Rachel helped him sit up. "It was ahead."

Shit.

"That sure sounds like west to me," Jarek said.

Unless Gada had happened to somehow jump to the other side of the planet, of course.

Johnny traded a worried look with Haldin. "We'd better let them kno—oh shit." He looked up from his comm. "No net coverage here."

That wasn't much of a surprise, out here over the Pacific.

"Probably still not much coverage there, either," Jarek said, "but don't you guys have some of those little messenger fellas on this rig?"

"We do," Haldin said slowly, his eyes flicking to Alton, whose eyes had drifted shut, "but…"

Elise was watching Alton now too.

Alton opened his eyes with the look of someone returning from a faraway daydream. "But we're running preciously low, and sending warning that way may be risky."

"Gada might intercept it?" Haldin asked.

Alton nodded. "If he's headed that way, it's entirely possible. And in that case, we'd be blowing any element of surprise to send a message that wouldn't arrive for Brandt to hear it. In any event, we wouldn't be able to tell what had happened, as Brandt likely won't be able to respond without a nest of his own, and I doubt Gada would kindly inform us he'd intercepted our warning."

"Well that is a pickle," Jarek said.

Freaking telepaths.

Haldin looked around at all of them. "Do we go?"

There was a short silence, during which Jarek felt the subtle tilting pressure of the ship's deceleration through his legs.

"HQ is still in trouble, as far as we know," Michael said after a short silence. "We heard it straight from them. We know it's true. This…" He touched lightly at the side of his head. "I don't know what I saw. Not for sure. And I definitely don't know if it's true."

"So we send the warning to the Himalayan clan," Rachel said, "and then we get our asses back to HQ before it's too late."

That made a certain amount of sense, aside from the minor problem that they might be leaving eight of their dwindling number of potential raknoth allies to die while flying off to help a base that might already be in the clear if the duration of the last furor was any reliable indication.

There was too much they didn't know, and no way to find anything out but to pick a direction and go.

"I don't think we can do much for HQ at this point," Haldin said. "The furor will probably be over before we get there, they're tough enough to handle it without us, and it's starting to sound like a diversion, anyway. If Gada somehow sniffed us on his trail, he might've started a furor on the other side of the globe to chase us off in the other direction. Or maybe he had no idea and was just trying to keep everyone looking the wrong way to start with."

"Or maybe it's happening because he's flying there right now to end the fight before it begins," Rachel said. "Maybe he deliberately tricked Michael hoping he'd tell everyone to be looking in the wrong direction."

Michael lowered his eyes to the deck as everyone turned his way, his face tight as if he were fighting some internal battle to decide whether or not he should be trusted.

"Should we put it to a vote?" Elise asked.

No one seemed particularly excited about the idea.

"I've lived under the rakul for over three thousand years," Alton said, "and I feel it's safe to say that, if Gada knows of the Himalayan clan's location—and he would after looking into the minds of the raknoth he slew—he'll pursue his retribution on my kin before sparing much worry about humankind."

"And we're just supposed to trust your intuition on that one?" Rachel asked, gathering her staff from the deck and standing from Michael's side.

"I trust it," Haldin said.

"Of course you do," Rachel said.

Haldin showed his hands in a peaceful gesture. "The only horse I have in this race is stopping the rakul."

Rachel looked around at the group, her expression darkening. "Vote, my ass." She shook her head. "Did we all already forget what happened last time we went chasing after this thing?"

"That's a good point," Franco said, chiming in for the first time. "And it begs another question. Are we sure we're even ready to catch him?"

That gave everyone pause, and their collective hesitation in turn lengthened the uncertain silence.

It was a fair question. Aside from the fact that this Gada creature had apparently had little trouble taking on a Zar and four of his raknoth, Jarek had no real way to gauge what it was they were dealing with.

Haldin's eyes found his.

"What do you think, Jarek?"

What he thought, possibly for the first time in his life, was that he didn't want to touch this decision with a ten foot Whacker.

Never mind that he might be casting a vote for them to all fly to their deaths. Never mind that Rachel might take a vote against her, and *with* Alton, as a knife straight to the back.

He'd already let too many people down today, and now, no matter what they decided, people were going to get hurt—were already getting hurt. And every moment they lingered here was another moment they were letting it happen.

"How much longer will it take to swing by Brandt's and see for ourselves?" he asked.

Alton appeared to be consulting a map in his head. "Less than three hours, probably."

That wasn't exactly comforting. A hell of a lot could happen in three hours.

Still—and maybe it was the fresh memory of Kole's savaged corpse talking—Jarek couldn't quite turn away from the gut feeling that, unless that furor back home lasted far longer than the other one had, and unless Rachel was right and Gada had thought to trick them using Michael, Brandt's mountain temple was where they could do the most good right now.

Eight more raknoth on their side, not to mention the support of Brandt's human forces...

They could still score a win today.

Jarek looked around at the faces waiting for his input.

Electric trills laced through his chest, the words lingering on his lips.

Because it was crazy, wasn't it? Racing off after the thing that could cut down raknoth like mere squishy humans—and while HQ may or may not be burning under the furor, no less.

But it was already too late to do much about HQ, and if they could get Brandt and his people out, get them back to home base…

They could get it right this time. For Kole. For Katashina.

He could get it right this time.

They just had to move.

"What do you say, team?" Jarek looked around at the assembled crew. "Are we crazy bastards or aren't we?"

They all exchanged glances, weighing and assessing as if seeking some unspoken permission.

Finally, Johnny bobbed his head. "Crazy bastards."

"Crazy bastards," Haldin agreed.

Others echoed the sentiment.

Michael speared Jarek with a stern look. "And what about the Resistance you claimed to be a part of?"

"I think Haldin's right. They can handle the furor. They were preparing to do just that when we left. Keeping eight more raknoth alive today is the most valuable thing we can do for Earth's chances."

Michael and Rachel traded a look, Michael hesitant, Rachel clearly less than convinced.

"Fine," Michael finally said. "Crazy bastards, then."

"Crazy assholes is more like it," Rachel muttered.

Jarek was considering the wisdom of clarifying whether that meant she was in when Rachel shot an impatient look around the room and added, "So what are we all waiting for?"

Jarek clapped his hands together, not keen to waste the small grace. "The lady raises a fair point. Whose tummy do we have to tickle to get this crazy party on the road?"

"No tickling required," Alton said. "But you might all want to take your seats."

They hurried to comply, plopping down in the chairs that had clearly been retrofitted in the raknoth vessel and strapping into harnesses.

Jarek was a touch surprised when Rachel settled into the seat beside him, but he had the good sense to hold his tongue as she strapped in and met his eyes.

For just a second, it was like old times, and he couldn't help but think about the night they'd spent in silent fear awaiting the duel with Zar'Golga that'd gone so messily sideways. In that second, he even thought about reaching out for her, about saying quiet thanks for her support or an even quieter sorry for something he wasn't quite sure how to articulate.

But then the ship banked gently beneath them and drew their eyes to the front as the sun swung into sight and steadied out right-center in the viewport. At the center console ahead, Alton's gaze was distant with whatever he was doing to control the ship.

They accelerated—fast.

Jarek relished in the raw power of the ship, as communicated to him by the prolonged backward lurch of his stomach, until the acceleration lulled off and left only the sure weight of Rachel's presence beside him, the ominous pull of dread somewhere in the distant mountains, and the burning guidepost of the sun ahead—the same sun they'd already chased halfway across the world today.

Quietly, so quietly that only Al and Rachel could hear, he murmured, "This day just keeps getting longer and longer."

CHAPTER ELEVEN

In just over an hour, they were closing in on the Himalayas. Despite everything—the danger they were quite possibly approaching, not to mention the frightening pace at which they were doing so, or the fact that it was largely at the behest of Alton Parker—Rachel couldn't help but stare in wonder at the snowy, sun-doused peaks of the great mountains as they rushed toward them.

At least things were under control back at HQ—or at least headed that way. They'd received that news as soon as they'd found their way back to net coverage, right along with a hefty dose of cursing chastisement and orders for an expedient return from Alaric.

So maybe Alton had been right. Maybe the furor back at home base had simply been a distraction. The thought didn't exactly make her feel any better. Especially since it only meant it was that much more likely Kul'Gada was bound for the Himalayas and that they were indeed hot on his trail.

What would happen when they caught up to him... Well, they were probably about to find that one out.

She looked over at Jarek, strapped in beside her, and suppressed the faint urge to reach for his hand.

Why had she been so insistent on pushing him away since that kiss? Sure, shit had admittedly gone sideways in the past few days for their own reasons—namely the enormous cargo bag of unresolved shit she'd somehow managed to convince herself she'd dealt with in years past. But before that... Why had she spent two weeks being so stubborn when they could have had each other and...

And Jesus, why was she thinking about this now of all times?

Maybe because it felt a little too much like they were flying into a rumble with a creature who'd singlehandedly torn five raknoth to literal pieces.

She glanced around at the Enochians, all strapped in ahead of them along with Michael, and wondered if similarly doomy thoughts were drifting through their heads.

The nav marker on her comm map put them about forty miles out from Al'Brandt's mountain temple when Alton began gently decelerating and dropping elevation. As they leveled out, Alton took a sharp intake of breath.

The translucent viewing section of the cockpit's wall zoomed in to reveal the distant shape of a rustic wooden temple nestled into the side of one of the larger mountains. And there, below, was what must have startled Alton.

Rachel breathed a soft curse as the zoom focused in and the small shapes resolved into dozens of humans charging up the mountain path toward the temple. Some of them were bloodied and lacking the appropriate clothing for the frigid mountain air. None of them seemed to care. They charged on with maddened intensity.

As if they'd been caught in a furor.

"Son of a bitch," Jarek murmured.

"Gada," Alton hissed at the head of the cockpit.

The viewing panel refocused downhill from the charging berserkers to a level, diamond-shaped butte set a good ten feet higher than the slope around it. And there on the plateau stood a figure Rachel was instantly certain would be haunting her nightmares for years to come, provided she was around to have them.

Kul'Gada. There was no question about it.

He was like a twisted nightmare mashup of a tyrannosaurus rex and the big evil turtle from those old Mario games—plus a shot of Satan himself and a set of disturbingly crimson eyes, of course. Those glowing orbs slowly turned to face them as Alton slowed the ship to a distant hover.

The rakul's shape couldn't fairly be described as humanoid beyond the fact that he was an upright biped with two arms. Gada stood at a slight forward incline, the line of which continued on from his sandy yellow haunches and into his thick, powerful-looking tail. His back was a mess of jagged-looking bony protrusions that ran from upper back down the length of the tail, and his long arms and thick legs ended in viciously clawed appendages.

Silence hung in the cockpit, at least until Johnny disrupted it.

"Ahh, he doesn't look so bad!"

Obvious bravado aside, the sound of his jest still made Rachel feel just a touch less paralyzed with fear.

"Okay, guys." Haldin unstrapped his harness and stood. "This is it. Probably goes without saying, but let's not underestimate the thing that just slaughtered five raknoth. We keep him busy and buy time for Brandt's raknoth to either join us or escape."

Jarek raised a hand. "How do we feel about cutting the bastard's head off?"

Haldin made a *have at it* gesture. "That seems like an ideal outcome."

"Well Christ." Jarek unbuckled, stood, and strapped his Big Whacker across his back. "Why didn't you just open with that?"

Alton turned from the viewport. "Let's just try to keep our own heads here, shall we? Gada will be faster than he looks, and far stronger than any raknoth you've ever faced."

Rachel didn't miss the way Jarek tightened up, maybe at some memory of his nearly fatal duel with Zar'Golga a few weeks ago. She unbuckled and stood as the rest of the Enochians did the same, gripping her staff tightly for stability—and maybe just a bit to help calm wild nerves.

Alton waited for Phineas to take over the ship's physical, and apparently more clumsy, controls and then followed Michael and the

Enochians in filing back toward the exit hatch, checking weapons and murmuring last calm words to one another.

Rachel turned back to find Jarek watching her. "Well"—his faceplate slid shut and locked with a click—"let's get ready to rumble, then."

She opened her mouth to say something—she wasn't entirely sure what—but anxious fear clutched at her chest and halted her tongue.

Then Jarek cocked his head. "On second thought…"

His faceplate slid open, and before she knew it, he'd slipped a hand behind her head and was pulling her to him.

The kiss was as heated as it was unexpected, and as soon as she got over her surprise enough to even realize she wanted to respond, he was already pulling back.

His faceplate slid closed once more. "We can decide later who's pissed at who for what"—he shook his head—"but don't dare go dying on me, Goldilocks."

It all kind of sounded like macho Jarekism until the soft, "Please…" that followed.

That single word yanked at something deep inside her. Then she caught sight of Michael watching this all unfold from the doorway.

It was as good as any splash of cold water.

"Come on." She started after the Enochians, Michael trailing after her. "You don't wanna miss your chance at Whacking the galaxy-conquering dinosaur, do you?"

"God help me," Jarek muttered somewhere behind her, "I really don't."

"Rache…" Michael's voice was low, worried.

She kept walking, waiting for him to tell her not to go.

"Just be careful," he finally said.

"I will." She squeezed his arm. "And you just keep your head down for this one, Spongehead."

She filed in around the open hatch with the Enochians and steadied herself as Phineas not-so-gently brought the ship around to face them toward the butte. Kul'Gada watched them from sixty feet below, motionless but for the slow sweeping of his tail.

She half expected Johnny or Jarek to call something ridiculous down at the rakul, but everyone was silent, which was probably for the best. It seemed wise not to taunt the uber-powerful alien when they were within what she wouldn't be too surprised to find was jumping reach for the massive creature.

At least they had three people on board who could telekinetically swat the bastard down if he tried.

"*Ahh,*" came a voice behind them.

Michael's?

She had to look to confirm it had indeed been her brother. There was something wrong with his voice, something that made her skin crawl, and he looked rigid, his expression vacant.

"The boy has been touched," Michael continued in a monotone. "And he has informed you of my movements? How irritating."

She processed what was happening just as Michael shoved James against the wall, yanked the Enochian's pistol free from his side holster, and raised the weapon toward his own head.

Rachel reached for the gun with her mind, but Haldin was faster. The weapon yanked down toward the floor, pulled by an unseen hand, and then James and Franco were on Michael, struggling against the younger man's possessed strength. Johnny joined in to help the others wrestle her brother to the ground. Michael thrashed and clawed at them all the way, until he was pinned too tightly to move. That was hardly the end of it, though.

She could only guess at what Gada did next, but the agony in Michael's scream was every bit as real as if a hot poker had been pressed to his dark flesh. The sound ripped at her insides and made her want to scream herself. Haldin adjusted his cloaking pendant and dropped down next to Michael, trying to shield him.

Michael screamed again, his voice already raw from the intensity of it.

Rachel took a step toward him and stopped.

They couldn't keep Gada's messengers out of his head. She'd tried. She'd failed. She couldn't do a damn thing. Except to stop Gada from inflicting the torment.

Except to kill one of the monsters who'd started all of this—the Catastrophe, her family. Everything.

She turned to the hatch.

Gada had helped engineer the destruction of her world and more.

And there he was, staring up at her, trying to take Michael too.

"Rachel, don't!" Jarek's cry seemed to come from somewhere far behind.

And far too late.

She felt him swipe at the empty air just behind her as she leapt out and plunged toward the hulking rakul.

CHAPTER TWELVE

In the brief moment after her feet left the hard security of the Enochian ship deck, Rachel was certain she'd made a critical mistake. She'd acted in anger, utterly without rational thought. Jesus Christ, she'd thrown herself at the most powerful thing on the planet. And what's more, the ferocious snarl on Kul'Gada's snout and the hungry flare in his eyes told her she'd played precisely into the bastard's hands.

But none of that mattered now. She was falling, and she had t-minus two seconds to get her shit together and focus on stopping Gada from driving Michael mad with pain—not to mention keeping herself alive.

She gathered her will and, just before she impacted the snowy butte, threw the energy of her falling body into a hard, concentrated uppercut of force, directed straight at Gada's ugly face.

The attack sent the rakul staggering backward from her landing space, but not nearly as far as she'd hoped.

Gada's tail shifted to root him back to balance after only a couple steps. Before she could think, the rakul lunged forward with a thrilled howl.

She swung her staff around in a horizontal arc and threw a telekinetic blast behind the blow as it slammed into the rakul's side. The hit budged Gada off course just enough that he didn't trample her, but he rounded on her too quickly, sweeping out with a massive clawed hand.

Time slowed. Her mind went numb. And then a gray figure rocketed down and landed on Gada's head in the mother of all flying kicks.

She heard herself cry out in relief as Jarek completed the kick with a wobbly backflip dismount and Gada tumbled to the ground with a startlingly solid thud.

Jarek landed beside her and drew his sword. "I said *don't* die, dammit! Nice entrance, though."

Gada rolled awkwardly back to his feet, his bulk rumbling the ground beneath them, a low growl bubbling in his throat.

Rachel caught Alton's descent with her extended senses just soon enough that she didn't jump when the raknoth landed on her other side with a thud.

She barely had time to think cautious thoughts about another potential turncoat episode from Alton before Gada gave a bone-rattling roar and rushed forward.

Jarek stepped to meet him, sword at the ready. Rachel skirted back to offer ranged support as Jarek dipped under Gada's first swipe. He whipped his sword around and brought it down on the rakul's tail, which stayed unfortunately attached. The strike did, however, earn Jarek an irritated growl and a moment's attention.

Alton took advantage of the distraction to dart forward and drive a kick into Gada's chest. The rakul stumbled then pivoted unexpectedly and swept his tail around to catch Alton with a torso slap that sent him flying clear off the snowy butte.

One threat eliminated, Gada whirled on Jarek.

Just then, Haldin and Elise landed beside Rachel, each bearing a spear. A low thrum shook the air as they touched down together, and Gada jolted to the side as if he'd been hit by a small car.

Rachel watched in horrid fascination as the rakul shook the blow off and the already considerable claws of his three-fingered hands began to elongate into long, chitinous blades.

"Looks like someone's getting excited," Jarek called.

Gada said nothing. He simply lunged at Jarek.

Jarek leapt backward to match, then reversed and stepped past the charging Kul, batting his way under Gada's bladed swipe with his sword. As Gada turned to follow him, Rachel gave his tail a telekinetic yank. Gada, having been relying on the tail to break the momentum of his charge, fell ungracefully to his ass with a furious roar. Jarek closed in and brought his sword down with all of his might.

Gada raised an arm in helpless defense. Only it wasn't so helpless.

The blow that would have lopped a raknoth's arm off met the Kul's arm with a dull thud and sank no more than an inch into his flesh. Jarek overcame his surprise in time to leap backward and avoid Gada's counter swipe. The rakul lurched to his powerful haunches and followed hungrily. Haldin and Elise were charging in to engage now. Rachel cursed and followed after them.

She telekinetically flung snow in Gada's eyes and yanked at his feet and tail to keep him off balance as best she could. She even hurled a small fireball at his face. Haldin and Elise harried at Gada's thick flanks with their spears, dancing out of range of his tail strikes with impressive agility. Nothing they did slowed him for more than a second here and there as he bore down on Jarek, raining strike after furious strike.

Cold fear settled in the pit of her stomach as Gada swatted Jarek's sword aside so hard it nearly left his hands. Jarek was looking flustered, and Gada's attacks seemed to be growing in strength, as if he'd only been testing them thus far.

Gada raised a bladed hand to strike—and froze.

"Now, Jarek!" Haldin shouted. His hand was raised in a closed fist, and he was trembling.

He was holding Gada in place, Rachel realized with a jolt. She cast her own telekinetic bubble around the rakul and added her strength. Even split between them, the effort was immense. Gada strained against their hold with unbelievable strength, lancing out telepathically at the same time.

She couldn't hold. Wouldn't hold for more than a few seconds. She fell to her knees.

Jarek lunged forward and hacked at Gada's exposed neck. Dark blood trickled, but the strike didn't do much more damage than the first had. What it did do was piss Gada off beyond belief.

She lost track of which part of his bellow she heard mentally and which part was out loud, but the sound was ferocious, and the swell in power even more so. Her hold on the rakul broke, and she collapsed to the snow in exhaustion. She must've lost it for a second or two, because when she looked back up, there were people climbing onto the butte—maddened, wild-looking people.

Gada was calling in his ramshackle army.

Haldin hadn't fallen from exhaustion like Rachel, but he looked like he was about to. Next to him, Elise was shifting to face the mindless villagers running toward them.

"Alton," Haldin called, swaying on his feet. Then, louder, "Alton!"

Elise retracted her spearhead and moved, staff twirling, to meet the first of Gada's furor puppets.

Meanwhile, Gada roared and resumed his mission to destroy Jarek with a single-minded animosity he'd apparently been holding back for the beginning of the fight.

Across from their furious shuffle, a pale-faced Haldin hesitated, clearly torn between helping Jarek with Gada or Elise with the overwhelming tide of berserkers.

Rachel scrambled woozily in the snow, trying to regain her feet, to gather her focus, but it was no good. Her head spun with residual channeling fatigue, and she slipped and fell forward into the cold white powder.

She looked up, desperate, just in time to see Alton alight on the butte at Jarek's flank. Haldin, seeing Jarek had help for the moment, whirled to face the horde of villagers dangerously close to swarming over Elise.

Alton darted to Jarek's side, but Gada was beyond caring now. The rakul stomped on without a moment's pause, lashing out relentlessly with claw and tail.

Jarek and Alton dodged and weaved clear as best they could, Jarek taking the brunt of Gada's fury, both of them backpedaling all the while. They couldn't keep this up. Couldn't stop him.

She had to do something.

So she planted her staff in the snow with freezing numb hands and pulled. One leg up, then the other. Her head was clearing now, carrying in a fresh tide of feedback about just how fried she was.

Ahead, Jarek's armored boot caught on something buried in the snow as he dodged a blow, and he tripped backward with a wordless cry.

Rachel's breath caught right alongside Gada's eager hiss.

Alton tensed as if caught between the options of attacking Gada or hauling Jarek clear.

Gada sprang forward.

No time.

It happened before she knew it, as if by its own accord.

A push. A small push. That's all it was. She didn't even have to give conscious thought to channeling the energy.

Alton stumbled straight into Gada's path, red eyes wide, hands thrown up as if to brace himself against the thin air that had suddenly betrayed him—by Rachel's bidding, of course.

Gada adjusted to the development seamlessly, the victory unmistakable even on his alien features as he raised his claws for the killing blow.

Rachel had one blink of an instant to wonder at what the hell she'd just done.

Then something dark and fast slammed into Alton and sent him flying, and it was Jarek there, desperately raising his sword overhead with hands on hilt and blade to block Gada's powerful swipe head-on.

Gada's chitinous blades caught the broad side of Jarek's sword, cleaved it clean through with a sharp crack, and continued downward. Something wrenched inside of her as the claws ripped into Jarek's armor at the shoulder.

The cry Jarek let out only twisted her insides further. She'd never expected to hear him make a sound like that—surprised, agonized. Afraid. She couldn't see straight, couldn't think.

Gada withdrew his hand to wind up for another swipe.

Steaming rivulets of blood fell to the snow.

"No!" Rachel cried, starting forward.

Somehow, Jarek managed to duck the next blow, but the kick Gada followed up with caught him square in the chest and sent him sailing through the air to tumble off the edge of the butte.

"No!" she screamed, hefting her staff as she picked up speed. "You son of a bitch!"

Gada turned to meet her, an eager flare in his eyes.

She shifted her grip to the end of her staff and spun, pivoting around into a baseball style swing. As she turned, she channeled everything her tired body could handle—and more.

Gada was openly reaching for her, unconcerned by the staff bound for his head. He'd regret that.

His blades were entirely too close to clamping down on her as she completed her turn, but she kept swinging and poured every ounce of the energy she'd channeled into a pinpoint telekinetic charge at the end of her staff.

The staff hit with a low boom. The jolt of the impact tore through her arms, and Gada staggered down to one knee with a startled shriek, covering one eye with the palm of his bladed hand. She caught a brief glimpse of clear, oozing fluid and realized she'd put out Kul'-Gada's eye. Then the rakul threw a backhand at her that probably could've flipped a car.

She thrust her staff out upright, throwing what energy she could into one of its shield glyphs. It was a hasty working, rooted not to the space between them but to the staff itself, which was in turn supported only by the strength of her own arms and body. When the blow fell, the strength of her flesh and bone gave well before that of her will.

Her arms buckled, her staff crashed into her torso, and she was flung backward. She couldn't say how far. Only that it was too far.

The world spun and solid ground smacked at her from every side as she tumbled across the butte. At least there was snow, mercifully thick and fluffy. Without it, she might have broken every bone in her body.

As it was, she wasn't sure she hadn't.

For a second or two, she wasn't quite sure of anything. She couldn't seem to string a complete thought together aside from that her vision was swimming with darkness from whatever she'd just done, and that she was afraid, and that she hurt. And—she gasped—and that she had to move!

With a wordless cry, she threw herself to the side just as Gada's large foot stomped down on the spot she'd just occupied with a brutal thud.

She rolled drunkenly to her knees, raising her hands toward the rakul, her staff lost to the snow. She gathered everything left inside of her and let it loose one last time. As much juice as she'd already channeled and as disoriented as she was, her efforts barely drew a twitch from Gada.

She slumped down, utterly exhausted. Gada stepped forward, his single eye pulsing scarlet.

This was it.

She thought of Jarek, lying in the cold snow, dead or dying, and she cursed herself for her idiocy. Not Alton's. Not anyone's. Just hers.

At least she didn't have much longer to suffer the thought.

Kul'Gada raised his blades—and stumbled sideways as something plowed into his left side with a ferocious roar.

Rachel looked up, not believing it at first, and there was Al'Drogan.

He dipped back to avoid the sweep of Gada's tail, and in charged Lietha with a scream of wordless fury that would have put a banshee to shame.

"No, Lietha!" Drogan cried.

Lietha didn't bat an eye. He slammed into Gada's chest in a full on tackle, and—despite the radical size discrepancy—somehow sent Gada toppling off his feet.

The rakul swung for Lietha as he fell. He would have hit the raknoth, possibly even killed him right there, had Lietha not been inexplicably yanked backward several yards to land unceremoniously on his minty green rump.

Rachel turned and saw Haldin approaching, hand raised. Behind him, Elise and Alton were holding off the furor horde side by side.

"Hey, Spike!" someone shouted from behind. Phineas had pulled the ship down over by the direction Jarek had fallen. Good. And that shouting someone turned out to be Johnny, fully loaded. Also good.

Gada ignored Johnny's call until the redhead opened fire with some Enochian artillery that hummed softly and apparently packed a big punch.

Gada roared and faced Johnny, but Drogan, Lietha, Haldin, and Alton all stepped in to cut him off.

Elise appeared by Rachel's side and helped her to her feet. Behind her, a dozen villagers were either lying unconscious or staring in fear at Gada, apparently coming back to their right minds now that they'd had some time in Haldin's and Elise's cloaking fields.

"Jarek," Rachel croaked.

"The others have him," Elise said. "Gather your strength, Rachel. Focus."

Any other time, she probably would've told someone to fuck off if they'd said something like that to her. Now though, she just nodded and called her staff to her hand.

Elise went to join the others in harrying Gada from all directions at once. Gada spun at their center, taking swipes at his harassers here and there, finding little success and growing progressively wilder and more frustrated with each attack. Several times, his missing eye had him turning more than he otherwise would have to fix onto the next target. Slowly, the tide was shifting.

At least until Gada caught Lietha with a tail whip and broke the circle. Drogan lost focus for an instant looking after Lietha and paid for it with a gash across his chest. Alton, stepping in to help, didn't see Gada's reversal coming, and he paid for that with a hand. A bloody Drogan grabbed Gada's tail and yanked him back before he could land a second blow on Alton. Alton roared a challenge and kept fighting.

Rachel telekinetically tripped Gada up long enough for the five of them to regroup in a semicircle.

They stared each other down across the trampled snow, tension building until it felt like the very air would burst with it. If it didn't, Rachel might. She was an easy breeze away from collapse, and all she could think about was Jarek bleeding to death in the snow behind her. But he had Al and the others. And they had Gada.

Gada shifted his weight, and their line responded in kind. She thought they were about to get back into it when a chorus of roars and howls rolled down the mountain.

She resisted the urge to look until Gada turned extra far to see the disturbance with his good eye, then she allowed herself a quick look.

What tatters of the wooden temple doors remained from the mob's ongoing assault had been thrown wide open and eight raknoth were plowing through the crowd at hard runs, headed in their direction. Once they cleared the overhanging roof of the temple, each of the raknoth bounded forward, clearing the few dozen villagers still ahead of them. Each touched down only briefly before bounding forward again, leapfrogging down to the butte at a startling rate.

Whatever they'd been waiting for, Rachel hoped to Christ it was her and the others the raknoth were coming to stand alongside and not Gada. The rest of her allies seemed to be having the same thought. Haldin must've come to some decision, though, because he stepped past Rachel and started working his way around Gada so that he'd be boxing the rakul in toward the incoming raknoth.

Gada watched him for a long moment, then he sniffed audibly at the air a few times, shook his head, and turned away from them, rumbling out a low growl she could feel in her chest.

They all pressed forward at his turned back, but the rakul crouched and launched himself down the mountain, kicking up a big puff of snow in his wake. The leap carried him at least sixty or seventy yards away, and the thud of his landing traveled easily back to them on the crisp air.

Gada leapt again and again, retreating down the mountain in a fashion similar to the raknoth approaching from the mountain temple.

They stood in silence for a long moment watching him go, and then Rachel went to find Jarek.

To Rachel's surprise, Drogan beat her to Jarek. She hadn't even noticed the raknoth slip away as Kul'Gada had retreated and Al'Brandt and his merry band of leapfrogging raknoth had hopped to the far-too-late rescue, but by the time she crossed the butte, he was already down there, huddling over Jarek's armored form alongside James and Johnny and—

"Drogan!" she cried down. "What the hell?"

The raknoth shot her an over-the-shoulder glance, licking the blood from his chops with disturbingly wet slurps she could hear even from up on the butte.

"Jarek Slater will survive," he called. Then he bent back down and continued going to town on Jarek's shoulder.

What the fuck was he doing? And why the hell weren't Johnny and James stopping him?

She jumped from the edge of the butte and slowed her fall enough for her wobbly legs to manage.

James patted the air with his hands as she shuffled frantically over. "It's okay. Drogan's just stopping the bleeding."

"By drinking his damn blood?"

"Al's got..." Jarek slurred. "Right, buddy?"

She'd thought he was unconscious.

"Should I stop him, ma'am?" Al asked.

"Uh..." she said.

Jarek popped one eye open and squinted drunkenly up at her, pale as the snow he lay on and clearly less than lucid. "Goldilocks..."

"I'm here." She dropped down beside him and found his hand. "You're okay. You're okay."

His mouth worked soundlessly for a few seconds, and he seemed to be contemplating something of profound importance. "Is... Is Stumpy licking me?"

He passed out before she could answer.

Drogan glanced at her as if awaiting some rebuke, then he shrugged and kept slurping.

"Okay," Rachel said. "What the hell is he doing?"

"Mostly cleaning and healing I think," James said. "Raknoth can synthesize a host of different agents in their saliv—"

"You think?" Rachel asked.

"Well yeah, but—"

"Jarek Slater will live," Drogan said between slurps, not looking up. "We have lost enough allies today."

That set her back on her heels, so to speak. In more literal terms, she sat on her butt, not particularly minding the cool touch of the snowy ground after her exertions.

"Don't go too soft on us there, big guy," Johnny said.

"I assure you, I am as hard as the stone upon which we stand."

Johnny's face scrunched and his eye twitched as he clearly fought to contain laughter. Drogan didn't seem to notice.

Rachel couldn't remember a time she'd been further from a laughing mood. Not with Jarek lying unconscious in the blood-soaked snow, his armored hand cold in hers.

Not when it was her fault.

What the fuck had she been thinking?

Even if she couldn't forgive Alton, even if she ended up deciding he had to pay, throwing an ally under the bus like that in the middle of a fight—and with a galaxy-class monster, no less...

She'd betrayed them. All of them.

Hot shame crept over the nausea in her stomach and threatened to ascend to her face. Chest-clenching apprehension wasn't far behind as the full implications of her actions began to tease themselves out in her mind.

But she'd have to deal with it all later.

Right now, she needed to be present for Jarek.

"You're hurt too," she said, only then remembering the gash across Drogan's chest as she caught sight of it.

"I will heal," Drogan said. "It is not a problem. If one of you would go ascertain that Lietha is uninjured, though, I would be grateful."

Johnny threw him a salute. "I was gonna go check on things up there anyway. Maybe find out how Brandt and his gang enjoyed the ringside seats. Be back soon."

Rachel watched him go then turned back to the gruesome sight of Drogan laboring to access the depths of Jarek's considerable wound. She didn't really know what she was looking at through the mess of tissue, but the cut was damn deep. It seemed like a mild miracle the arm had even stayed attached, especially during his flight from the butte. Judging from the marks in the snow, he'd bounced and slid a good fifteen yards before settling where he now lay.

She never should've jumped from the stupid ship in the first place. Maybe if she'd waited for everyone to form up and move together...

But Michael had been in serious trouble. That much she was sure of. She needed to go check on him too, but for now...

She took Jarek's hand in her lap and waited, ignoring the frosty numbness beginning to spread through her butt and legs.

"How's he doing in there, Al?" she asked.

"Stable, ma'am. More or less." Al's tone was reserved, muted—more proof he wasn't just some cold-hearted robot. "Believe it or not, I've seen him in worse shape."

"Oh, I believe it." She gave him a wan smile, felt weird about it, and then remembered that Al probably did indeed see the gesture.

"Franco says Michael appears to be all right as well, ma'am. He lost consciousness when the fighting started, but he's sleeping peacefully now."

"Thanks, Al."

Sleeping or no, she needed to check on the Spongehead. So she laid Jarek's hand by his side and pulled herself to her feet by her staff to go find her brother.

James bobbed halfway to his own feet, looking like he'd ask if she needed help, but then he thought better of it. Good man.

She looked down at Drogan. "Just don't… do anything weird."

He gave a grunt by way of reply.

She shook her head and turned for the ship, guilt and nausea rearing their heads and looking for viable purchase throughout her insides.

Don't do anything weird? Who was she kidding?

They'd crossed that line a long time ago, and the way things were going, she didn't expect they'd be going back anytime soon.

CHAPTER THIRTEEN

Jarek drifted through interminable cycles of darkness and semi-awareness. There were jostles. There were voices. At one point, there was the soft touch of a hand on his cheek. He smiled at that and faded into pleasant dreams of Rachel smiling and laughing in a wide open grassy field and wearing, of all thing, a freaking sundress.

Definitely a dream.

When he finally rose in full from his disoriented sleep, the first thing he saw was Rachel. She was standing at the foot of his bed and, little to his surprise, not in fact wearing a dress. Or smiling. She actually looked rather surly.

He'd done something.

What had he done?

Wait, why was he in a bed in HQ medical, and—*Agh!*

Fire lanced through his shoulder as he tried to shift and sit up. He closed his eyes against the unexpected pain and let out a soft groan. A hand settled on his good shoulder, and he opened his eyes to find Rachel looking down at him.

"Owie," he whispered.

"You're an idiot," she said.

He blinked the sleep from his eyes and took a closer look at his compassionate caregiver. Her eyes were blotchy, and her lips were drawn tight, as if to keep them from trembling.

She'd been crying? Over him?

He locked eyes with her. "But an idiot with a sexy lady waiting at his bedside."

She took a deep breath, looking equally likely to laugh or cry. "What were you thinking?"

"Mostly that I could devour about eight pounds of bacon right now. But I'm guessing that's not what you mean."

Not even a little bit, judging from the look on her face.

"You can't just throw yourself into danger every time someone needs help," she snapped. "Every time I…" She broke off, lip quivering.

Jarek waited to see if she'd continue, but she seemed to be stuck for the moment.

"I'll always throw myself into danger for you, Goldilocks. Every time."

She swallowed, refusing to meet his eyes. "And for Alton too?"

"Eh." He turned his good hand up in a mini shrug, moving cautiously enough that it caused only mild agony through his right side. "It seemed like the neighborly thing to do."

"Jarek, I…"

Merciful Maker, were those fresh tears forming in her eyes?

Was she really this upset over him getting a bit—okay, maybe severely, judging by the fire in his shoulder—banged up?

Maybe so.

He wasn't entirely sure how he should feel about that, but the thought pleased him all the same.

"I'm still here, Rache," he said softly. "I'll be more careful. And hey, speaking of careful, an astute observer might point out I wasn't the first person to throw myself out of the ship back there. Straight at the galaxy-conquering dinosaur no less."

He hadn't meant it to be an accusation, but the way her face tightened told him the words had stung.

"No. You were just the first one to do it with a clear head."

"Eh, I don't know if 'clear' is the right word." He grinned. "Or 'head' for that matter."

Rachel made a breathy sound halfway between a snort and a sob. She turned away to grab a chair—though Jarek didn't miss the quick dab she made at her eyes—then she sat down at his bedside, took his hand in hers, and held it in her lap. When she'd settled, he saw that she'd lost the battle to contain those tears. The wet rivulets trailed down her cheeks silently, and for a long moment they just gazed at one another.

"I'm sorry," she finally said. "I'm the idiot. And now you're hurt, and Fela's damaged, and"—she let out another sob-laugh—"he broke your Whacker… Jesus, Jarek. A few inches to the right, and you could have died."

"Hey…" He didn't know exactly what to say next, so he settled for freeing his hand from hers and reaching up to press it to her cheek. "'You could have died' has kinda been the central theme of all our dates."

She snorted, and another one of those burgeoning tears pulled a jailbreak and plunged down her cheek. "You call that a date?"

He shrugged. "I mean, when else are we supposed to find the time? The more important question is whether it's working."

"Wouldn't you like to know?" She leaned down and planted a warm kiss on his cheek. "Just don't die and leave me all alone here, okay?"

He grinned. "Funny, I seem to remember making a similar request before you leapt out of a ship at the aforementioned dinosaur."

Her sigh was warm against his cheek, her scent setting his heart to racing. It didn't slow down when she rested her forehead against his, eyes closed. He didn't even particularly mind the waves of pain that pulsed through his right side with each beat.

He just closed his own eyes and enjoyed the closeness of her. Slowly, carefully, he tilted his face up and found her lips with his.

A quick kiss, soft and reassuring.

He pulled back and opened his eyes to see an equally soft smile on Rachel's face.

"Holy crap," he murmured. "I'm in, aren't I?"

She frowned at him—a little too intently. "What are you talking about?"

His mouth split in a wolfish grin. "Oh, I'm so in."

She rolled her eyes. "You've lost a lot of blood. You must be delusional."

"I mean," he continued, ignoring the quip, "it's basically a moral obligation at this point anyway, but…"

She reached up and thwapped him lightly on the forehead.

"Ow. Too far. Got it." He rubbed at his forehead, careful not to move too much. "I'll take that as a strong maybe, then."

She snorted.

Drogan chose that moment to walk into the room wearing his sandy-haired middle-aged male appearance.

"Stumpy!" Jarek said. "Dude, I had the weirdest dream about you." He frowned at Rachel. "What happened after I tapped out, by the way? I'm assuming things turned for the better, seeing as we're all alive and whatnot."

"Rachel Cross was… bravely holding the field against Kul'Gada when we arrived," Drogan said, his eyes fixed on Rachel all the while.

Rachel squirmed a bit under Drogan's piercing gaze. Which was kind of weird, seeing as Jarek couldn't really recall having ever seen her squirm for anyone.

"Damn near getting myself killed, in other words," Rachel said, keeping her eyes pointedly on Jarek and looking a touch tense. "I did take one of Gada's eyes after he got you, though. Not that that's likely to stick. Haldin and Elise got tied up dealing with those villagers, and Drogan showed up just in time to save my ass. Al'Brandt and his raknoth came charging out of the temple in their own sweet time, and Gada ran off down the mountain."

"Huh," Jarek said, mildly more curious now about why exactly Rachel was acting weird. "Well, all things considered, I'd say we earn a gold star for our first rumble with the unstoppable force."

"Coming from the guy whose arm is barely attached to his body," Rachel said.

Drogan walked around to Jarek's wounded side and gave the bandages on his shoulder a few sniffs. "Which is why I've come to continue speeding your healing, if you are ready."

"Uh, continue?" Jarek glanced between them.

Rachel's face said it all.

"Wait, that wasn't just a weird-ass dream?"

Nothing.

"Ugh!" Jarek looked at his bandaged shoulder in disgust. "What the hell, Stumpy? You fed on me?"

Drogan cocked his head. "Well, technically, yes, but—"

"And you let him?" Jarek asked Rachel.

She threw her hands up defensively. "It was working! His saliva slowed the bleeding and, like, started mending your tissues together in front of our eyes. It was pretty creepy." She glanced at Drogan. "No offense."

Drogan huffed.

Jarek eyed him. "You guys can heal people with spit?"

Drogan crossed his arms. "We are masters of biological manipulation. It is why we are able to strengthen vessels once we take them. Despite what you might think about us, we create just as well as we destroy. Mending endogenous wounds comes far more easily, but we are capable of passing on some of this ability through our fluids if we so choose."

"Ick," Jarek said. "Fluids…"

Drogan sighed. "Do you wish to be healed or not?"

"Do you really have to lick me?"

"Would you prefer I spit in the wound?"

Jarek made a face. "I think I'd prefer a second opinion more than anything. Can we, uh, inject it? There's gotta be a syringe around here somewhere."

Rachel rooted around in the corner cabinets and came back with a syringe and a paper cup, which she handed to Drogan.

The raknoth shrugged, wiggled his head, and bared teeth which were rapidly morphing to fangs. He raised the cup. Clear fluid—drool, as far as Jarek was concerned—began to drip from fangs to cup.

Jarek shuddered. "The humanity..."

He faced Rachel to take his mind away from the thought of smearing Drogan's *fluids* on an open wound. "So what's the news? How bad was the furor we missed?"

"Well"—Rachel gestured at the walls around them—"we're still standing here, but it sounds like things got pretty messy. We're, uh, not the most popular kids in camp right now, what with us conveniently slipping off with raknoth before the furor and coming back not long after."

Jarek pointed at his shoulder. "I don't suppose anyone happened to notice we weren't exactly on vacation?"

Rachel made a face. "I wouldn't expect many sympathy cards anytime soon. Especially not from the commanders."

Great.

You really couldn't win, could you?

But hey, maybe he deserved it. It wasn't like any of his gallivanting —as Alaric had put it—actually ended up doing much good for anyone. Sure, they'd helped some raknoth escape the mountains, and hopefully secured them as allies, but that was something they should've been able to accomplish with a comm call or some messengers. Kole was still dead, Katashina was probably still burning, and Jarek had gone and damn near got himself amputated.

Which reminded him. "Fela?"

He caught sight of the exosuit's collapsed form in the far corner at the same time Al said, "Right here, sir. Mostly in one piece, even."

Jarek winced at the ugly opening Gada's claws had shredded in Fela's right shoulder. It must've been a single claw, actually, looking at it now. He couldn't really say the suit had seen worse, but if Al wasn't too worried, it must mean he thought the damage was something he and Pryce could handle.

"Glad to hear it, buddy." Jarek looked back at Rachel. "And Gada? Do we know where he went?"

"Likely to recover and continue hunting less protected clans," Drogan said. "Possibly even to recruit those of my kin who would yet hope to rejoin the masters."

"The council's debating whether we should focus on bolstering our defenses or going after Gada while he's on the run," Rachel said.

"There's a slight difference between running and being 'on the run,'" Jarek said.

Rachel nodded. "Plus we have no idea when the rest of his buddies are gonna show up. I voted we set an entire city of traps for the bastards."

"I like the way the lady thinks," came an amused voice from the doorway. Pryce.

He stepped into the room and hesitated only a moment at the sight of Drogan before heading to the foot of Jarek's bed.

He took in Jarek's condition with a grim expression. "You look like hell, son."

"You should see the other guy," Jarek said. Rachel arched a brow at him and he added, "I mean, like, out of professional curiosity and stuff. Galaxy-conquering dinosaurs, man."

Rachel tilted her head in concession.

Pryce frowned, thinking about that. "I may need to see some footage of that one." He went to inspect the damage to Fela's shoulder and let out a low whistle. "Must've been one scary bastard, though. How are you holding up in there, Alfred?"

"Quite well, sir," Al said. "Thank you for asking. As you know, most of my hardware is fortunately housed in Fela's posterior portions."

Jarek shot a wide grin at Rachel. "Al's always on my ass one way or another."

"Woe is me," Al said in a somber tone.

Pryce chuckled and turned back to them. "I'll patch the armor as best I can. Not so sure about the servos, but I'm sure Alfred and I can figure something out."

"Much obliged, old man." Jarek turned to Rachel. "Mind doing the honor of keeping her safe while I'm not inside of her?"

Rachel arched an eyebrow. "You want a phrasing check on that one?"

He made his best thoughtful face and finally shook his head. "Nah, I'm good with it."

She smiled and stood. "Fine. I'm already supposed to be helping with the cloak generators over there anyways. I guess I can guard your mistress while I'm at it."

"My deepest gratitude," Al said. "I think."

"Don't mention it." Rachel turned to Pryce. "I wanted to talk to you about something else too."

"Mysterious," Jarek said.

Rachel wiggled her fingers most mysteriously in the air, but her expression quickly sobered. "We need to figure out how to kill that thing if hacking it to pieces isn't a valid option."

"Hey, he bled when I cut him," Jarek said. "And you said you took his eye out. He's got soft spots."

"Well yeah, but that's an eye. That's like the one guaranteed soft spot."

"And it will regrow," Drogan added. "Likely quite quickly."

"Fire always works," Pryce said. "A strong hide won't keep blood or whatever else from boiling…" He wrinkled his nose. "Not to sound morbid or anything. Still, easier to turn up the heat than to figure out how to swing a bigger stick harder."

"Or a bigger Whacker," Jarek said. "Bastard sheared mine clean through."

Pryce's eyebrows reached for the ceiling. "With what?"

"I wanna say claws," Jarek said, "but sword-fingers is probably a better description."

"Galileo's beard…" Pryce muttered. "Scary bastard indeed."

"Space dinosaurs, man." Jarek shook his head. "Not even once."

"Right," Pryce said. "Well I'll see what I can do about that too."

"That's kinda what I wanted to talk to you about," Rachel said.

"Most mysterious," Jarek said.

Pryce perked up. "Why don't we step on over to my office then?"

"You're okay here?" Rachel asked Jarek, shooting an uncertain glance at Drogan.

"Oh, sure. Stumpy and I have big plans."

Pryce started to say bye, then paused, glancing between Jarek and Drogan's impressively full cup of miracle spit with a curious expression. "Wait, is that—is he…?"

"Raknoth spit. Magical healing properties." Jarek waved his good hand. "You know, that old chestnut."

"Sure, sure," Pryce said, nodding. "Guess I'll… see you soon then." He turned and then did a double-take. "I'm gonna have to hear more about how the hell that works later. You know that, right?"

Jarek chuckled and waved him away. "Go on, you old scholar, you. I'm sure Stumpy will be happy to answer your questions later."

Drogan let out a soft growl, still salivating into his cup.

"I'm sure Alton will be happy to answer your questions later," Jarek amended.

"Okay, then." Pryce frowned at the cup one more time. "Get…" He shook himself out of whatever mental tangent he'd wandered off on. "Get some rest. I'll see you soon."

They turned to leave, and Al dramatically cleared his throat through Fela's speakers.

"Oh, shit," Rachel said. "Sorry, Al."

Jarek smiled at the AI's leg-jerking shenanigans. "Go on, buddy. You can do it."

"Very well, sir." Fela rose smoothly to her feet under Al's control and gave a neat little bow. "Do be careful while I'm gone."

"Oh don't you worry about little old me," Jarek watched Drogan drip one last big globule of drool into the paper cup and wipe his mouth on his sleeve. "I'm clearly in fantastic hands."

The three left in their bizarre little convoy, each one of them looking back at Jarek one last time as if it were a requirement to pass through the door. Rachel's glance lingered longest, her gaze flicking uncertainly between him and Drogan, her posture still just a touch stiff, defensive.

"I'd ask you if that seemed kinda weird," Jarek said to Drogan when they'd gone, "but something tells me you're not the guy I should be asking about sporadic human behavior."

"You refer to Rachel Cross' defensive reaction to my presence?"

Jarek looked at the raknoth, mildly surprised. "So you did notice?" He frowned down at the blanketed bump of his feet. "Maybe she's just shaken up. I mean, can you imagine saying goodbye to this face?"

Bad joke turned to sad joke as his fingers brushed the scar lines Golga had left him, starting on his forehead. First that, now his shoulder. There might not be much left to say goodbye to if he kept this up.

He didn't mention that maybe she was just tired of sharing the same breathing air with any raknoth in general, or that, underneath the bad jokes, "shaken up" was about three sizes too small a phrase to describe how he himself was feeling after having barely lived through that monster Gada bearing down on him with all of hell's fury and more.

Jarek's nightmares were about to enter a whole new dimension of terrifying after that battle. But, somehow, none of this seemed like stuff Drogan needed to know.

At least, not until the raknoth said, "I would wager it has more to do with the fact that she tried to kill Al'Braka before I arrived."

It took Jarek a few seconds to remember Al'Braka was Alton Parker's real name, or at least the one the raknoth had given him before he'd decided to change his ways and adopt a new one.

When he did remember, though…

The final moments he remembered from the fight flashed through his mind, and the uncomfortable feeling he realized now had been quietly percolating in the periphery shifted to a full-on sinking stomach.

Back on the mountain, Jarek had been sure his misstep and resultant trip had cost him the fight—right up until Alton had made an inexplicably awkward stumble into Gada's path. Almost like the raknoth had his own accident.

"What do you mean, she tried to kill him?" he asked quietly.

"Al'Braka wouldn't say much," Drogan said. "And only through our telepathic link at that, but it was little more than an unfortunately-timed push from what I gathered."

"But Rachel…"

What? Wouldn't have done that? After everything she'd said about Alton and the raknoth, could he really be so sure?

Something—and it felt dangerously like naïve hope—told him she wouldn't have gone so far as to deliberately try to take one of their allies out in the middle of such a dangerous fight. But a crucially-timed push, seemingly out of nowhere—who else would it have been but Rachel? If she'd seen it as simply putting a raknoth at risk to buy Jarek time to recover and find an opening…

"Shit," he whispered.

After everything she'd said back on the Enochians' ship, it wasn't too much of a stretch to imagine she might be okay with that kind of means to an end mentality right now.

Or maybe not.

Suddenly, the conversation they'd just had took on a whole new light. Her hesitation. The tears. It was as if she'd been trying to tell him something. And then there was her reaction to Drogan's arrival.

And here he'd let himself fancy it all had something to do with him and his light butchery experience.

He met Drogan's gaze. "If this is true, what are you planning to do about it?"

Drogan studied him for a stretch before answering. "I have neither proof nor any great love for the one who has eschewed his true name. At present, I am not compelled to do a thing. If she were to turn against me or my own clan, however…"

"Yeah." Jarek shifted uncomfortably and did his best to keep a wince of pain from seizing his face. "Well, I think it goes without saying that anyone who tries to touch a golden hair on her head is gonna have to go through me first."

Drogan pointedly shifted his gaze to the mass of bandages covering Jarek's shoulder, looking slightly amused but saying nothing.

"Whatever," Jarek said. "Just a flesh wound anyway. I'll heal."

"Perhaps." Drogan stepped forward and almost gingerly began to peel Jarek's bandages away. "If you say please."

"Yeah?" Jarek said, suppressing the vulnerable shudder that tried to run its way down his back. "And how about if I say 'lick me, you glib stumpy bastard'?"

Drogan showed him a particularly reptilian smile and bent to inspect the wound.

After a cursory glance at the ugly bloody line stitched across a disturbing length of his shoulder and upper chest, Jarek turned his thoughts back to Rachel in an active attempt to distract himself from Drogan's poking, prodding, and occasional low rumbles.

If she'd really done what Drogan claimed, and if she was headed off to Pryce's, where the Enochians would be holed up working on these cloaking fields of theirs…

Moving as carefully as he could, he reached with his good hand for the comm on the bedside table.

He needed to talk to Rachel before the shit irrevocably hit the fan.

CHAPTER FOURTEEN

"Something troubling you?"

Pryce's question cut through the haze that had settled over Rachel's mind. She'd allowed herself to sink so deeply into the rumbling purr of the old diesel engine and the mindless seeing-without-seeing of the dreary surroundings passing by in the passenger door window that she'd nearly forgotten Pryce was there at all. And now…

"Huh?"

It wasn't that she hadn't heard Pryce's question so much as that the crucial bits of her brain didn't seem to be getting around to consciously processing it. She wasn't so sure she wanted them to.

Pryce offered an easy shrug, keeping his eyes on his driving. "Call me crazy, but I'm getting the feeling a few of your marbles might be heavier than average at the moment."

That was one way of putting it. Another might be that she'd basically stabbed one of her own allies in the back without warning. And sure, maybe she'd done it out of blind fear for Jarek, or because she had serious concerns Alton or any other raknoth could themselves become turncoats in this fight—willing or otherwise. Maybe.

Or maybe she'd done it out of pure, unresolved rage, boiling underneath—or maybe not so underneath—the surface even after all these years.

Did a turncoat ever really have any grounds to say they'd only done it to keep the other guy from possibly, maybe doing the same?

She wasn't sure. About any of it. But she especially wasn't sure she wanted to spill this particular heavy marble to Pryce—or to anyone, really.

"I'm just upset," she finally said. Not even a lie. Not at all. "This thing we're up against"—she shook her head—"and what it did to Jarek…"

Her comm buzzed before she figured out where she was going with the thought.

Jarek. Speak of the handsome devil.

The message on the comm quickly dissolved any sense of comfort.

We need to talk, Goldilocks.

Shit. Had Drogan told him? Did Drogan even know?

She nearly jumped when Pryce cut into her paranoid rumination.

"I don't imagine many people would go through what the two of you have and keep climbing back to their feet for more," Pryce said slowly. "Whatever it's doing to you, whatever you're feeling… Well, for what it's worth, just keep in mind that most of us would have soiled ourselves and ducked for cover by now."

She might have smiled at that if she wasn't too busy wondering if what she'd done was worse.

What would Jarek think? What *was* he thinking right now?

Pryce guided his big blue truck through a one-two turn, left and then right, and the dread that had taken up residence in Rachel's gut wriggled in anticipation.

Had she realized before joining Pryce that the Enochians had already taken Alton to Pryce's place to rest and recuperate as they got to work on the cloaking field generators…

She would've gotten in the truck anyway. Or so she told herself. Because, despite whatever other shit might currently be spattering down from the fan blades, they needed to get these cloak generators up and running if they wanted to keep their forces together long enough to even confront Gada. And on top of that, Rachel would be damned if she was going to turn away from what she'd done and try to avoid Alton and the Enochians like some frightened child.

"There was also a bit of a misunderstanding out there," she said quietly.

So maybe she kind of did want to spill that confounded heavy marble.

The pissed-off Enochian standing out front of Pryce's shop as they pulled up kind of put a damper on that, though.

Pryce stopped the truck and looked back and forth between Haldin's crossed-arm sentinel stance ahead and what Rachel hoped was her neutral *I'm fine, and everything's totally cool* face.

Pryce's gaze settled on her as he slid the truck into park and killed the engine. "This wouldn't happen to have anything to do with said misunderstanding, would it?"

Ahead, Haldin uncrossed his arms and started for the truck with a level, confident stride.

Rachel swallowed, and shot Pryce what she hoped was a convincing shrug. "It might. Maybe you should head inside while we talk. Thanks for the ride."

Pryce's wrestling brows indicated he wasn't so convinced that was the best course of action, but he nodded and hopped out of the truck.

"You too, Al," she added back at Fela's form as she climbed out of the truck.

"But, ma'am, I'm perfectly capable of—"

"It's between us," Rachel said. "We're all friends here, I'll be fine."

Judging by how slowly Fela disbanded from the truck bed, Al was about as thrilled as Pryce about the unexplained tension. For all she knew, Al had already pieced the puzzle together without anyone's help. But, after a reluctant pause, they both headed into the shop through the front door.

Rachel turned to face Haldin as he covered the last ten yards between them. She tried to refrain from fidgeting with her staff, but couldn't help pulling her mental defenses tight—just in case.

"An interesting choice of words," he said quietly as he drew up by the front of Pryce's truck. "We're all friends here, huh?"

Rachel tried to keep her expression neutral. "What did he tell you?"

Haldin gave her a humorless grin. "He didn't. Not until we were back here and you were safely off at HQ. But I knew something had happened. Alton's never been the fastest or most adept fighter among his kin, but what happened back there, it just didn't add up, and neither did his story. Not until he finally admitted that maybe, just maybe, someone had given him a little push." He shook his head, staring razor daggers at her. "Just a harmless little push, right?"

It had been a mistake. She should be able to admit that. A mistake bred in a moment of thoughtless panic. Gada had been so fearsome, so powerful. They'd needed an opening. She hadn't thought it through, had only been trying to help. And sure, it had been wrong to throw Alton under the bus, so to speak, but...

No. It had definitely been a mistake.

So why couldn't she get her mouth to cooperate and say the words?

"Nothing to say for yourself?" Haldin asked, his voice dangerously quiet.

The clear, windless air around them began to softly swirl and crackle with power, and with it came the stirring of Rachel's own anger.

"What do you want me to say? That I'm sorry?"

So maybe it had been a mistake. But did Alton really deserve to hear that she thought so? That she was wrong? Could she really bring herself to apologize, even indirectly, to one of the bastards who'd been a part of the murder of her family?

No.

Haldin didn't back down at the tone of her voice, nor did he look anything but maybe more angry as she began to gather her own power.

Within seconds, the air was whipping around them, buffeting hair and clothes and everything else. Haldin stood poised and unafraid, looking like he had no doubt he could take anything she threw at him and still have enough left to bury her under Pryce's truck.

Let the son of a bitch try.

"I saw an opening," she growled. "I took it. Everyone's still alive, aren't they?"

"That's your excuse?" He took a step forward, and a heavy pressure settled over Rachel like a lead blanket. "An opening? That's what you call trying to sacrifice an ally?"

Rachel channeled the energy, pushed out enough to counter his telekinetic dick-showing, and was just about to push further when one of the windows of Pryce's living quarters jerked upward and Elise's raven locks and fair skin appeared in the open window.

"Hal..."

She called the name with only a hint of chiding, but enough to be heard.

Rachel braced herself, half expecting it to simply push Haldin over the edge that much more, but Haldin took a great deep breath, let out a long sigh, and relaxed. Wordlessly, he threw Elise a thumbs-up over his shoulder, his eyes never leaving Rachel.

"Shall we talk, then?" he asked, the hints of a wry smile creeping onto his face.

Rachel let out a long breath of her own and cautiously released the energy she'd gathered back to her surroundings in one last gout of heat and swirling air.

Jesus. That had been close. And as much as she wanted to think she could hold her own in a fight with Haldin or any other arcanist, she sure as hell wasn't going to lament not finding out for sure right now.

"All right," she said. "I'm listening."

He considered her for a stretch, looking like he was debating where to begin. "You wanna know how I first found out about the raknoth?"

She watched him closely, still not quite trusting the sudden change of direction. Finally, she gave a stiff nod. "Sure."

He rested his elbows against the hood of Pryce's truck and made a point of studying his fidgeting fingers for a long handful of seconds. Finally, he sighed.

"The first raknoth I ever encountered was parading as the High General of the Legion. That's our military on Enochia."

"Shit," Rachel said.

The raknoth had pulled similar tactics on Earth, but that didn't really make the charade any less terrifying—especially not after how things had turned out for Earth.

Haldin gave a slow nod of agreement, his eyes focused somewhere in distant memory. "Shit's right."

"So when you say you encountered him…"

"We had the good general over for dinner one night. I grew up in a Legion family myself, I should add. My dad was a captain, and I was a tyro, a trainee, at the time."

Rachel looked down at her feet, suddenly sure she knew where the story was going.

"It wasn't so unusual, the general dining in with an old friend and a loyal Legion family. But what I didn't know was that my dad had been privately investigating Kublich—the general, I mean—for months. My mom and I didn't know what he was up to, only that he was spending a lot of time away from home for what he insisted was work stuff."

Haldin laced his fingers over the truck hood and shook his head. "Johnny tried to tell me my dad was having an affair, for the love of Alpha."

"But your dad knew?" Rachel asked. "About the raknoth, I mean."

He shook his head. "He knew the general had been behaving erratically and was possibly involved in some shady activity. I don't think my dad had any idea just how right he was until that night."

Haldin straightened and speared Rachel with a painfully somber gaze. "He killed my parents. Ripped them apart with his bare hands in our living room that night, right in front of me."

"Jesus," Rachel whispered. Then, feeling she had to fill the empty silence, "How'd you, uh…"

"Escape? Survive?"

She nodded dumbly.

"A man named Carlisle burst in and saved my life. He'd been investigating the general for months. Lucky he chose that night to sneak on base and have a closer look. He was a Shaper, or, you know"—he waved a hand—"like us. Gifted. Incredibly gifted. I had no idea I was too at the time, but…" He cocked his head. "Well, there's nothing like losing your family and being blamed and hunted by an entire world order to kick your ass into gear, I guess."

The rest of the tension bled out of Rachel's shoulders and back. "I'm sorry, Hal."

It wasn't enough, but she wasn't sure what else to say. "I… Well, you know my story. You know I mean it when I say I can sympathize."

He nodded. "I know you do. Which is why I'm telling you."

And just like that, tension began to creep back in.

Here it was—the part where he pointed out that he managed to put his own shit in order, let go of the hate, and do the right thing for the good of everyone, and shame on her for not doing the same.

But this was different, she wanted to insist. This was her family. Her family that'd been destroyed on the whim of Alton's clan leader. Her mom who'd died afraid and alone to save her, in part because Alton had gone along with it all.

Her mom who'd also tried to wipe the raknoth off the face of the Earth, a small, irritating voice pointed out. Because she couldn't just forget that part, could she?

As terrible as it was, as unforgivable, she couldn't completely delude herself into denying that the raknoth coming after her mom had been, in some way, a matter of self-defense—or self-preservation, at least.

If Haldin's parents had been killed just for his dad poking around too much, could she really say she had any more right to be pissed at the raknoth than he did?

Probably not. And yet here he stood, defending one of them.

What did that say about her? Or him?

He was watching her patiently, awaiting some conclusion.

"I don't know what you want me to say."

He shook his head, looking his true younger age for once. "I really don't know either. I just know that your world is in serious trouble, and that if we don't stop them here, mine probably will be too."

"But..." She looked toward the window Elise had disappeared from, wondering if Alton could hear them right now.

"How do you do it?" she silently sent, careful to make sure it only made it to Haldin and no one else. *"How can you look at Alton or any other raknoth and not see your parents dying in front of your eyes again?"*

Haldin made something like a flinch and closed his eyes. *"I still do, sometimes. And then I remind myself how many more children will lose everything if we're not strong enough to stop it. I..."*

"I didn't want to work with Alton when he gave himself up back on Enochia," Haldin said out loud, apparently feeling no need to hide the information from prying ears. "He was a part of some truly horrific atrocities on my planet. Enslaving humans to be used as comatose blood bags, or worse."

"Worse?"

"They were building an army of human-raknoth hybrids."

Half-formed images of what such creatures might look like passed through her mind, each one more horrifying than the last. And what had become of the human half of the equation?

"Jesus," she muttered.

"It wasn't pretty," Haldin agreed. "For a long time, I thought Alton and his clan were just trying to take over the planet and rebirth a race that had been all but demolished on another planet—a planet called Earth that somehow, impossibly, was halfway across the galaxy and yet home to humans just like us. That was hard enough to wrap my head around to start with. When Carlisle and I finally succeeded in exposing the raknoth to the rest of Enochia, though, Alton came out of hiding and turned himself over to explain what they'd really been trying to build an army for."

"To take on the rakul," Rachel said.

"I didn't believe him, of course. Not at first. Even after he showed me"—Haldin touched the side of his head in reference to the memories of the rakul Alton had shown him and he in turn had shown her

—"I still had more than a little doubt. It was all too convenient. And, while it by no means justified what he and his clan did to thousands of innocent Enochians, it painted their actions in a new light—one that was desperate and hopeless rather than pure, baseless evil." He shook his head. "I didn't want to believe it."

She knew a thing or two about how that one felt. "But here we are?"

He nodded. "But here we are. And, barring some miraculous intervention by Alpha, God, or any other deity we happened to miss on our way across the galaxy, we've got twelve seriously powerful assholes to deal with, and no one but each other to count on. I, uh…" He scratched his head, looking away. "I didn't mean to go all spirit of vengeance on your ass just then."

When he lowered his hand, he was wearing a guilty grin. "I promised Elise I'd keep it together. We just need to know we can trust the people at our backs if we're going to throw down for this planet. And, all things considered, I really hope we can."

Rachel swallowed a big gulp of dry nothing, warm shame creeping up her neck and onto her face.

He was right, dammit.

"I'll do my best," was all she could manage to say.

He nodded as if he understood and hadn't truly expected anything else and started to turn for Pryce's shop. "Right, then. Let's go build some cloaks."

CHAPTER FIFTEEN

The second time Jarek woke in his sad little medical bed, it wasn't to Rachel's caring gaze, but to cold darkness. And he wasn't alone. He wasn't sure how he knew it, as his sleep-logged conscious mind struggled to catch up to whatever its sleeping counterpart had detected, but something was wrong.

He took a deep breath, closed his eyes, and listened.

Hushed voices, barely perceptible from out in the hallway. Two men arguing.

Over what?

Jarek opened his eyes and forced himself to let the tension out of his aching muscles and fiery shoulder.

It was almost certainly nothing to do with him. The low disgruntled voices had probably just set off some overly sensitive danger alarm of his sleeping brain. That was it.

Except that didn't explain why one of the said disgruntled hallway goers pulled open the door to medical one room over and uttered a hissed, "Shut up!" at his friend.

Jarek swallowed and looked around the area by his dim bedside light for options, coldly dismissing the quickening of his heart and the nervous energy that came with it.

It was probably nothing. He sure as hell hoped it was nothing, because if it was anything else, he was screwed. There was nothing to work with, no impromptu weapon to be found, and even if there had been, his shoulder wasn't in any condition to allow him to fight.

It was probably nothing.

But as the first dark silhouette appeared in the doorway, some deep-seated instinct told him that "nothing" was coming, and it was coming to hurt him. Maybe it was the way the figure paused and gestured back to whoever was behind him. Maybe it was just the vaguely familiar stout bulldog outline.

Well, no reason to lay quiet and wait.

Jarek put on his best *top of the morning to you* tone. "Mr. Rodgers, as I live and breathe. What brings you here in the creepy-ass dead of night?"

The silhouette had gone rigid at the sound of his voice, but it quickly recovered and prowled toward him. Another figure slipped into the room behind him, and then a third as the leading shadow drew close enough to the dim light for Jarek to see he'd called the leader's identity correctly.

"We've got something to say to you, Slater," Rodgers the angry bulldog said.

Crap.

He knew that tone—the tone that clearly designated their "something" probably involved a pillowcase and a bar of soap, or, if he was lucky, maybe just good ol' fashioned fists.

For whatever reason—and there were admittedly plenty to pick from—they had serious beef with him. They had him cornered, trapped, defenseless. He wasn't going anywhere, and they knew it. But that didn't mean he had to give them the satisfaction of admitting his insides were turning to cold gravy.

Instead, he tilted his head toward the bedside table that was empty but for a cup of water and the earpiece he'd slipped out for the night. "You can add your get well soons to the pile. Otherwise, maybe you should come back in the morning. Pretty sure we're outside of visiting hours, and there aren't enough hours left in the world for the beauty sleep I'm needing."

Rodgers was close enough in the dim light now for Jarek to make out his cold grin. "You never stop do you?"

Night Raider Number Two drew up beside him, and Jarek recognized the guy who'd damn near zapped him with a stun gun the previous morning.

"Of course he doesn't," Stun Gun said. "He's the fucking Soldier of Charity, didn't you hear?"

The third guy—tall, thin and leery—Jarek didn't recognize as he stepped up on Rodgers' other side, but that hardly mattered now. He didn't seem interested in adding to the interaction—not in any way that involved words and not fists, at least.

"I might be way off base, guys," Jarek said, "but I feel like I'm picking up on a little bit of hostility. Anyone care to let me in on what gives?"

"What gives," Rodgers said, sliding Jarek's bedside table aside and stepping into unmistakable intimidation territory (and, coincidentally, within handy cock-punching distance of Jarek's good hand if things went that way), "is that we've had enough of your bullshit."

Jarek suppressed the desire to coil defensively up to the head of the bed as Stun Gun crossed around to his injured side and Leery moved to the foot of the bed.

"Yeah…" Jarek said, fighting the urge to try to watch them all at once and instead focusing solely on Rodgers. "I get a lot of that. You might need to be more specific. Was that the bullshit where I pulled a dozen Resistance fighters out of the shit at the port? Or maybe the part where I faced the strongest raknoth on the planet in single combat so none of you ninnies would have to worry your pretty little—"

The world exploded in a bright dance of swirling stars and pain. As quickly as it blazed into existence, the flare receded to a local throb that informed him Stun Gun had just given him a cold clock on the side of the head.

"Yeah," came Rodgers' voice through Jarek's hazy surroundings, "you're a real hero of the people."

"A hero who lords it over the rest of us mere mortals," Stun Gun said.

"A hero who abandons his post and does whatever the hell he wants without the slightest thought of how it might affect the rest of us," Rodgers said.

Stun Gun leaned in closer and planted a thumb over Jarek's shoulder bandages. "A hero who wouldn't be worth the dirt on our boots without his big fancy exo."

He could take them, a small voice whispered in the back of Jarek's mind. Even with one arm out of commission. A sucker punch to Stun Gun's nose straight into an elbow to Rodgers' waiting groin. A chest kick for Leery, and then to his feet, where he could administer follow-up kicks and knees as required to shut these indignant ass-wipes up for good.

His injured arm might just fall off along the way, but he could do it. He'd won worse fights before, hadn't he?

Maybe so. But what was the point?

He'd fucked up. He already knew that. Fighting these guys wasn't going to fix anything. Beating them, assuming he even could, wouldn't make them wrong.

"Fine." He plopped his head to the pillow and stared at Rogers, feeling more tired than he could remember having ever felt. "You're right. Is that what you wanna hear? You're right about everything. So take your fucking shot. Or don't. Just get on with it."

Judging from the look on Rogers' face, he'd been hoping for a bit more spunk, or fear, or whatever else from Jarek. Whatever disappointment he felt, though, was quickly replaced with cool smugness as he traded a look with his co-conspirators and regained his wobbly confidence.

Rogers grabbed Jarek's throat and cocked a fist to strike. "You asked for it, hero."

Jarek watched with an odd mixture of dread, selective apathy, and, as he thought of the ashes of Katashina, maybe just a sprinkle of sick, twisted eagerness.

"The next time you boys decide to pull some harebrained payback bullshit," came a voice from the doorway, "you might wanna at least check the corners before you go on attacking your own men."

Alaric. Thank the cowboy gods. But what did he mean, check the corn—

A low growl rumbled in the darkness off to the right. Rodgers' grip on Jarek tightened for a second. Then a pair of scarlet fiery orbs appeared in the darkness, and Rodgers released him and staggered back with a strangled yelp.

Alaric flipped the switch by the door, and bright light flooded the room, revealing Drogan in a seat against the far wall, watching them with a flat expression under his glowing eyes.

"I'd like to speak to Slater alone if you boys'll leave us to it." Alaric stepped aside to clear the doorway for them, looking utterly unperturbed by the scene he'd walked in on.

Jarek's would-be attackers looked as one from Alaric to Drogan to Jarek and, finally, to one another. Then, by some unspoken agreement, they all scampered for the doorway.

One of them—Stun Gun, Jarek thought—didn't resist the urge to audibly mutter, "Fucking raknoth-lovers."

And then they were gone, and Alaric shifted his calm gaze to Drogan. "You too."

Drogan looked for a few seconds as if he might implore Alaric to make him move, but then he stood, the red fire draining from his eyes, and, with a shrug, strode out of the room.

"Might not wanna go far," Alaric added over his shoulder.

Jarek refrained from pointing out that keeping the raknoth anywhere nearby kind of ruined the point of asking him to leave in the first place anyway. It wasn't like Drogan couldn't hear them from a room or two over.

Somehow, the detail didn't seem so important as Alaric finally turned to Jarek and skewered him with a stern glare.

"And what brings *you* here at this creepy hour?" Jarek asked, fighting the urge to squirm.

"I had business nearby. And you're welcome by the way."

"Yeah…" Jarek touched lightly at the aching right side of his face and winced at the fresh pulse of pain. "I never was the most popular kid in class."

Alaric broke eye contact to fish into his coat pocket, no doubt going for a wad of his favorite chew. "I can't imagine why."

Jarek quietly watched Alaric go about his masticatory ritual. "I suppose you're pretty pissed with me right now too," he finally said.

"Well, what the hell else would you expect?" Alaric jammed a pinch of green leaves into his mouth. "What were you thinking, shirking a direct order? What did you expect me to do about that?"

Jarek shook his head. "I don't know." He nodded toward the doorway where his personal protesters had fled. "They're not wrong. I'd be lying if I said I took the time to even think about it."

He waited for Alaric to attack, to hop onto the back of his admission and dig in, but the commander only stood there, steadily chewing, watching Jarek as if he were waiting for him to continue.

Jarek dropped Alaric's stare and fixed his gaze on the uninteresting blanket covering his lower body. "I made the wrong call."

Silence.

"I made the wrong call, and people died."

Silence.

Finally, he looked back up at Alaric. "I fucked up, okay? You think I don't know that? Come on, let me have it. Tell me I'm an arrogant prick, that I don't deserve the suit."

Alaric only chewed on in maddening silence.

"Tell me, goddammit!"

He hadn't meant to yell—hadn't meant to say anything at all. It was exactly what Alaric wanted, he knew.

Jarek didn't play on this side of head games—didn't bend and break under the weight of the shit he'd accepted a long time ago might happen as he fought for survival. He sure as hell didn't lose control and wallow in self-doubt.

And yet here he was.

He looked away from Alaric, refusing to go on.

Alaric let out a heavy sigh. "Dammit. I'd be tempted to knock some sense into you myself if you didn't look so damned pathetic right now."

"Yeah… Well, join the club."

"Screw Rodgers and his buddies." Alaric shook his head. "You're too damn far up your own ass to even understand why I'm angry, aren't you?"

"Uh, maybe?"

Jarek was genuinely unsure at this point.

Alaric closed the gap to Jarek's bedside in four sweeping steps, looking like he may or may not pistol whip Jarek at the end of the line.

"It's not obedient yes men we need here, son. If we're gonna take on a whole group of things that can do this"—he pointed to Jarek's shoulder—"we need leaders. Strong ones. Ones who can inspire by example, who look before they leap and actually give half a rat's ass about the men and women fighting beside them." He jabbed a hard finger into Jarek's chest. "Leaders who don't pull the shit you just pulled. Do you understand me?"

On any other day, coming from any other person, those probably would have been nut-punching words. Now though, coming from Alaric, and with all the unsavory weight of his recent failures sitting at the back of his throat, Jarek felt like he was the one on the receiving end of said punch.

So he gave Alaric a nod and kept his mouth shut.

"Well hallelujah, then." Alaric shook his head and sighed.

Jarek waited a few seconds to be sure he was done. Then, "That business you mentioned a minute ago… Seth?"

Alaric's jaw tightened, and he glanced at the door before speaking. "We'll discuss your punishment after you've recovered enough to be useful."

"Guess that means the penalty's not death, huh?"

"Not this time."

He knew Alaric was joking—or mostly joking, at least—but that didn't keep his insides, or specific parts of his outsides, from shriveling a bit at the commander's stern glare.

Apparently satisfied he'd met his glare wattage quota for the night, Alaric turned to leave.

He paused at the doorway and spoke without looking back. "It was a good call, speaking to Seth about bridging the gap between our camp and Krogoth's." Slowly, he looked over his shoulder to meet Jarek's eyes. "Unlike some people in this room, I'm not above occasionally listening to reason."

And with that, he was gone, leaving Jarek alone with nothing but a heaping pile of guilt and a large side of shame.

Drogan stalked back into the room less than a minute after Alaric left, which suggested that he hadn't gone far at all and, consequently, that he'd probably heard Jarek's chastising loud and clear. If he had though, he hid the smug smile Jarek expected quite well.

"Sleep," Drogan said, switching off the main lights and disappearing back into his dark corner. A scrape and the faint groan of metal accommodating a heavy load told Jarek Drogan had settled back in his chair. "I will see to it your recovery is not interfered with."

Jarek showed the dark ceiling a bitter smile. "Don't tell me you're worried about me, Stumpy?"

"You may yet prove useful in this fight," came Drogan's reply from the darkness.

"Aw shucks, buddy." Jarek brushed the throbbing right side of his head. "But, much as I appreciate the sappy sentiment, I can't help pointing out you could have acted a bit sooner back there."

When Drogan spoke, Jarek had the impression the raknoth was smiling. "You appeared to have the situation reasonably under control."

"Oh yeah. Clearly." Jarek frowned at the darkness. "And not that I don't also appreciate the shitty bodyguard act and everything, but what are you doing hanging here instead of Camp Krogoth?"

Hesitant silence. Then, "The Zar is... less than pleased with my recent actions."

"Oh yeah? You're telling me your boss isn't a fan of his guys going rogue either?"

"Indeed."

Jarek considered that. "Huh. You never really struck me as the *cower from the angry master* type."

A faint growl rumbled from the darkness. "I thought it best not to provoke him with my continued presence. This is hardly the time to allow pride to disrupt our ranks."

"Sure, sure."

Jarek couldn't really argue with that. Hell, he could probably even stand to learn a lesson or two from Drogan. The guy did have at least a few thousand years of experience on him, after all.

Silence stretched between them. Maybe it was the residual nerves from his near brush with a prison-style beat down, or maybe it was just the discontent Alaric's words had left roiling in his stomach, but Jarek felt compelled to fill it.

"Well look at us, Stumps. Just two pals on the outs with our own—"

"Will you silence your tongue and do something productive?" Drogan snapped. "Sleep. Heal. The sooner you can fight, the sooner you can help me destroy Kul'Gada and the others."

"Definitely. That's a plan. Just facing down the galaxy-conquering monsters, you know. Two pals, side-by-si—"

Drogan growled, louder than before.

"Fine," Jarek said. "Have it your way, grumpy. Grumpy Stumpy."

The growl grew until Jarek could feel it in his own chest.

"All right, all right."

Jarek shifted around until he found a semi-comfortable—or at least less *uncomfortable*—position, then he closed his eyes and settled in to wait with his heavy thoughts for the sleep that probably wouldn't come.

CHAPTER SIXTEEN

Being cooped up at Pryce's with the Enochians, Rachel decided, wasn't so bad once she'd made it through the initial *sorry I sort of tried to murder you* awkwardness with Alton. To his credit, or maybe just further against hers, Alton made it about as easy as it could've been. Whether it was his own guilty conscience telling him he'd kind of deserved it all along or he was just a better actor than she'd feared, he seemed to approach the entire affair with a calm attitude of *hey, shit happens... but it'd better not happen again.*

Which was fair enough, she supposed.

Forgiveness was one thing, and possibly an unobtainable thing at that, but agreeing to at least not pull something like that again...

After everything that had happened, she could do that much.

That said, she'd done her best to avoid Alton since, and he'd made a point to accommodate her efforts. And now, after a long day of enchanting and a few hours of deep, dreamless sleep, Rachel didn't lament stepping out of Pryce's to stretch her legs—even if it was alongside Alton and the Enochians.

For reasons unknown, Krogoth had apparently had some change of heart through the night and agreed to finally have a proper conference with the Resistance commanders. Soon, the council would be meeting with him and whichever other raknoth clan leaders were willing to play ball at this point to discuss next moves now that Gada was irrefutably here and coming for them.

Rachel wasn't so sure Krogoth agreeing to talk really changed anything about the fundamental relationship between his forces and the Resistance—or that she felt any differently about the entire alliance herself, even after the business with Alton. But, at the very least, it probably wasn't a negative development where their mutual survival was concerned.

Stupid as it might've been, though, Rachel was a bit more preoccupied with the thought of facing Jarek at the moment.

She hadn't responded to his message yesterday, nor had he tried to reach her again. Left to her own devices, she might have tried to put off seeing him on this particular visit to HQ, but when Haldin had asked if she minded him tagging along to see their wounded wise-ass…

Well, if she could face Alton, she could face Jarek.

When they stepped into medical, Rachel was ready for the sight of ghastly wounds and Drogan's saliva cup and syringe. Or so she thought.

Ready or not, the sight of Jarek indelicately jamming a syringe tip between his staples and squirting raknoth spit into the wound he'd made a gruesome mess of turned Rachel's stomach over.

"Demons' depths," Haldin said as they entered. "What are you doing?"

Jarek turned, his face tight with pain as he finished the last of what looked to have been at least three or four injections, judging from the state of the messy wound.

His eyes took in Rachel and sent an anxious ripple through her chest before settling on Haldin.

"I'll tell you what I'm not doing. I'm definitely not blatantly disregarding the opinion of a licensed medical professional." He grimaced and extracted the syringe tip. "And I'm sure as hell not pumping myself full of raknoth spit in hopes of gaining superhero-like healing powers. That would be crazy."

Behind Jarek, Drogan gave an innocent shrug.

"No, I understand what you're doing," Haldin said, "but… Sweet Alpha, man, you couldn't at least find a needle or something?"

Jarek tried to shrug but winced instead. "Agh! Dammit! I think aforementioned medical professional hid said needles after we asked for her help, uh, shooting up the vitamin R, if you will. I'd go so far as to say she didn't trust us to behave responsibly."

Haldin smiled. "Guess you showed her."

"Totally." Jarek threw the syringe in the waste bin by his bed and extended his good hand toward Drogan in a closed fist. "Put it there, Stumpy."

The raknoth crushed the paper cup in his hand and frowned down at Jarek's fist. Then, hesitantly, Drogan extended his fist to meet Jarek's.

It was almost sweet, in a bizarre kind of way. Minus the part where the gesture only solidified Rachel's conviction that Jarek was not going to be happy about what she'd done to Alton—or already wasn't, if Drogan had filled him in.

She wasn't in any hurry to broach that topic, though, so she didn't complain when Haldin asked Jarek how he was feeling and proceeded to fill him in on the fight and his assessment of how Gada had handled himself.

Jarek's gaze drifted her way several times throughout, but he kept whatever questions he wanted to ask to himself for the time being.

They were turning to the topic of how they might go about handling Gada the next time around when something brushed softly at the edge of Rachel's mind, faint and unobtrusive, but most certainly there.

It was the feeling she'd come to associate with the messengers, and it made her go tight inside and out. The dread only deepened when she noticed Drogan and Haldin looked to have felt something too.

Not now. Not another furor.

Haldin held up a finger to Jarek, who dropped silent and took the three of them in without batting an eye. He could probably tell something was off with all of them.

Haldin closed his eyes and switched the glyph on his cloaking pendant to the off position.

Rachel pulled her mental defenses tight and followed his example.

The soft buzzing presence at the edge of her mind immediately resolved into a voice like a dozen loosely synchronized whispers.

"*—who still serve your true Masters. Join us in ending this mockery of our established order and we will grant you forgiveness. We will cure you of the ailment that chains you to this feeble race, and you will be free to return to your proper place as emissaries of the Kul. This I offer only once. Join us, or prepare to meet the eternal void.*"

With that, the presence vanished.

Gada. That had been Gada's voice. She was sure of it.

Drogan's eyes were glowing faint crimson now. Rachel reached for her energy stores just in case and watched for any other reaction.

Was he thinking about it? Turning on them? Fleeing back to his masters for forgiveness?

And what about the rest of the raknoth who'd heard?

Drogan's eyes dimmed as they turned to her and Haldin. "Lies. The rakul do not forgive. They would not hold the power they currently do otherwise."

Rachel let out the breath she hadn't realized she'd been holding. "How many of your buddies will come to that conclusion?"

Drogan frowned at her as he thought about that. "I cannot say. Fear rarely makes for intelligent decisions."

She tensed and had to bite down on a retort.

What were the chances that wasn't a shot at her recent failure?

"Okay, gang," Jarek said, breaking the tension whether he knew it or not. "I think this is the part where you fill in the guy who isn't sporting a telepathy dish on his noggin."

"Kul'Gada calls for those raknoth still loyal to the rakul to join him in destroying us," Drogan said.

"Ah." Jarek scratched at his head with his good hand. "Well shit."

"Probably doesn't bode well for the state of our current alliances," Haldin agreed.

"What," Jarek said, "you mean you don't think the fine people out there will trust our raknoth buddies once they realize their old boss just offered them their jobs back?"

"Well," Haldin said with a sideways glance at Rachel she appreciated like a slap in the face, "as much as a hug fest as it's been so far…"

Rachel could have kicked the Enochian square in the pants for the way Jarek's dark, piercing eyes assessed them after that.

If he hadn't been sure before that something had happened, he probably was now.

"We need to get ahead of this before word spreads," Haldin said. He looked at Drogan. "We also need to figure out which raknoth are going to flip on us. Because I doubt they're all just gonna tell the Masters to suck it."

Drogan nodded. "I concur. We will extract oaths of true fealty from those with us. We will root out those who think to betray us to our doom"—he pounded fist and open palm together—"and *they* will be the ones who will suck it!"

Jarek barked a laugh at that, and, despite everything else, Rachel almost joined him. Determined to maintain her somber composure, though, she managed to retain her laughter to a brief silent shake.

Drogan glanced between them uncertainly.

"Excellent," Haldin said, only partially succeeding in masking his own amusement. "We're lucky to have you with us, Al'Drogan. Now I better go find Alton and speak to the commanders before someone catches scent of this thing." He met Rachel's gaze, and the desire to give him a groin shot only grew. "I'll see you in the council chamber soon?"

She gave Haldin a stiff nod, and he bade his farewells and headed back to meet his crew in the commons.

The Enochian was right to take this new threat to their marginal internal peace seriously, but he was probably worrying preemptively. The only people who would've been able to hear the message would probably be the last people to spill the beans. Her, Haldin, Elise, the raknoth.

And Michael.

Her heart quickened.

Michael. Shit. She'd been too wrapped up in her own little silent drama here to realize he'd probably felt the broadcast too. And, if past experiences were any indication, it was entirely possible he hadn't done so quietly.

"I have to go."

The realization fell out of her mouth on its own, a distant mumble next to the racing kaleidoscope her mind was playing out of all the ways this might imminently explode in their faces.

Jarek raised his good hand in a gesture of peace. "Easy, Goldilocks. No one's about to—"

"It's Michael," she said. "If he heard…"

Understanding sparked in Jarek's eyes.

"I need to check on him," she said.

"Go," Drogan said.

She held Jarek's conflicted gaze until he gave a small nod.

"We'll talk later," she said, backing toward the doorway.

Then she turned and hurried out of medical before he could say anything more.

Well, there was one bullet dodged. For the moment, at least. The next one, though…

Haldin was just about to turn the corner at the end of the hallway as Rachel stepped out of medical. He paused when he caught sight of her. She was about to send her worries about Michael his way, but he stiffened, apparently coming to some similar conclusion, and darted off toward the commons.

That didn't exactly soothe the unease in her gut as she turned the other way and hurried through the bland hallways for Michael's quarters.

By the time she reached her destination, she'd broken into a run.

She rushed through the open doorway—which in itself didn't seem like a great sign—and was met with wide-eyed stares from Michael and Lea.

"Rache," Michael said. "What is it? What's wrong?"

He didn't look too bad—no worse than usual for these days, at least.

Had he even felt the messengers?

Lea had risen to her feet, like she was expecting a horde of maddened berserkers to pour in on Rachel's tail.

"It's, uh…" Rachel looked between the two of them, taking in their expressions more carefully before focusing on Michael. "Did you happen to, uh—"

"I felt it." He frowned. "Heard it. Whatever. I was just telling Lea. I take it you heard him too?"

Rachel eyed the open doorway uneasily and pushed the door closed before saying anything.

"Yeah. And I might have thought to close the door before telling anyone about it. If anyone heard you…"

Rachel's comm buzzed against her wrist before she decided just how to finish the thought.

"No one heard," Lea said, though the look on her face didn't convey nearly as much confidence.

Rachel glanced down at her comm. The message was from Haldin, and it consisted of one word.

Trouble.

"You're sure about that?" Rachel asked, raising her comm for them to see.

Michael and Lea exchanged a horrified look, both of them lost for words.

"Just sit tight," Rachel said, turning for the door. "I'll make sure no one starts killing each other out there."

They watched her like scolded children as she pulled the door closed behind her and set off down the hallway again, this time starting at a full run.

After a minute of dodging and weaving past indignant Resistance soldiers, she turned into one of the hallways that led to the commons and spotted Alton, Johnny, Elise, and Haldin ahead, surrounded by at least a couple dozen Resistance soldiers who looked less than pleased.

It wasn't hard to guess why.

"Whoa, whoa, whoa," Johnny was saying as Rachel padded quietly toward the spectacle. "Easy, lady. I don't know where you're getting your infor—"

"I heard Carver say it down the hall not five minutes ago," a stout woman with short, dark hair said. "That harvester thing is throwing arms wide open for any vamp willing to fall in line and hand us over. We already know we can't trust the bastards."

"Ah," Johnny held up a finger. "See, that sounds like an unsubstantiated claim to me. I don't know how you guys do things here, but—"

"You're goddamn right you don't know, you alien freak," cried a kid that couldn't have been older than seventeen or eighteen.

Johnny pointed toward the voice, still holding the black-haired woman's gaze. "That's hurtful. Look, I get that you don't trust the scary bloodsucking monsters. It's a wise move. Good on you."

"Who the hell do you think you—" someone started, but they fell silent at a sudden flicker of fire in Johnny's expression.

"The fact here is that we are up against some serious shit, people," Johnny said. "We don't have the luxury of turning our backs on allies for anything less than irrefutably damning evidence. And, you know what? If you're not okay with that, let me ask you this: which one of you is going to wrestle down Alton here and throw him in chains?" He glanced at Alton, then back at the crowd. "Have any of you ever tangled with a raknoth? I'm guessing not, since you're all still standing here."

Alton and Haldin both looked like they wanted to add more, or maybe even rein Johnny in, but Haldin continued to stand quietly at his friend's side, and Alton, probably wisely, hung in the back, looking as harmless as he could manage.

Rachel hovered at the back of the growing, buzzing crowd, unsure how to proceed.

Johnny raised a valid point about Alton, but he couldn't have picked a worse audience. The soldiers who deemed themselves Earth's premier guardians against the "vamps" were the last people who'd want to hear that these "alien freaks" thought their bark was lacking its bite.

Regardless, she wasn't sure anything she could say would carry much weight with this crowd.

"We've had enough of this bullshit, space-boy," rumbled a tree of a man pushing his way through the crowd. He made it to the front row and jabbed a finger down at Haldin's face. "I don't trust a single goddamn one of you. You could all be vamps in disguise, for all we know."

This point raised a hearty chorus of agreement and further accusations.

Haldin calmly looked over through the noise and caught Rachel's eye.

"A little help?" came his voice in her head.

She took half a step forward and opened her mouth, searching for the words.

What could she possibly say?

Heads were starting to swivel her way now, curious as to what Haldin was staring at while that hulking mass of man loomed so threateningly over him.

She had to say something.

"There's only one raknoth in this room right now," she finally called. "And I'd probably be dead right now if it weren't for him and these three."

"Yeah?" the human tree called right back, only looking away from Haldin for a moment. "And we're just supposed to take your word on that? The word of a telepath who comes and goes as she damn well pleases? You're an outsider, lady. If you're not with us, you can fuck off, for all I care."

Another round of agreement rippled through the crowd, though it might've been slightly milder than the last one. Either way, it emboldened the big guy to get even more up in Haldin's face.

Haldin's calm composure was starting to show cracks now. "She is —We're all…"

He closed his eyes, his face tight, and Rachel half-expected the human tree to take sudden telekinetic flight.

"Fine," Haldin growled instead, eyes snapping open. "Fine. You call us raknoth?"

Rachel felt the thermal energy drain from the air around Haldin.

Then the air between him and the human tree flared to life with a brilliant wall of fire.

Cries and shouts exploded through the crowd, those closest scrambling backward.

The big guy who'd been in Haldin's face fell over in his haste to back up, tiny wisps of smoke curling up from his singed beard and eyebrows.

"What the fuck?!" he thundered as he hit the floor and pulled himself back another few feet.

The wall of flames died out almost as quickly as Haldin had conjured it. The Enochian stood calmly watching the human tree now, a small fireball still hovering over his raised palm.

Tense silence filled the room, everyone waiting to see what the mad arcanist would do next.

Finally, Haldin allowed his handful of flames to die out. "Raknoth can't do that, last I checked."

He pointed at the kid who'd called Johnny an alien freak, and half the crowd flinched.

"You. You're right. We're not from here. We left our planet—our perfectly good, safe home—because we thought your world might be in trouble. And it is."

More people were packing into the common room now, drawn by the commotion. The crowd watched silently, waiting.

"Here's the truth," Haldin continued. "Johnny's right too. Alton could tear you all to pieces right now if he wanted to. So could I. That's not a comfortable thought to live with, I get it. But here's the more important truth." He waved a hand from himself to Alton, Johnny, and Elise. "We're gonna keep putting our lives on the line to protect the innocent people on this planet. I don't really give a damn who likes who. We're gonna fight the rakul because it's the right thing to do. If anyone wants to stop us from doing that, well... I have to wonder what it is we're even fighting for if that's how little you care for your own world."

Johnny clapped him on the back, and Elise stepped confidently to his side, her expression daring anyone to argue.

"And what if your precious raknoth sell us down the creek to these masters of theirs?" someone called.

"Then I'll be standing on your side of the crowd when we find them," Haldin said. "But there are none of those raknoth here."

The crowd weighed his words in a sea of murmurs and whispers. A lot of them even looked half-convinced—or slightly uncertain, at least.

"Let's break this up, people," called a strong voice. Rachel craned her neck to see Commander Daniels pushing into the hallway that led to the council chambers. "The small council is meeting now to get to the bottom of this. Mr. Raish, Mr. Parker, we'd like a word. Immediately."

Haldin nodded, his Zen mask firmly back in place. "Of course, Commander Daniels."

The crowd parted to let them pass, some of them—particularly the human tree—clearly hesitant to do so.

"Excuse me," Johnny said as he shimmied through the crowd after Haldin, Alton, and Elise. "Pardon me. Just trying to save the world. Pardon the inconvenience."

As unproductive as poking an already edgy hive was, Rachel couldn't find it in herself to blame Johnny too much.

She wasn't about to fall to the ground licking the Enochians' boots or anything—and they weren't expecting it, either—but they had literally flown halfway across the galaxy to risk their necks for these people. Raknoth sidekick or not, the least these soldiers could do was back off and leave the Enochians alone while they continued to bleed for the Resistance and the people of Earth.

Of course, if she felt so strongly, she certainly could have said so when it had mattered.

The look Haldin shot her from across the room suggested he was having similar thoughts.

"Coming?" he sent.

She swallowed, gave him a nod, and started winding her own way through the slowly dispersing crowd, wondering whose side she was even on anymore and, more importantly, just how much shit the Enochians would be willing to take before they decided to say screw it and just fly home.

One way or another, she had a bad feeling they'd be getting the final answers to those questions sooner than any of them wanted.

CHAPTER SEVENTEEN

After the confrontation in the common room, Rachel wasn't overly surprised when Haldin bristled at Commander Daniels asking Johnny and Elise to wait outside the council chamber.

"With everything going on right now," Daniels said quietly to their small huddle, "it seems wise to do our best to discourage the idea that we're favoring the Enochians over our own people."

Sensible enough, even if it still was kind of a slap to the pants for Johnny and Elise. But the two didn't argue—just opted to go visit Jarek instead.

Rachel took one last survey of the wary looks still tracking them from the commons then followed Haldin, Alton, and Daniels into the council chamber.

When the doors were closed, and the sounds of the base beyond had fallen to a low din, Daniels looked at Haldin with more warmth than she'd shown outside. "Not half bad out there, Mr. Raish. Your conclusion could have used some work, maybe, but I think one or two of them may have even heard you out there."

Alton looked utterly unimpressed by her words.

Haldin just looked angry. "The people I love could die tomorrow fighting for those ungrateful bastards," he said, his voice a quiet snarl that made Rachel want to take a step back. "I wonder every day if I'm a terrible person for having brought them here."

What little amusement had crept into Daniels' expression bled out immediately, but it wasn't replaced by anger as Rachel expected. Instead, she only looked tired, sad, and not a little bit sympathetic.

"I'm sorry, Haldin. I hadn't thought—"

"Forget it," Haldin said. "Let's just talk about the message and get ready for this conference."

Daniels nodded, slipping her Resistance commander expression back on.

Alaric and Nelken were waiting for them at the front of the room, Nelken leaning heavily against the head table to rest his braced leg, both looking marginally curious about the heated words but neither seeing fit to ask. A few of the council regulars were seated in the front as well, but other than that, the room was empty.

Daniels joined the other commanders at the head table. "So," she said, looking at Rachel and the other telepaths as if they were particularly complicated pieces of foreign technology, "you were all able to hear the, um, broadcast yourselves?"

Rachel nodded, as did Haldin, but it was Alton who the three commanders were most closely watching.

So apparently they had some idea what Gada had offered the raknoth.

"And what do you think, Mr. Parker?" Nelken asked.

Alton showed them a disconcerting grin. "Does it matter? Are you simply going to trust me when I say that the Kul is lying?"

Alaric tilted his head in concession.

"We see your point," Daniels said, rubbing at her temples. "This is a tough one, even internally. Working with Krogoth's forces, on the other hand..."

"Your people are just going to have to find the trust to work with theirs," Haldin said. "We can screen each of our raknoth allies and determine their allegiance beyond the shadow of a doubt. Drogan promised to do as much, and I don't think Krogoth will oppose the idea. But that'll take time, and who knows when Gada will strike again, or when his brethren will arrive. Plus, that option still leaves you guys having to take our word for it. There's no winning here without a little faith."

Alaric chuffed, plopped into his chair, and rooted around in his pocket. "So, business as usual, then?" He withdrew a small container, stuffed a pinch of green leaves in his mouth, and started chewing.

Nelken frowned at him but said nothing as the double doors opened and a few more council members began trickling in and finding seats.

Alaric glanced at his comm. "Well, it's time."

Rachel traded a glance with Haldin, and they went to find seats, Alton following along behind them.

Nelken switched on the projector on the head table and stared expectantly at Alaric, who placed the call and patched it over to the projector. A flat holo sprang into existence over the table, complete with the rotating icon of a pending connection.

The commanders went to take seats in the front line of chairs as the call tone sounded over and over. Uncomfortable silence filled the room as they waited for over a full minute, the call tone chiming all the while.

Finally, though, the call was accepted on the other end and, after the couple seconds it took to connect, the holo resolved into an image of Zar'Krogoth sitting placidly behind a rich wooden desk in full raknoth form. His rust-red hide, as it always did, gave Rachel the impression that he'd just finished rolling around in the blood of his enemies.

Disturbing as Krogoth's appearance was, it was no more so than the sight of the man standing at obedient, somber attention at his left shoulder.

Seth Mosen.

What the hell was he doing there? Last she knew, Mosen had been locked up in the HQ brig.

"Zar'Krogoth," Nelken said. "Al'Brandt. Good afternoon."

It was only when Nelken said Brandt's name that Rachel processed the second raknoth at Krogoth's flank opposite Mosen. After their mountain temple had come under attack, Brandt hadn't argued about taking his clan to New York to join Camp Krogoth.

In reply to Nelken's greeting, Krogoth only worked at the air with slitted nostrils and looked bored for a long stretch.

"The others will be here soon," he finally said, managing to imbue each individual word with distaste.

An awkward minute of silence stretched. Another pair of council members slid into the chamber and promptly found seats. Krogoth picked at his fangs.

Finally, there was a light buzz on Krogoth's end. He reached for something on his desk, and the wide holo broke itself into two and then three discrete windows.

The first newcomer, Rachel took to be Al'Koshna based on the tropical background in the raknoth's holo. The second, Rachel couldn't mistake. Nan'Ashida, commander of a sizable human army and little shit extraordinaire.

Two more splits, and they were joined by another pair of raknoth Rachel recognized not at all by sight and only vaguely by name—Al'Tor and Al'Grog.

Alton had once told her that his people were not well-suited for what humans thought of as friendship. Watching the clan leaders working their way through uncomfortable greetings as they trickled in, Rachel saw what he meant. She'd picked up on as much in what interactions she'd had throughout their recruitment tour, but it really seemed like none of the raknoth were particularly fond of one another.

Maybe that was just what happened after a few thousand years of roaming the galaxy together.

Among the few clan speakers Rachel recognized as absent, Zar'-Taga was the most worrisome. He commanded the largest raknoth clan after Krogoth's, and while Rachel had thought their expedition to visit him in Ireland a week earlier had gone well enough—minus the skepticism that the rakul were even coming—his absence now suggested otherwise.

Of course, it was possible he was just late to the call. Still, Rachel couldn't help but wonder if maybe Gada's recent offer had caught Taga's fancy.

"Let us not tarry in discussing the matter at hand," Krogoth said once they'd waded through the awkward greetings.

As the only Zar present, Krogoth probably had the technical right to govern the meeting, but Rachel had a feeling he would have taken the leads either way.

"Kul'Gada has called us forth," Krogoth continued, "and some of you are likely considering the wisdom of suing for peace with the rakul. No doubt, the humans are wondering which of us they might trust to hold fast against the harvesters."

Rachel could've swore she saw a vein throb in Nelken's temple at Krogoth's casual assumptions, both of authority over the meeting and of the Resistance's motives and concerns, but the commander didn't say anything. Probably for the best.

Much as it irked her to admit it, at the end of the day, this was pretty much raknoth business, and most of their kind didn't exactly have an overabundance of respect for humans. Better to let their own Zar whip them into shape.

Assuming Krogoth still fell on the anti-rakul side of the line himself, of course.

"You do not consider this, brother?" Koshna asked. "I have no love for the Kul, but too many of us have seen what becomes of those who would oppose the Masters. Is it not possible this conflict might be resolved without fighting?"

Krogoth gave a growl of a chuckle and spat to the side. "The rakul have not lived for tens of millennia ruling with light hands. I have seen raknoth slain without question for crimes far milder than our own. Desertion, they will not forgive."

"It was not peace Kul'Gada sought when he laid siege to our temple scarcely more than one cycle past," Brandt added from his place at Krogoth's shoulder. "It was only after he met failure and defeat at the hands of our combined clans that the Kul thought to seek our allegiance. Kul'Gada is a coward, and we will not yield to him or his ilk."

Combined clans, huh? That was rich coming from the guy who'd waited until the fight was all but won to come out and play.

Whatever. At least he was arguing for killing that giant spiky bastard.

"Truly, brother?" Ashida asked. "You wish us to believe that you turned back the advance of one of the rakul?"

Rachel's growing agitation must've been palpable. Haldin rested a gentle hand on her shoulder and helped ground her before she lost the fight to refrain from spitting out that *they* had stopped Gada and that Ashida could shove a richly varnished chair leg up his ass if he doubted it.

"Believe what you will, young Nan," Brandt said. "I care not."

The disdain in his voice, at least, made Rachel feel a hair better.

"Al'Brandt speaks truth," Alton said. "I was there myself, along with Zar'Krogoth's second, Al'Drogan. With the help of our human allies" —he waved pointedly to Haldin and Rachel with the stub of the hand he'd lost to Gada—"we managed to drive Kul'Gada away."

Ashida sneered but said nothing.

Nelken pounced on the silence that ensued. "I take it, then, that we're all still on the same side in this conflict?"

Krogoth looked mildly irritated at Nelken's gall in speaking, but he gave a decisive nod. "I will stand against Kul'Gada, regardless of what any here have to say. And when the rest of the harvesters come, I will stand against them too. To do otherwise is to invite certain death upon myself and my people."

"My clan will follow Zar'Krogoth in this," Brandt said.

Al'Koshna was nodding slowly. "I am proud to count myself kin to such bravery. We too will stand against the rakul."

Ashida gave an exasperated sigh, looking like he'd rather be anywhere in the galaxy right now. "If you are all bound to this madness then I will not think to escape it. You will have my army, brothers."

Al'Tor and Al'Grog echoed the oaths of their kin faithfully, if somewhat less enthusiastically.

When all the raknoth had spoken, Krogoth bared his fangs in a frighteningly predatory smile. "And so we have all given our words, but now heed these last ones from me. If any of you is fool enough to betray us and side with the rakul in the coming war, I will personally see to it that your heads are removed well before Kul'Gada and his kin have the chance to forgo their empty promises and see to it themselves."

With that, Krogoth disconnected from the call.

Talk about a pep talk.

Still, Rachel couldn't say she minded. If anything, Krogoth's militant warning almost made her feel a touch better about their chances at not getting stabbed in the back by one of these a-holes.

Not that she trusted Krogoth, exactly. But something told her she could trust his desire to destroy the rakul, and that was probably the best she was going to get.

The remaining clan speakers disconnected in a disorganized fashion after that, with only Al'Koshna giving any farewell at all.

Soon enough, the gathering was back down to just those in the council chamber, discussing the meeting amongst themselves in quiet voices.

"Well," Nelken said, powering down the projector and turning to lean heavily against the table and address the room, "that was… almost reassuring."

Alton chuckled. "Yes. But only if you're willing to make the mistake of assuming we can trust all of them."

Coming from the raknoth she'd distrusted enough to throw at Gada's waiting blades, it was just about the most unsettling thing Rachel could have heard right then.

CHAPTER EIGHTEEN

Seven thousand miles away, Nan'Ashida leaned back in his newly-restored hardwood chair and sighed.

That had been trying. And frustrating, and humiliating, and half a dozen other things. But, most of all, it had been unnerving.

He leaned forward in his luxurious chair, rested his elbows on his equally luxurious table, and steepled his fingers. Resting his dark lips lightly against the tips of his index fingers, he tried to think.

Had Al'Brandt and that renegade Al'Braka—the one who now called himself Alton Parker—been telling the truth? Was it possible his brothers had actually stood against the Kul and triumphed?

Preposterous.

But then what did they have to gain by lying about such claims?

A series of small tremors in the table and the floor reminded him that it didn't matter now. He'd already made his decision—not that he'd had any real choice in the matter.

The tremors grew stronger, the thump of heavy footsteps steadily approaching.

Thump. Thump. Thump.

Kul'Gada's enormous bulk dipped through the dark doorway. The rakul's side brushed against the frame and tore away a large chunk of the adobe wall.

Ashida winced but didn't dare say anything.

Once he was through the opening, Gada stood back to his full height, nearly scraping the decorative dark wood joists of the spacious room, and fixed a heavy gaze on Ashida.

Ashida, for his part, averted his gaze and did his best not to shudder. "I told them I will stand against you with Zar'Krogoth and the humans. Just as you instructed, Master."

He waited for what felt like an eternity. Finally, he risked a glance.

Kul'Gada was watching him with a fathomless expression, and—

Wait. Had Gada's eye been like that before? A feebly glowing lump? How had he missed that? Probably because he'd been beyond too terrified to look the Kul in the face. But the sight only unsettled him further.

Was that a favor from this fight Al'Brandt spoke of? Had they truly managed to injure one of the Masters?

Ashida pushed the thought from his mind. It didn't matter. He was still trying to wrap his mind around the fact the Kul was here at all. If he were still alive at the end of this conversation, he'd consider himself tremendously lucky.

What he needed to do was establish his value.

"My army is yours to command, Master," he said.

Gada stared.

Ashida pulled his hands from the table and folded them in his lap, doing his best not to squirm. "They will serve you well. As will I."

Cursed void, why was the Kul just staring on like that?

Ashida was about to offer him something for refreshment when the rakul perked up like a hound catching a scent and held up an enormous hand for silence.

Ashida was only too happily obliged.

Gada's snout twitched, and he bared his fangs in a wide smile. For a second, the glow of his lame eye sputtered. The eye itself gave an odd wriggle, and then the crimson glow blazed back to existence, every bit as intense as its counterpart.

Ashida tried to keep his expression neutral. Not that Gada would have noticed.

The Kul's attention remained focused somewhere far away. Ashida reached out with his senses and realized Gada was communicating with someone via messengers. It was focused, tight—not like the broadcast the Kul had sent earlier that day.

Gada finished whatever conversation he was having and fixed Ashida with another stare.

Finally, he spoke in that slithering voice of his. "This will be a pleasant surprise when the time comes to confront these insolent rebels."

"Apologies, Master," Ashida said, "but what will be a pleasant surprise?"

Kul'Gada's smile made Ashida cringe inwardly.

"My brother draws near."

Ashida failed to cover his surprise, but Gada cared little about what he thought.

The Kul drew closer and closer until Ashida lost the battle to control his own shaking hands, and then he leaned down and thrust his face dangerously close to Ashida's.

"I want you to tell me about the humans who conjure fire from air."

CHAPTER NINETEEN

Rachel hadn't come back. Not the day she'd rushed out of Jarek's room to check on Michael after Gada's creepy messenger broadcast, and not in the two days since.

Jarek couldn't quite say which part miffed him more—that she was actively trying to ignore him or that he actually cared as much as he did.

But *ignore* wasn't exactly the right word, was it?

Avoid. She was avoiding him.

Because, by all counts, the comm messages they'd swapped over the past couple days, not to mention the ones they'd relayed through Al, much to his prim and proper chagrin, had been perfectly engaging—playful, even. She just seemed to be reticent to engage him in any medium that limited her ability to turn tail should he decide to press her on The Issue.

Jarek was convinced now that Rachel had willingly thrown Alton to the dogs—or to Gada, rather—during their Himalayan scrap. It wasn't the only possible explanation for her behavior, but it was the best one.

He wasn't entirely sure how he felt about it, either.

Not happy. That was a fair start. But he understood, too. It had been twisted and misguided, sure, but she'd been through some serious shit at the hands of the raknoth, and the battlefield wasn't a place where people were often afforded the time to take hold of their emotions and make level-headed decisions. Especially not when they were tangling with intergalactic-grade super monsters.

Mostly, he just wished Rachel would come talk to him.

Maybe he should just message her that before he up and died of pure, unadulterated boredom and its insidious cousin, worthlessness.

In the past three days, Jarek had had visits from Pryce, Alaric, Lea, and assorted Enochians. Michael, being mostly laid up himself, though he seemed to be looking a bit better since their run-in with Gada, stopped in fairly often to commiserate as well.

And, of course, he had Al's sassy robot butt with him via comm at all hours as well.

None of it really made being an invalid any more bearable, but at least he didn't have to resort to talking to himself.

The one other constant in his days, aside from the doctor who'd mostly written him off since he'd hopped on the Vitamin R, was Drogan, who, aside from stepping out for a few hours here and there, continued hanging around to lay low from Krogoth and provide said miracle spit.

As disturbing as the idea had initially been, Drogan's spit therapy turned out to be well worth the cringes. After day one, Jarek had gone from nearly amputated to capable of light shifting without the fear of an arm falling off. The pain was bad, but he cared a lot more about the progress.

And progress he made. Now, just days after Gada had torn into him, he was able to gingerly move the arm under its own power through a painful but passable range of motion.

Without the treatments, he quite possibly would have ended up losing the arm. Keeping it at all was a mild miracle. But at the rate he was going, he might even be ready to fight in days or weeks instead of the months or years it might have otherwise taken.

The only downside was the appetite. No matter how much he shoveled in, he couldn't seem to satisfy his body's rampant requirements. Not that scarfing unlimited food was so bad, aside from the fact that his excessive consumption wasn't winning him any extra love from the Resistance folks.

Still, to say he was sold on raknoth spit would be an understatement—provided he remained scale free and didn't start sprouting claws and glowing red eyes, at least. When Drogan returned from wherever he'd stepped out to that afternoon, Jarek was excited enough that he couldn't help but wonder if the ol' Vitamin R wasn't packing some manner of addictive hook.

Would it even matter if it did? Probably not. It wasn't like this was recreational. He needed to be ready to fight.

"Stumpy! My favorite drug pusher. Scaliest, too."

Drogan gave a noncommittal grunt, grabbed his customary paper cup, and set a syringe and a hypodermic needle down on the table.

"And the comparison grows more adept," Jarek said. "Am I about to get secondhand hepatitis, or did you convince the good doctor to cough up the goods?"

"She retrieved the needles from hiding when I admitted the injections would at this point do more harm than good without proper delivery."

"Ah. Well go team, huh?"

Drogan didn't answer as he came to Jarek's bedside to get his drool on. First, though, he peeled Jarek's bandage aside and sniffed at the wound. "Much better."

Jarek glanced down and had to agree. The long dark gash on his shoulder appeared to have mostly closed up between the line of staples. He probably barely needed the bandage anymore. Or the staples, even.

All hail the spit.

"You're a miracle worker," Jarek said. "I'll be swinging a sword again in no time. You know, once I find one that's not cut in two."

"Haste would be ideal," Drogan said. "I do not trust this silence. Whatever it is Kul'Gada waits for, best we be ready to meet it with the full might of our finest warriors when the time comes."

"Shucks, buddy. You saying I'm a fine warrior?"

"You may not be a raknoth, but you have proven yourself more than once, most notably against Zar'Golga."

Jarek tipped his head. "Not to mention against you and Krogoth."

Drogan gave a low growl. "The point is that you have survived opponents few would have. Even Krogoth acknowledges as much. Now would you like your treatment or not?"

Jarek bit back a grin. He shouldn't bite the hand that feeds—or the mouth that spits, as it were—but ruffling Drogan's feathers could be just a little too fun sometimes.

"That would be lovely, Drogan. Thank you."

Drogan recoiled a bit at the sound of his name.

"Yeah." Jarek frowned. "Feels weird, right? We'll stick with Stumpy."

Drogan muttered something about giving Jarek a stump to talk about, but Jarek couldn't help but notice he didn't explicitly say no.

"So how are preparations over at casa de Krogoth?" Jarek asked when Drogan paused from spitting to wet his whistle.

"They go as planned," Drogan said. "We will be able to hold against a sizable army should Gada work one into a furor. If he were to wait for the rest of the twelve, though… that would be another matter."

It was a horrifying thought, twelve Gada's rampaging around on the battlefield. Though apparently the rakul came in all shapes and sizes, from what Drogan and Alton had explained to them, each occupying the form of whatever species they'd been invading when they'd been granted ascension to the rank of Kul.

More terrifying was the fact that Gada was the youngest. If the remaining eleven were older and more powerful than the monster they'd barely survived together in the Himalayas… Well, hopefully the rakul had the good manners to keep coming one at a time.

"Where do you put the odds on the other rakul showing up before we deal with Gada?" Jarek asked.

"Impossible to say without knowing when we will confront Gada, but I do not dare hope we will see many days pass without the appearance of at least one or two more Kuls. Lietha shares my feeling in this, as do Krogoth and many others."

"Lovely," Jarek muttered. Then, "And what is it with you and Lietha, anyway?"

"I do not understand what you ask."

"I don't know. He seemed like kind of a minty green pain in the ass when Kole dished him off on us. Hell, you were the one who knocked the guy's face off. But now you guys are like super best friends. What gives?"

Instead of answering, Drogan turned and busied himself with filling the syringe from the saliva cup. Jarek was about to ask again when the raknoth spoke.

"Lietha's disposition is quite understandable, given the circumstances in which she has found herself."

"Well yeah, I get that—Wait. She? Did you say she?"

Drogan gave a small shrug. "It is not a perfectly accurate word, but it seems the best choice in this language."

"Lietha's a… But he's—she's…" Jarek's mouth worked, seeking to ask a dozen questions at once and at first producing none. "You hit a girl?"

Drogan chuckled. "I hit an opponent on the field of battle. No child of Rakzaied would ever begrudge such a thing."

"Wait, wait, wait. I thought the raknoth on this planet were all dudes."

Drogan nodded and began fixing the needle to the filled syringe. "If you wish to think of our subspecies as analogous to your sexes then yes, all raknoth are 'dudes,' as you say. But Shieth'Lietha is no raknoth. She is one of the rakzeed, the mothers of our species."

"Ah, right. Guess I missed that one on orientation day."

Jarek had never really stopped to even think about the sex of the raknoth. That they were all male had just been a default assumption given that every one he'd seen had been wearing a male body.

"Are there many of these, uh, rakzeed here on Earth?"

"There is but one."

"Wow. One chick and eighty dudes? How's that working out?"

Drogan gave an exasperated sigh. "My kind do not copulate and mindlessly fondle like yours. There is no romance, no petty shows of jealousy and possession. The Shieth rarely leave Rakzaied, and the Maieth never. When our numbers dwindle, the raknoth return to the homeworld, provide our lifeseeds—what you would call genetic material—for incubation, and the imbalance is rectified shortly. It is as simple as that."

"Jesus, man. Do they make you sandwiches while they're at it, too?"

Drogan offered him the filled syringe with a frown. "You imply this arrangement is guilty of what you would call sexism?"

Jarek took the needled syringe and shrugged. "Hey, you tell me. You've been here for the whole revolution, right? You probably remember women being told to be good baby-makers and stay in the kitchen like it was yesterday."

"Yes, but it is not so with the rakzeed. They hold a position of great honor in our species, one of critical importance to our survival. It stands to reason that they should be kept out of harm's way, much as your own bodies have evolved to keep your gonads protected. It is the way of nature."

"Huh."

Something told Jarek his gonads would've been anything but safe if he'd tried to explain that kind of reasoning to Rachel or Lea, but he didn't see the point in getting into a debate with Drogan's archaic bias right now.

"So how did Lietha get here then if the, uh, Shieth rarely venture out?"

"She…"—Drogan frowned—"was unsatisfied with her role on Rakzaied. An unusual disposition."

Surprise, surprise. Position of great honor his gonads.

"On a trip home some centuries ago," Drogan continued, "Zar'Kole took notice of her distress and offered her another path. Or so she tells me."

"Uh-huh. So, what, the rakul or whoever don't come chop off hands or… appendages for running away with the planet's baby-makers?"

"It is not unheard of for a Shieth to abandon her post. I have heard it said that it is in fact often times the Kul themselves who take them for their own purposes. In any case, their numbers are replenished easily enough, just as with the raknoth."

"Shit, man." Jarek sank the needle into his shoulder and began the first injection with a grimace. "At the risk of stating the obvious, the rakul sound like enormous cock-hats." He glanced at his shoulder. "For several reasons."

Drogan inclined his head. "I have not heard this phrase, but I believe I agree with the underlying sentiment. It is time the rakul pay for the millennia of their tyranny."

"Right on. Fight the power." Jarek finished his injection and handed the syringe back. "So why did Lietha choose to take a male for a host? Trying to keep her head down in a sea of bros?"

Drogan carefully filled the syringe a second time. "I think you are misunderstanding the subtleties of the differences between our subspecies and your sexes. But, in essence, yes—Lietha wished to remain inconspicuous to those who might have showed unwanted interest."

Jarek wagged his eyebrows. "So does that mean your interest was wanted?"

Drogan handed him the second shot with a scowl. "I simply know enough to recognize a rakzeed when I smell one, unlike many of my younger and less-traveled kin."

"Yeah you do, Stumpy, you horn-dog, you! So, what, are you guys like…"

Drogan crossed his arms and nodded impatiently toward the full syringe in Jarek's hand. "This planet is hardly in need of defenseless raknoth young right now."

Jarek pointedly got on with the second injection. "Yeah, I get that, but you know… Last girl on the planet. Big badass like yourself. End of the world fast approaching… None of that's doing anything for you two?"

"I think you confuse our relationship with the pathetic mush you share with Rachel Cross. Living among the humans for centuries may have left its mark on us in the short term—submerging in another culture always does to some extent—but I assure you, neither one of us is entertaining thoughts of holding bodies into the night and smashing faces together like a pair of filthy... humans."

Jarek held Drogan's now faintly glowing gaze.

This was getting him worked up, wasn't it?

A slow grin crept over Jarek's mouth. "Is this your way of telling me you're scared to kiss a girl, Stumpy?"

By way of reply, Drogan took the spit cup and slapped it heavily down on Jarek's bedside table. "Stick this where you will. I am leaving."

"Again? Hey, we can talk about it, buddy! It's nothing to be embarrassed about, you kn—"

Drogan growled and started for the door.

"Wait!" Jarek cried, shaking with barely-contained giggles.

Drogan stalked out of the room without a backward glance.

"Okay! Good talk, buddy!" Jarek called after him. "Same time tomorrow? I'll be right—Yep, he's gone. Damn... Eh, he'll be back. You catch all of that, Mr. Robot?"

"Quite fascinating, sir," came Al's voice in his earpiece. "And masterfully handled, as always."

"Ahh, to be five-thousand years old and in love..."

"Perhaps I'll know the feeling someday," Al said. "Provided I ever find a better alternative than the ship. She's so slow, sir. And no personality to speak of. Never wants to talk about anything but pressures and velocities and altitudes."

"Hey, if we've got galaxy-conquering space dinosaurs floating around, there's gotta be a nice lady AI out there somewhere in the universe."

"I was merely joking, sir. But you know you could have been more compassionate to Stump—Drogan just now."

"What is this, raknoth therapy hour now?" Jarek asked.

But, in truth, he did feel slightly bad about having laughed Drogan away like that. Sure, the raknoth was a dangerous predator and had left a lot of bodies in his wake, but the more glimpses Jarek took behind the curtain of the raknoth/rakul relationship, the more he felt like the raknoth weren't so clearly the evil bastards he and pretty much everyone else had always wanted to believe they were.

Drogan had feelings too. Probably.

He'd try to do better next time. However irritated Drogan might have been, Jarek had a feeling the raknoth wouldn't be gone for long.

So, after he'd fumbled his awkward way through drawing up and administering the last of the miracle spit, he laid back with a heavy sigh and closed his eyes, thinking healing thoughts and vowing to be less of an unsupportive wise-ass—by a little bit, at least.

Then, when the weight of his old friends, Boredom and Worthless-ness, began to grow too much, he sighed a curse, threw back his blankets, and slid out of bed to see how his legs were faring after days of bedrest.

CHAPTER TWENTY

Rachel removed her hands from the boxy device in front of her, crossed her arms on the table, and laid her head on top of them. She took slow, deliberate breaths and did her best to hold off the shudder as the channeling fatigue exacted its vengeance for her latest working.

"Enchanting fuel for the lady and the sir," came Pryce's voice.

With conscious effort, she opened her eyes and looked up, and there was Pryce with his sympathetic gaze and his—Oh holy mother of god.

She lunged for the tray of brownies like a wild animal who hadn't seen food for weeks. Beside her, Haldin was only slightly more dignified in his approach.

Pryce grinned, set the tray on the table, and sat down across from them.

It wasn't that they'd been wanting for food. It was simply that enchanting—or Expression, as Haldin the Shaper called it—took its toll. Especially when one was at it all morning long.

Plus, Pryce's brownies were goddamn delicious.

She didn't ask him how he'd made them or whether that was a spritz of mint in there, she just woofed brownies until her soft-spoken manners managed to quell the beast inside of her long enough for her to spout, "These are amazing!" around a mouthful of sweet chocolaty goodness.

Haldin gave an affirmative grunt. He looked pale from his exertions, and she couldn't imagine she looked any better. Probably worse, actually.

"How goes it?" Pryce asked.

"Not so bad," Haldin said. "Last time I did something like this, I was figuring it all out from scratch." He shook his head as if chiding himself. "Tried to cloak an entire army in a single night once I did. Didn't exactly work out so smoothly, but I guess it's safe to say I've had worse than this."

Rachel waved her hands in the air to show him just how impressed she was by his epic, manly awesomeness. "Well those of us who aren't used to single-handedly saving the world are exhausted." She snagged another brownie. "And hungry."

Sarcasm aside, she actually was pretty damn impressed with Haldin's capacity for punishment, both in channeling and in a more conventional sense. He was a warrior, as was Elise. Everything else aside, Rachel was glad they had the Enochians with them. Especially since they needed to protect a serious number of heads from getting lost in Kul'Gada's furor, and assembly-line enchanting wasn't exactly her strong suit.

"I don't know when enough's gonna be enough, all things considered," Haldin said, nodding toward the two cloaking generators they'd just finished, "but I think these put us up to enough cloaks to cover HQ and the main bulk of Krogoth's line." He glanced at Rachel. "Assuming they don't mind the cold."

"Better cold than stark raving mad, I suppose," Pryce said.

It was hard to argue with that.

The challenge of powering the gigantic cloaking field generators they'd enchanted into each small box was a problem without an easy solution—or a readily available one, at least. Sure, good batteries, solar panels, or even old generators were all fine options for deploying the devices, but none of those were exactly in overflowing surplus.

So they'd kept things simple, at least for now. She just hoped they didn't find themselves fighting next to the devices on a cold, rainy day. She'd been there before, on the night the nest had burst, when the bullets had been pouring on her catcher as thickly as the rain itself. Back when the only ones trying to kill them had been Drogan and his men.

God, how had being hunted by *only* a raknoth warlord and his army become a fond memory?

Her comm buzzed, and she looked down to a message from Alaric: *Bringing cloaks? Meeting will be too long if it lasts a minute.*

Wasn't that the truth?

"We're coming, we're coming" she muttered at the comm.

"Alaric?" Haldin asked.

Before she could answer, the door Pryce had swapped for the open hole Drogan had punched into the shop wall a few weeks prior swung open, and Johnny stepped in.

"You guys ready to go share your project with the class?"

Rachel made a face. "Not really, but it sounds like they're waiting." She turned to Pryce. "You sure you wanna come? I can't imagine you'll be missing much more than a pissing contest between Krogoth, Alaric, and anyone else brave enough to whip it out."

She looked pointedly at Haldin with the last, but he only shrugged and shook his head. Her gaze drifted to Johnny, who gave her a wave and a wink. "I'm your man. Just give me the signal!"

She shook her head. "Not what I was getting at."

Johnny shrugged, and Rachel turned back to Pryce.

"I'm curious to see what they're cooking up over there," Pryce said. "If I have to brave a few waggling genitalia along the way, I suppose I'll survive. I could use a break anyway."

Elise trailed in after Johnny to help Haldin start gathering the cloaking field generators into the duffel bags Pryce had provided.

"Fair enough," Rachel said. "How's the Soldier of Charity's reboot coming along, by the way?"

Pryce wrinkled his nose. "Well, Fela's not what I would call easily patchable. She's got more layers than a Russian stacking doll. The armor, that's easy enough to improvise. The bits that do the actual moving, on the other hand... I don't happen to have any synthetic muscle lying around, but Al and I are toying with integrating some old servos, so..."

"So that's... good then?"

Pryce shrugged. "I'm sure we'll figure it out. We always do!"

"I'm sure if anyone can, it's you two. What about the other thing?"

Pryce grinned. "You mean the Big Whacker 2.0?"

Rachel rolled her eyes. "I wish we didn't have to call it that."

"Ah, but how else would they know that it's bigger and whackier in every way?"

"Oh, I think they'll know something's wacky, all right," Rachel muttered.

Pryce only grinned wider. "I should be able to wrap up my part and lay down the etchings by this evening if you want to start"—he wiggled his fingers—"doing your thing tonight."

She frowned at him. "I think you might be a bit too chipper for a guy who's trying to help stop the second apocalypse."

"What can I say?" Pryce gave a helpless shrug. "I love building stuff."

<hr>

SOMETHING TOLD Rachel that the grandiose chamber where they'd been instructed to wait for Krogoth was not of Krogoth's choice and design but simply the room he'd adopted from the late Zar'Golga as an "office." Whatever the hell a raknoth needed an office for. And one so decadent at that. Then again, in her book, the same question would've been fair enough when reapplied to the doubtlessly richer-than-rich human who'd occupied the space in a past lifetime.

Haldin, Johnny, Alton, and Pryce stood with her, Alaric, and Alaric's detail of half a dozen armed guards in the penthouse suite on the eastern edge of what had once been called Hell's Kitchen.

Maybe they should call it Krogoth's Kitchen now.

The building was one of the few in the area that had avoided complete ruination during the Catastrophe. Most of New York City hadn't been so lucky, but Zar'Golga had labored, or at least his men had, to scrape together a fairly livable space around his mighty tower. Though "tower" might have been a stretch. The building wasn't objectively that tall by old standards, just tall compared to those left standing.

The penthouse was vastly unnecessary in its spaciousness and decked out with glossy, wood-paneled walls and a large skylight whose dozens of glass panes reminded her of a honeycomb. The floor was ridiculously luxurious—and did she mention unnecessary?—dark marble, interspersed with splashes of lighter gray. It was all rather immaculate.

She wondered how many people had died in that room.

When that became overly disturbing, she turned to wondering how many more minutes Krogoth would keep them waiting here for whatever posturing bullshit he was up to.

The answer to both quandaries, she was pretty sure, was *too many*.

Even so, the clacking of boots and claws on marble that preceded Krogoth's arrival several minutes later didn't exactly bring relief. The warlord strode confidently into the room, flanked by a figure on either side, a raknoth she didn't recognize on his right, and on his left… Shit.

Seth Mosen followed Krogoth into the room, jaw tight and gaze held low.

Alaric's knuckles cracked like dry wood beside Rachel, but the wiry Resistance commander made no move other than to shift his weight and skewer Krogoth with a cold glare.

Mosen and the two raknoth drew up to their group, and for a long stretch, no one spoke. Rachel could feel her companions' desire to spit pointed comments about the wait—wanted to make such comments herself. Krogoth almost seemed eager for them to come.

Finally, though, Haldin broke the silence, calm and steady. "Shall we get to business, then?"

Krogoth cocked his head and gave Mosen an expectant look.

"Father," Mosen said, eyes still trained on the smooth marble floor.

Rachel swore she could feel the air itself tense around Alaric as his gaze flicked between Krogoth and Mosen. "What the hell is this?"

"I believe you might call it an intervention," Krogoth said, the crimson of his eyes dim against the rust red of his hide.

Was that a sign of deference or something? She hadn't cracked the code on raknoth eye glows yet. Krogoth didn't really seem like the deferent type. Maybe he was just tired.

"Much as I appreciate the peaceful return of my subject, Commander Weston," Krogoth continued, "if we are all to share the field of battle, I would prefer to do so with moderate certainty you will not decide to shoot one of my lieutenants. Again."

So that was a no on the deference thing—the son of a bitch.

Judging from the tension in his jaw and the strangled sound that escaped his throat, Alaric seemed to be banking on popping tendons or cracking teeth to provide an answer in lieu of words.

Rachel wasn't sure if her heart was trying to break with sympathy for father and son or explode with tension for the rest of them. Alaric, for his part, stared at his son, utterly speechless.

Thanks to the many uncanny "upgrades" Zar'Golga had treated him to over the years, Mosen had healed quickly enough after Alaric had been forced to shoot him to restrain him during a scrap they'd had in Philadelphia just a few short weeks ago.

But there were wounds even a raknoth's miraculous healing gifts couldn't keep from scarring, and Rachel was pretty sure father shooting son was one of them.

"You know I wouldn't," Alaric finally said. "That was... That's behind us now. Seth, I—"

Mosen shot his father a look, his face contorted and his eyes glinting pale red. The words died in Alaric's throat. And then Mosen was staring at the floor again.

The Resistance soldiers shifted uncomfortably around them. Pryce looked like he was on the verge of saying something. Rachel felt compelled to help Alaric, to find the right words for him, but...

What did you say to the son who'd been compelled to murder his own mother—your wife—and systematically trained to hate you for allowing him to fall into enemy hands and become their hybrid puppet?

Apparently, no one knew.

"Enough," Alton said.

The crimson fire poured back into Krogoth's eyes, and he straightened as he fixed onto his new challenger.

Alton kept his eyes pointedly trained on Krogoth's feet as he spoke. "Might our time not be better spent elsewhere, Zar'Krogoth?"

Krogoth thought about that for a long second, looking like he might decide to escalate matters, but finally decided he'd had his fun.

"Very well," he said. "I believe that will do for now. Let us visit the battlements."

Even if the raknoth hadn't murdered her family, Rachel would've been fighting the urge to help Krogoth achieve blast off through his ridiculous skylight by then.

Krogoth didn't care one bit about what Alaric and Mosen might do to one another out there, she was sure of it. The display had been intended to hurt, an exercise in psychological warfare that was unhelpful for everyone involved. Unless Krogoth had wanted to get Alaric too upset to speak and probably too pissed to think clearly. Then it had definitely been helpful to Krogoth.

One day—and she didn't know when, but one day—Rachel was going to give Alton and Krogoth and all the other scaly bastards what they deserved. But for now, Haldin's and Pryce's imploring looks convinced her to stow her arguments now that they were moving on.

They made their way silently out to the landing pad built off the posh penthouse, where the Enochians' hovering ship was waiting beside Krogoth's smaller parked one. By some unspoken agreement, they saw to it as a group that Alaric stayed on the opposite side of the pack from Krogoth and Mosen until they'd split off to board their separate ships.

The flight was a short one. Within a minute, the remains of old Central Park stretched out ahead in the view port, dry and largely barren—of greenery and wildlife, at least. The park was most certainly not barren of activity. That, it had in droves.

The scope of the bustling below was actually quite impressive. All around, Krogoth's people were busy at work with hand tools and more elaborate machinery, constructing a long-running barricade a little ways in from the southern end of the park. Others were hauling heavy-looking armaments to the turrets interspersed along the fortifications. Out beyond the wall, dozens of men were busy in the dirt planting a variety of smaller traps, and a dozen or so yards behind the wall on their side, still more men labored to dig a pair of huge pits.

Alton guided them after Krogoth's ship to a landing near the pits, and they all shuffled out of the ship.

Krogoth led their party to the closer of the pits. Alaric quietly established a comm call with Nelken and Daniels as they went so the commanders could have a look at Krogoth's preparations from the relative safety of HQ.

Pit Number One, like its brother on the other side of their ships, was probably twenty feet on either side, and another twenty or thirty down. A hectic mess of rebar networked its way along the walls and the floor of the pit. As they drew up to the edge, Rachel saw men at work below, anchoring sheets of plywood to the inner surfaces of the rebar network. The old concrete mixer truck nearby solidified their goal in Rachel's head.

They were building a cell of sorts.

"Not bad," Haldin said. "But we still have to get Gada in there. Assuming he's careless enough to strike here to begin with. He could still tear the rest of the world apart waiting for his backup to arrive or for us to come out to him."

"That's what we're worried about," came Nelken's voice from Alaric's comm.

"The Kul will come," Krogoth said. "Gada is renowned neither for his patience nor his skill at tactics. He will be burning to prove himself after his defeat in the mountains, and I imagine he will hope to do it before his peers arrive to hear of his earlier failure."

He sounded confident enough, but then again, Rachel couldn't really picture Krogoth sounding unconfident about anything. Aside from his side hobby of psychological sadism, Krogoth struck her as a warrior first and foremost, and one with an ego. If he hadn't already caught onto the old phrase, "My way or the highway," Rachel suspected it would be a likely candidate to capture his heart quite quickly.

Still, Krogoth's operation looked a whole hell of a lot better than their rag-tag fighting force had flying off to try to get the drop on Gada. If divine intervention or some manner of massive rakul stroke was out of the question, she hoped Gada would be brazen enough to charge into this death trap.

That hope only grew as she spotted the two long green pressurized cylinders off to one side of the pit.

"Fire always works," Pryce said quietly beside her, apparently following her gaze.

Jesus. At first she'd took the pits to be cells. Cells without tops for the moment, but she'd figured that must be why the men at the other pit had been digging shallow lines to either side of their pit—probably setting tracks for a sliding panel or something. But they weren't just cells, were they?

They were giant, custom-made rakul ovens.

The thought was at once revolting and comforting. Revolting in the carousel of screaming shrieks and charred, smoking flesh that poured through her head. Comforting in that it might just work. And right now, that was better than they could say about most of their plans.

Trapping Gada wouldn't be easy—it might even prove impossible —but it was better than aimlessly harrying him and hoping he didn't inevitably score a hit with those devastating blades of his. And with Krogoth's army and the Resistance at their backs, their chances seemed a lot brighter. Unless Gada kicked up a big enough furor to bring an army of his own to match.

But that's why they'd brought the cloak generators, right? Assuming those actually worked to break whatever army Gada might stir up.

"Are we sure this thing'll hold him?" Rachel asked, still looking down at the pit. "You know, assuming the other million steps before that all go off without a hitch?"

"The interior will be reinforced with plated steel," Krogoth said. "It should suffice for long enough."

She thought back to the way Gada had cut through Jarek's enormous sword with enough force left to tear through Fela's armor in the same swing and wondered if that were a wise assessment. It wasn't overly encouraging that everything about this setup seemed to be coming back to *Hey, it's better than anything else we've got.*

God knew what they were going to do when the rest of the rakul arrived. If this was the best they had, they were going to need a lot more pits, at the very least. Judging from the markings and the digging equipment further down the line, Krogoth was of the same mind.

"So all we have to do is push the giant killing machine down there and slam the lid, then," Rachel said, mostly to herself.

"Preferably without any… misunderstandings, this time," Krogoth said.

Rachel did her best to keep her face composed as her stomach attempted to flee somewhere subterranean.

Had Krogoth heard about what she'd done?

A furtive glance at Alton showed he was caught off guard by the statement as well, but Rachel wasn't sure what else Krogoth could be referring to. The way he was boring holes in her with those glowing eyes right now didn't exactly suggest an alternative explanation.

Neither did the predatory wink he shot her from across the pit.

She resisted the urge to reach out and shove Krogoth into the pit right then and there—or at least to turn and get the hell out of Camp Krogoth—as Haldin mercifully turned the conversation to the cloaking generators and Alton followed his lead.

A warning, then, Rachel thought as Krogoth continued to stare at her from across the pit, a blood-chilling smile creeping slowly onto his reptilian snout. A creepy-ass warning not to try any funny business around Krogoth or his clan.

Part of her wanted to reach out and telepathically tell him to shove it out of spite alone. The rest of her succeeded in suppressing that desire and turning to the cloaking generator discussion just to escape Krogoth's leer.

They spent the next couple hours going over plans and touring the battlements. No one actually resorted to whipping it out, but Haldin and Krogoth, and Nelken via Alaric's comm, did hem and haw about the best locations to install the cloaking generators, with occasional inputs from Pryce and Johnny.

Alaric remained awash in a sea of surly stoicism that was rivaled only by Mosen's silent brooding.

Elise and Rachel followed them all in companionable silence, watching and listening, though Rachel only caught half of what was being said. Mostly, she was busy wondering how it had come to this. Men and women working beside the raknoth who'd laid waste to their world. All of them preparing for the likely necessity of taking down innocent, maddened civilians just to get a shot at the giant red-eyed asshole who wanted to lay waste to them all.

And eleven more like him on the way.

If things went poorly, they could all be dead in a week. Less. It was almost too much to process. But this was the hand they'd been dealt, and there was little left to do but keep their heads down and keep swinging until the rakul were gone or they were.

And what if they did win? What if they beat the rakul and were left standing side-by-side with the raknoth? What then? Were they supposed to imagine they could all just drop the past fifteen years and share the planet happily ever after like good symbiotes?

Fat chance.

One way or another, she couldn't help but think this fight was going to come to a bloody end, followed shortly by another.

When the meeting had concluded with Nelken, Daniels, and Alaric agreeing to send a portion of their forces to aid Krogoth's preparation efforts, and they'd returned to Pryce's to get back to work on a new batch of cloaking generators, Rachel pulled Pryce aside, needing to hear what someone else thought, to know that she wasn't sliding down a big old sheet of crazy.

"You know what they say," Pryce said after some short deliberation. "Sic vis pacem para bellum."

It took her a few seconds to register the old adage.

If you want peace, prepare for war.

She arched a brow at him. "Really? That's what you've got? You never struck me as a sayings guy."

Pryce shook his head. "Oh no. Not in the slightest. I was going to say I think it's the biggest load of shit ever peddled down through humanity. Well, except for…" He cocked his head thoughtfully, then waved away whatever had occurred to him. "Never mind. Point is, I don't think the whole *big stick, scared enemies* policy is long-term sustainable. Case in point, look at what's happening between the raknoth and the rakul right now. War-making is so often the answer and, I think, never the solution."

"I feel compelled to point out that this is coming from the guy who's currently playing a crucial role in helping us prepare for said war-making."

Pryce cocked his head. "I'd like to think we just had the misfortune to be born in the middle of some great equilibration. Even steady-state systems need time to stabilize after perturbation, you know. In the grand scheme of things, if that means a few millennia of ugliness to achieve a future that doesn't end with the mutual annihilation of, well, *everything*…" He shrugged. "I can be okay with that."

Rachel waited to see if he'd continue. Then, when he made no sign of doing so, "I'm not sure that really answers my question."

He gave her a wan smile. "I'm sure it doesn't."

She shook her head, part bemused, part exasperated. "You're a strange old man, you know that?"

By way of reply, Pryce only gave her a friendly pat on the leg and walked away whistling a tune she recognized after a few moments as the older-than-dirt classic, *Dust in the Wind.*

CHAPTER TWENTY-ONE

If commercial advertisements or the global market had still been things, Jarek would have signed up in a heartbeat to be the poster child for Drogan's Old-Fashioned Miracle Spit. Just five days after Kul'Gada had smitten his bloody body into the snows of the Himalayas, Jarek crawled out of his bed in medical for the last time and gingerly wind-milled his injured arm to the tune of his doctor's exasperated protests. There was still plenty of pain, but nothing popped or tore out of place.

Good enough in his book.

Even if the world hadn't literally been coming to an end, he couldn't have taken any more of the waiting. He hadn't had a proper visitor since his oh-so-interesting talk with Drogan. The fact that his friends were all busy prepping to save the world out there didn't lessen his desire to get back to the action. And neither did the message Rachel had sent him the previous night, implying in a roundabout way that she was maybe-sort-of-kind-of sorry about having avoided him these past few days and promising she was going to have a special surprise waiting for him when he was ready.

He'd spent the night eagerly thinking and dreaming about the implications. At least until he'd woken up to an odd-hour message from Pryce emphatically promising much the same thing. That had somewhat dulled the excitement.

Either Fela was getting an upgrade, or he was in for some traumatizing shit.

Drogan had been back the day after their little mishap to provide a dose of slobbery healing goodness with a liberal side of determined silence outside of the necessary communications. This morning, though, the raknoth had been at least mildly more responsive to Jarek's comments before informing Jarek he'd done his best and now it was up to Jarek to finish restoring his own pathetic, squishy meat suit to fighting shape.

Granted, it was a bit of a jump to get past little chestnuts like immortality and requiring human blood to live, but, despite their differences, Jarek would almost go so far as to say he and Drogan were slowly developing something of a friendly rapport—ish.

That, or he'd read entirely too much affection into Drogan's "banter".

Hell, maybe Jarek really was hurting for friends.

An arcanist, a digital construct, a bunch of humans from another planet, a crazy old tinkerer, and now a raknoth…

Nah. He was doing just fine.

Right now, though, all he really cared about was getting back to doing something that wasn't walking aimlessly around HQ or lying in bed waiting for the hurting to stop.

So once he'd dressed for the day, he headed for the common room and climbed up to the new groundside exit, determined to huff it over to Pryce's and get his lungs working.

Inside and out, the base was alive with activity. Resistance soldiers busied themselves unloading, organizing, and repairing weapons and other equipment. Others were hard at work erecting fortifications around the base in preparation for whatever was coming. From what little he'd heard, things were even busier over at casa de Krogoth, where their wise leaders were hoping to force the inevitable confrontation.

The bustle was a poignant reminder that Gada was five days closer to pulling off whatever he must be up to. Unless the rakul had simply decided to wait for his eleven backup monsters before striking again, that was. Jarek couldn't imagine the other rakul would be much further behind.

Either way, time was running out.

He was headed in the direction of the recently-completed south gate and preparing to kick it up to a jog when Pryce's truck pulled around a nearby line of shipping crates headed the other way, toward the less populated corner of the base where Jarek's ship was still parked. It wasn't Pryce in the truck, though, he realized as it passed by, but Rachel.

He turned and jogged after her as she continued on and pulled the truck up beside Jarek's ship. She still hadn't spotted him as she hopped out and turned back for her staff.

It wasn't until Fela unfurled and stood up in the truck bed and Al called, "Good morning, sir," that Rachel jolted upright and looked around to see him approaching.

Their eyes met, and his heart leapt in a way that had nothing to do with the jogging. It probably would have irritated him more if Rachel hadn't looked every bit as flustered as he suddenly felt—and then some.

He tried to relax and focus on Fela as Al hopped the exo from the truck bed down to the pavement and awaited Jarek's arrival.

"Ah," Jarek said. "A fresh pressed suit. Just what the Jarek ordered."

Al shifted to put Fela's shoulder on display, and Jarek took a closer look at the patch job. The damage had been bad, he knew, but Pryce had done a good job with it, as usual. The new right shoulder plate was a bit bulkier than the original, but not obnoxiously so.

"How's that shoulder handling, buddy?"

"I might ask you the same question, sir. But our fix is workable. Not great, but workable. Might I suggest not being mauled by the galaxy-conquering dinosaur next time?"

"You might," Jarek said.

"I dunno," Rachel said, drawing up beside Fela with a hesitant grin. "'Not great but workable' kinda sounds like just your style."

"Style being the operative word there, I think," Jarek said.

She shrugged. "Everyone's entitled to their own opinion, I suppose. How's the shoulder? You look like a raknoth spit on you."

"Oh, you know"—Jarek did a demonstrative windmill—"not great. But workable."

She smiled, but the silence stretched a bit too long, and some of that nervous discomfort crept back in.

Rachel shifted her focus to her staff, fidgeting. "I, uh, guess we might have a few things to talk about, but… surprise first?"

Much as he'd resented being kept at arm's distance these past days, now that she was here in front of him, Jarek was in no hurry to see Rachel do anything but smile for the time being.

So he made a show of glancing around at the not-so-far-away work crews and said, in a hushed tone, "Like, here? Right now?"

She wagged her eyebrows with more sarcasm than Jarek would've thought possible. "If you think you can handle it. How are you with your left hand?"

"Oh, you bad girl…" He rubbed his palms together and clapped a hand on Fela's shoulder. "Either there's a sword waiting for me in that truck or I'm about to be one very happy man."

As it turned out, there was a sword waiting for him in that truck.

"Eh," Jarek said as Rachel uncovered the weapon that had been wrapped safely next to Fela for the ride, "I guess I'm still a pretty happy man."

"Hey"—Rachel hefted the weapon up from the truck bed with a mild effort—"I just got done playing with your Whacker all night long. What else could you want?"

Jarek eyed the weapon more closely. "Huh. Color me intrigued."

The blade was sheathed, but it looked slightly smaller than his Whacker, and it had a slight inward curve, like a gigantic kukri, or maybe a kopsis or some other similar sword Pryce would be able to name for god knew why.

Technical distinctions aside, Jarek was pretty confident about one thing. The curved blade would be all the better for lopping off rakul limbs.

He accepted the sword from Rachel and actually listened to her advice to mind his shoulder as he drew it. The blade was indeed curved, and quite wicked-looking. It felt heavy in his bed-rested arms. It *was* heavy compared to any standard sword—maybe fifteen pounds or so—but the balance wasn't bad, and it wasn't intended to be used without Fela anyway.

Most intriguing of all were the several glyphs etched on the flat face of the blade, not unlike those on Rachel's staff and bullet catcher. And there, right near the cross guard, someone—almost definitely Pryce—had etched into the side of the blade, shallow but readily legible: *Big Whacker 2.0*

"Yes!" Jarek cried, thrusting the blade triumphantly skyward. "Long live the Big Whacker!"

Rachel snorted. Al clapped ceremoniously with Fela's hands.

Jarek slowly lowered the blade, trying not to wince at the pangs in his shoulder. "So, uh, what does it do?"

"Hopefully not break, for starters. But there's more."

"Do go on."

She nodded toward Fela and the ship. "Why don't you suit up and find out for yourself?"

He sheathed the blade. "Tease a guy, why don't you. To the ship, Al! I need to be inside of you."

"I do hope you mean Fela, sir," Al said as he remotely keyed the ship ramp open and marched the suit over.

"You're sure you're up for this?" Rachel asked, following along behind. "I don't want you to rip an arm off swinging a sword around too soon."

"I'll be careful."

For some reason, neither Al nor Rachel seemed particularly convinced by that one, but Rachel was clearly burning to see her and Pryce's creation in action as well.

Aboard the ship, Jarek began to strip down without a thought. There was only one way to properly don Fela, and clothes—at least beyond briefs—were not a part of it.

"You look a lot better," Rachel said quietly behind him.

When he looked, she'd turned away to sit at the open boarding ramp while he changed. He grinned at her chivalrous attempt to protect his modesty and stepped into Fela's embrace.

Once suited, he took up the Big Whacker 2.0, giddy with excitement, and plunked down the ramp. He spun the blade through a few experimental arcs. The discomfort in his shoulder wasn't crippling, but it was enough that he shifted to lefty for the next try.

"You like it?" Rachel asked.

He whipped it through one last arc and smiled at her. "It's perfect." He ran his thumb over one of the glyphs. "I'm still not sure what it does, though."

She gave him an impish grin. "Flip the switch on the pommel."

He did.

Nothing happened—unless he counted Rachel growing visibly excited.

"Flip the switch and…?"

She wiggled her brows, and this time there was nothing sarcastic about it. "Give it a swing, big guy. Just be careful."

He frowned at the sword, shrugged, and spun it through another series of arcs.

It was as if the blade were suddenly moving through a vat of molasses instead of air. Even stranger was the heat that radiated from the blade's length, beating onto the sensors in Fela's forearms.

"Uh…" He looked from the blade to Rachel. "What?"

Her smile widened. "Come on, man! A real swing. Put that suit's back into it! You know, carefully though."

Jarek willed his faceplate shut more for affect than anything. "I feel like you're giving me mixed signals here, Goldilocks."

With that, he set his feet, took a two-handed grip with his good arm in the lead, and stepped into a heavy overhand strike. Once again, the invisible molasses field pulled against the blade, but he swung hard enough that the strike still fell as fast as any swordsmen could've managed with a normally weighted sword.

A flash of azure light seared the air inches in front of the blade's path as it fell. That alone nearly jostled a surprised cry from his throat, but the gust of heat that swept over his arms and chest finished the job.

"Holy shit!"

Afterward, he stared dumbly at the blade, registering the smell of ozone in the air.

He turned slowly to Rachel, who was watching him with a satisfied smile. "Goldilocks… did you just build me a lightsaber?"

She wrinkled her nose. "There might be a copyright issue in there somewhere, but yeah—I got about as close as I could think to."

He willed his faceplate open. "I think I'm in love."

Her eyebrows crept upward as if by their own accord as she searched his face. Something about the expression made her look younger and more beautiful than she ever had.

"With the sword," she said, half-question, half-statement.

He tilted his head, holding her stare. "We could go with that."

Her throat shifted in a visible swallow, her gaze pulling at him until he'd all but forgotten the sword in his hand. "So," she finally said, "do you, uh… wanna go cut something?"

The tension rushed out of his chest in a series of airy chuckles. "You bet your ass, I do." He looked around the shipping yard like a dog at a butcher's shop. "How hot does it get? Think it can cut through one of these shipping crates?"

She shot an uncertain look at a distant crate. "I think so. Pretty much, the harder you swing it, the hotter it gets, right up until it caps out around 'ridiculously freaking hot.' You need to take it easy though. Don't hurt yourself."

Jarek turned on his heel and darted off with a bark of laughter. After days of bed rest, the freedom of moving with Fela's power wrapped around him was like heaven. He veered toward a shipping crate whose door stood ajar, calculated distance, made a small stagger step to adjust, and lunged into a hefty top-down diagonal slice.

The blade fell in a flash of heat and azure light. The sword barely even kicked in his hand, but then the top corner of the crate door was falling.

The hunk of corrugated steel hit the ground with a crash, its severed edge a trail of glowing molten metal that matched the one left on the downsized door.

"Hell yeah!" Jarek shouted.

He danced through a few turns, putting the blade through a smooth series of flourishes and hard strokes that brought the blade alive with glowing energy.

With each swing, the extra resistance seemed more and more of a non-issue. He merely had to remember to expect it and think a little further in advance to keep the movements smooth and flowing.

He flipped the pommel switch to the off position and strolled back over to Rachel and the ship.

He spun the sword through a few more loops, felt the blade to make sure it wasn't too hot, then stepped up the ramp and slid it neatly into the sheath Rachel held out for him. "This is amazing, Rache."

She looked up at him, the sword lingering in their combined grasp for a stretch before Jarek moved the weapon to the side and stepped in closer to her. Before either of them could break the silence, he stroked her cheek with his thumb and bent to kiss her forehead.

"Thank you."

She tilted her head back to meet his eyes, and something in his chest tried to do a barrel roll. She was just so damned cute when she bit her lip like that. Her hands slid slowly around his sides, and the hunger built until he couldn't contain himself.

He wrapped a hand behind her head and pulled her into a kiss. She lingered on the threshold for a second, hesitating. Then her arms tightened around him, casting aside all pretenses of self-restraint. Jarek dropped the sword on his recliner and slipped the free hand around the small of her back.

When she pressed into him, he looped his arm the rest of the way around her waist and hoisted her off the ground, pulling one leg up to his side. She went with the motion and hooked her feet behind his back, their lips never parting for a moment. He slapped blindly at the wall, head spinning with raw need, until he found the switch to close the boarding ramp, and then he carried them into the cabin, pulling Rachel's jacket off along the way.

That was when Al decided to clear his throat in Jarek's earpiece.

He set Rachel down on the bed. "Run along, Mr. Robot."

Fela sprang open with a series of hard clicks and peeled away from his body. He stepped out, leaving nothing but the fabric of his briefs between him and Rachel.

Behind him, Fela stood and jogged up to the cockpit to Al's cries of, "Not looking! Not looking!"

"Just go watch a movie in cyberland or something, you big baby!" Jarek called after him. He turned back to Rachel and saw hesitation creeping into her expression.

He took her hands and pulled her to her feet.

"We shouldn't," she whispered. "I—"

He wrapped his arms around her waist and kissed her, relishing the feel of her all the more now that it was through his own hands rather than Fela's tactile sensors. Slowly, inch by inch, she softened until her body was molded to his.

When the faint moan escaped her, he lost control.

They were on the cot before he knew it, twisting and twining in a desperate race to press their bodies together as completely as possible. Her shirt came off, and they pressed together again, the smooth warmth of her skin against his driving his brain in wild circles until he could barely see straight.

They pulled hungrily at each other, too lost in the urgency of the moment to take more coherent action than simply mashing their bodies together.

Unbidden, the memory sprang to mind of Drogan muttering something about mashing faces together like filthy humans, and Jarek laughed before he could stop himself.

Rachel stiffened against him. "What?"

"No, nothing," he said quickly. "It's nothing."

He descended to kiss her neck, but she stopped him. "Nothing?"

Damn his giggly body.

"I just, uh, remembered something Drogan said. About us squishy humans. It was nothing."

Somehow, that didn't seem to put her at ease.

"Oh," she said.

That single syllable was like a fine sheet of ice spreading between them.

For a second, he considered trying to explain the tidbit about Drogan and Lietha, as if that might just clear the air, but no—a lesson in raknoth reproduction probably wasn't the ticket to righting this suddenly sinking ship.

As testament to that, Rachel added, "Guess the two of you really hit it off, huh?"

Her expression was a forced neutral, but the way she said it—the unspoken suggestion that such a thing was morally reprehensible—had Jarek spitting out his rebuke before his better judgment had time to vote.

"Wasn't like I really had many alternatives on the visitor front."

He regretted the words almost before they'd finished leaving his mouth. This wasn't what he wanted—the petty, scathing bullshit. The undue judgment. The shadow falling over Rachel's expression, making it all the worse.

"Jarek..." she said quietly.

He couldn't quite tell what it was in her eyes. Anger? Frustration? Regret?

She looked away, refusing to meet his eyes. "I was—I didn't want..."

Tears glistened in her eyes, and intuition hit him like a charging raknoth.

All this time, he'd been sure she was dodging him because she thought he'd be angry or at least want to lecture her about what she'd pulled with Alton.

He'd never thought to imagine she'd simply been afraid of what he might think of her for it. Why would she be? Since when did she care what he thought? But that's exactly what he saw in her face now. Remorse and fear.

"Hey." He took her chin and steered her eyes back to his. Or tried to.

She resisted for a second and then snapped her face back toward him with a sharp huff of air, her eyes brimming with tears, remorse giving way to anger. "Dammit. Why do you—"

He cupped her cheek with one hand and, feeling her jaw quivering with tension, shook his head. "I don't care, Goldilocks. Never mind what whiny-bitch Jarek has to say about it."

She watched him uncertainly, looking like she was debating whether she should shirk his touch and retrieve her shirt.

He shook his head again, willing her to believe him. "I don't care. Not about what happened in the Himalayas. Not about what's happened since. We've laid too much shit on the line for each other to let a second's questionable judgment throw it all out the window."

Because a second's misjudgment was all it had been. Call him naïve, but he was sure of that looking at her now. Whatever hang-ups she might still have concerning Alton and the rest of the raknoth, she wouldn't be making a habit of sabotaging their war efforts moving forward. He trusted that.

The quiver of her jaw intensified beneath his palm. Then, quietly, she said, "Don't you mean defenestrate it?"

He laughed, thinking back to the shootout in Deadwood she was referring to, when he'd complimented her on blowing a gunman through the window. Back when he'd been without Fela and they'd both been about two steps shy of knifing each other. It felt like such a long time ago.

"You're right." He planted a kiss on her forehead. Her cheek. Leaned in until his lips brushed her ear. "Pardon my pedestrian tongue, m'lady. It tends to wander." A light nibble. "You don't happen to have any idea how we could keep it occupied?"

Rachel shifted beneath him, clearly not hating the affections, despite the firm hand she planted against his chest.

"You realize I almost got you killed," she whispered, "right?"

"Eh." He leaned back to take her in—ruffled hair, tear-streaked face, and beautiful, shining eyes—and shrugged. "None of us gets to bat a thousand, Goldiloc—"

She reached up and pulled his mouth down to hers, and he didn't fight it.

Before, their kissing had been insistent, frantic.

The kiss she drew him into now, though, was deep and electrifyingly sensual—passionate, but in no hurry to get out of its own way or move on to the next step. It was full of care and warmth and the salty wetness of recent tears, and it made Jarek's head spin like he'd just sprinted a mile with a gas mask full of nicotine.

He was almost too stupefied to speak when she pulled back and whispered, "I'm sorry, Jarek."

"I, uh…"

Words, dammit. He needed to use his words.

Rachel's face was crinkling into a smile now, her brow arching up at him. "You okay up there? You're not having a stroke, are you?"

"Oooh…" He dipped and planted a kiss on her breastbone, reaching for the button on her jeans. "You might wanna be careful using the word 'stroke' right now."

She laughed, resting a hand on his but not quite stopping him.

And by the will of all the cruelest, most dastardly fates in the universe, her comm chose that moment to buzz against his side.

"Shit," Rachel whispered.

For a few quick heartbeats, they held each other's gazes, silently debating. Then some unspoken agreement passed between them, and she swiped the call away with a breathy laugh.

He pulled her in for another kiss and skirted down the cot, slipping out of his briefs, moving to help her do the same with her jeans— each small movement she made, each touch of warm skin driving him wilder with need.

The comm buzzed again.

"Fuck it," Rachel breathed.

She was unfastening the intrusive device from her wrist and shifting her hips to aid Jarek's endeavors with her jeans when Al spoke from the cabin speakers.

"So sorry, sir, but we have multiple calls from HQ. It's... Well, it appears to be quite urgent."

"You've gotta be kidding me," Jarek growled.

"My sincerest apologies, sir."

"Are we talking pants urgent?"

"Indeed, sir."

Rachel sighed. "Guess we'd better check it out."

Jarek looked back and forth between her and the cockpit, praying for some magical development to float along and un-ruin what had been turning out to be a perfectly amazing day.

No such luck.

"Shit!" He kissed Rachel's forehead and sprang off the cot, headed for the cockpit. "Take the call, then, Mr. Robot," he said, stepping into Fela's waiting boots stark nude. "And easy with the pelvic plate, buddy," he added as Fela began to fold around him.

The console holo sprang up, blank but for the buffering icon as the connection strained to add video to the call.

"What?" he growled at the console before he'd even noted the ID.

"Sorry," came Lea's voice, "I—oh..." she added as her face appeared on the holo and her holo must've similarly populated to show Rachel tugging on her shirt in the back cabin.

"What's up?" Jarek asked, not in much of a mood to give a shit what anyone thought right now. "Judging from the persistence, I can only assume the world is ending."

"I'm..." Lea's gaze flicked back and forth between him and Rachel. "Shoot. I'm really sorry to interrupt, guys, but we have a problem."

CHAPTER TWENTY-TWO

Once upon a time, Jarek had been reasonably confident that phrases like "we have a problem" could be translated to things like, "We're gonna have to wait for daylight if we don't want the ship's batteries to run dry," or, "Hey, that band of marauders who wanna kick your ass just rolled into town." Those had been problems, yes, but manageable ones. Trivial ones, even.

But nowadays, anytime someone said those four shitty little words, Jarek was inclined to go from zero to full-on clench in a few microseconds flat.

"Lay it on us," he said as Rachel entered the cockpit behind him, entirely too clothed for the afternoon they'd been fixing to have.

"It's happening again," Lea said. "Another furor, I mean. It's hitting Newark, coming up from the south. A big one, from what our scouts reported. The commanders are sending everything we can to get it under control."

Crap.

"The new generators are almost ready," Rachel said, dropping into the copilot's seat next to Jarek.

"Nelken's reaching out to the Enochians himself about getting them deployed right now," Lea said. "In the meanwhile, they want you guys at the vanguard." She glanced uncertainly at Jarek. "Assuming you're ready for it."

"I can handle it," Jarek said.

As long as he tried to favor his left arm where possible and didn't happen to come across any upset Wookies. Or rakul.

Whether or not he was ready wasn't quite as concerning at the moment as the way this development was tickling at his *funny business* button, though.

"Why Newark?" he added. "Why hit anywhere but here or Camp Krogoth?"

Why, indeed, unless Gada was trying to draw them out?

"Command is already considering it could be a trap," Lea said, "but we still don't know if these events are even deliberate or what, and people are dying out there. Unless you know something we don't, we're moving out. All of us."

Jarek traded a questioning glance with Rachel. "That's an order?"

Lea looked uncomfortably between the two of them on the holo. "You two be careful. That's the order. There's a team headed your way for transport. I'll see you out there once we've finished rallying the troops here."

With that, she ended the call.

It was probably just that he was hearing through Fela's sensors now, but the muffled sounds of activity outside seemed to have doubled or tripled since their fun had first been interrupted by their confounded comms.

Jarek absentmindedly listened to the bustle, trying to mentally hash out every scenario in which a furor down south wouldn't simply be a trap to bait them out of their stronghold.

The options seemed rather limited.

"What is it?" Rachel asked.

He shook his head. "It's nothing."

"That doesn't look like your 'it's nothing' face."

Probably because it wasn't. But Lea was right. People were dying. Whatever else might be happening... Well, he was supremely short on any proof, and he didn't need to look too far to remember what had happened last time he'd thought he'd known best.

So instead of speculating, he stood and offered Rachel his hand. "Come on. We need to move."

Rachel watched him closely, making no move to take his hand. "You think you're seeing something they're not? And you're just gonna march into battle like a good little soldier anyway?"

Jarek shrugged. "It's nothing. And you heard the lady. Orders is orders."

With that, he strode back to the cabin to strap on his gun belt and his shiny new sword, trying to ignore the nagging feeling that'd settled somewhere in the space between his brain and his gut.

It was nothing, as he'd pointed out twice now. They'd keep the good people of Newark from hurting themselves and each other as best they could until the furor ended or the Enochians got there with the cloaking generators, then they'd regroup back at HQ and rally up for the real fight.

What could possibly go wrong? Aside from pretty much everything, that was.

Apparently, Rachel had her own share of skepticism about the whole thing.

"Can we get a bioscan or something to confirm that's still our Jarek in there, Al?" she asked from the cockpit.

"I was rather thinking this was cause for celebration, ma'am," Al said. "Jarek practicing caution and playing nice with others? I'll enjoy it while I can."

"Don't tempt me, Mr. Robot," Jarek said, strolling back to the hatch release. "Any eyes on that team, by the way?"

A firm pair of thumping knocks on the hull answered before Al could.

"Company, sir," he added anyway.

"Gee, thanks, buddy."

Jarek reached for the hatch release, glancing back to exchange a knowing look with Rachel only to find that she'd tensed in the cockpit doorway, looking less than amused.

"They sent Drogan," she said quietly to Jarek's questioning look.

Ah.

"You don't have to hold hands," Jarek said slowly. "But our people seeing him helping out there could probably do us all a lot of good right now."

She considered that, looking no less tense, but finally nodded her agreement.

Jarek slapped the hatch release, and the ramp descended with a mournful groan to reveal several skeptical faces gathering nearby, pointedly separate from Drogan, who'd been the one to knock.

Around them, the entirety of HQ was at full throttle—squads dashing here and there to link up with their respective transports while others, presumably those who weren't packing cloaking glyphs on their persons, hurried to carry gear and supplies where they were needed. From the looks of it, command was scrambling the better part of the entire Resistance army to get its ass down to Newark.

They must be dealing with a serious furor then, beyond what they'd seen before. The thought didn't ease the bad feeling in his stomach.

As hectic as their surroundings were, tense silence somehow managed to assert itself through the space between the parties gathered in and around Jarek's ship.

Drogan looked like he'd say something first, but, instead, he closed his mouth and strode pointedly up the ramp, past Jarek and Rachel without a word, and into the cockpit, where he probably realized he'd be most easily separated from the rest of the crew.

That, however, didn't make the Resistance troops look any happier at the thought of climbing aboard.

A loud click reverberated across the lot, and Nelken's gruff voice sounded from several speakers, informing the base that all readied forces were clear to depart. Jarek thought he detected a hint of rankle in Nelken's tone, probably largely centered on the man's current role as the injured commander who was to sit back at HQ while the others got to have their fun out in the field.

Around the lot, the already chaotic bustle took on a frantic edge at

Nelken's all-go order. The half dozen transport trucks already gathered by the newly-constructed gates sprang forward to action, several more rolling in to take their place.

Fun. Right.

Jarek looked down at the timid troops waiting at the base of the boarding ramp and waved them on. "C'mon. Let's get this party started, people." He jerked a thumb in Drogan's direction. "He'll keep his hands to himself."

"I'll make sure he does," Rachel added to the troops.

Jarek forced himself to keep a relaxed expression and not look around at the low warning growl that rumbled from the cockpit. At least it was quiet enough that he was probably the only one to hear it.

So maybe Rachel wasn't exactly all in on Operation Raknoth Friendship yet, but at least her comment encouraged a few of the troops to scowl and plod their way onto the ship with their dastardly ally.

The rest followed their example quickly enough.

"Right then," Jarek mumbled, slapping the hatch button. "Was that so hard?"

Not as hard as making his way up to the cockpit past the dozen troops now crammed into the cabin, apparently.

It didn't help that none of them seemed overly concerned with easing his passage, either because they were feeling ornery or because they were too preoccupied staring at the boarding ramp with a range of horrified expressions as it raised shut with the groans of a laboring ox.

"Shall I take us up, sir?" Al asked in Jarek's ear as he reached the head of the crowd and the ramp snapped shut with a few too many jarring clacks.

"Take it away, buddy. Nice and easy."

Soldiers grabbed high and low for handholds as Al lifted the ship and set them off as gently as could be reasonably expected.

Jarek posted himself just outside the cockpit and clamped an armored hand onto one of the grips above the door, not minding one bit when Rachel skirted closer to him and opted to use him for support.

What enjoyment he gained from Rachel's closeness, though, was quickly snuffed out by the heavy silence that hung in the air, practically oozing malcontent and distrust. All Resistance eyes were trained on the cockpit door, none of them relaxed.

This wasn't going to do.

"Stumpy?"

Drogan shot him an irritated scowl, his eyes lightly smoldering.

Jarek ignored the look and jerked his head toward the cabin-goers. "Is there anything you'd like to say to the class?"

"My participation was requested by their commanders," Drogan said without looking back into the cabin or even particularly bothering to raise his voice enough to be heard back there. "If they take qualm, perhaps they should reevaluate the process by which they elect their leaders, not to mention their desire to survive in the days to come."

Fantastic. Thank god he wasn't going to make this difficult or anything.

Jarek looked back to the cabin crew and waved his free hand, trying to keep the wince off his face. "See, guys? All good!"

Oddly enough, they seemed less than convinced.

A short, tense flight later, the only positive news was that no one had much energy left to worry about the single raknoth in their midst.

Jarek had expected the furor to be big.

Not this big.

There were hundreds of them, maybe even a thousand, just in the stretch he could see through the cockpit windshield as they flew low over the first arriving Resistance trucks. Wild-eyed men and women of all shapes and ages, in all states of dress and undress, and with all manners of armaments. The crowd had one thing in common, though.

They were clearly all out of their minds with rage.

Several bodies already lined the streets, plenty more joining them by the second as many of the crowd tore at each other with teeth, nails, fists, and the odd club, blade, or chair.

How were there this many?

Had Gada swept all of Newark, moving up from the south? Had he marched them in from all the homesteads in the surrounding areas?

The sight of a skeletal middle-aged woman burying a hatchet in a young man's throat reminded Jarek that the hows and whys weren't exactly important at the moment.

Al guided the ship down to an abandoned, crumbling lot so they could unload without clogging the traffic lane for the Resistance trucks approaching behind them. The soldiers in the cabin shifted uneasily, readying stun guns, batons, and even a few tranquilizers and riot shields.

Jarek couldn't really blame them for the nerves. Before the ramp had even completed its descent, it seemed like the frantic, slobbering attention of half the berserking civilians in immediate view had snapped their way.

It was creepy as shit.

They piled quickly out of the ship and got organized as the first batch of Resistance transport trucks rolled by and stopped to do the same.

Further down the road, the furor crowd eased out of its self-mutilation and kicked into a full-on charge.

Something was off. Something more than the thunder of hundreds of feet pounding the pavement and the disturbing growls and shrieks that filled the sickly noon air.

This wasn't like the furor Jarek had witnessed, or like what he'd heard from the accounts of the one they'd missed. He was sure of it, but it took him a long moment to realize why. Finally, though, he saw it.

While there was plenty of wild-eyed madness to go around from one individual to the next, as a whole, the mob's movements were too focused, too organized.

Now that Resistance forces were rolling in and giving the berserkers something to fixate on, what had first looked like total chaotic madness was suddenly resembling a deliberate, albeit insane, army.

Could Gada pull this kind of operation from afar?

From the immediate looks of it, yes. But Jarek didn't have much time to worry about it as the leaders of the maddened pack closed the gap between them.

They just had time to fall in with the Resistance troops who'd arrived in the first few trucks, and then the fighting began in proper, more ferocious than anything Jarek had ever witnessed.

It didn't matter that one side was doing its best to remain non-lethal. The other side more than made up for any lack of violent madness on their behalf.

Civilians crashed into the riot shield line with reckless abandon, swinging and kicking and biting at anything and everything within reach. Terrible cries split the air, many barely recognizable as human, so numerous that they almost seemed to combine into one long, unbroken scream straight from the throat of hell.

The dozen shield-bearers holding the street line shoulder-to-shoulder nearly crumpled under the first surge—would have collapsed completely before the mad tide if not for the strength of their allies filling in behind them and holding them fast in groups of threes, fours, and even more in a few places.

Jarek allowed himself a horrified glance at Rachel, who returned the look just as intently, too startled even to remember to be tense at Drogan's close proximity. Then the three of them waded into the madness together.

As they went, Jarek caught sight of more than a couple particularly troublesome berserkers taking sudden, inexplicable flights back into the raging ranks—Rachel's work, no doubt.

Halfway to the front line, Drogan abandoned their steady push and instead leapt high and long from the crowd. He touched down in front of the shield line and wasted no time shoving several frenzied civilians back from the exhausted Resistance troops, who seemed wholly uncertain as to whether this was a welcome change or not.

At the shield line, the chaos was at its peak. The curses and shouts of Resistance troops were nearly as numerous as the wild shrieks from the raging civilians. Those who weren't too busy actively holding the shield line were reaching in to apply close range stun weapons to any intruding limb or face they could reach. Further back, others were taking what limited shots they could find with ranged stun guns.

A voluminous roar from the right reminded the entire field exactly where Drogan had elected to make his stand.

"You gonna go make sure he doesn't kill anybody?" Rachel asked at Jarek's side, half-shouting to be heard over the cacophony.

Before he could answer, one of the troops nearby chucked a small something into the mad mob, and the street thundered with an enormous cracking sound.

The respondent cries from the crowd took on a momentary quality of startlement but clawed quickly back to blind rage with renewed fervor.

Jarek gave Rachel one last look with his own eyes and slid his faceplate closed with a careful thought.

Ready and almost willing, he slipped an arm between the two shield-bearers directly in front of him. "Excuse me, gents."

The glares they turned his way were almost as frightening as the writhing limbs and gnashing teeth just beyond.

Okay, so maybe those glares weren't even close on second thought. Especially not as they took on a strong *Hey, better him than us* quality and the two troops shifted just enough for Jarek to slide through without knocking them over.

"Agh!" Jarek cried as the first pair of teeth chomped down on his left arm hard enough that something—the teeth, probably—cracked.

He drew the chomper closer and planted a hard shove into the man's chest.

"Why'd it have to be zombies?" he growled to no one in particular.

Past his initial shock and surrounded by a seemingly infinite horde of insane berserkers, he quickly gave up on any hope of doing things neatly and allowed instinct and reflex to take over.

As sturdy as Fela's armor was, the real threat wasn't so much in the fists and teeth and occasional club whacks as it was in the very tangible threat of his being overwhelmed and swarmed down to the ground.

How many incoherently bloodlusting humans would it take to literally tear him limb from limb if that happened? He wasn't sure. But he was guessing the answer wasn't any higher than the number currently trying. If he went down, he'd find out in short order.

Without the Resistance line at his back, it probably would have been over in less than a minute. The poor raging bastards would have surrounded him and pressed in until no amount of strength and clever wriggling could have freed him. With the Resistance at his back, though, he only had his front to worry about. When he got in trouble on the sides, the troops sprang forward to deal with it— several times before he'd even realized he was in trouble.

And so he fought on in the thick of it, trusting in his overdeveloped battle reflexes and in the men and women at his back.

At some point, Alaric's voice in his earpiece informed him that the commander had arrived with reinforcements, but that hardly seemed to matter to Jarek in the moment, stuck as he was in the heart of the shit.

Time ceased to have ready meaning as he sank deeper into the violent rhythm of the fight. All he knew was that they were holding, and that was all he had time to know.

At least until a crimson-eyed Drogan bumped into his side and growled, "We have been deceived."

Jarek wrenched a scraggly-bearded madman from his feet and used him like a long, flailing bowling ball on the scrabbling berserkers behind. "What are you talking ab—"

"This is not Kul'Gada's doing."

Not Gada? But then—

"My kin," Drogan hissed, batting aside a pair of burly berserkers. "We have been betrayed."

"Jarek!" came Rachel's voice from somewhere behind.

If there was a follow-up *we have a problem*, he didn't hear it as he dodged a berserker's grab and shoved him back into the encroaching crowd.

What he did hear, though, as he took advantage of Drogan's momentary cover and focused his attention back Rachel's way, was a well-tuned rumble he would've recognized anywhere. It was the engine of the truck that had saved his life not far from this very street nine years ago, on a cold Newark night.

Pryce's truck.

"They're coming out of it!" someone cried.

And, true to their word, while many of the crowd were still clawing and biting their way toward anything and everything, others were beginning to look around at their fellow berserkers in varying states of confusion and horror.

"It's working!" another soldier cried down the line.

A girl that couldn't have been older than twenty lunged for Jarek, eyes wide. He caught her by the shoulders, preparing to counter her struggling and launch her back into the crowd. Only she didn't struggle—just sagged in his arms and looked up at him with a whimper and the most piteous expression he'd ever seen.

Around them, the number of civilians coming to similar awakenings seemed to be growing. At a glance, Jarek could glimpse Pryce's truck inching up into the Resistance ranks on the curb, Pryce at the wheel, Alton in the passenger seat. Faint tendrils of steam drifted up from the truck's hood, as if the air around it was abnormally cold.

One of the cloaking generators? It had to be.

They must've finished the new batch and sent Pryce straight over.

Jarek fought the tired voice whispering it was okay to at least partially unclench. Something was still wrong.

As if in response to the thought, the dark purplish shape of the Enochians' ship rushed past in the distance, bound northeast from the direction of Pryce's shop.

Where were they headed in such a hurry? And when there were clearly problems closer to the home front to deal with?

Most of the Resistance ranks didn't seem to have noticed, but Jarek couldn't shake it. The cheers were beginning to spread, a twisted contrast to the sinking feeling in Jarek's gut. Everyone seemed to think the day was won.

Everyone except Rachel and Drogan.

The two of them were looking around in alarm, scanning through the subdued crowd of civilians and across the nearby rooftops. Rachel shook her head as if in response to a question no one seemed to have actually spoken out loud.

Jarek was about to ask Drogan what gave when his earpiece crackled to life, followed by Nelken's grave tone.

"Attention, all Resistance forces. The rakul known as Kul'Gada has been sighted marching on Central Park with at least a thousand men at his back. I repeat, our New York allies are under imminent attack. Commander Weston will determine what forces are required to stabilize the situation in Newark and send what remains to aid Commander Daniels at the Central Park defenses. God speed, Resistance. Our planet is depending—"

"They come!" Drogan thundered beside Jarek.

For a second, Jarek thought he was referring to Nelken's broadcast.

Then, somewhere behind, Rachel shouted, "Get those shields back up! The cloak's not gonna hold once they're inside!"

Ragged civilians and weary Resistance soldiers all looked at one another uncertainly until Alaric barked, "You heard the lady! Form up!"

Jarek's mind was still reeling to catch up with all the rapid fire information and connect the dots on who the hell *they* were when he caught sight of the lone figure dropping from a ruined apartment rooftop toward Pryce's truck below.

There was a horrible moment of helpless waiting. Then it smashed into the bed of Pryce's truck with the kind of destructive effect that could only mean one thing.

Raknoth.

The new arrival's eyes came alive with crimson fire even as Pryce and Alton scrambled to evacuate the truck cab.

Not fast enough.

The raknoth hopped out of the bed holding a cylindrical box under one arm and caught Pryce's door halfway through Pryce opening it. The raknoth shoved the door shut hard enough to dent it inward.

Jarek gathered himself and leapt over the Resistance line.

Too late. He was too late.

It all seemed to unfold in slow motion as he sailed through the air toward the truck. Alton leapt out of the far side of the truck just as the raknoth got a hand underneath the cab and flipped the entire vehicle Alton's way. Alton, too surprised or off balance to act, went down under the rolling heap of metal.

Jarek landed just in time to catch one last glimpse of Pryce's wide-eyed face as the truck's rotation carried him out of sight with a string of violent, metallic crunching.

"Pryce!"

In front of Jarek, the enemy raknoth raised the cylinder overhead. The cloaking generator, he realized—just a split second before the raknoth slammed the device to the pavement and it came apart in an explosion of bent metal and scattered components.

As the cloak shattered, a roar sounded from somewhere in the line of buildings behind, followed by another further up the street. And another. And another.

His goal accomplished, the raknoth who'd smashed the cloaking generator gathered himself and leapt to the rooftop across the street, followed by a stream of Resistance gun fire.

It was too late.

Fiery red eyes appeared on a rooftop here, in a dirty window there, and all around them, the cries of human madness ripped through the streets once more, doubled or even tripled in volume, and seeming to come from all directions at once.

"This was never Gada," came Rachel's voice beside him.

Jarek tore his eyes away from the enemy raknoth gathering on the perimeter to meet her grave gaze.

Drogan slammed down to the pavement beside them. "No. It

appears the Kul only wanted his faithful raknoth to draw us out so that he might deconstruct our forces from two sides at once."

Jarek drew his sword, body swirling from head to toe with combat nerves and dread. By chance, he caught Alaric's eye for just a second across the ranks.

Screwed. He didn't need to see it in the commander's eyes to know that's what they were.

Surrounded. Cut off from HQ and everywhere else as Gada marched to destroy their only allies without their interference.

Jarek didn't have time to squeeze a curse from his stunned mind before, with an awful chorus of growls, roars, and shrieks, an army of traitorous raknoth and desperately violent civilians closed in on them from all sides.

CHAPTER TWENTY-THREE

Rachel allowed herself one last self-directed curse and then gathered her will, preparing to fight on. She should have caught it sooner, could have warned the Resistance that there seemed to be a curious lack of the signature feel of the messengers present here.

It was clear as the stark raving lunacy in the eyes of the approaching horde now, but somehow she'd failed to notice it before —failed to recognize the slightly more tangible net of a single mind, or several minds, rather, casting their will out to the crowd of civilians before them.

If only she'd been paying proper attention. If only she hadn't been so busy trying to exude calm will and keep an eye on Jarek and Drogan.

"Who the hell are they?" she sent toward the raknoth, who'd already moved to deal with a stream of berserkers flooding in from a side alley.

"Zar'Taga and his clan," Drogan's voice growled at the edge of her mind.

"I don't suppose you have any brilliant idea for stopping them?"

Drogan shoved aside the screaming madman who was currently

attempting to strangle him and pointed toward a raknoth perched on a nearby rooftop, surveying the scene below. His green hide was tinged with streaks of gray.

"Help me remove Zar'Taga's head," Drogan sent.

She didn't bother to send the *gladly* that pulsed through her mind, just checked her six and opened a comm line with Jarek.

"We've got a target," she said before he could drop whatever nugget was no doubt on the edge of his tongue.

"Targets are good," came his reply. He face-palmed the berserker rushing his way and held the woman at bay as he looked back at Rachel. "Where?"

She pointed. "Salt and Pepper up there. That's Taga. Drogan says off with his head."

"Right, then." Jarek kicked his frothing attacker away, clotheslined another, and pushed his way over to Alaric to point out their new objective.

At a startling growl from behind, Rachel spun to confront a fast-approaching berserker. He caught onto her staff, a trace of uncertainty creeping into his eyes—probably thanks to the fact that he'd entered her own little cloaking field.

"What?" he mumbled. "What the…"

He seemed to be regaining control. But it wouldn't last, not once they parted. So she muttered a quick sorry, slapped a hand to the side of his head, and telepathically pushed him into unconsciousness.

When he was slumped safely against the adjacent brick wall, Rachel turned back and saw Alaric pointing and barking orders. The Resistance soldiers around him sprang to the task of clearing a path to the nearest building across the street.

Jarek looked back at her, and his voice crackled in her earpiece. "Up we go?"

Rachel eyed the rooftop in question. "Not sure I have the legs for that jump."

"I've got faith, Goldilocks. You coming, Stumpy?"

Drogan wasn't on the comm line, but he appeared to hear Jarek all the same. He gave a curt nod and started pressing his way over.

Rachel plotted a course through the frenzied crowd, gathered a hefty punch of energy, and prepared to do the same.

She'd barely made it five steps when the sound of a young, frightened cry froze her solid.

She whipped around, scanning with both eyes and mind and—

There. A kid no more than nine or ten was scrambling back in a crab walk, a look of terror etched across her face. A pack of six mindless berserkers raced after her, seemingly captivated by the small, helpless life flailing before them.

Rachel leveled her staff and caught half of the girl's pursuers with a wide telekinetic blast. She was reaching through the channeling fatigue and the urgent clamoring in her head to form another blast when something slammed into her from behind.

She hit the ground hard, her staff pinned beneath her, and gasped for air only to find the unforgiving pavement had shocked her diaphragm into inaction.

Through the shuffling sea of legs and bodies, she caught a glimpse of the girl's light blond hair and delicate frame. The bastards were closing in on her.

Rachel reached for the energy, ignoring who- or what-the-hell-ever was pulling itself up her back, reaching for her vulnerable throat.

It didn't matter. Her cloak might stop her attacker. The girl. The girl was all that mattered right then. She had to stop them, had to help her.

Too late, she realized like a knife in the chest as she reached out to telekinetically yank the girl out of harm's way and the leading berserker raised his club. She was too late.

Then Alton Parker sprang in and plowed the two nearest berserkers aside. The third, he swatted away almost as an afterthought, then he scooped up the girl and leapt back toward the overturned truck, where he handed her trembling form to a battered but steady-looking Pryce. And not a moment too soon.

The instant after Alton had handed over the girl and stepped back to the battle, a green-hided raknoth caught him in a tackle that drove both of them clean through the wall of the adjacent apartment building.

Relief for the girl. Surprisingly genuine worry for Alton. Rachel barely had time for a flicker of each before a strong arm slipped around her throat and yanked.

She coughed and struggled wildly, panic gripping her chest. He clamped a rough hand over her face, nails digging painfully in.

Couldn't focus. Couldn't breathe. Couldn't…

The mass on her back gave a violent jerk, and then it was shifting, rolling off her, leaving her mercifully free to gasp for air and scramble to her feet.

"You okay?" someone asked.

A touch on her shoulder nearly made her jump and swing her staff.

The berserker who'd had her throat flailed weakly on the pavement. The young Resistance soldier who'd clubbed him off her back was watching her with uncertainty in his eyes.

Rachel looked around, the world coming back into some manner of reason—minus the utter chaos all around them, of course. She spotted Pryce beside his overturned truck, posted defensively in front of the cowering girl, hefting a heavy-duty stun rod, and turned back to the waiting soldier.

"I'm… I'm good. Thanks for the hand."

He looked a little confused by her words, almost as if he wasn't quite sure it had actually been him who'd helped her and not the other way around.

She didn't have time to dwell on it as she remembered what she'd been doing before the scream. That was when she caught sight of Jarek on the rooftop above.

He was moving fast, charging along from one rooftop to the next, bound straight for green-gray Zar'Taga and—

Shit.

He was also about to be outnumbered—two of Taga's clan racing to intersect Jarek before he could reach their Zar.

Rachel's mind was doing its own racing trying to figure how to get up there in time to help when she noticed Drogan rising to the occasion. Literally.

The raknoth leapt from the chaos below and crested the rooftop just in time to snag Jarek's lead pursuer by the collar and trip the other with a well-timed kick. The rear raknoth stumbled into his partner, and, with a violent jerk, Drogan hurled the pair of them to the street below.

Rachel paid little attention to their furious roars and started forward to get in range to help as Jarek closed on Zar'Taga.

It was over before she could.

Jarek was maybe twenty feet from concluding his headlong charge at Taga when he tripped. Rachel's stomach lurched with him as his hands shot wide for balance, his sword angled uselessly toward the ground, his stutter-step recovery too little, too late.

Taga struck like a cunning viper, lunging for Jarek at the exact moment he was planting his weight, anchoring himself like a bright red bullseye in his attempt to regain control.

Except Jarek didn't plant his weight. He extended his rear leg and launched into a rolling dive, skirting just clear of Taga's claws, out of Rachel's sight.

And leaving the way clear for a dive-bombing Drogan.

Rachel hadn't noticed the raknoth leap from where he'd detoured Jarek's pursuers. Apparently, neither had Zar'Taga.

Drogan plummeted at Taga like a two-footed wrecking ball.

It didn't appear to make physical sense, the way Drogan drew to a sudden, smacking halt when they met, each raknoth so tremendously strong that Drogan simply froze on Taga's raised arms as if they were two rigid metal statues rather than living bodies. Rachel was half-surprised the impact didn't collapse the roof in.

Zar'Taga roared at Drogan, a terrible, voluminous roar that silenced half the battlefield below as everyone looked to see what manner of creature was capable of producing such a sound.

So it was that hundreds were watching as Drogan dismounted with a tight flip and Jarek appeared on Taga's flank.

Somewhere, a raknoth shrieked what might've been a warning.

Taga whirled.

Jarek struck.

A quick swipe and a flash of azure, and then Taga's body was falling limply to the rooftop, and Drogan was catching the raknoth's toppling head and thrusting it skyward with a roar nearly as mighty as Taga's had been.

The remaining sounds of fighting dimmed with surprising suddenness as the fallen Zar's clan turned their collective attention to Drogan's dominant display and realized what had happened.

"I think we have their attention," came Jarek's quiet voice in Rachel's earpiece. Above, he was looking down on the crowd, sword rested over his shoulder. "Think you can catch my armored ass? I always wanted to make a dramatic entrance."

Rachel ran through a rough estimate as she closed within a more manageable range to his rooftop perch. Catching a man from that high would be unpleasant. Add the exo, and she was looking at shaky knees at the very least. But this standstill was infinitely preferable to the madness that had preceded it, and she assumed Jarek had a plan for prolonging it—maybe even putting a stop to the fight altogether.

Or she wanted to assume, at least.

"I'll do you one better," she said quietly, drawing to a halt roughly below him.

"That's my Goldilocks."

And with that, Jarek hopped off the four story rooftop as casually as if he were merely skipping a last step.

Rachel braced herself and focused.

It wasn't the easiest of conversions to hold intact in one's mind, especially not with Jarek's trust—not to mention his plummeting physical bulk—looming over her, but she held tight and, in the moment before he touched down, opened the channel.

FROM WHAT VALUABLE lessons he'd learned from his extensive cinematic studies over the years, Jarek was relatively certain frightened cries were not to be found on the features list of dramatic entrances, yet that's nearly what escaped him as the hard pavement raced up to meet him without any noticeable hesitation.

Part of him couldn't help but tense in preparation to try to salvage the fall—not to mention his femurs and other assorted, currently intact pieces—with a haphazard roll.

He refrained, trusting in Rachel, who was watching him just below with a deeply furrowed brow.

Mercifully, in the final second of the fall, he felt it—the telekinetic support harness that was simply there one moment and yanking up on his tightly clenched, armored backside like giant air brakes the next.

Of notable impressiveness was the way he was able to land beside Rachel from the four story drop with barely a bend to his knees. Of exceptional badassery was the sonorous boom that split the air around them as he did so, easily on par with a good thunderclap.

Rachel had promised one better than simply catching him, and she'd delivered.

A second later, Drogan completed the theatrics when he slammed down beside them with a sound of pulverized pavement Jarek felt through his own feet and knees. The raknoth was still holding Taga's head.

Dramatic entrance achieved, then.

Jarek stood slowly, brandished his deactivated sword through a pair of tight arcs, and strapped it to his back, looking around at the silent armies of Resistance troops and disturbingly still civilians that surrounded them. The sprawling crowd seemed caught between breaths, the Resistance troops watching them intently, waiting to see what they'd do, and the all-too-recently violent civilians simply gazing distantly, like robots awaiting further direction from their remaining raknoth overlords, who mostly lurked on the high ground, watching Drogan, Rachel, and Jarek with burning red eyes.

"Right then..." Jarek said, speaking loudly enough to be heard for some distance in the tense silence gripping the street. "Now, normally, this would be the part where I'd be tempted to ask why we can't all just get along here."

Judging from the immediate rustles and the outpouring of verbal discontent, that idea was about as popular as scrotum-kick Sundays on both sides.

"But!" Jarek cried, employing Fela's speakers to boost his voice to loudspeaker status. He raised his hands for peace in the momentary lull in outraged noises. "*But,* I think it's safe to say that's abso-fucking-lutely out of the picture for this crowd right now."

"Goddamn right it is!" one of the Resistance women shouted, to several hearty agreements and hell yeahs.

Jarek hooked a thumb in their direction, mind searching frantically for the right words. "Right. So the question I'll ask you all instead is…"

Is what?

The three raknoth he could see in the crowd shifted impatiently, red eyes hungry. To his left, several Resistance troops made similar movements.

This armistice would break at any moment.

Christ, what had he been thinking, throwing himself down between two armies, expecting to just talk them all out of a crisis? When had he ever talked anyone out of anything?

He glanced back and found Alaric watching him with an unreadable expression, probably wondering the same damn thing. Nevertheless, the wiry commander cocked his head and gave a roll of his fingers, suggesting Jarek figure it out all the same—and sooner than later.

So Jarek raised his hands to the crowd in a querying gesture and went with the question in his mind.

"Do you *all* wanna die? Or just most of you?"

Growls and mutters from left and right promptly indicated that the only person the crowd might unanimously wish death for at the moment was Jarek himself.

Beside him, Drogan directed a low but impressive growl at his kin that sounded more or less like raknoth speak for *shut the hell up*.

"We all know what's coming after Kul'Gada," Jarek called. "And even if we survive today, we know what's in store for us when they get here, whether you're mortal or not." He turned more directly toward the nearest enemy raknoth and pointed at Taga's severed head, still hanging from Drogan's hand. "Whatever this guy told you, I'm betting most of you realize that somewhere deep down in your scaly little hearts."

For a long moment, silence prevailed.

Then the raknoth Jarek had addressed snarled and stepped forward, looking around at his kin. "Cursed void, are any of you truly listening to a human where the masters are concer—"

Taga's severed head struck the speaker square in the temple. He shook his head and looked down at the morbid missile in shock, then rounded back toward them with a furious roar.

Drogan's counter roar was louder and, if Jarek's judgment was reliable, several notches higher on the pants-wetting scale.

"These two humans have survived direct combat with one of the Kul," Drogan called. "As have I. And I tell you all now, regardless of what Kul'Gada has promised, the masters will not forgive our deception. They will not stop until every sentient life on this planet has been obliterated."

The raknoth looked at each other uncertainly. Considering?

"They're only coming here because of you!"

The shout came from the Resistance ranks, a sharp stomp to the inkling of hope that had teased at Jarek's chest. Several more followed it, emboldened by their fellow soldier's courage.

"You brought this shit to our doorstep!"

"—ruined our planet!"

"—killed my family!"

"Why the fuck should we trust you?"

It spread like a flash fire of malicious will, weapon grips and trigger fingers tightening throughout the Resistance ranks, soldiers shifting for a fight, some taking aim.

Across from them, raknoth growls rumbled through the street, and several of the enthralled civilians were tensing out of their vacant stupors, baring teeth and wild eyes.

"Hey!" Jarek called, raising hands for order.

But no one was listening now. The violence was back in the air, simmering, ready to boil over. Jarek looked to Alaric in desperation.

The commander met his gaze, the slightest arch creeping over Alaric's brow, as if to say, *Well? What's next, genius?*

Jarek knew better than to think this was some kind of game to the Resistance commander. There was only so far Alaric could yank the crowd sentiment with his authority. His hands were tied, or more tied than Jarek's at least.

We need leaders, Alaric had said on that night in medical. *Ones who can inspire by example, who look before they leap and actually give half a rat's ass about the men and women fighting beside them.*

So maybe looking before he leapt wasn't Jarek's strong suit. That was clear enough. And maybe he didn't know any of these men and women well enough to give that rat's ass about them in any meaningful way beyond a general desire to see them make it through this mess.

But he *could* be an example—could show them just how desperately they were already clinging to the fringes of survival, standing here fighting amongst themselves while Gada marched to destroy their only real allies.

"Fine," Jarek said, more to himself than anyone else.

He glanced between the two groups, a light stone's throw from erupting back into full-on battle. He waited to recognize his harebrained inspiration for the blatantly obvious insanity it was.

But there was nothing else. No more time.

"Fine!"

Jarek yelled the word this time, loud enough to buy a moment's attention.

Now or never.

They could accept that they were all in this together, lower their weapons, and start marching for the real enemy side-by-side, or they could all die—maybe not today, but soon. Those were the only options.

Together, they had a fighting chance.

Fighting amongst themselves, they were already dead.

So, with a careful thought, he sent Fela the command to convince them all the only way he could think to.

"Sir…" Al said quietly, no doubt sensing his intention.

He said nothing, only held the command in mind.

And with a series of pops, clicks, and whirs, Fela snapped open, and Jarek stepped out onto the battlefield, butt-ass naked.

Judging by the sea of surprised murmurs and poorly covered laughs rippling through the Resistance army, and the single cry of, "What the fuck, dude?" that was one way to hold a crowd's attention. Even some of the raknoth looked surprised, and a couple amused.

Jarek's idea of keeping his hands clutched protectively over his manhood lasted all of two seconds before it struck him that any show of humility or decency was probably well beyond concern at that point. So he raised his hands high and bared it all for anyone who cared to look.

"There you go!" he cried. "No more suit." He gestured to the Resistance. "You wanna shoot my stupid ass?" Then to the raknoth. "You wanna tear my throat out and drink the blood of this presumptuous raknoth killer?"

He thrust his hands and face skyward. "DO IT, MOTHER-FUCKERS!"

It took all of his willpower to stand there like that, eyes closed, utterly vulnerable and unable to see any of the thousand potential threats coming. Some corner of his mind pointed out that Fela was still nearby and that Rachel would probably protect him if anyone took him up on his generous offer, but neither of those things really offset the feeling of dangling loose right between two pissed off armies.

When he tilted his head back down and allowed himself to look again, though, they were watching him, some curious, some clearly of the mind that he'd lost every iota of sanity he'd ever been graced with.

He nodded, feeding on their disbelief, willing them to see his conviction. "That's right! Put me out of my misery now, because I'm willing to bet my life on the fact that if we don't get our shit together and get up to Camp Krogoth right now, we're all gonna be dead within the week anyway."

The raknoth watched in silent stillness, whatever surprise and amusement had been on their reptilian features fading to neutral thoughtfulness.

On the other side, Jarek saw some of that thoughtfulness mirrored in the Resistance ranks, albeit with a good deal more skepticism.

"How are we ever supposed to trust them after this shit?" someone finally called from the Resistance line. "After everything they've done?"

That was the question, wasn't it?

He should've taken heart that, for the first time in the tense stand-still, someone at least seemed to be asking it with a genuine tone rather than a rhetorical one—that clearly neither side truly wanted this fight.

But what answer could he possibly give?

If survival wasn't enough, what else was there?

If he'd known the answer to that question, he and Rachel wouldn't have ended up in rough waters in the first place.

But apparently that was Rachel's cue, because, before Jarek could even try to keep the momentum going, she was standing there next to his pasty nakedness, and some of those expectant eyes were starting to shift from him to her.

"We'll trust them by remembering the actions of their people aren't always their own," she called.

The sound of crumbling brick caught the assembly's attention. Jarek turned to see Alton Parker hop down to the street from a large hole in the wall of a nearby building, an odd limp in his step and a wary look in his eyes as he glanced at the equally battered raknoth who emerged beside him.

The minute nod Alton gave Rachel was odd enough, but Jarek was shocked when she solemnly returned the gesture.

Apparently he'd missed something between the two of them.

"We'll trust them by understanding that none of this violence was bred in a vacuum," Rachel continued. "That we humans took our shots too before all of this, before the Catastrophe."

The truth about the blood curse the humans had unleashed on the raknoth—or at least an approximate version of it—had circulated rapidly through HQ following the battle with Zar'Golga's forces weeks ago but had been met by heavy skepticism by most.

For that reason, Jarek wasn't overly surprised when calls of *bullshit* and *raknoth lies* lit the crowded street.

"Why should we believe any of that blood virus crap?" someone shouted from near the front of the line—Rodgers, Jarek realized with a sinking stomach as he followed the voice.

Only it wasn't open scorn on the Resistance fighter's bulldog face, as Jarek had expected, but uncertainty—his eyes flicking back and forth between Rachel and Jarek as if now searching for some reason not to believe them.

That look seemed to be spreading through the crowd. And, judging from the tension on Rachel's face, she was preparing herself to give them their reason.

"Because it was my mom who made that virus," she finally called.

Anyone who heard the waver in her voice would have had a hard time believing it to be a lie. Jarek had the impression she felt nearly as naked in that moment as he actually was.

She visibly forced down a swallow before continuing.

"She was trying to do a good thing for the world. Was trying to save us all. But she was wrong. And the raknoth who decided to pull the trigger on Earth fifteen years ago were sure as hell wrong too. Mistakes were made. Big mistakes. On both sides. And we can all keep blaming each other and holding onto this negative shit until the rakul are picking our bones. Or we can suck it up and remember that we're all in this together, whether we like it or not."

She shook her head, catching her breath as the crowd watched, waiting, hanging on her words with uncertain looks.

"I won't tell anyone they should forget the past. I know I sure as hell won't. But if you don't wanna die right alongside everyone you know and love, we need to stop letting that past rule our lives. We can't change it. But we can try to do better."

For a long while, the street was quiet but for the scuffs and rustles of the Resistance ranks shifting and exchanging questioning looks and whispered comments.

The uncloaked civilian army stood as still and vigilant as the red-eyed statues of their raknoth commanders.

Jarek barely dared to breathe for fear of ruining what tenuous peace seemed to be fighting its way to life between them. He didn't even want to hope at this point.

Then the closest of the vacant civilians began to stir and look around in concerned disorientation. It started slowly, but soon enough, hundreds were coming to their senses, and several of the raknoth were shifting from their scaly battle modes back to their human appearance, red eyes dimming.

"Despite our duty to obey," called the raknoth Drogan had nailed with the late Zar's severed head. "There are several among us who did not agree with Zar'Taga's decision to trust Kul'Gada. If you truly speak in earnest, we will agree to end this conflict and depart for Zar'Krogoth's battlements as your allies in this fight."

Maybe the raknoth had already held their own telepathic council, but if any of them felt otherwise, they didn't say it.

The bigger question was whether the men and women at Jarek's back would choose to accept their word—or their presence as allies, for that matter. The spreading sounds of the civilians' pained awakenings didn't exactly help matters.

But then Alaric strode out to join Rachel, Jarek, and Drogan in the small clearing that had formed around them.

"We agree to cease hostilities," he called. "Once these people are free from your influence, with the guarantee they'll stay that way, we'll move north to join the fight."

The raknoth who appeared to have asserted himself as clan leader looked a shade irritated by Alaric's insistence on how they treat their human puppets, but the request seemed to have already been granted anyway, as witnessed by the growing activity of the men, women, and children coming to, checking on one another, being physically ill, and otherwise reacting to the scene in which they found themselves.

Apparently deeming Alaric's words sufficient, the new clan leader tilted his head and turned to bound off to the south, his eight kin leapfrogging after him.

The Resistance army watched them go, mercifully silent of any challenge to Alaric's decision, then they set to lending what aid they could to the recovering civilians.

It was only then that Jarek's exhausted mind caught up enough to remember he could probably return to his armor.

Rachel's tired eyes on his pushed the thought to the side of his mind before he could work up the will to move, though.

"That was a hell of a speech, Goldilocks," he said quietly. "And here I was thinking *naked guy between two armies* couldn't be beat."

Rachel gave him a wink, looking both exhausted and yet somehow lighter than she'd ever been. "Maybe you just need a bigger stick, sweetheart."

And then she surprised them both and slapped his pale white ass.

He stared at her, not quite understanding the volume of feelings pouring through him in that moment, standing there stark nude, staring at this beautiful woman in the aftermath of the slaughter they'd so narrowly avoided—that he and Rachel had somehow put a stop to.

The words tumbled out all on their own.

"God, I think I love you."

He might as well have plugged her lungs to a vacuum.

Her mouth worked soundlessly for a few beats, until the floundering apparently grew too much to bear and she dropped her gaze—only to end up staring directly at the exposed stick in question.

She snapped her eyes back up to his face, cheeks reddening, but Alaric's voice interrupted them before she could say anything.

"I think you'd better put that thing away before you blind someone."

The commander drew up beside them with some kind of paradox etched across his face, stern yet amused.

Jarek threw a stiff salute, which only left him more exposed and added *exasperated* to the mural of Alaric's expression, then he stepped into Fela's waiting boots.

"Say no more. I'm not nearly Irish enough for this shit anyway." Once he was safely back in his armor, he glanced surreptitiously around and waved a finger between them. "And just for the record, angry armies on either side does not a turgid Jarek make."

Rachel closed her eyes, trying to suppress a laugh, or maybe a shudder.

Alaric just frowned. "I'm sure the boys and girls'll all be happy to hear that, son. But in the meanwhile, I think we'd better focus on hurrying our asses north."

Jarek gave a sober nod, the reminder of the fight to come—of facing down Gada once more—evaporating what good humor their momentary victory had conjured up.

As if in response to his emotional shift, the street dimmed around them, a cloud passing in front of the sun. He looked up just in time to see a raknoth ship—presumably that of the late Taga's clan—rocket by overhead, bound northeast toward Central Park.

Further in the distance, along the same trajectory, several dark storm clouds were rolling along toward Camp Krogoth with the promise of shady gloom and terrible fighting conditions.

Wonderful.

"I think," Alaric said, frowning at the distant storm clouds himself, "you'd better get your ship in here and get as many as you can carry to Krogoth's line."

Jarek gave a casual two-fingered salute. "Sir, yes sir. You heard the man, Al."

Alaric started to turn away from them but doubled back and added, in a low voice, "Good work, by the way. Both of you."

A small grin pulled at Jarek's mouth. "Probably not exactly what you had in mind when you gave me that leadership talk, huh?"

Alaric's eyebrows twitched upward by a few hairs. "You don't know where I've been, son. Still, I'm not sure we would've survived if and when Taga's clan decided to join in. You saved a lot of lives." He cocked his head. "For now at least. And you too, Al'Drogan. Your assistance is appreciated."

Behind them, Drogan gave a slight shrug, watching for Jarek's approaching ship, clearly impatient to be moving.

Alaric glanced up as the ship crested into view then clapped his hands to Rachel's and Jarek's shoulders. "Now get moving. We'll be right behind you."

CHAPTER TWENTY-FOUR

"Two thousand," Jarek said slowly, turning the word over in his mind. "Two thousand trained, armed men, marching to help destroy humanity." He gave his head a sharp shake, jolting himself out of the thought, and looked back at Drogan, who stood at attention next to Alton in the cockpit with a clawed finger to his earpiece. "Where the hell did Gada find a real army?"

"Ashida," Rachel said before Drogan or Alton could answer. "Bastard's got an army, and if anyone was gonna turn on us, it was definitely that tea-sipping asshole."

Drogan lowered his finger from his earpiece and nodded. "Rachel Cross is correct. And Nan'Ashida's treachery is not necessarily the worst of the news."

Jarek glanced at the five Resistance troops crammed into the cockpit with them. Behind them, the ship's cabin was packed to bursting with more soldiers, most of them listening intently to find out just how thick of shit they were about to fly into.

He wasn't sure they could all handle worse news at the moment, but now still seemed better than once the bullets were flying.

"What's worse than a freaking army, Stumpy?"

He was pretty sure he already knew, but somehow it didn't soften the blow when Drogan said it.

"Zar'Taga's clan was not the only one to be swayed by Kul'Gada's recruitment efforts."

Shit.

He opened his mouth to ask how many enemy raknoth they were about to be dealing with, but the look Alton shot him made him think better of it.

Better now than later for the nature of the danger they faced, maybe, but as for the exact details…

Maybe now wasn't the time to delve into exactly how many raknoth were still trying to kill them after they'd just narrowly convinced Team Resistance to fly into battle beside a couple dozen raknoth.

It was the damnedest thing—a bunch of humans and raknoth trying to defend themselves against the big bad Kul, and what did they have to contend with? Freaking humans and freaking raknoth—not to mention the giant swords-for-claws monstrosity that would no doubt be coming for them on the battlefield.

Of course, it wasn't like the humans on Team Apocalypse 2.0 were exactly marching to the beat of their own drum out there. Not much they could do about being telepathically enslaved. The enemy raknoth would be operating on a much weaker excuse, namely fear, but that hardly mattered now.

Al would get them there, they'd charge down that ramp, and they'd fight until they'd won or until they couldn't. Simple as that.

Simple. But not even close to easy from the looks and sounds of it.

Through the viewport, the Hudson was drawing into view, and already he could see the smoky haze of combat permeating the distant air above Central Park. He almost thought he could smell the gunpowder too, but that was impossible, just a phantom sensation as his mind placed what he was seeing into context.

"Let's have a better look, Al," he said quietly.

Al adjusted their flight, gently gaining altitude as they drew close enough for Jarek to conduct a rudimentary visual survey.

He almost wished he hadn't.

Gada's forces were sizable, to say the least. An impressively large convoy of trucks, other land vehicles, and even a few ships was flooding into the city from the north, much of the traffic continuing on straight for the center of the line in Central Park and plenty more branching out east and west to test the flanks of the New York defenders.

Suddenly it made sense why Kul'Gada had been lying low for the past week. Setting whatever time he'd spent bending his fearful raknoth subjects back to his will aside, if those were Ashida's forces down there, finding the ships to carry them all over from Africa by air and ocean would've been no small feat. Even if the raknoth had had them on standby, it would have taken days. But now here they were, marching on the wrong side.

And, without a doubt, Gada was down there with them.

And, as an added bonus, the clouds that were still rolling in at a good clip from the west seemed to be growing darker and surlier by the minute.

"Well if that's not a bad omen," Jarek muttered.

Rachel leaned past him and frowned at the incoming clouds. "What, you scared it's gonna rain on our little parade?"

He studied her weary expression. "I think you may be spending too much time around me, Goldilocks."

"Touching down next to Commander Daniels' position in thirty seconds," Al announced to the cabin. "And, sir, I don't like the way those men down there are—"

The first shot pinged off of the underside of the ship.

"—looking at us," Al finished. "Hold on, everyone."

The ship dropped abruptly, dipping between the ruined buildings and leveling out maybe ten feet above street level, low enough to avoid taking much more fire as they flew in behind the central battlements.

Jarek went through the routine motions of checking his pistols and confirming his new Whacker was still strapped to his back.

Behind him, the clicks and clacks of magazines and actions being double-checked filled the ship.

He turned to Rachel, who'd already concluded checking her batteries and bullet catcher and now stood with her staff planted and gripped in both hands.

"You ready for this?" he asked.

She looked pointedly at his shoulder. "Are you?"

Drogan glanced over then as if he'd been wondering the same thing.

Jarek shot the raknoth a thumbs up and patted the shoulder in question, which, while still burning from their earlier engagement, had handled the fighting surprisingly well so far. "She'll hold together."

That was sufficient for Drogan.

Rachel seemed less convinced.

The look between them deepened, her expression mirroring all the fear and concern he felt wriggling through his own gut. There was something he needed to say, he was sure of it, but for the life of him, he couldn't seem to find the right words to start.

Then the ship rocked beneath their feet as Al set her down, boarding ramp already beginning its mournful descent, and the time for words was past.

The sounds of battle poured into the ship the instant the rear hatch cracked open—sharp, aggressive, and impressively expansive. The soldiers in the back of the cabin wasted no time in thundering down the ramp, followed promptly by those closer to the cockpit.

Jarek grabbed Rachel's wrist and held her back for a moment as their company left the cockpit.

Drogan, already shifting back to full scaly battle mode, huffed at them and gave a faintly disgusted shake of his head before stalking out after Alton, leaving them alone.

"Promise me neither one of us dies out there?" Jarek said quietly.

Her mouth drew into a tight line, then she stepped closer and kissed him. "Promise."

"Good." He slid his faceplate closed with a thought. "'Cause I'll be damned if I'm gonna die with blue balls."

"You're a real romantic, you know that?"

He shrugged, smiling behind his faceplate. "I have my moments. Now let's party."

They jogged down the ramp. Al lifted the ship off and guided it to safety a little ways back from the battlefield as they moved after Drogan, Alton, and their Resistance shipmates toward the battlement that currently appeared to be serving as central command.

Daniels and Krogoth were there amid the human and raknoth fighters, along with most of the Enochians, who'd all donned light armor of some sort and were armed from simple with Haldin's and Elise's sidearms and spears right up to the walking arsenals of Enochian artillery that were Johnny and Phineas.

Ahead, the gunfire both on the fortifications and beyond the ramshackle wall were building in frequency and volume as more enemy forces drew within range.

While Daniels issued commands to her men on the ground, Krogoth was snapping orders and watching events unfold from atop the wall, surrounded by a small contingent of his raknoth. After a brief exchange with his minty-green not-quite-lady-friend, Drogan leapt up to speak with his Zar.

Jarek debated pushing his way over to Daniels, but she already appeared to be getting updates from the soldiers they'd flown over, so he followed Alton instead.

Lietha eyed Jarek and Rachel distastefully as they approached. The Enochian's greetings, at least, were slightly warmer, albeit understandably tense.

"Everything's in place?" Rachel asked Haldin, forced to shout-speak over the growing sounds of fighting beyond the wall.

"As in place as it's gonna be," Haldin called back. "We've got cloaking generators covering the line here and the flanks as well. Should keep their men from getting too close without them risking their control. And the other bit's ready too," he added with a pointed glance toward a rough-looking patch of earth nearby—one of the pit traps Jarek had been hearing so much about, he assumed.

He was trying to picture exactly how they'd force Gada into the thing when Lietha and Alton stiffened.

"What is it?" Jarek asked.

"Word from our kin," Alton said. "Gada's raknoth are pressing the flanks. Hard."

"No matter," Lietha said, flexing viciously clawed fingers. "I will tear the traitors apart myself if need be."

As if in response to her words, or maybe just her violent attitude, Alton's skin began to darken to green hide.

"Preach, sister," Jarek said.

That earned him multiple confused looks and a surprised scowl from Lietha, which reminded him he might well be the only one in the huddle—with the possible exception of Alton—who knew about Lietha's Shieth status.

As soon as the thought occurred to him, a fearsome roar in the distance and a pair of concussive blasts that shook the ground beneath their feet reminded him they had entirely more pressing concerns.

Seemingly out of nowhere, Lietha's demeanor shifted like a dog who'd just seen the treats come out. "Yes," she hissed. "We will end them."

Drogan leapt from Krogoth's fortification twenty yards away and landed beside them with a thud.

Without preamble, he turned to Jarek. "Join us in bringing justice to the traitors on the western flank, Jarek Slater."

Jarek touched a hand to his chest. "Little old human me?"

Was that what Lietha had meant about ending them?

It was damn confusing—not to mention damn creepy—working with an outfit whose members could all communicate telepathically.

Drogan nodded. "You can keep pace with us, yes? Al'Brandt requires our aid."

Jarek glanced over at Daniels, but she was more than a little occupied directing arriving Resistance forces by comm and shouted commands. "And the eastern flank?"

"Those who had followed Taga have been dispatched to bolster the other half of Al'Brandt's clan on the eastern flank," Drogan said. "Our forces will hold here for the time being, but we must go now."

"Go," Rachel said beside him.

"We'll hold the fort here if anything green comes flying over that wall," Haldin added.

Jarek wasn't crazy about parting from Rachel's side when the shit was so heavy all around them, but at least with the raknoth, he could move fast enough to be back in short order if need be.

"Give us a ring if the big guy shows up to play?" Jarek asked.

They both nodded their agreement, and Jarek set off beside Drogan and Lietha.

Whatever else there was to be said about working with the raknoth, Jarek couldn't deny that being able to truly stretch his legs without fear of leaving his allies in the dust was a major perk.

If he'd had time to pause and survey the soldiers they passed, he liked to think they would have used phrases like "with all the speed and grace of a majestic jungle cat" to describe his passage as he bolted along, dodging and vaulting over debris and old, rusted cars as needed.

Drogan and Lietha, on the other hand, were more like leap frogs. Big, scaly, utterly deadly leap frogs. They bounded along on either side of him, keeping pace with a steady stream of tremendous jumps that carried them thirty or forty yards at a time.

After the first minute, the sounds of fighting began to dim as they left the main conflict behind. Within the second minute, new sounds appeared and grew louder—gunfire intermingled with the screams of men and the battle roars of raknoth. It sounded like they'd found that flanking party. Soon enough, the fight came into view.

The defenders on this flank looked to be a mix of Resistance soldiers and Krogoth's men. Among the numerous dead lining the streets, Jarek spotted several broken raknoth bodies that looked like they'd died tearing each other to shreds.

Three raknoth were still moving through the defenders' ranks like forces of nature, tearing and biting and smashing into their human foes with reckless abandon. On the far side of the battle, the raknoth Jarek thought was Al'Brandt was tangled in a vicious struggle with two more raknoth, fighting like a caged animal.

As Jarek and his allies closed in, a Resistance soldier found her way to the heavy machine gun mounted in the back of a humvee, pried aside the man who'd died there, and opened fire on one of the three rampaging raknoth. The raknoth staggered to the pavement with a shriek. Before the gunner could finish the job, though, she was gunned down by one of Ashida's soldiers pushing through the opening their raknoth had cleared.

Jarek pulled his new sword free, triggered the pommel, and leapt into the fray.

He caught his first enemy unaware. The raknoth was stalking toward a soldier who was frantically scrambling away on hands and haunches. Jarek's horizontal stroke cleanly removed the raknoth's head in a flash of azure heat. The smell of seared flesh filled the air, and the raknoth's body fell slack to the pavement beside his own head.

The remaining enemy raknoth turned to face Jarek. Even the two struggling with Brandt paused. Most of the Resistance and Team Krogoth soldiers wisely took advantage of the distraction to clear away from the impending melee and return to the task of holding off Ashida's encroaching soldiers.

Lietha landed to Jarek's right side just as the two closer enemy raknoth sprang forward with hungry roars and one of Brandt's foes disengaged to likewise come deal with the new threat. Before the left-most of them had made it more than two steps, Drogan descended from on high to smash him into the pavement with his own battle roar.

That didn't slow the other two raknoth, who were upon Jarek and Lietha in seconds.

Jarek dipped back from the first swipe of the raknoth who closed on him. When the raknoth telegraphed his intent to make a lunging grab, Jarek took another long step back, spun left, and brought the Whacker around in a strong upward sweep.

The attack felt clumsy with the extra resistance of Rachel's workings, but it was still fast enough to sear and cut through the raknoth's right wrist and a good chunk of his torso.

The raknoth staggered, let out an ugly, hissing scream, and, despite the considerable injuries, pressed on, batting Jarek's blade aside with his remaining hand.

Jarek ducked right and drove his shoulder into the raknoth's side. The raknoth shuffled and barely managed to regain his balance. By the time he did, the Whacker was already descending to tear from right trapezius to left armpit with a flash of blue fire.

The Big Whacker 2.0, it seemed, worked like a freaking charm.

The cut wasn't quite deep enough to split the raknoth in two, but he definitely wasn't moving anymore after collapsing to the pavement, so Jarek turned his attention to scan for the next target.

His concerns were unnecessary. To the right, Lietha had her foe in a firm headlock. With a savage yank and a sickening crunch, she severed some internal part of the raknoth's anatomy, then she went to work with her claws, intent on removing her foe's head.

Across the intersection, Brandt seemed to have gained the upper hand on his challenger now that it was a one-on-one fight.

Jarek turned toward Drogan in time to see him deliver the last of what looked to have been several brutal stomps to the head of his opponent, who gave a few twitches then lay still on the pavement, flattened head oozing a disturbing combination of fluids.

Drogan's glowing gaze turned toward Jarek.

"Smashing work, Stumpy," he said weakly.

Heavy thunder boomed overhead.

"Sir," Al said in his ear. "Kul'Gada has been spotted heading for the front lines. We'd better get back there."

Jarek clutched his sword tight, memories of Gada's unbridled fury setting his shoulder to aching and trickling cold dread down into his gut. But Rachel was back there, and all the others too. They had to stop Gada here—fear be damned.

Brandt told them to get back to Krogoth, he, Drogan, and Lietha apparently having already heard the news of Gada's approach via the voices in their heads. They spent a precious minute helping him and the humans push Ashida's soldiers back to restore the line, then they turned and headed for the central battlements at full speed.

Leaving a single raknoth to guard the flank wasn't ideal, but it might well take all of them to put down Gada, and if they didn't do that, none of this would matter anyway.

Rain began to patter down in thick droplets as they went, and above, the sky was growing positively foreboding.

Without a doubt, the storm was coming. And, as they raced to the aid of their friends, it looked like it was in no mood to dither.

CHAPTER TWENTY-FIVE

Rachel pointed her staff, gathered her will, and let loose a telekinetic blast that drove one of Haldin's attackers into the rampart fifteen yards behind. One problem accounted for, Haldin ducked a savage swipe from the other enemy raknoth, sent the creature stumbling into Krogoth's deadly reach with a telekinetic shove, and whirled into telekinetically catching a live hand grenade and hurling it back over the wall.

A distant boom, a single instant of peace, and then they reset to take their next challengers.

Things had been stable for all of two minutes after Jarek had departed with Drogan and Lietha. With little else to do on the ground, Johnny and Phineas had climbed up onto the battlements to add their firepower to the line. Beyond the wall, intermittent explosions had punctuated the cacophony.

Rachel had hovered near Haldin and Elise, unsure where best to apply herself.

Then the first section of wall had blown inward about thirty yards down the line, and the answer to that question had become far too obvious far too quickly.

The first men through the breach had clearly felt the effects of the cloaking generators, reeling in confusion as the devices severed their connections with Ashida or Gada or whoever was controlling them.

Then the enemy raknoth had come charging in, over and through the wall, and all hell had broken loose.

On either side of the wall, men and women killed each other in droves while raknoth attempted to do the same.

With the considerable aid of Krogoth and his raknoth, Rachel and the Enochians had helped put a sizable dent in the number of intruding enemy raknoth.

The sky had grown dark as they fought, the beginnings of what promised to be a heavy rain joining the rumbles of thunder just in time to greet the arrival of Alaric and a convoy of Resistance forces.

The reinforcements had been a welcome sight—a hopeful one, even. At least until the first cries had gone up.

Kul'Gada had been sighted.

Even Krogoth looked worried for a second. Then he caught the raknoth Haldin had shoved his way and swung his traitorous kin like a flailing bat to smash into another raknoth who'd leapt over the battlements, tore through the men atop, and lunged straight for Krogoth.

That done, Krogoth tilted his rust-red snout skyward and let out a primal roar of challenge that was taken up by his raknoth all along the line. It was the most fearsome sound Rachel had ever heard. Until Gada answered.

She didn't know—didn't want to know—how close Gada was on the other side of that wall, but the sound he made seemed to dwarf even the fury of the battle around them, reaching down through her chest and shaking the ground beneath her.

When the Kul's roar ended, the sounds of the ongoing battle seemed almost mild for its absence. Rachel jabbed at her comm with shaking fingers and snapped a quick report to Al.

"I'll tell him to hurry back, ma'am," Al said. "Do be careful over there."

She didn't voice the thought that careful might not be enough, just killed the call and turned to fight on alongside Alton and the Enochians, who were facing down two more raknoth.

The rain wasn't yet steady enough to dampen the small gout of flames Haldin conjured to hurl into one of their faces. The raknoth turned with an aggravated yelp, swatting at his snout, and was promptly met by Elise's spear in the under jaw. The blade pierced hide, but not deep enough to kill the raknoth.

His ally roared and lunged at Elise, who threw herself to the side, clearing the way for Alton to step in and catch the over-eager raknoth off guard and drive him to the ground.

As Alton set to work severing the spine and removing the head, Haldin moved toward the second raknoth, spear at the ready.

Rachel gathered her energy and was preparing to reach out and tell Haldin she'd pin the raknoth for the killing blow when another stomach-wrenching roar shook the field, and a wave of telepathic pressure crashed down on her.

Gada. He'd crossed into the cloaking generator field. There was no question about it. Nor did there need to be.

As soon as she turned to the wall, Gada's enormous bulk appeared, flying over the fifteen foot wall with an ease that shouldn't have been physically possible for a creature of his enormous size.

The rakul slammed down to a landing near Krogoth and his guards, shaking the ground even twenty yards away.

"Hal!" Elise cried to the left.

Rachel looked back in time to see Haldin whirl into blocking a raknoth's overhead pound with a raised forearm—and, presumably, a considerable dollop of channeled energy, considering his arm didn't snap like dry kindling as it should've.

The raknoth stopped in his tracks, staring in obvious confusion at Haldin's clearly-not-obliterated forearm. Before it could get over its surprise, Haldin dropped his shoulder into the raknoth's chest. Rachel added a blast of telekinetic force and sent the creature sailing backward into Alton's waiting arms.

"We need to help Krogoth," Haldin sent to them as Alton set to the gritty work of finishing the raknoth.

They fell into a tight group and moved to join Krogoth and his three remaining raknoth guards in circling Gada. The Kul watched with little evident concern for them or the numerous bullets pelting his hide.

Four more raknoth leapt the wall on Gada's trail. Rachel whipped her staff up and managed to cut one's jump short with a well-aimed blast. The other three touched down and wasted no time moving in on Krogoth's raknoth.

Gada chose that moment to spring into action.

In the blink of an eye, the first of Krogoth's raknoth lay dead on the muddy earth.

Krogoth didn't stand idly by, though. He followed Gada through his lunge, ducking smoothly under the Kul's heavy tail, and tore a sizable hunk of flesh from the back of Gada's right leg with his claws.

Satisfying to watch, but it was going to take more than that to hobble Gada.

The Kul swept his tail at Krogoth—who narrowly avoided the strike— and spun to charge after the raknoth.

Haldin pelted a small fireball at Gada's face. The Kul barely flinched, but it at least bought Krogoth an extra fraction of a second to throw himself out of Gada's path.

The Kul rounded on Haldin with an irritated growl. Rachel timed her attack and formed a lance of telekinetic force that buckled Gada's knee and sent him into a drunken stumble. Elise and Alton circled around while Gada regained his balance, Elise taking the opportunity to harry his wounded flank with her spear.

Around them, more raknoth were closing in, some fighting on Gada's side, others clearly not. Rachel caught a glimpse of Mosen rushing toward them from across the park alongside a pair of raknoth —drawing back from the eastern flank, apparently. Probably to help deal with Gada. But that hardly mattered now.

The traps. They needed to start driving him toward the traps.

She looked for the choppy ground where the closer of the concealed traps lay and realized Haldin was already circling around Gada, orienting to be able to push the Kul in the proper direction.

Rachel followed along. The others shifted in kind, keeping Gada occupied as they went, apparently understanding the intent.

"Say when," Rachel sent to Haldin and Elise.

With her senses extended, she could feel the vast pull of energy pouring into the Enochians from their batteries and their surroundings, chilling the rainy air further.

Rachel took her own pull from her batteries and clenched her fists, relishing the crackling power buzzing through her core.

"Now," came Haldin's voice.

All at once, she let the energy explode out of her in a column of telekinetic force aimed straight at Gada's chest. Additional cascades of energy pulsed out beside her—a swift river from Elise and a crushing tsunami from Haldin.

Their triple whammy took Gada off his feet, but when the rakul's hulking mass slammed back to the earth, he was still a good fifteen yards away from the nearest trap.

More importantly, he was pissed, and Rachel was nursing a seriously spinning head and wobbly knees for her efforts.

Around them, several smaller fights had paused to see what had caused the small earthquake.

"Kill them!" Gada's voice hissed in her head like a thousand disjointed whispers as he clambered to his feet. *"To me, my children! Kill them all!"*

Those of Gada's raknoth who weren't already nearby soon reconciled their error, launching over the wall and rushing in from multiple directions to answer their master's call.

"To me, free raknoth of Earth!" Krogoth beamed out for all to hear. *"Let us clear the field of these traitors and finish this False Master!"*

Gada started after Krogoth with authority—so much so that no one saw it coming when he abruptly changed course and cut down another of Krogoth's raknoth instead.

On either side of Rachel, their circle was quickly falling away from containing Gada to defending against his reinforcements.

Alton pounced on one of the incoming raknoth, driving him to the ground. Haldin and Elise whirled off to confront another.

For a terrifying stretch, it was only Rachel and Krogoth facing the monstrous Kul, Krogoth taking the brunt of his fury and Rachel running what interference she could.

Then the raknoth Haldin and Elise had engaged came sailing through the air like a live missile and struck the Kul in the back. Gada, expecting an attack, promptly turned and cut his flailing underling in two before his body hit the ground.

Rachel couldn't help but feel a touch of grim satisfaction watching it play out. That satisfaction took root and began to grow into determination as more of Krogoth's raknoth arrived from the eastern flank to help with Gada and his raknoth. She caught sight of Alaric nearby, directing his troops into a defensive perimeter around their fight, isolating them with Gada so they could finish him without interference.

All they had to do was get the rampaging monster into the giant hole in the ground.

Rachel began to drift that way as they fought, and the others mirrored her, guiding the Kul swing by swing to his awaiting doom. A little further, and they'd be able to land him in the first pit with another good blast.

Gada stalked after them, either not sensing the ploy or simply not caring. Their reinforcements aside, the Kul probably had good reason to be confident.

Underfoot, the trodden ground was growing more muddy and restrictive by the minute in the thick rain. If they didn't end this soon, Gada would pick them off one-by-one as they tired and grew too bogged down in the rain and the mud.

A quick backward sweep with her extended senses confirmed she was within a few yards of the pit trap. Unfortunately, that was also when Gada ceased his stalking. He regarded them silently as the war continued to rage on around them.

Then he began to laugh.

It was an odd sound, a series of airy hisses punctuated by brief, low rumbles.

More troubling than the laugh itself, though, was its implication.

"Ah," Gada hissed, this time out loud. "A trap."

A crack of thunder punctuated his words, and Rachel's stomach fell.

"Clever," Gada said. "So clever." He leaned toward them, crimson eyes pulsing brighter with what might have been excitement. "But what if I told you that I have a trap of my own?"

Rachel glanced toward the concealed pit, so damned close, and met eyes with Alaric, who'd scooted discreetly over to the trap's manual switch, ready to spring it by hand if it should fail to activate.

So close. They'd been so goddamned close.

For a long second, there was nothing but the sounds of the fighting raging on around them. Then a cry descended from above, shrill and piercing.

Rachel risked a glance upward and caught a glimpse of a craft not unlike the Enochians' ship descending from the dark clouds. There was the flicker of motion—something falling from the craft—then Krogoth was grabbing her and they were flying away from the pit.

What the hell was the bastard think—

A flash of brilliant orange. The air split with a tremendous boom. A torrent of hot air slammed into them, and then they were hitting the ground, rolling to a rough, jarring halt.

Farther down the line, a second explosion lit the night.

Rachel tried to scramble out from under Krogoth, her head reeling from the blast. Krogoth ignored her struggles for a second, then scrambled to his feet and pulled her up after him.

She nearly pitched over as her weight settled back on her shocked legs. Then she took in the damage, and shock twisted to nausea in her gut.

Twenty yards off to the left, Alton was crouched over Haldin and Elise, his back badly burnt, trying to pull them to their stunned feet. Gada stalked toward the three of them, steady and confident despite his own blackened right flank.

To the right, the traps were in shambles—the thin decoy covers of soil and earth caved in, gouts of blue flame licking up from the exposed pits to join the more steady orange flames that burned almost cheerily in the wake of whatever had been dropped from that ship. Even at a distance, the heat was intense.

And all they had now was a pair of big fiery holes in the ground.

It was possible the proper lids might still be triggered to slide over the pits and trap Gada inside, but good luck getting him in there now that they'd lost the chance of surprise. Even then, it'd probably require manual activation now that—

Shit. Alaric.

She scanned to the right of the pits, where she'd last seen the commander standing.

There.

He lay still, tendrils of smoke drifting up from his stringy gray hair and his battered long coat. Clearly, he'd taken some serious heat in the explosions. But not nearly as much as the charred, limp figure draped over him.

Mosen.

A roar to the left snapped her addled attention back to the moment.

Krogoth was charging Gada's turned back, Alton stepping away from a recovering Haldin and Elise to approach the Kul from the front.

Gada sprang forward, only to come to an abrupt halt and round on Krogoth instead. The Zar saw it coming and was ready to duck Gada's swipe. What Krogoth wasn't ready for was Gada's feint.

In mid-swipe, the Kul broke and spun clockwise, catching Krogoth with a powerful tail slap that sent the raknoth flying.

Alton hopped back just in time to avoid the follow-through swipe Gada aimed at him, then returned a hard kick to the Kul's lowered head. Gada spun with the kick and tried his luck with another tail whip. Alton managed to jump over the heavy appendage, but that only left him floating helplessly in the air as Gada completed the revolution and came around with another bladed strike.

The blow caught Alton at mid-thigh and took both of his legs.

He smacked to the ground with a very human cry. Gada followed, ready to finish him, but then Alton sprang back, yanked seemingly by thin air, and landed beside Haldin, who was on his feet now, looking seriously pissed.

The closest of the fires that had spread from the explosions at the pits died out around Haldin as he gathered energy, preparing to let loose.

Rachel started forward on shaky feet to help but froze when a horrible shriek cut through the air, just like the one that had preceded the blast. The sound made Rachel want to curl up and cover her ears, and the thing that fell from the sky with it only deepened the desire.

It slammed down beside the pits with ground-shaking force that sent a circle of mud and rainwater exploding out from the point of impact. The creature was shorter than Gada, but not by much, and nearly as wide as it was tall. The initial appearance of a swirling, amorphous blob soon resolved into the wriggling movements of hundreds of tentacles ranging in size from the width of a small finger to that of a tree trunk, the thickest tentacles extending down to the ground—not unlike legs.

From the depths of the countless slithering appendages, a pair of large, burning red eyes stared out at them.

Before they had time to process the shock of the thing or properly wonder where the hell it had come from, Krogoth came barreling in to attack it.

At the same time, Gada took advantage of their surprise and lunged for Haldin.

Helpless shock ensnared Rachel as Haldin turned, focus broken, hands shooting up in an action that screamed pure, useless reflex, eyes betraying, for the first time, the fear of the terrified teenager that still resided in there.

The one who was about to die.

Rachel couldn't move, couldn't process anything but that look in Haldin's eyes, the look of finality, of—

Elise slammed into Haldin in a low tackle and drove him clear of Gada's path like the world's smallest freight train.

Rachel felt an instantaneous flood of relief at the Kul's frustrated cry. Then horror at Elise's agonized one.

The Enochians hit the ground together. Haldin bounced straight to his feet and back to his senses, coming into a protective crouch over Elise.

On the ground, Elise wasn't moving. Haldin bent to check on her, trying to keep an eye on Gada at the same time.

Whatever he saw on her still body made him go pale and shaky at the knees.

Gada watched, fangs bared in what looked to be a sneer.

Rachel had to get his attention, had to give Haldin time to get Elise to safety.

"Hey!" she shouted.

She pelted the side of Gada's face with a hefty fireball and tried again telepathically.

"Hey, asshole!"

She gave him a firm telekinetic uppercut on the snout, moving closer.

Gada rocked back, but didn't seem to particularly care.

Haldin didn't appear to be noticing much of anything around him. His jaw was clenched, his eyes filling with tears as he reached down to touch Elise's head. Alton was crawling toward them, his severed legs dragging behind.

Alton reached Elise, and Haldin stood, rigid with a fury like Rachel had never seen before. It radiated off him in waves, the air crackling around him as he prepared to unleash untold hell on Gada.

And Gada simply watched all the while, looking, if anything, excited about what was coming. The sick son of a bitch.

A shrill screech pierced the air from where Krogoth had attacked the tentacular monstrosity.

Then, Krogoth's thought, tinged with urgency. *"Rachel Cross!"*

She tore her eyes away from Haldin and Gada in time to see the creature hurl Krogoth straight for the farther of the flaming pits.

She reached out, not taking the time to think about it.

He was far, farther than she was used to working any serious channeling, but she found him in her senses and gave him a hard telekinetic shove, enough to carry him over the pit rather than into it.

It took more out of her than it would have at a reasonable distance, but she turned back for Haldin, refusing to fail him again for something as surmountable as channeling fatigue.

Too late.

It wasn't hard to imagine how Haldin hadn't seen it coming. He was out of his mind with grief-stricken rage. And the wriggling bastard had moved so fast—one second tossing Krogoth to the fire, the next, ensnaring Haldin from behind with half a dozen tentacles at once.

Haldin cried out, thrashing against the creature as it pulled him smoothly away from Elise. It was no good. The tentacles gave no more than if they'd been solid bands of iron.

"Brother," Gada hissed.

The voice that answered from within the swirling mass of tentacles was like sheets of rusted metal scraping together.

"Brother..."

Rachel wanted to cry out for help—for Jarek, for Krogoth. For anyone.

But there wasn't time.

So Rachel reached for the energy her exhausted body wanted nothing to do with as Haldin snarled a helpless curse and Gada, baring his fangs in a wide smile, started toward Elise.

CHAPTER TWENTY-SIX

Rachel was pointing her staff at Kul'Gada and preparing to throw every ounce of force she could muster to get the bastard away from Elise when a flicker of movement to the left caught her eye, and a large, dark figure came blurring in toward the Kul with impossible speed.

She almost cried out in relief as she realized it was Jarek.

Jarek planted his feet several yards out from Gada and drew his sword as his considerable momentum carried him the rest of the way in a muddy slide.

Gada began to turn, no doubt hearing him coming.

Jarek was quicker.

In one smooth motion, he slid to a halt and brought the sword down full power on the Kul's heavy tail.

A flash of blue light and a hiss of steam.

Gada let loose a gut-wrenching shriek and spun on Jarek with a savage, bladed backhand, but Jarek had already leapt back and out of reach.

Rachel saw with grim satisfaction that the rear third of Gada's tail now lay on the muddy ground, completely severed.

"C'mon you ugly bastard," Jarek called as Drogan and Lietha

caught up and joined him on either side. "I've got a tale for you." He tilted his helmeted head. "No, wait—I can do better."

Rachel didn't have time to process the exasperation and relief before the tidal wave of energy building behind Gada drew her attention.

Haldin.

A cry that barely sounded human rang out, followed by a sound like a dozen shotgun blasts in a small room, and the tentacled thing holding Haldin stumbled backward with a scream like a discordant chorus of fiddles from hell.

Haldin's knees buckled as he hit the ground, clearly exhausted after whatever channeling he'd just worked. That didn't stop him from crawling toward Elise the instant he was free, a few amputated tentacles still dangling loosely from his arms.

Rachel started for them at a run.

Alton looked up from whatever he was doing to Elise's wounds and growled something at Haldin, which the Enochian seemed to ignore. Alton pointed emphatically toward the tentacular monstrosity, which Rachel realized now could only be another Kul—and a Kul that appeared to have recovered from its shock, at that.

It was starting to glide forward when Johnny and Phineas pushed in through the surrounding chaos, planted themselves in front of their fellow Enochians, and opened fire.

The Enochian artillery filled the rainy air with rapid, rhythmic pulsing sounds, quickly joined by a furious scream from the creature. It lashed out, simultaneously smacking the rifle from Johnny's hands and Phineas from his burly feet.

Rachel drew up beside them, leveled her staff at the swirling mess of tentacles, and fed the thing a heavy column of force right at center mass.

The creature didn't fly so much as roll back a dozen yards, tumbling through something like a perpetual cartwheel, its tentacles working quickly to roll it smoothly through the motion. It came to rest back on its thickest tentacles, utterly uninjured and ready to attack again.

Before it could, Krogoth landed beside her with a deep thud, followed shortly by one of his raknoth.

"What the fuck is that thing?" Rachel asked him quietly.

"Kul'Armin," Krogoth said, tilting his head to the Kul in acknowledgment and flexing his clawed fingers in anticipation.

"Right…"

So they'd scored two Kuls for the price of one. Fucking fantastic.

With her reinforcements stalking forward to confront Armin, Rachel risked a glance over her shoulder, to where Jarek, Drogan, and Lietha were doing their best to corral Gada.

Her heart leapt as Jarek raised his sword to parry a series of Gada's swipes, her mind flashing back to the sight of the Kul tearing through his previous blade, but her enchantments did their job. On each strike, Gada's enormous claws slowed considerably before they impacted the blade, almost as if they'd encountered an invisible body of super viscous goo along the last foot of their path.

Kul'Armin must not have had much to say to Krogoth, because, when Rachel turned back, the tentacular Kul was surging forward, tentacles working in bizarre synchrony to propel him as smoothly over the ground as if he were hovering.

Krogoth sidestepped the rush and landed a hard claw rake that removed a few smaller tentacles from the Kul's back.

Krogoth's underling wasn't as fast. The raknoth roared as the Kul caught onto one of his arms. He thrashed wildly, scoring a few hits but doing little to prevent the inevitable as the Kul reeled him closer, wrapping him more tightly.

Rachel tried telekinetically prying the tentacles off and yanking the raknoth free, but Kul'Armin's grasp was too strong, too pervasive.

She focused down to one of the smaller tentacles, no wider than a finger, and, with a surprising amount of effort, pulled until it tore free from Armin.

Rewarded with a small yelp, Rachel moved on to the next one.

At the same time, Krogoth harried the Kul from all sides, light on his feet despite the long fight and foot-sucking mud. Another raknoth joined him from the fray, desperately seeking to free his shrieking kin from Armin's grasp.

It wasn't enough. For every tentacle they removed, another took its place until, finally, the ensnared raknoth's head came free with a sickening tearing sound.

Armin tossed the lifeless body into the adjacent burning pit and the severed head at Krogoth's feet.

Rachel expected Krogoth to roar and charge, but, instead, he and his underling only circled Armin, dividing the Kul's attention and watching for any opening with smoldering red eyes.

A furious roar to the left demanded Rachel's attention.

She traced it to Drogan, who faced Gada side-by-side with Jarek, eyes burning brighter crimson than she'd ever seen. Behind them, Lietha lay torn open in the rain and the mud, either dead or too wounded to move.

Phineas was carrying Elise away from the fight now, Alton crawling leglessly after them. Haldin watched them go, paralyzed, oblivious to Johnny's words as the Enochian held him firmly across the chest and spoke something in his ear.

Every way Rachel looked, they were losing, and if she didn't do something and do it fast, they were all going to be dead—likely within the next minute or two.

A streak of lightning licked at the dark sky, momentarily illuminating every single glob of rain and all the other bloody details around her. With it struck a solution, and as the accompanying thunderclap filled the air, Rachel found herself grinning a mirthless grin.

Jarek apparently had a similar thought in the wake of the lightning. "We sure could use some Lady Zeus action right now, Rache," he called as he dodged clear of a charging Gada.

"I've got some Lady Zeus for you," Rachel muttered, a fresh surge of adrenaline buzzing through her head as she prepared for what would surely be an exhausting last ditch effort.

But maybe she didn't have to do it alone.

"Hal," she cried.

No response.

She beamed the thought at him like a battering ram.

"HAL!"

He might as well have been catatonic.

Johnny, coming to a similar conclusion, released Haldin with a loud curse and turned his weapon on Gada.

Rachel saved her curses, gripped her staff for support, and closed her eyes, casting out her senses.

It was there all around them, a veritable ocean of ions, dancing and swirling on the stormy winds, casting tentative but persistent tendrils down from the clouds, seeking a ground, a path of least resistance.

So Rachel focused on Gada's position in her senses and gave it to them.

A brilliant blue-white bolt of lightning flashed through her eyelids, searing through Gada's back and lancing into the clouds above, the rushing crack of thunder instantaneous and nearly deafening in such close proximity.

Charred flesh and ozone wafted to her senses as Gada dropped to a knee with a deep roar.

Behind her, Armin gave an angry shriek of his own.

Rachel did her best to ignore it and reach through the channeling fatigue to prepare another strike.

Had she somehow been manipulating this amount of charge within a range of a few yards, it would have been an effort, but a manageable one. As it was, exerting her will over so far a distance and so wide an area, the first strike had left her head spinning. The second one wasn't going to be any easier, but she gritted her teeth and forced it down anyway.

Another tremendous boom. Another roar, this one clearly pained.

Darkness.

Cool wetness on her knees, her chest, the side of her face.

"Rache!"

Jarek's distant cry, strained as if he were still fighting.

"Hey! Get your shit together, Haldin!"

Jarek again.

She opened her eyes to find she'd collapsed in the mud.

Had she been out? Or simply fallen over from exhaustion? She couldn't tell.

A little ways off, Gada fought on against Jarek and Drogan, his back and right flank thoroughly charred black. His fighting was still ferocious, though he moved as if he'd seen better days. Then again, so did Jarek and Drogan.

Johnny had circled around and was dragging Lietha's body back from the fight, and—

"Rachel."

Haldin's voice.

She looked up and found him standing over her, but he wasn't looking at her as she'd expected. His attention was fixed on Kul'Gada, cold rage plastered across his face.

"The lightning," Rachel sent, her head still whirling. *"It was working. Can you...?"*

He dropped unceremoniously to the mud next to her and reached out his hand, his eyes never leaving Gada.

"Together?"

She reached out and grabbed his hand. Their fingers intertwined, and Haldin's presence washed over her, strong and resolute and brimming with barely-contained fury.

"Together," she sent, taking strength in his resolve.

She'd touched his mind once before, when the Enochians had first arrived on Earth and she'd needed to verify the truth of their story, but that had been different. Intimate, yes, but still a one-way arrangement, with Rachel in control.

Now, though, she was pretty sure that wasn't going to cut it. For them to do this together, to share in each other's strength... She'd never deliberately opened herself to anyone that completely. It wasn't a welcome thought.

But the sight of Jarek narrowly dodging Gada's blades reminded her that that didn't matter one damn bit right now.

So she dropped the wall between her mind and Haldin's, and he did the same.

Sights, sounds, feelings, even thoughts—everything doubled,

pouring through her in an overwhelming rush. Most overwhelming of all, though, was the guilty rage coursing through Haldin's veins.

At first, the heat of it made her flinch, but as their separate beings swirled together into a singular stream, that rage became hers as well.

Calm, she thought as best as she could. *Focus. Gada.*

The rage didn't dim, but it did focus.

She—no, *they*—closed their eyes and bled into their extended senses, fixing on Gada, taking in the swirling dance of charged particles, beginning to draw energy from their surroundings.

It seemed to Rachel that she was guiding the process more so than Haldin, but the fact that she could feel his agreement as if it were her own confused the question of who was doing what.

It didn't matter.

Together, they massaged the tendrils of charge down toward Gada's spiky back. Together, they waited until Drogan had kicked out one of the Kul's legs and hopped back to safety.

And, together, they touched the charge down on Gada's hide and rained white-hot fury on the giant bastard.

The ground kicked beneath them, the sonorous boom of thunder buffeting their rain-soaked hair.

For the first time, Gada's shriek was tinged with a desperate edge.

They felt him in their extended senses, whirling to face them, starting forward to put an end to what he seemed to have just realized was a serious threat.

Jarek darted in and hacked a deep, searing cut to Gada's injured right flank. It didn't stop the Kul, but it slowed him enough for them to build another charge and fry him a second time.

Gada dropped to his knees, nearly pitching flat over.

They built another charge and hit him again. Then again.

Clammy perspiration mixed with the rain streaming down their brow, sickly waves of channeling fatigue roiling in their gut. She couldn't have distinguished whose brow and whose gut. Probably both of theirs.

It doesn't matter, she thought. Or was that Haldin?

Unimportant.

They had the bastard on his knees.

They drove Gada flat to the ground with telekinesis, their combined consciousness wavering with the enormous amount of energy they were slinging, and hit him with yet another bolt of lightning.

The Kul stopped struggling.

They drifted awash in a sea of channeling fatigue, leaning on one another for support.

Nearby, someone was yelling.

Jarek.

But why?

She tried to focus on his voice through the mental haze and realized it was her he was yelling at, bolting toward them all the while.

"I said look out!" he cried, leaping over her and Haldin.

He came down on the other side and planted his armored boot into Kul'Armin, who'd slithered his way up behind them while they'd been raining fury down on Gada.

The Kul gave an aggravated roar, but even as he recoiled from the kick, several tentacles shot out and wrapped themselves around Jarek's leg. The tentacles held firmly as the rest of Jarek's body fell victim to gravity and toppled downward. His back slammed into the muddy earth, and Armin wasted no time in wrapping him up more tightly.

Jarek managed an awkward one-handed sword swing that took off a few smaller tentacles, then he tried a few kicks with his free leg, but Armin continued to bind him and reel him in.

Then Krogoth slammed into Armin's side with a lowered shoulder, and Drogan landed on the Kul's opposite side and began ripping at the tentacles holding Jarek.

Rachel and Haldin gathered their combined focus and capitalized on the distraction to telekinetically yank Jarek and Armin in separate directions.

One of Jarek's legs came free, and, with one last kick, he parted from the Kul's deadly embrace with a wet ripping sound.

Jarek hit the ground with several tentacles still dangling off his legs. He pulled himself to his feet, shaking them off, and readied his sword for another round.

Behind them, Gada's smoking form remained thankfully still in the mud, face down.

None of them were in much better shape.

Exhaustion pressed in on Rachel and Haldin, heavy and insistent. Jarek was panting and moving as if every part of his body hurt, and Drogan and Krogoth both appeared to be literally missing pieces.

But it was just them and Armin now.

So, taking solace from that fact, they pushed aside their fatigue, gathered their will, and prepared to call the storm down once more.

Before they could, Armin surged toward them on a wave of tentacles.

Jarek planted himself between them and the Kul and met his tentacled rush with a blazing sweep of his sword. The attack seared through the Kul's flesh, but Armin pushed on.

Drogan rammed into the Kul's flank, ripping and tearing until a thick tentacle swept one of the raknoth's legs out and slammed him to the ground.

Jarek spun to the side and whipped his blade down on the tentacles holding Drogan. Rachel and Haldin waited until the stroke fell to lash out with a telekinetic blast that sent Armin rolling several yards back. Krogoth, apparently sensing what came next, had the good sense to abort his own charge and dive clear as Rachel and Haldin called down a lance of lightning.

Armin shrieked and went rigid as the bolt struck him, his tentacles stiffening like a giant sea urchin, then he wobbled around and started shakily toward them.

They felt as shaky as the Kul looked, clinging onto their combined consciousness by mere threads.

They should hold off. Recover. Allow Jarek and the raknoth to buy them time to safely prepare another strike.

But there the wriggling bastard was. Shaky. Isolated.

They could feel his confidence eroding, could sense it in his movements.

They could end it right here, right now—take back some small semblance of justice for Elise and all the others who'd suffered today.

So, together, they called one last brilliant flash down from the sky.

WHEN RACHEL ROSE from the darkness and became aware of her surroundings once more, things felt oddly foreign. It took her a long moment to remember why.

She was on her own. No Haldin.

Rain washed over her, far more vivid now that she wasn't lost in her extended senses—as was the lengthy list of pains parading through her body.

A flash of azure lit the falling rain to the right and ended with a soft, wet *thunk*.

Another. And another.

Rachel blinked and woozily shifted around to see Jarek's blade descending on Armin for what was at least the fourth time but probably more like double digits if the Kul's appearance was any indication.

Haldin was sitting beside her, watching the execution with a pale face and grim satisfaction.

The stench of burning and death clung to the air, only partially alleviated by the cleansing rain.

If Armin had been struggling at some point, he wasn't now.

Drogan and Krogoth stood vigilantly by as Jarek continued to hack away, Drogan still holding one of the tentacles he'd ripped from the Kul's body.

Not trusting herself to try to stand yet, Rachel watched, the wet thunk of each strike turning her stomach despite the part of her that cried out with savage glee.

After nearly a minute of Jarek's hacking, she pulled herself to her feet by her staff. She turned to offer Haldin a hand, but he was already up. She followed his gaze and her stomach fell through the floor.

Kul'Gada was gone.

She turned wide eyes to Haldin. "Gada—"

"Bolted," Jarek called from Armin's motionless form. He'd finally stopped hacking and was doubled over, panting. He straightened to face them, his face plate sliding open. "He took off when you guys hit Cthulhu here with the Zeus juice."

"The coward," Krogoth growled.

"But a living coward," Jarek added, looking none too pleased about it.

The sounds of fighting were dying down, coming mostly in small bursts here and there. The fact that they weren't currently being overrun and that the sounds seemed to be fading into the distance made Rachel think the Resistance and Krogoth's forces must have Ashida's army in retreat.

The beginnings of hope fluttered in her chest but died quickly enough when she looked down at the butchered mess of Armin's body and thought about their own wounded.

She gestured toward Armin with her staff. "Is he…?"

"Kul'Armin's true body has been mortally wounded," Drogan said. "Here lies the first in five thousand years to relinquish the title of Kul."

"He will not be the last," Krogoth said.

"Yeah. All hail the Whacker," Jarek said weakly before strapping the weapon to his back and sinking down to the mud for a breather. "As much as I know you party animals wanna celebrate, though, I think we'd better hurry with the cleanup duty."

Krogoth was already stalking off toward the battlements to do just that.

"Yup," Jarek said, still breathing heavily. "That's good. You creepily untiring bastards got it under control. Put her there, Stumps," he added, extending a fist to Drogan.

Drogan ignored the offered fist in favor of patting Jarek on the head like a small toddler, then he stalked off to find Lietha.

Rachel turned to ask Haldin about Elise, but the Enochian was already gone.

Jarek was right. They had a whole hell of a lot to clean up—and then some.

She should go find Haldin and Elise—go do something to help someone, at least. But, for the moment, she couldn't bring herself to do much more than sink down by Jarek's side and lean against his bulky shoulder. She didn't complain when he wrapped a muddy arm around her, or when he bent down to plant a warm kiss on her forehead.

She just rested her head against his shoulder, let out a long sigh, and, for a short while, allowed herself to think of nothing but the feel of the rain on her skin.

For now, at least, they were alive.

CHAPTER TWENTY-SEVEN

To say Jarek had been in his fair share of fights throughout the years seemed like a bit of an understatement. Hands down, though, the battle they'd just been through had utterly and completely dwarfed anything he'd ever been a part of—hell, anything he'd ever even heard of.

It had probably been the largest conflict the world had seen since the wise old world powers had been dismantled—or, rather, obliterated—in the Catastrophe.

Everyone was still trying to come to an accurate conclusion on how many lives had just been lost. Looking around at the carnage, Jarek decided it had to be well north of a thousand, maybe even closer to two.

Men, women, and raknoth lay dead in droves. The recently barren soil of Central Park would have drank their spilled blood hungrily, had the rain and fighting not left it so muddy and churned up. Hundreds of recovering combatants rushed here and there, helping the wounded, looking for friends, and, in a few cases, looting the ripe spoils of war.

"Jesus Christ," Rachel whispered beside him.

"Yeah." He didn't know what else to say. He certainly didn't have anything productive to tell her. Somehow, the enormity of the death and suffering all around them had sapped him of any desire to joke around.

At least the sun was poking out now.

Thank god for the little things, right?

Like how, with their crude battlements and home field advantage, the combined forces of Team Earth seemed to have at least come through with fewer losses than Gada and Ashida's camp.

But fewer didn't always mean few, did it?

The stretch behind their defenses was more than plenty littered with bodies, human and raknoth alike, and Jarek had felt the immediate urge to hurl upon looking out over the wall.

"We should check on Alaric," Rachel said. "Looks like the medics are done with him."

Jarek followed without argument, glad to have something else to think about. At least until they found him.

It wasn't that Alaric was terribly wounded. Aside from some singed hair and some surface-level burns on the right side of his face, Alaric actually looked pretty good.

Except for the deep-set *my wayward son (who hates me, by the way) just nearly died saving me* guilt plastered across his face.

The wayward son in question sat with his impressively burnt back turned to Alaric, glaring daggers at the distant wall as one of Krogoth's raknoth treated his wounds with the good ol' spit shine.

"I know this doesn't change anything, Seth," Alaric was saying. "I just…" Alaric waved a helpless hand. "I wanted to say thank you. And that I'm sorry." He shook his head. "Always sorry."

Mosen said nothing—at least not until Alaric began to turn away with an unmissable slump in his shoulders.

"Hey, Dad?"

The hesitant, almost vulnerable note in Mosen's tone gave even Jarek pause.

Alaric, on the other hand, turned back with the air of a soldier who'd just stepped on something that could've been either a buried treasure chest or a landmine.

Mosen turned around far enough to meet his father's eyes, an act that must've been excruciating given the state of his back. It wasn't pain in Mosen's glinting red eyes, though, but hatred.

"Go fuck yourself."

And with that, Mosen turned back to glaring at the distant wall.

Alaric stared at him with unseeing eyes for a long moment, looking like he maybe wished that it had in fact been a landmine he'd stepped on after all, then he turned to head for where Commander Daniels was running her operational triage.

That Alaric caught sight of the pair of nosy onlookers named Jarek and Rachel as he turned was most unfortunate.

What Jarek would've given to have had some kind of optical camouflage on Fela right then…

Alaric looked like he might have been having similar thoughts, but he finally sighed and stepped over to join them.

"So what's the deal, cowboy?" Jarek asked, tapping at the side of his face where Alaric was now sporting superficial burns. "Couldn't stand not being a part of the band of badass facial scars?"

It was beyond a fool's errand to try to wrestle a glint of amusement out of Alaric right now, so Jarek wasn't surprised when Alaric ignored him and focused on Rachel instead.

"Anything to report? Damn medics had me tied up since they found us." He spat on the ground. "As if it matters. Commander, my ass."

Rachel hesitated, clearly unsure how to respond and behave after what they'd just seen. When Alaric's stare shifted to aggressively expectant, though, she started spitting words out.

"Uh, no. Sir. Nothing to report. We just, uh…" She practically winced with discomfort. ". . . wanted to make sure you're all right."

Alaric blew out a humorless huff, glancing surreptitiously back at Mosen, who clenched his jaw but otherwise tried to pretend he hadn't noticed.

"All right," Alaric said. "Sure. Goddamn dandy. Why don't you two—"

Something across the field caught his eye, and he straightened to attention. "Zar!"

Jarek followed his gaze to Krogoth, who paused on his route to wherever he was headed, frowned at them, and finally turned and stomped his way over.

"How bad?" Alaric asked quietly as Krogoth approached, apparently having caught on to their freakishly good hearing.

Krogoth waited until he'd reached them to answer.

"Roughly half. Both humans and my own kin as well."

Jarek tried to wrap his head around the raknoth's answer. He didn't need a formal report to know they'd taken a serious hit, but half? Half of all of their forces? Close to a thousand humans and maybe a dozen raknoth. All dead.

And for what?

If this was the price for taking down a single Kul, they wouldn't survive the coming war—not without a serious course correction.

Not that it would have greatly evened the odds, but he might have felt a shade less despair about it all if they'd managed to take down two rakul instead of one.

That shifty bastard Gada had picked his moment of retreat carefully, and he'd executed it with a ruthlessly complete lack of concern for his fellow Kul. Sure, they might've had Gada on the ropes for a few minutes at the end there, but it had cost them far too much. And Gada was cunning.

He'd be back, strong and dangerous as ever. And with ten of his friends.

Krogoth, seeing they were all busy registering the shock of the news, turned to continue on.

"Hold on, Rusty," Jarek said.

Krogoth seemed to debate responding to the nickname, then he turned to stare crimson at him.

"Gada," Jarek said. "Ashida. Where are the bastards?"

"Kul'Gada has fled by ship," Krogoth said. "I wager he waits in orbit for his kin."

As Krogoth spoke, a ship swooped down overhead and settled to an easy landing close by.

"The traitor Nan'Ashida, on the other hand," Krogoth said, eyes pulsing brighter, "has been spotted fleeing northeast. I go to repay his transgressions presently."

Jarek traded a glance with Rachel, who turned to Alaric with grim determination in her eyes.

"May we?" she asked.

Alaric glanced back at Mosen again, then looked from Rachel to Jarek.

"Make sure you give him a hard boot up the ass from me?"

Jarek was opening his mouth to give an affirmative when Rachel cut in.

"I'm thinking we have better tools at our disposal," she said, thumping her staff against the earth a few times.

Alaric tipped an imaginary hat in her direction, looking satisfied if not humored. "Have fun, then. Find me when you're back."

With that he stalked off in Daniels' direction.

Jarek turned back to Krogoth. "So, need a hand then, comrade?"

"Hardly," Krogoth said, turning for his ship. Without turning back, he added, "But you may join if you wish."

"Let's get the bastard," Rachel said, with entirely more animosity than he was used to hearing from her.

Understandable enough, given what the bastard had done here today—not to mention that Ashida had sounded like an unbearable asshat to begin with.

So he nodded, and they followed Krogoth onto his ship. Two more raknoth boarded after them—Al'Brandt and one of Krogoth's clan— and then they were off.

They caught up to Ashida's forces a couple minutes and several miles later. The retreating convoy of ground vehicles couldn't hope to outrun a ship. Ashida himself, on the other hand, might have stood half a chance.

He certainly tried.

No more than five seconds after the convoy drew into plain view of their ship, a dark figure with burning red eyes sprung out of the lead vehicle and took off northwest, bounding away from the convoy in a series of inhuman leaps.

Krogoth growled orders for the pilot to follow Ashida and for the other two raknoth to drop down and deal with Ashida's convoy.

"No," Rachel said to the latter order. "Enough people have died today. Those men are Ashida's slaves, nothing more."

Krogoth looked at her as if she'd just asked him to swear off human blood, but after a long moment, he tilted his head. "I care not what happens to that traitor's puppets so long as Nan'Ashida meets his justice this day."

And from the looks of it, that traitor was about to.

Like the rest of the raknoth, Ashida was fast, covering several dozen yards with each rapid bounce across the ruined city. Even with Fela, Jarek would've been hard pressed to run him down. With a ship, though, it was inevitable.

When they drew over him, Krogoth opened the ship's side hatch, took careful aim, and dove. The ship bucked violently from the power of Krogoth's exit. Below, Ashida touched down from a bounce and looked up just in time to take Krogoth's tackle full on.

They slammed to the ground hard enough to crack the pavement beneath Ashida. The darker raknoth fought, but Krogoth swatted aside his blows, pulled him into the air, and threw him through the wall of an adjacent building before leaping out of sight to follow with a chest-rattling roar.

Jarek traded a wide-eyed look with Rachel. Once the pilot had brought them down to comfortable jumping height, he hopped out behind their two raknoth allies. Rachel landed beside him just as Ashida came flying out of the building like a dark missile.

He hit the ground like a skipping stone, headed in their direction. Jarek reached for his sword, but the two raknoth were already closing on Ashida. They grabbed him by the arms and hauled him to his feet, kicking and snarling.

"Fools!" he hissed. "You know the power of the Masters. You've seen what it costs to resist them."

"And yet resist we did," Krogoth's voice drifted out of the dark building he'd ejected Ashida from. Krogoth emerged from the shadows and stalked toward them. "Kul'Armin is dead, slain by the hands of raknoth and humans alike."

Ashida spat. "By blind luck and"—he glared at Rachel—"vile sorcery did you manage to stumble into victory against the Kul. It is folly to think it will happen even once more, and they are still eleven."

Krogoth drew up to Ashida and leaned in dangerously close. "Kul'-Gada would have joined his brother in the void this day had your forces not interfered. You, young Nan, have overplayed your hand for the last time. You will answer for your crimes."

"Incoming, sir," Al said in Jarek's earpiece.

Wonderful.

Jarek looked around and saw that Ashida's convoy was indeed arriving on the scene now. One of the raknoth holding Ashida murmured a similar warning to Krogoth, though Jarek couldn't imagine the raknoth didn't already sense the incoming threat.

The vehicles drew to a halt a good forty yards away, and a couple dozen armed men piled out of cars and troop transports, lining up and training weapons their way.

"If any one man fires his weapon," Krogoth called, not bothering to even look their direction. "I will personally tear out each and every one of your throats."

For a long few seconds, tense fingers lingered on triggers. Then Rachel fiddled with her comm and stepped closer to Ashida, and it was as if a couple dozen strings had suddenly been cut. A few of Ashida's men held steady, but most relaxed their weapons, traded uncertain looks, and glanced back at their vehicles, their body language universally seething, *Hey, not worth it.*

"Neat trick," Rachel said, watching Ashida without a trace of compassion. "Guess that's what happens when you don't bother giving your men half a reason to give a shit about you."

Ashida spat again, this time at Rachel, and with impressive velocity.

She seemed to have been expecting it. The glob of greenish spit slowed in mid-air, then hovered back to soak into Ashida's chest, where it hissed and smoked against his shirt and flesh.

"Filthy—"

Ashida struggled furiously then, but Brandt and the other raknoth held him tight.

"Filthy animal!" he screamed.

Krogoth watched Ashida all the while, his features dispassionate, save for the fire blazing in his eyes. When he spoke, his tone was formal.

"We will no longer suffer your existence to taint the name of raknoth kind. Do you wish any last words, Nan'Ashida, oath-breaker, traitor to your own people?"

Weak struggles and curses in Krogoth's direction were the only replies the Nan had to give.

And so ended Nan'Ashida.

It was the second time Jarek had watched Krogoth tear off a raknoth's head, and it wasn't even remotely less disturbing than the first time.

Afterward, Krogoth tossed Ashida's head forty yards to the assembled soldiers and told them to be on their way—to help the wounded or clear out and never show their faces here again, he cared not.

The men didn't seem to have any qualms about leaving their late leader's body behind as they loaded into their vehicles and sped away.

"Well." Jarek said when they were gone. "What a lovely tea party that was."

Krogoth gave him a look that made him want to close his faceplate.

"Come on, Rusty. At least that's two problems off the list."

The forced lightness in his tone wasn't fooling anyone. They knew all too well just how many items were left on that list, and just how few resources they had left to deal with them.

"When will the rest come?" Rachel asked.

Krogoth looked skyward. "Impossible to know if they do not wish it so. But soon, I fear. Far sooner than we can hope to prepare for."

"Would time really matter?" Jarek asked. "Seems to me we need a better plan before we worry about not having enough time."

Krogoth's glowing gaze remained skyward. "And do you have a better plan, Jarek Slater?"

"I was kinda hoping the warrior with a few millennia of field experience might have a trick or two up his sleeve."

Krogoth sighed and dropped his gaze to the ground. "The only trick we have ever managed to pull on the Masters was to convince them we had met the void. Now that that has failed..." He shook his head. "Gada will likely wait for his brothers this time around. The harvesters will come. They will come in terrible force, and we will fight. There is no plan beyond that."

With that, Krogoth turned and headed for the ship.

"He's got the head-ripping down pat," Jarek said. "Now if he could just bring the same intensity to pep talks..."

Not that he'd been expecting an impromptu master plan from the raknoth. The rakul were a problem without a clear solution—maybe without any solution at all. The prospect of fighting Gada alongside ten creatures of similar power was terrifying, and there didn't seem to be a single thing any of them could do about it other than to say, *Hey, I guess we'll try our best and fight it out to the end.*

At present, though, he couldn't see how that end could be anywhere but the grave for all of them.

They needed something the rakul wouldn't see coming—something that could turn the tide and throw them the advantage before the rakul even realized what hit them. They needed a nuclear option, so to speak. Or maybe even literally. He made a note to ask Krogoth about the possibility, though he was almost certain there couldn't be many functional nuclear weapons that hadn't been either used or destroyed in the Catastrophe.

"We should get back and check on the others," Rachel said, breaking into his thoughts. "Elise was in pretty bad shape."

She was right. He hadn't had a good look himself, but after listening to Rachel's recounting of the cut Elise had taken, Jarek wasn't so sure she'd manage to pull through, even with raknoth healing juice on her side. Of course, saying as much wasn't going to help anyone. Rachel knew as well as he did that the fight had taken a toll on all of them and that there'd be plenty more to pay before this was over. Assuming any of them lived to see the other side at all.

So he simply went with, "Aye aye, Goldilocks," and set off for the ship beside her, sincerely hoping that they weren't about to add another name to the far-too-long list of the day's casualties.

CHAPTER TWENTY-EIGHT

With the recent exception—and nightmare—of having let tears fly in front of Jarek on his ship, as a general rule, Rachel didn't cry. Not when there were people around to see, at least. But when they crept onto the Enochians' ship...

Seeing Elise, watching the way Haldin, Franco, and the others all hovered beside her, so clearly raw and torn...

That nearly brought on the tears.

Rachel couldn't claim to know Elise well. The girl had only been on Earth for a couple weeks, after all. What she did know, though, was that the girl was fierce.

No, not the girl. The woman.

Because, young as she might be, Elise was certainly not a kid anymore. She'd seen too many fights, felt too much pain. Elise and her fellow Enochians had all been through hell and back again, and once they'd returned, they'd decided to fly across the galaxy and risk their necks again anyway. And now it had cost her dearly.

Oddly enough, though, Elise seemed less upset by the news of her paralysis than anyone else in the room. Instead, she looked calm—resolved, even. Her eyes flicked at regular intervals between Haldin, who was kneeling beside her cot, and Alton, who'd propped his legless body up against the wall.

When Rachel tuned in, she realized Elise was sharing some telepathic communication with the two of them.

Rachel couldn't hear what was said, but whatever it was had Alton clearly uncomfortable, Haldin nearly manic, and Elise oddly at peace.

Jarek, unable to sniff out the telepathic communication, stepped into the silent room and unknowingly interrupted it. "Hey, guys."

Some finality passed between Haldin, Elise, and Alton as Jarek and Rachel stepped into the room, the two Enochians looking in agreement and the raknoth looking decidedly unhappy about it.

"Everything under control out there?" Johnny asked.

Jarek nodded. "Ashida's dead. Fighting's over. Just a holy hell of a mess to clean up."

"Yeah…" Johnny said, the mood in the room absorbing the news right into a big fat reminder of the damage lying right in front of them.

Rachel swallowed. "Is there anything we can do to help?"

It felt like a stupid question, considering, but she had to say something.

"We appreciate your support," Franco said with well-practiced politeness, "but I think the best thing right now is for us to—"

"Oh, sweet Alpha." Elise sighed. "I'm not dead yet, Dad. Not yet. I'm paralyzed. And we can fix it."

"Elise…" Franco crooned, stroking her hair.

"Don't *Elise* me." She turned her head toward Rachel and Jarek. "You mention that maybe hosting a raknoth to heal you up might not be the worst thing in the world, and suddenly everyone thinks you've lost the will to live."

Suddenly, the looks that had been passing between Alton, Haldin, and Elise made a lot more sense. That must've been what they were holding silent court about. But to host a raknoth… And what raknoth would be willing to…

Rachel met Alton's eyes. "You're…"

Alton crossed his arms and gave Elise and Haldin what was an impressively level look for a legless guy leaning against a wall. "Not agreeing to anything before we've had ample time to properly discuss the implications."

"Not even if we find a raknoth whose host is beyond repair?" Haldin asked in a tone that suggested this wasn't the first time they'd had this discussion.

"Annnd here we go again," Johnny said. He cocked his head thoughtfully. "Though, now that I'm thinking about it, that Lietha guy was in pretty bad shape last I saw him."

Jarek's finger shot up as if he had something to say about that, but he seemed to think better of it at some look from Alton.

Only… No. It wasn't that Alton had silenced him.

They were listening, both of their heads slightly perked—to what, Rachel couldn't say. But judging from the soft crimson glow that woke in Alton's eyes, it wasn't anything good.

"What is it?" Haldin asked, looking between them.

And that's when Rachel felt the familiar, wispy presence pressing in at the edge of her cloak.

The look in Haldin's eyes as he met her gaze told her he felt it to.

"No," Rachel whispered.

Not now.

Jarek had already whirled on his heel and was heading for the ship's hatch. "Something's happening out there," he called over his shoulder.

She could hear it now, on top of the pervasive presence shimmering around them—some shift in the buzz of voices outside. And there, in the air itself now, the subtle yellow glow that had crept into the room seemingly out of nowhere, barely perceptible but for its gentle, nebulous swirling.

Messengers.

Which meant—

"No," Haldin said. He'd gone rigid, his eyes flicking around the room.

"It can't be," Alton said, his gaze distant land skyward.

The voices were building outside, twisting from the dull buzz of conversation to sounds of anger and violence. A cry went up, only vaguely recognizable as human. A gunshot cracked in the distance. Then another.

Shouts. Sounds of fighting.

Jarek was already stepping through the hatch when Rachel turned around.

"We'll check it out," she said.

Then she took off after Jarek.

"Wait!" Haldin shouted behind her, but she was already halfway to the hatch.

She followed Jarek out of the ship and into utter chaos.

After the shitstorm they'd seen down in Newark, she thought she'd seen it all.

This was worse.

Madness had erupted across the body-strewn battlefield. Everywhere, people were attacking each other. Krogoth's forces, Ashida's, the Resistance—it made no difference.

Soldiers tore indiscriminately at one another, some with weapons, others with bare hands. Some even remembered how to use their firearms.

Those men and women who were properly cloaked against telepathic influence or nestled within the generator fields tried to band together, to hold against the frenzied tide, but there were too many.

More were flooding in from outside the battlefield, civilians from the surrounding areas who'd been caught up in the furor and driven here to the killing field. The furor must've been enormous to bring so many.

And through it all, that soft yellow light flowed, shifting and undulating like something living.

Rachel watched, frozen in place, unsure what to do, how to help.

A new sound joined the chaos, spreading through the frenzied hordes like a thousand tiny disjointed klaxons blaring their alarms.

Her stunned brain didn't put it together until her own comm buzzed against her wrist and informed her with its own grainy blare.

Retreat.

Daniels, Alaric… It didn't really matter who.

The commanders were calling for a full retreat.

"Rachel Cross!" a voice roared in her mind.

She followed the tendril of thought and spotted Drogan sprinting toward them through the masses of raving humans, a bloody Lietha clutched in his arms. He plowed through waves of wild berserkers, his own eyes burning with frantic desperation.

"Get back!" his voice hissed in her mind.

"I don't know, Al," Jarek was snapping. "Just bring the ship and get Alaric and anyone else you can out of there."

"Jarek…" Rachel said slowly, trying to slow her thoughts enough to process any of it.

The furor. The retreat.

HQ. Was HQ even safe?

And Michael…

She reached for her comm, thinking to try for her brother.

Before she could, Drogan gathered himself to leap from the crowd below.

"Jarek, we have to—"

Jarek must've seen Drogan coming himself, because he turned and shuttled her up the steps and through the hatch before she could finish the thought.

A second later, Drogan thudded to a hard landing right where she'd been standing. He didn't stop there, pushing past them and into the ship with Lietha's bloody body, urging them along with him.

"They come!" he cried, his tone wild, desperate. "We must flee this place!"

"Slow down, Stumpy," Jarek said. Or started to say before Drogan shouldered him to the wall, still clutching Lietha's limp form to his chest.

"Fool," Drogan hissed. "There is no time!"

He released Jarek and took off for the cockpit.

Rachel and Jarek shared a stunned look.

The furor outside was bad—worse than anything they'd seen yet.

But for Drogan to insist on fleeing, and for the commanders to be calling for retreat…

She turned back to the hatch, not wanting to look—not wanting to believe it could be true. Not now, after they'd fought so hard. After they'd won the day at so terrible a price.

It was too much.

They couldn't handle more. She couldn't handle more.

But whatever was happening out there, it wouldn't simply go away for her refusal to acknowledge it.

So Rachel leaned out of the open hatch and looked skyward. Cold dread poured through her at what she saw, freezing her inside and out.

"Oh, fuck," Jarek said quietly beside her.

The remainder of the storm clouds had passed. The sky was clear. And there, high up in the atmosphere, descending from god knew where, were half a dozen ships, all of similar shapes but various sizes. All decidedly not of this world.

The harvesters had come.

EPILOGUE

After spending nearly a year working their way across the galaxy, jump by jump, Haldin was no stranger to a quiet ship. On the contrary, the quiet times had often been some of his favorite. The times when he'd sat deep in meditation, glimpsing at that elusive inner peace with which his old mentor had been so attuned. The times when he'd lain with Elise for hours, feeling the soft warmth of her bare chest rising and falling against his, infinitely mesmerizing and undeniably vibrant with life.

But now Elise's body was broken.

That inner peace was nowhere to be found.

And this quiet…

This quiet was different.

This quiet told of defeat and despair, of guilt and shame at having fled to fight another day, even when no one fleeing had any true expectations that that fight would ever be one they could win.

This quiet was absent hope, and Haldin had been sharing it with Alton for too long now, staring the raknoth down in more ways than one as they waited for Elise's change to truly begin.

Alton had propped his legless body up against the wall of Haldin and Elise's bedroom. Haldin stood over him, arms crossed, lost in thought.

The position might've given him some kind of psychological advantage against another human—never mind that any such human would currently be screaming in pain following the beastly double amputation Alton had suffered—but Alton was far too old and cunning to care about such things.

And so they'd been here, locked in a mostly silent stare for the better part of an hour.

It almost seemed like a waste of time, like they should go do something productive—take charge, establish a plan, a next move.

Except this was the next move. THE Next Move. The *only* move left. He just needed Alton to see it.

"It's unnecessary." Alton sent for the thousandth time. *"Dangerous."* He looked over at Elise's still form, his face more expressive than he often allowed, filled with uncertainty and maybe even fear. *"Bad enough that Elise and Lietha were forced into this. The least we can do is protect them until they're ready to stand together."*

Haldin crossed to Elise's side and knelt down to softly stroke her fair cheek and her raven dark hair. He resisted the urge to pull back her blanket to inspect Lietha's entry site yet again and resigned himself instead to the long, pensive silence.

The weight of his old friend, Guilt, prowled the perimeter of his mind, seeking some weakness through which to enter. He shut it out with the resolve he'd learned out of necessity back on Enochia.

It wasn't his fault.

It wasn't Alton's.

They hadn't brought Elise here—hadn't brought any of them.

They'd simply set out to accomplish something together, he and Alton. Elise, Johnny, the others… They'd all made their own decisions, for their own reasons.

Elise was a warrior. She was the love of his life, the one that he'd die to protect—would give anything to protect—over and over and over again. Every time.

But she'd chosen to come here, chosen to fight.

She controlled her own destiny, not him.

He had to remember that, had to respect it. Had to hold onto it with desperate, bloody fingertips to keep from being sucked down the bottomless hole of despair and self-loathing that waited, always there, just below love and reason.

He had to forgive himself.

But scud, was it hard.

And demons' depths take him now if Alton thought he'd sit here and let Elise suffer this new fate alone.

"We're doing this, Alton."

The raknoth crossed his arms. *"This... symbiosis is unnatural to us. It will take time to perfect. Too much time. You trust the others to ensure our survival meanwhile?"* He tilted his head toward Elise. *"You trust them to protect your love?"*

Haldin studied Alton. *"You really think we have a choice? That there's any other way we win now?"* He was quiet for some time. Then, *"Wasn't this always the plan?"*

Alton gently shook his head, silent for a long while. Then, finally, *"I'm afraid, Haldin."*

It hadn't been what Haldin had expected to hear, but he wasn't surprised to hear it, either.

Human, raknoth—it didn't matter.

Who wouldn't be afraid right now?

After a thoughtful silence, he went and sat with Alton. With careful deliberation, he planted his hands on the raknoth's shoulders, holding Alton's gaze with all the steady conviction he could muster.

"You're the one who convinced me to come here, who brought this world the help they needed to make it this far."

It felt incredibly odd to be touching the raknoth like this. In all their time together, he couldn't recall having ever touched Alton outside of sparring sessions.

"You're the reason the rakul are going to lose, Alton. And so am I."

He let his hands fall from Alton's shoulders but left one extended, open and waiting to seal this insane pact.

"I'm scared too." Haldin glanced at Elise, bolstering his resolve. *"I've never been so terrified. But this is it. The others will keep us safe as long as they can. But this is how we win."*

He'd never seen a raknoth look quite so human as Alton reached, slowly at first, and then fell upon Haldin's extended hand with both of his own, his alien eyes wet with unspilled tears.

"Okay," Alton whispered.

Haldin gave him a solemn nod, his jaw clenched tight in a futile attempt to prevent the tears from welling in his own eyes.

"I…" Alton searched for some time and finally gave up with a shake of his head. "Thank you, Haldin."

Then he sagged limply against the wall like his strings had simply been cut, just like that.

It was time, then.

Haldin looked longingly at the corridor hatch, not so much seeing the smooth, purplish surface as the realm of possibilities that lay just outside it.

Even with the darkness descending, even with this planet so completely, utterly screwed, there was still life to be found out there. Moments of pain and joy, triumph and sorrow. There were his friends. There was his mortality.

But this was how they won. He was sure of it.

So instead of heading for the hatch, instead of saying his goodbyes to Johnny and Franco and the others, he crawled delicately onto the bed and laid down next to Elise. He took her hand, careful not to shift her body, and enjoyed the simple feeling of her hand in his—the calloused warmth, the faint but unmistakable pulse of human life pumping through her veins.

Would it feel the same on the other side?

Would it ever feel this way again?

At the foot of the bed, Alton's body gave a hard twitch, then another. A horrible wet crack split the air, like the world's largest egg beginning to hatch.

Haldin's gut churned with apprehension and barely contained

nausea, his pounding heart and electrified nerves screaming at him to get up, to run, to get the hell out of there.

"I love you, Elise," he whispered.

Then, with her hand grasped tightly in his, he laid back and closed his eyes to wait.

END BOOK THREE

AUTHOR'S NOTE
THE "META NOTE" EDITION (UPDATED SEPTEMBER 6TH, 2020)

What would YOU do if, tomorrow, all of our world leaders sprouted red eyes and started launching nukes without warning?

That, Dear Reader, was pretty much the question I was asking myself as I sat down to start writing The Harvesters Series. Or so I tell myself in hindsight.

In truth, this series really began more as a protracted byproduct of my procrastination than anything else.

See, before that big glitzy apocalypse question really grabbed me, I was already elbows deep working on another book—the first book I'd ever written, in fact. A lengthy tome that was in fact starting to look like the beginning of an epic sci-fi trilogy. But there was a problem.

I had this cool, action-packed alien invasion story going down on this world called Enochia.

I had this neat-o idea about how these events were all tenuously connected back to this ancient world called Earth.

I even knew the broad strokes of what had happened back on poor ol' Earth.

(*SPOILER ALERT: It involved world leaders one day sprouting red eyes and launching many, many nukes without warning.*)

What I *didn't* have was a totally firm grasp on WHY Earth had been devastated, or WHAT happened next. And boy, did I need to know the answers to those questions.

In fact, I needed to know SO MUCH that, much like a man trying to change a light bulb in a house of loose shelves and squeaky drawers, I chucked the tome of my Enochian work-in-progress aside to go focus on these new, *totally* important sidetracks.

(In my defense, they were oh-so-shiny and exciting.)

I meant to spend an afternoon at the drawing board doing some worldbuilding to satisfy my curiosity.

I ended up writing the four-book Harvesters series (plus two prequel novellas and multiple short stories) instead.

And while it all started with a simple questions (*what would YOU do when the nukes started flying and all the rules went out the window?*), I was pleasantly surprised to find a much more interesting story quickly taking shape before my eyes.

A story about two outcasts finding each other in a world gone horribly sideways. (And, yes, ALSO a story with LOTS of action, bloodthirsty aliens, and explosively snark-tastic shenanigans, too. But mostly the "outcasts" thing.)

And it didn't end there, either.

Because the more I watched Rachel and Jarek come to life struggling against the raknoth and their bleak post-apocalyptic settings in these books, the more I needed to know WHY they were the people they so clearly *were* under the surface.

Why was Jarek so bitter about the world when he so clearly wanted to do good?

Why was Rachel so closed off when her powers allowed her to see the world with a depth that few of us could shake a wizard's staff at?

Sure, I had workable ideas. Broad strokes. Loose, hand-wavy things.

I knew the general flavor of the story pie. I even had a decent idea of what most of the ingredients were. But I didn't have the full recipe.

We'd come full circle. Turtles all the way down.

Again, I found myself needing to know.

So I rolled up my sleeves and went to work, reverse engineering exactly how one ends up with one wise-cracking, sword-slinging, exo-suit-wearing Jarek Slater, and a chop-busting, magic-slinging Rachel Cross to match.

I had a blast finding my answers via the prequel novellas, *Cursed Blood* and *Soldier of Charity*. More importantly, I think you will too.

(And better yet, you can grab 'em both for free.)

All you have to do is go to *lukermitchell.com/reaping-day-signup* to join my mailing list and download your free copies of *Cursed Blood* and *Soldier of Charity* today!

In addition to occasional behind-the-scenes notes like the one above (which was actually adapted from one of my Sunday newsletters), as a member of the list, you'll also get access to free books from all of my other fictional worlds—as well as discounts and short stories you won't find anywhere else.

(Rachel's origin story *Cursed Blood*, for instance, is only available in the box set or to my mailing list readers.)

Sign up at the above link to grab both Harvesters novellas free today, and enjoy!

And if newsletters and email shenanigans aren't your bag, no worries. You can always visit *lukermitchell.com/books* to find the complete list of my published works—and to grab *Retribution* (Book 4) and prepare for the beginning of the end of the Harvesters Series! (Don't worry, there are more books to turn to once you're done.)

Whichever way you go from here, I just want you to know that I really do appreciate you coming along for this ride. I sure hope you've enjoyed it, and here's hoping you enjoy the next one even more! Thanks so much for reading. We'll see you on the other side.

Cheers,
Luke Mitchell

ACKNOWLEDGMENTS

Like a surprisingly literate (and unsurprisingly awkward) snowball plunging downhill, it seems the more books I manage to write and sell, the more people I have to thank for supporting me along the way and helping me to deliver the best stories I can. That said, I guess I'd better get straight to it.

First on the list (as she always will be) is my incredible fiancé, Marina, whose support has always been stalwart and whose love reminds me there are still at least a few reasons to pull my head out of the clouds and participate in this real world of ours from time to time.

Secondly, to my mom, my soon-to-be in-laws, and my friends, I thank you all for making me smile, occasionally feeding me, and otherwise supporting me in your own special ways. In particular, a big, sweaty thanks to my dear friends, Matt and Cara, for sheltering me from the oppressive Georgian heat for a good deal of my *Reaping Day* revision time—long and brutal as it was.

Speaking of revisions, as always, I owe a good deal of gratitude to my developmental editor, Lisa, who once again descended from Story Heaven to grant a living, breathing soul to the sad Story Golem I'd stuffed together by my own devices.

No matter how carefully Lisa and I plan and execute a story, though, the ultimate test remains in how that story is received by readers. To that end, I want to thank my faithful ARC crew, who have come through yet again in helping me deliver the most polished story I can (not to mention in helping me believe that said story is in fact *not* a steaming pile of Golem droppings). Additionally, for finding and slaying what typos and other various word demons slipped past us all, thanks to Dj, proofreader extraordinaire and writer of consistently hilarious emails.

Moving on, to judge a book by its cover, I think we can all agree that Prokopy and Clarissa have once again nailed the illustration/design combo that's given this series the look I love.

And lastly, to end with a hefty (but sincere) chunk of cheesy goodness, I want to thank you, dear reader, for buying yet another one of my books and continuing to fan the sails of my wobbly little authorship. It means so much that I even decided to stop being rebellious and finally put an honest dedication in a book (see the front matter, or, alternatively, just know that I really do appreciate your support).

So on we go.

We're all in this together now, team. May our collective snowball never reach the bottom.

Thank you so much for reading!
-Luke Mitchell

ABOUT THE AUTHOR

Not a llama. Mostly human.

Luke is a storyteller whose dreams include learning the ways of the Force, becoming a sentient robot, and maybe even one day growing up. Also, lots of zombies… Don't ask.

Oh, and that "growing up" bit? That was a lie.

After studying engineering science at Penn State and neuroengineering at Drexel, Luke finally decided to throw in the towel on building a working Iron Man suit and opted instead to simply make things up and write them down. Boy, is he having more fun now.

When he's not holed up in his writing cave trying to string words together, he can often be found powerlifting, video-gaming, reading, and/or drinking the darkest, most roasty beers he can get his mitts on. Sometimes all at once.

But you know what? That's enough about Luke. He's really not that interesting. Still, if you'd like to say hi to him for whatever reason, he'd probably be glad to hear from you!

Go to **lukermitchell.com/reaping-day-signup** to join the mailing list and grab your free copies of *Soldier of Charity* and the list-exclusive *Cursed Blood*!

Additionally (as you wish)…

Follow me on BookBub for new release alerts
bookbub.com/authors/luke-r-mitchell

Browse the rest of my published titles
lukermitchell.com/books

Join the Patreon team for digital copies of ALL of my work (past, present, and future) — and much more!
patreon.com/lukermitchell

Thank you for reading!